WITCHESKIN

The Lunar Shadows Universe

Book One

Witcheskin
By Nem Rowan

Published by Gurt Dog Press

All rights reserved. No part of this book may be used or reproduced in any manner without written permission of the publisher, except for the purpose of reviews.

Cover design by Nem Rowan
IM Fell English font © Igino Marini
A Black Crown font © Wahyu Eka Prasetya

This book is a work of fiction and all names, characters, and incidents are fictional or used fictitiously. Any resemblance to actual people or events is coincidental.

Copyright © 2022 Nem Rowan

Digital ISBN 978-91-986187-8-5
Paperback ISBN 978-91-986187-9-2
Hard cover ISBN 978-91-986434-0-4

*For April and Linn,
whom I love, whatever form you take.*

Witcheskin

Nem Rowan

One

Flies crawled and spun, pale wings buzzing, liquorice bodies zooming forward, and stopping abruptly like poorly animated cartoon characters as their tiny, robotic legs scuttled mechanically over the bristling fur in which they laid their eggs. The air was polluted by their presence, more so than the stench coming from the corpse. It was going to be a hot summer's day, and although the heat from the morning sun had yet to fully emerge from its slumber, the insects were out in full force. An undulating breeze ebbed and flowed over the cliffs, washing over the jade fields and emerald forests, but it did nothing to reduce the rotting, putrid ripeness humming beneath the hanging boughs of the trees.

A fly pitched on my cheek, and I slapped it away, unable to control the shudder of disgust that ran through me. No matter how many times I did this, the presence of the flies never got any easier. I always walked away feeling as though my skin was alive with the buggers. Itching, scratching, and scraping my nails through my hair never did me good. Only the sea wind, when I made it onto the cliffs on the way home.

She had fallen on her side, poor thing. Entrails had been dragged, unravelling like ribbons from a sewing box, torn and shredded, towards the trees. Blood soaked the grass, and flies, flies were everywhere. Rigor mortis had set in, causing her legs to go completely stiff, and her hooves to stand out in the air; she looked like a toy cow that had been thrown to the ground, frozen in a standing pose.

I could see her eye, bulging, wide open. Fear had left an imprint on her, like it did all the other innocent animals that had fallen victim to this epidemic of cattle mutilation. The only reason I knew she was here was because I had heard my mother talking on the phone to the farmer, so I had come running early in the morning, to get here with my camera before they came with a tractor to pull her sorry corpse away for disposal.

I crouched, careful not to press my knees to the blood-saturated ground and watched as the sunken tent of the cow's empty torso came into focus, eyes squinting down at the screen of the digital camera. I had to get pictures from every angle. They were evidence, proof that something was happening here, and if no one else would document it, then I would have to. I felt like it was my duty to do this. It didn't matter that I hadn't grown up with manure in my ears like the rest of the villagers liked to brag—it was about the animals. There was a reason I was vegetarian. I was powerless to stop the slaughter of the cow sand sheep by the men who farmed them, but this was something else, something much darker and more mysterious.

Something roamed these woods, emerging in the middle of the night to attack, only it didn't devour its victims. It simply mauled them, took parts it wanted, and then left behind a crime-scene worthy of a horror movie with bits and bobs lying all over the place. I had hundreds of photographs, and even so there were dozens of other deaths I hadn't been able to document. That's just how prevalent this had become, and still no one was speaking about it. They were all just burying their heads in the ground, pretending it wasn't happening, or making excuses.

If anyone asked questions, they were shut down, told it was just a dog on the loose. Probably some poorly trained mutt from the city, brought to the area by campers, and left behind to run wild, never mind how ridiculous it sounded. Anything to keep outsiders from sniffing around was good enough.

We don't want no media presence round by yere, they said. *We don't want strangers, we don't want intruders.*

That's what I felt like I was, even after living here for four years. A stranger, an intruder, an outsider. They had welcomed my mother back with open arms, but me? No, I wasn't like her.

Banishing my bitter thoughts, I swiped another fly from my freckled cheeks and stepped around the cow, boots squelching in the crimson mud as I took more photos. Instead I turned my mind to thoughts of what the papers would say when this all came out. What the newsreaders would say at breakfast. I had collected archives of documentaries and films from America, interviews with cattle ranchers who blamed the deaths on anything from aliens to El Chupacabra, footage of animals that'd had parts extracted with surgical precision.

It wasn't that I didn't believe in aliens or El Chupacabra. It's just that that wasn't what was happening here. There was no surgical precision in these deaths. Only blood lust and destruction, as if whatever was doing it took great enjoyment in its nocturnal activities and relished in the grotesque buffet of meats it had left behind. A sort of Jack the Ripper for cows and sheep.

Suddenly I heard the chugging of an engine. I turned, looking up towards the top of the field where it crested into a hilltop, and I saw the black shape of the tractor heading this way. It was time for me to leave. I replaced my lens cap and climbed the wooden fence into the woods, camera hanging on its strap bumping against my chest as I hurried off through the trees, boots still creating audible squishing sounds in the gory mud. I followed the bloody stain deeper into the woods, leaving behind the noise from the tractor, until finally it was replaced by the twittering of birds, my red carpet turning to green grass and wild garlic.

I breathed deep. My dad used to say he always went into the woods to breathe in the scent of the garlic when his asthma was bad. He said it cleansed his lungs better than any medication ever could. I breathed deeper. My clothes stank of iron and bile, and my skin was itchy as usual, but I restrained the desire to scratch, instead shoving my hands into the pockets of my hooded jumper and watching for tree roots as I meandered through the woodland. Sunlight glittering through the crisp leaves overhead dappled everything in sight. Pairs of butterflies whirled together their chaotic dances of love. I enjoyed seeing them; it was reassurance that there would be many more butterflies to come. The grass tickled my bare legs when I moved through it. There was no path, but I could hear the sound of the tide on the beach, which mean I was getting close to the coastal path.

The wind started to bluster, and the branches of the trees swished and swayed. The wind always made me feel cleaner after visiting the crime scenes, and even if we didn't live on the seafront I still would have chosen to come down here to wash myself of the scent of death. It was just a shame I had to share the house with my mother's boyfriend, Geraint. Otherwise it would have been perfect.

There was a little house across the bay, a tiny cottage on the hillside overlooking the edge of the cliff, and often I would look across at it and wish I lived there instead, far away from Geraint's teasing, and the daily chore of listening to him moan. Sometimes, at night, the lights in the cottage would be on, and I would gaze at it from my bedroom window, wondering who was there and if they were gazing back.

My whole life had been like that. Gazing at other

people, wishing I could be them instead, wishing we could trade places, trade bodies. It took a lot of effort to remind myself every day to be grateful for the body I was born with. It was the only body I had; I would never have another.

The bay was a small alcove surrounded by much larger ones all along the Welsh coast, but that didn't mean it was without its fair share of visitors in the summertime. The locals didn't mind. They were here for the sunshine and fresh air. They'd buy ice cream and surf at the beach. At sundown, they'd drive off and leave the bay as quiet as it had been when they'd arrived. Tourists didn't interfere in the matters of the village. When I first came here, I had tried to befriend visitors whenever they appeared, but I eventually realised that even if I made friends with them, it was only until sunset, and then I was alone again. It was a hard lesson.

There was no one left in this countryside to be my friend—no one human anyway. Only the animals didn't judge me, and so only the animals were my friends. There were no jobs for someone like me, and so I was unemployed, which made me poor as dirt. I never understood why Wenda, my mother, had brought us back here. It felt like she had condemned me to a life of nothingness, just a constant drifting from here to there in search of a meaning to my life. Sometimes I thought it was because of this unending void that I had become so lost, since I had only become this way after we moved here. This village, a miniscule speck on the map where she had lived for many years, and where my father had been born. I heard his voice in the words of the locals, his friendly Welsh accent, his jovial banter and comical dialect. Every day I was reminded of his absence.

I was a child of the Red Dragon, but I didn't feel that she loved me. England was where I had grown up till the age of twenty-three, where I'd had many friends and done well at school. If ever I was bored or needed a kind ear to listen, I could step out the front door and find myself surrounded with places to go. It wasn't like that here, and the isolation was unbearable at times, especially during the colder seasons when tourists were less likely to visit. People saw the carrot-coloured hair I had inherited from my parents and thought I belonged here. I wanted to belong, but I couldn't.

The village was a club I couldn't buy a membership to. Sure, they called me by name, and greeted me sometimes on the path, but there was a wall separating us. They occasionally took the time to peer over at me, but it was not a wall I could climb.

I tended to stay out of the way of the village anyway. It was a tiny place and made it too easy for people to spot me, so I mostly wandered the cliffs and fields in the surrounding area. There was a pub, a post office, a grocery store, and that was about it really, besides the caravan park on the hill, and the tiny souvenir shop that sold sweets and surfing gear. Mum worked at the caravan park as a cleaner. It was a twenty-five-minute walk from the house, and sometimes she brought me with her when there was over-time available. It was the only time I made money of my own, and I was lucky the man who owned the site was happy to pay me cash.

That was mostly in summer and autumn. For the rest of the year, even Mum was short on hours, and if it wasn't for the money Geraint made from the taxidermy animals he stuffed, and the odd-jobs he did for the locals, we would have had nothing. This fact alone gave him license to pester and torment me on a regular basis. He delighted in reminding me that it was his house I was living in, his food I was eating, and his water I bathed in.

I huffed as I zipped up my hoodie against the chill in the breeze. There I was again, thinking negatively. I had been teaching myself ways to switch off those bad thoughts whenever they came, listening to guided meditation tapes and reading how-to books. I was figuring it out, learning to say no to my brain, and choosing my emotions, but it took a lot of mental strength. At times I found myself just laying on my bed and staring at the ceiling, my ears trained on the ticking of the clock in the hall.

I looked out across the bay as I walked the rocky pathway between the shrubs and whip-like reeds of tall grass that grew along the cliff's edge. I could see the little white cottage from here. Beneath it, at the bottom where the rocks met the sand, there was a hole. I had heard it led to a cave network under the ground. Old legends said a witch had lived down there, and that she had been killed by a group of knights who saw her spirit rise out of her body. So it was said that any who should enter the cave would be cursed by the wandering ghoul. This tale was the only reason I hadn't been down there yet. It wasn't that I genuinely thought I would be cursed. No. I just liked to believe there was some truth in old stories.

Our home was just along the way, and as I climbed the stone-strewn road up the hill, the ivy-tangled fence came into view, followed by the peaked roof of the house and its many narrow windows that faced out to sea. More ivy clung to the white exterior, twisting up over the stained-glass porch and hanging its tendrils from beneath the upper window sills as the weather vane jutting from the tall chimney swung and creaked in the sea wind. To either side a fence separated the front garden from the back, a wrought iron gate allowing access to the rear where Geraint kept his animals, mainly chickens and a couple of goats.

The house itself wasn't as old as the many shoebox cottages that were tucked away all over the farmland here. Built in the Victorian era, it looked quite out of place. Geraint's family had bought it in the 1950s when it had been separated off from another piece of land upon which a work-house was built. The owners of the work-house had lived in this imposing building, a field and a half away from the source of their wealthy income, until finally workhouses were abolished, and the owners were forced to sell. The work-house had since been converted into a home for the elderly.

Geraint had gone to Cardiff, which meant I had the house to myself, a time for which I was incredibly grateful, as I could move about unhindered by the fear that he could be lurking in any of the rooms. I had a key, finally. When we had first moved here, even though I was an adult, Geraint had refused to give me a house key, so Mum had to copy hers for me otherwise I would be sat waiting on the doorstep for either of them to let me in. The key always felt warm in my pocket. For me, it was a small triumph against Geraint, and a symbol of my close relationship with my mother who had always been there to support me. Even when I wasn't going out, I carried it about with me.

The little bronze key glinted in the sunshine as I took it out and opened up the door, greeted by Jojo, Mum's Jack Russell terrier, who was overjoyed I had returned. Her dense, leaping body jumped up against my legs as she barked and wagged her tail, so I paused to reach down and pet her before closing the door on the blustering wind outside. Her claws pattered on the wooden flooring as she followed me along the cave-like hallway where I hung up my black hoodie, and after fighting with my laces, I pulled off my footwear.

"Who's a good girl, Jojo?" I grinned at her as she climbed up on my leg, stumpy tail vibrating while I struggled with my second boot. Her eyes always twinkled. They were dark and glittering, like the pebbles down on the beach when the tide washed over them. Her scruffy white fur was patched with brown, and her shiny black nose reminded me of a fruit pastel that'd had the sugar sucked off it.

Upstairs, I pulled my bedroom curtains open to let the sun in. My room was relatively organised, and not as messy as Geraint liked to believe, although there was the odd pair of socks lying about the floor, and a few cobwebs in the corners. But I liked the lived-in look. My bed was pushed right up to the window so that at night I could sit under the duvet and look out to sea. Beside it was my giant bookcase, crammed full to bursting with all my precious books and ornaments. Facing the bed was the wardrobe, whose doors I was never able to close, mainly because there was so much clothing that the doors couldn't sit in their frames properly. To the left was a full-length mirror, and another cabinet where I kept the rest of my clothes.

Pictures of animals I had cut out of National Geographic magazine were stuck in a clustered mosaic to the wall above the bed, and the other walls were peppered with photo frames and movie posters. I didn't have a desk anymore, so I did most of my work on my laptop at the window sill. It was the smallest bedroom in the house, but that in itself didn't bother me in the least. It was that Geraint made me feel guilty for occupying it without being able to pay him rent.

Jojo flew onto the bed and padded around for a comfortable spot while I took off my clothes, still scratching at my skin as the hum of the flies in my head reminded me of the itch I had felt earlier. I wasn't planning on going anywhere today, which meant it was pyjama time. As I pulled off my shirt, I looked at myself in the mirror. It didn't matter that it had been seven years since the operation; the scars never stopped looking ugly, and my body never looked right to my eyes. With my clothes on, I could fool anyone if they didn't know, but standing naked before the looking glass, I was confronted with all my personal demons, and boy did they taunt me.

The scars created two horizontal slash marks across my chest, starting near the middle, and going right up to my underarms. My nipples were pale and numb, mostly hidden by the thick coppery hair that grew all over my body. I at least had that going for me; my body hair was part of my identity now. I quickly put on my pyjama shirt. No matter how many years passed, no matter how I smiled at the psychiatrist and held my head high in the street, there were always moments where I saw the body I used to navigate this world with, and it made me shudder just as much as the flies did.

I had put on my plaid lounge pants and was pulling on my bed socks when I heard the front door slam open. Mum's voice was audible from the hall downstairs, coupled with heavy breathing and noisy footsteps. I put on my glasses after cleaning them on my sleeve and went to listen at the door. It sounded like someone was with her.

Blood was trailing along the hallway towards the kitchen, and I stopped at the bottom of the stairs, alarmed by the sight of it. I'd had a bloody morning so far already, without this emergency situation popping up. Jojo squeezed past me and trotted along the hall, her paws leaving tiny prints on the wood as she headed towards the source of the commotion, so hesitantly I followed her, creeping to the very end where the door to the kitchen was. I heard groaning and gasping, and Mum was shrieking, her voice shrill with panic. I had never heard her speak like that before and it frightened me. Cabinet doors slammed, and the tap was running. It took three steps down a small flight of stairs into the kitchen as the room was built deeper due to the slope at the rear of the house, so when I peeked in, I found myself looking down onto the scene. The blood trail moved across the black tiles, spots like splashes of paint.

I pressed tight to the wall and peered through the crack towards the wooden dresser where Mum was taking tea towels from the drawer. Her short ginger bob was wind-tossed, and there was wet sand on her work trousers from where she had walked along the beach, damp patches on her knees, and sunburn on her round nose and cheeks. Her grey eyes were wide as she turned and went to the kitchen table where the stranger was sitting, his leg lifted up on the table to keep it elevated, and I saw then the source of all the blood: a gaping wound in his calf was being held together by his thick, deeply-veined hands.

"Get out of the way, Jojo!"Mum cried when the little dog crossed her path to try and sniff the strange man. She yelped and bounced aside when Mum's foot went to shift her by her furry bottom, her dainty paws taking her back to the doorway where I lurked.

I watched Mum wrapping the man's leg tightly in a tea-towel. For some reason he was completely naked except for Mum's fleece jumper, which she had tied around his waist to try and maintain some modesty. His skin was dark, creamy, and coffee-coloured; his hair was jet black, and fell in wavy reams to his shoulders. I had a vague idea of who he was because he tended to stand out amongst the Caucasian locals.

I moved to the other side of the door to try and catch a glimpse of his face, just to confirm it was who I thought, and I saw his large nose, his angular jaw, and his dazzling lime-green eyes. He was about the same age as Mum was, perhaps slightly younger. In typical small village fashion, everyone else called him 'the Persian' or 'that Iranian fella,' I had never heard his actual name, and had only ever seen him from a distance when he was working in the fields. I admired his strength, because it seemed no matter how much work-load the farmers piled on top of him, he continued to toil away in all weather.

"Owen!"Mum exclaimed, my head jerking to look at her. Damn, I'd been spotted.

"What's... What's happening, Mum?" I stammered apprehensively, wondering if she was angry that I had been hiding outside when I could have been helping her.

"Get in yere now boyo! Come, and help me!" she shouted at me, the volume of her voice startling me. "Stop stroking your beard and fetch me down the First Aid kit from the bathroom."

"Mum, I don't think a plaster is gonna—" I began

before stopping suddenly, realising that he was looking right at me. Up close, I was amazed by how green his eyes really were.

"Keep your leg lifted."She ignored me as she shifted his leg, black droplets of blood splashing on the table top. His face creased in a grimace of pain, and he clutched at the towel wrapped around it, the veins in his muscular forearms bulging.

I fetched the First Aid kit, wondering why Mum had brought him here. It seemed strange that she didn't just call for an ambulance when she was probably carrying her mobile phone in her pocket. Wisely, I chose not to ask any questions while she was still fussing around him, and instead helped her to clean the wound and bind it tightly. I kept my eyes trained strictly on the job at hand; otherwise they would float across to his bare chest, and his eyes gazing across at me. I could feel him staring, feel his presence so palpable at my side, as though he was silently trying to get my attention, but I chose to ignore it, feeling nerdy and unattractive. Mum did a good job of cleaning and binding the wound, wrapping it in bandages, and making sure it was tidy and secure.

"I'm still disputing your choice to stay here, Maredudd," Mum muttered as she cleared away the blood-soaked tissues and cotton balls while I hovered at her side, with bundled up tea towels in my red-stained hands.

"And I'm still disputing your choice to nag me, Wenda. I don't need to go to the hospital, it'll be fine," the man replied stubbornly as he rested his hands in his lap. He looked tired, and there were dark circles under his eyes.

I looked between them, getting a strange feeling that they knew each other already. They exchanged words with a kind of familiarity reserved for brothers and sisters.

"Put the kettle on, Owen, and I'll finish up by yere,"

Mum answered, deliberately not replying to his dismissal.

"Okay..." I nodded, awkwardly placing the heap of towels on the table top and going to the sink to wash my hands. The blood was like oil, difficult to wipe from my skin, engraining itself in all the tiny cracks around my fingernails. As I turned off the tap, I managed to hazard a glance at Maredudd, momentarily marvelling at how masculine he was, only for that marvel to be swiftly followed by a pang of jealousy.

With the kettle hissing and bubbling as it heated behind me, I leaned against the counter and watched Mum bustle about, trying to prevent my eyes from returning to him. That's when my gaze fell upon a wet-looking pelt I hadn't noticed before draped over the back of one of the chairs. It was greyish-black, the fur short flat-laying like the pelt of a seal; there was also blood on it. All sorts of confusion arose in my head, and as I turned to pour the hot water into the mugs on the counter, I mentally thumbed through the many myths legends I kept stored in my brain until I came upon the Selkie.

In Celtic lore, primarily from Ireland, the Selkie was a seal that could transform into a human and walk on land. Sometimes they were known to marry humans, usually men, and would bear their children. The husband would have to hide the Selkie's pelt, otherwise she would find it turn back into a seal, running away to dive into the sea be with her kin, never to be seen again. I was anxious to take a closer look at the skin that was hanging on the chair, but that would attract everyone's attention, and I didn't have the confidence to go asking awkward questions when Mum was in military-mode, cleaning everything around us. Instead I stirred the tea, my mind becoming a whirlwind of excitement fascination.

"I'm gonna have to call Alison; she's probably wondering where I've got to," Mum told me in a hushed voice as she picked up her cup of tea with a grateful smile. "Will you be all right for me to leave him yere with you? He's no harm."

"You're going back to work?" I asked, glancing over her shoulder at Maredudd sitting at the table still.

"He's no harm, Owen. You'll be fine. I'll only be gone four hours," she said as she sipped from the mug, not caring to blow away the steam. We called her Asbestos Mouth for a reason.

"Mum, please stay here with me," I whispered, not wanting him to hear although it was highly likely he was listening to our muffled conversation. "What if Geraint comes home?"

"He's not due back until Sunday. Now, I have to go make that call, and then I better get going, otherwise Alison is gonna be tamping," she patted me on the arm, gently, but firmly rubbing my shoulder to reassure me.

I looked at her despairingly as she turned and wandered out with her mug lifted to her face, wishing that she would stay take care of him instead.

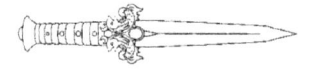

Maredudd's luminous eyes regarded me emotionlessly as I appeared at his side holding a t-shirt pyjama bottoms. The clothes were mine, and I couldn't very well have him walking about naked. Besides, there was no way he was going to wear anything from Mum's pyjama drawer, so mine would have to do, even if they were a bit on the baggy side. I held the folded clothes out, offering them to him.

"Here. You can wear these," I answered shyly, trying not to make eye contact with him. He stared right at me, almost unblinking, and I found that difficult to handle. Face to face eye contact had always been a struggle for me.

"Thank you. You must be Owen. Sorry we didn't get

to introduce ourselves properly earlier." He accepted the clothing after placing his empty mug on the table. Although his hands were still red with dried blood, they left no marks on the fabric.

"Your name is Maredudd?" I replied, taking the used cup and placing it in the sink for later. It was a relief to turn my back on him, but his presence was still a pressure against me, like the roaring of a waterfall striking rock.

"That it be," he agreed. His voice was rough, but gentle, and when I wasn't looking, his accent made him sound strikingly similar to Dad. It caused an uneasy twinge in my heart that I was quick to push aside.

"Earlier it sounded like you and Mum knew each other already," I commented, unsure of how to breach the subject with him.

"That's correct," he agreed again.

I looked at him over my shoulder, finding his blunt responses to be rather unyielding. Perhaps he didn't want to talk about it. Dad was considered dead, even though no body had been found. We'd had a funeral, and everything; there was just nothing to cremate or put in the ground. If he had been Dad's friend too, maybe it hurt him to talk about it.

"Mum never told me about you before," I told him as I leaned against the counter. I tried not to look accusing, but it was difficult.

"Maybe she might have if Geraint and I hadn't had a falling out." He reasoned with a slight shrug. "I'm sorry I didn't get to meet you sooner. You're the spit of your dad, you know that?"

I couldn't stop myself from blushing. To be told I looked like my dad was a compliment that reached down to my very core. I had spent most of my life being told I looked like my mother, and I didn't think we really looked all that alike. Both of my parents were ginger, so people could have said I looked like either of them, really. My mouth opened, and I just sort of mumbled a little, and stared at the floor, speechless.

"Think you could help me put these trousers on?" He changed subject, distracting me from my moment of flattery as he lifted the pile of clothing I had given him.

"Uh—sure, sure." I snapped out of it, stepping forward awkwardly, and helping him lift his damaged leg down to the ground.

He grunted with discomfort, startling me with the sudden noise, and I did my best not to suddenly drop his foot on the tiles. I chewed my tongue, not wanting to speak, not wanting to look up at him. He passed me the trousers, and bent forward, both of us making a haphazard teamwork of pulling the trouser leg over his firmly-bandaged injury. With that done, I allowed him room to put the other trouser leg on.

"You're gonna have to help me up." He made a wry smile that caused the corners of his eyes to wrinkle.

Blushing, I held out my freckled hands, and his strong ones clasped them, the abrasiveness of his palms surprising me as he allowed me to pull him upright. I turned my head away, eyes half-closed, and he pulled the pyjama bottoms up whilst balancing on his good leg. Mum's jumper was thrown on the chair, droplets of blood falling from the wet fabric.

"Thanks, Owen." He slapped me on the back, and I was momentarily winded as he threw me forward, shocked by the impact as I hadn't seen it coming.

"No problem." I watched him pulling the t-shirt on over his head, embarrassed that it was quite baggy on him. "So what happened to your leg? Did you have an accident or something?"

"You could say that. Hurt myself while swimming," he said in a rather nonchalant manner, and I got the feeling he didn't want to talk to me about it. His eyes glazed over, and he looked past me towards the kitchen window.

"Oh, that's unfortunate. Good thing Mum got you to safety," I remarked, lowering my eyes to the floor. His evasiveness made me feel embarrassed that I had asked.

"Your accent? Bristol, is it?" he asked as he dusted himself off, standing there in the mismatched wolf-print t-shirt, and striped bottoms, his feet bare on the tiles.

"Yeah, but I guess it's faded a little since we moved here." I smiled back, relieved that he had recognised it. A lot of people thought I was from Plymouth or Cornwall.

We both looked down as Jojo scuttled over to sniff Maredudd's leg, her pebble eyes regarding us with caution after Mum had told her off, but when neither of us shooed her away, her stump tail began to wag, and her little head bobbed back and forth as she stole additional sniffs of his trousers.

"I'd bend to pet you if it weren't for my leg."He chuckled.

"That's a thing. You should come, and sit in the living room, it's more comfortable in there. You can put the telly on," I gestured towards the door, realising it would be rude to expect him to sit to the table all evening.

"I'd rather without the telly if that's all right with you. It's like spraying black paint on your third eye."He chuffed as he limped towards the kitchen door, Jojo jovially trotting behind him.

He managed to climb the steps rather gracefully, all considering. I turned and put the kettle on a second time. I put Mum's cup in the sink, contemplating what must have happened before she brought him here. There was sand on her clothes, so she must have found him on the way to work. She always walked along the beach, and then up the hill to the caravan site, just as she had probably done so again when she left the house half an hour ago. It was the only explanation I could think of.

I needed another cuppa. Even though it was warm outside, the kitchen was always freezing cold, and my feet were chilly. It didn't help that the tiles were damp after having mopped the floor of Maredudd's blood. While I waited for the water to boil, I crept over to the kitchen table where the pelt was and lifted it from the back of the chair before holding it up and spreading it out. It smelled strongly of something, a stinking herbal scent that assaulted my nostrils. I was right though, it was a seal pelt, complete with flippers, claws, and whiskers, holes in the head where the eyes had been. It was still damp, but the fur was so glossy, and smooth. I was pretty sure it wasn't one of Geraint's taxidermy projects because he'd never leave it in the kitchen, so it must have arrived accompanying Maredudd. I had visions in my head of him wrapping it round his naked body and transforming into a seal before shooting into the waves and vanishing.

I placed it back where I had found it, gently organising the silky flippers so that it wasn't clumsily dumped on the chair, which I assumed was how Mum had thrown it down mid-emergency. I felt a greasy residue on my hands, and when I looked at my fingertips, I saw a greenish coating on them, accompanied by the stench I had smelled when I had lifted it. Fortunately, it dissipated when I washed my hands.

"Would you like the radio on?" I asked as I popped my head round the door.

Maredudd was sitting in Geraint's armchair, his wounded leg propped up on the footstool with Jojo already making herself comfortable in his lap. His hands rested upon her firm, sausage-body, and his eyes were closed as though he was sleeping. They opened when I spoke, and for some reason I felt I had interrupted him in the midst of something important, my clumsy movements, and noisy footfalls shattering the peaceful quiet that filled the room he inhabited.

"No, that's all right," he whispered, his eyes closing once more. "I'd prefer it to be quiet."

"Oh... Okay. Well... I'll be upstairs in my room then,

if you need anything," I replied. I could feel my voice going wobbly with nerves. I didn't understand why his presence made me go like that. Like I was walking a tightrope. Maybe it was the fear of his judging me.

"Thank you, Owen. Much appreciated." He breathed deeply, his chest visibly rising, and falling beneath the t-shirt.

A warmth seemed to radiate from him, like I had stepped out into a summer shower, hot sun, and tepid rain luring me into running free beneath the clouds. A strange sort of mischievous joy. It was almost so intense that I wanted to be in his presence and flee from it all the same. It wasn't the first time the intensity of someone's presence had made me want to move away, to step aside from the heat of the burning fire within them, because being so close was starting to get uncomfortable. Mum said it was because I was introverted and could only stand to be around people for a short amount of time before I got annoyed. Dad used to say it was my hidden eye, and I was seeing the furnaces inside people where the heat generated, where the power to exist came from.

"Just call if you need me... Okay?" I excused myself, ducking away into the hallway, and climbing the wood staircase up to the next floor.

Like leaving the vicinity of a house fire, his energy still clung to me like tendrils of smoke as I escaped, streaming from my shoulders, and wisps twisting from my heels. I lay on my bed, the door closed, and the curtains open, gazing across the bay, trying to make out the blocky shapes of the houses, and white specks of sheep on the distant hillsides. The sky was pale, but the sunlight blazed, and seagulls made little black ticks on the watery blue canvas. I had tried to read, but my brain couldn't focus. The book was discarded on the floor, and I couldn't bring myself to do anything constructive. Instead my mind whirled, and blustered, a turbulent wind scattering coherent thought. The clock turned to four, and I rolled to my feet, a yawn stretching my mouth wide. At least doing chores would be a welcome distraction.

Two

The old goat turned his head to the side, allowing me access to scratch behind his ear, right in those difficult-to-reach spots where he often could find nothing long enough to scratch himself with. Of all the animals we kept, he was my favourite. When we had first moved into the house, he had taken a liking to me immediately, and ever since, he had been delighted to see me, and would wait by the gate when it was feeding time.

I had never really had much of an affinity for goats until I met him. He hadn't even had a name back then because Geraint had no need of it. He kept him simply for the use of breeding with the females he used for milking, and considered him disposable, which was a pity because he was very handsome for a goat. Quite large, muscular, and covered in a thick mottled coat of cream, and ochre, with large pointed horns sprouting from his bony head. Mum called him Roger, and the name had stuck. Every day I went out to feed Roger, and the other animals, the chickens, and the couple of turkeys, carrying buckets of food for them to sprinkle on the ground or tip into troughs. It was one of the only tasks I had been assigned that I actually enjoyed.

Roger's velvety nose sniffed my sleeve, puffing as he sucked in the scent before attempting to lip at it, and draw it into his mouth, chuckling I moved my arm away, and offered him some cauliflower leaves instead. While he stood there munching on those, I opened the gate, and entered, the demure females gathering about me with their heads craning towards the buckets of food waste. There were three of them, all of them white with splashes of black across their backs; their names were Mary, Sarah, and Winnie. Roger only spent time in the pen with them when he was meant to be mating with them; otherwise they were kept separate, and I often wondered if he got lonely living by himself in the other pen, because he would occasionally stand outside under the light of the moon, looking this way in a rather dejected manner. It took a lot of effort to stop myself from letting him into the house just to keep him company.

I heard Mum's voice drifting on the breeze, distorted by the swishing of the trees overhead as the wind blew the sound in my direction, and I looked over the pen's boundary towards the gate at the side of the house where she was standing. One of the farmers was there, old Mr Thomas with his shaggy white beard, and droopy, broad-brimmed hat, his spindly body clad in green plaid. He must have followed her up the garden path as she arrived.

"Geraint's not home, Mr Thomas, I'm sorry. He won't be round yere until this weekend," Mum was saying to him, her freckled face wearing an apologetic expression.

"Can ye give him a call for us? Please, Wenda?" the elderly man begged, his milky eyes weary with fear. "I can't set the traps myself. Can barely manage on these old legs these days without this happening. He said to come by yere any time his help was needed. Please Wenda, a call is all I ask of ye."

Mum sighed, her hands on her hips as she looked about herself, and she briefly caught my eye. I saw from the look she gave me that she knew the cogs in my head were turning. She turned towards Mr Thomas and nodded.

"Alright. I'll give him a call, but he won't be back now until Sunday. Are you alright to wait until then?" she asked, no doubt feeling guilty for attempting to turn Mr Thomas away when he looked so pitiful. "What's occurring, then? So I can pass the message on?"

"Another cow I found, over by the stream..." he began to explain, and I turned my back on them, my ears tuned to their conversation as I pretended not to be listening.

We didn't need to be looking at each other. We always knew just what was going through each other's minds. Often it was like we were perfectly synchronised, and often I found it very frustrating. As I was tipping the bucket of feed into the trough, I heard her boots approaching on the path.

"No, Owen. Do you hear me? I won't have you going there." She pointed a finger at me when I stood upright, bucket in hand, the goats clustering around my legs.

"Going where?" I feigned innocence.

"To Mr Thomas's field, that's where! I know you heard what we were talking about. I saw your pointy little ears pricking up." She pouted at me.

"I told you already, I haven't been going to any fields, and I won't be going to his field either." I shook my head, but she could see through my facade with minimum effort required.

"I know you've been going to look at those other rotting corpses, Owen, I ain't stupid! The clothes you put in the wash basket yesterday were honking! They smelled like death, just like they always do when you've been fulfilling this bizarre hobby of yours," she exclaimed, following me along the fence as I went towards the gate.

"Mum, I'm not doing anything dangerous! I know

you think it's bizarre, but that's all it is, a hobby. I'm not doing anything wrong or hurting anyone." I reasoned as I shut the gate behind me and put the bucket on the grass.

"You've been trespassing before though. I had Mr Walters coming up to me in the market last week saying he saw you round by his farmhouse on the hill, and his dog chased you. Is that true, Owen? Were you trespassing on his land?" she questioned, marching at my shoulder as I picked up the other bucket, and headed towards the chicken run.

I grumbled a murmur in response. I couldn't deny that I had been there, and the sheepdog had chased me. But he didn't catch me, and the only reason he thought it was me was because other farmers said they had seen me photographing the dead animals. I knew what I had done was stupid, but if I didn't get the pictures then the deaths of all the animals would be swept under the carpet and ignored. Mum blocked the entrance to the coop, and I sighed, stopping before her.

"I know you think I'm nagging all the time. But I do it because I care about you. I don't want you to get attacked by dogs or shot by a farmer because he thinks you're a thief or whatever. That's all. I don't care that your hobby is weird, I just want you to be sensible, and safe." She stared at me beseechingly, and I couldn't meet her eyes.

I looked down at the grass to the side of us, reluctantly acknowledging her words. "I'm sorry, Mum. I know you care about me."

"You're a twenty-seven-year-old man. It's about time you started acting like one and took better care of yourself. I dread having a copper coming by the house late one night saying something awful has happened to you." She reached out and stroked my hair gently. "I'm sorry for losing my temper with you, but I can't help it when you've got me worried half to death all the time.

It's because I care about you."

I nodded with a grim smile, and she patted my arm.

"Look. I thought that perhaps next time someone comes round about it, I will ask them for permission for you to go and see the animal. They probably wouldn't mind, and there's no harm in asking," she suggested, bending slightly so that she could catch my eyes, and I looked at her smiling face gratefully. "I'm sure if Mr Thomas was asked, he'd say yes. They aren't all your enemies."

"But they act different when you're not around. They're always friendly when you're with me, but when I'm alone, they're not very friendly then," I explained, watching as she lifted the bucket, and went into the chicken run to scatter the feed.

"They just think you're a bit odd. Let's be honest, all they know of you is that you like taking pictures of corpses, and what's not odd about that?" She grinned, the ruffled bodies of the chickens bustling beneath her hand as the seed rained to the floor.

"They know my old name though. Sian in the Post Office, and that man who cuts the hedges keeps calling me Cerys. That's why they think I'm odd. The dead animal photos are just the icing on the cake." I grunted as I leaned against the door frame, frowning as I thought of all those people who politely mocked me to my face. "It's Geraint's fault. If he hadn't said anything, then..."

Mum stepped out onto the grass beside me, and pulled the wooden door closed behind her. She took hold of my hands and squeezed them in hers.

"They would have found out anyway. That's what it's like in small communities. It's difficult to hide your secrets in places like this."

"I suppose that makes it okay? Maybe I should have stayed in Bristol," I murmured, looking down at our hands through half-closed eyes.

"You know you wouldn't have coped if I'd left you on your own in the middle of your transition. Maybe we never should have gone to Bristol in the first place. Then you would have grown up here, and everyone would know you the way they know me." She lifted my hands and kissed my knuckles. "Now look here, Mister. Someone needs to start dinner, and someone needs to go, and see to Maredudd. Choose wisely."

"I'll..." I began, but I closed my mouth.

I wanted to see to Maredudd, to talk to him more, but I was shy. I felt embarrassed just going and speaking to him when I could think of no good reason for my motivation, no way of validating it. I always felt like people thought I was communicating with them for some ulterior motive rather than just to be friends. I isolated myself whilst hating being isolated. A self-fulfilling prophecy.

"You can go and see to Maredudd. Besides, you never bake the pasta for long enough. Last time I got a piece stuck in my tooth." She giggled as she moved away from me.

"But I followed the recipe to the dot!" I called after her, bending to pick up the buckets before hurrying off along the garden path.

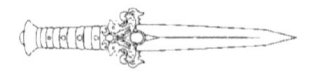

Fortunately, I was able to make it to the crime scene on Farmer Thomas's land before nightfall. I had to hurry, because I had stayed behind to help Mum do the washing up after dinner, which delayed me further. Thoughts of Maredudd filled my head as I half-jogged down the hill, camera bouncing on my chest, and the glowing lantern of the setting sun turning everything lemon, and clementine.

Maredudd's mood hadn't changed since he had

made himself comfortable in the living room, even after Mum had put on the television, and was listening to the news, seemingly unaware of the fact that he preferred the silence. I had expected him to be annoyed, but as before, he was still, and placid. The fire that had been crackling and popping when we had spoken before had died back somewhat, and instead was replaced with a coolness. I wished I could be so calm, and exude such wisdom, but I was like a newly born foal, staggering and stumbling through my life, collapsing here and there, and fighting to get to my feet again.

Checking up on his wound while Mum cooked in the kitchen had left me shrinking with shyness, and I hadn't been able to utter a word to him the entire time. When I was finally able to make eye contact with him, he smiled, and I felt his kindness within me, and around me, like a blanket thrown around my shoulders on a cold night. I liked the wrinkles at the corners of his eyes, and the veins in the backs of his hands. I liked the sound of his voice. I felt there was something special about him. We were still strangers, and even so, thinking of him made me smile to myself as I made my way through the grass, down towards the narrow brook that cut through the field.

The animal was fresh, and someone had already been here, and attempted to move her, probably Mr Thomas on his own, but he had given up. Footprints in the earth circled the body. There wasn't a great deal of smell coming from the body just yet, only the flies. The tiny winged devils that left me trembling with itchiness.

The camera lens whirred as the little machine did its magic, zooming in close, closer than I'd ever desire to get myself, close enough to see the shiny insects crawling amongst the hairs. I could feel my boots were sinking into the marshy ground, so I steadied myself by taking a step back, my eyes trained on the small screen of my camera as I focused the shot. I pressed the, button, snap. The evidence of strange ways was forever captured, another image to add to my growing collection. Sighing, I turned the camera off, and put the lens cap on, hanging its heavy weight against my ribs as I stood upright. The sun was beginning to wane, and here lay this sleeping giant, a dairy cow that just yesterday had been grazing, and walking about as normal. Now she was on her side, tongue missing, nether regions extracted, puncture wounds here, there, and everywhere. I felt so sorry for her, felt guilty photographing her like this, but the evidence would do her justice one day when everyone realised I was right.

I heard the sound of the tractor engine as it came up over the hill, leaving a trail of gouged tyre-marks beneath its thundering wheels, and I squinted into the sanguine sunlight, picking out the silhouette of the person driving it. I didn't want to stick around to see him towing off Daisy's carcass, so I made a swift, and silent exit.

The sun began to fade quickly as I walked through the trees, fox musk, and wild garlic perfuming the air, the evening birds singing the songs of their soirée, and shadows creeping out from amongst the leaves. It was a long path through nowhere to return to the house; the sky was dimming, and although I wasn't afraid, I couldn't help moving on fleeting steps through the wood. Blankets of bluebells covered the hillside, and it felt a sin to wade through them. I enjoyed walking the woods here at dusk as it was cooler, and quieter than during the day, and there was less chance of bumping into hikers or ramblers, so I could wander as I pleased without being disturbed.

My hands held my camera steady as I meandered down into the dip of the valley, birds still cheeping, and chitting above me in the branches, and twigs crunching under my dirt-caked boots. As the sun began to slink away, and the night gradually made its entrance, I felt an uneasiness inside me, a dark flower blooming, and I realised I kept looking over my shoulder.

Perhaps it was a fear I had been carrying with me yet denying the whole time. The images I had captured twenty minutes ago on my camera told me that something out here was dangerous, and if it could do that to a cow, imagine what it could do to a puny human such as myself? I kept my focus on the earthy path that lead towards the coast, occasionally pushing my spectacles back up my nose, and ignoring the desire to turn, and look behind me. I felt as though I was being watched. It wasn't the first time I had had such a sensation whilst walking alone through the countryside, but it had always turned out to be nonsense, and so I chose to ignore it at my peril. My nose picked up the scent of the ocean seeping into the forest on the breeze, but I knew I was still another fifteen minutes away from the coastal path if I continued heading on at a consistent speed.

But I also picked up another scent, a strong chemical stench that burned my nostrils. It reminded me of a foul aftershave the Post Office manager used to wear that sent all the old ladies hurrying out of the shop with their noses pinched in their fingers. That's when I heard the sound of heavy footfalls, and felt my throat constricting. A strangling, aching heat burned in my chest as I fought the urgency to run. Someone was walking nearby, someone big, foliage snapping, and bushes rustling as they moved past, but I couldn't make out which direction it was coming from. I thought I should stop, and call out, to see who was there, but my hands clutching my camera told me to keep going, to head for the cliffs. I heard my own heavy breathing, and my pulse pounding in my ears, and the smoulder of adrenaline continued to pump through my chest as I broke into a jog.

There came a rough, undulating puffing sound that

soon became louder than my own breathing, and if I hadn't known any better, I might have thought there was a steam train coming towards me. The feet that struck the earth made the noise of a gallop. It wasn't a *someone*, but a *something, and* it moved on all fours. That's when I began to run.

Branches scratched at my shoulders, and bushes slapped my shins as I fled. The pounding in my chest had swelled, and it now filled my body, propelling me on, urging me to panic. Suddenly I burst through the undergrowth and found myself on the pebble-strewn pathway overlooking the beach, and I heard a strange, shrieking grunt that perhaps might have been that of a horse, but it was unlike any horse I had ever heard. The path became steep, and my legs wobbled, and lost their coordination as I navigated the tilting slope. Stones, and clumps of sandy soil spat out beneath the soles of my boots, and the sea wind tore at my hair, threatening to flip my glasses from my face as my jacket was blown into the billow of a sail.

The thundering footsteps were beating after me, keeping up at a steady pace. The pathway was dipping towards a piled stone wall that began to rise higher the further along I went. I stole a glance over my shoulder, trying to seek out what was following me, but all I saw were the leaves, and boughs of the trees beyond. There came that bloodcurdling screaming again, the cry of some unknown horror that my mind was only too happy to give form to, and only when I twisted my ankle did I realise I was making my own kind of screaming, breathless cries for help, escaping my open mouth like plumes of smoke.

My boot hit a large rock in the path, and it turned my ankle inwards. The momentum I was running at continued, sending me tumbling, rolling, clattering down the slope, my body spun round, and round by the relentless dip. My camera strap choked me, and stones, and pebbles struck me like bullets from all sides. I lost my spectacles somewhere along the way, and each impact caused my precious camera to shed glass, and plastic, tiny pieces of debris blown away behind me like a comet entering the Earth's atmosphere.

It's funny how you don't quite comprehend how long, and steep a hillside really is until you find yourself at the mercy of gravity upon its tilted face. It seemed an eternity I was falling, and when I finally hit the bottom, I was bloody, and bruised. I landed on my back, and for a moment I could only stare up at the purple sky, and the tiny dots of stars winking down at me, until the reality of my situation reared its head again, and I managed to struggle back to my feet, wheezing, and in agony. I expected to see it then, whatever had chased me, but there was only silence.

Blood streamed from my nose, and I licked it away, cringing at the soreness of my split lip, looking this way, and that up the hill, but I found myself alone. Then I remembered my camera and found it in tatters. Tears filled my eyes, but I fought them back, refusing to cry. After all that had happened to me in the past, there was no way I was going to cry now. My body ached in lots of places it never had before, and I turned, and began making my way along the cliffs, limping, and sniffling, my ears ever alert should the shrieking recommence. There was a disappointment in myself that I hadn't been brave enough to stop and lift my camera. Perhaps I might have got a photo and been able to identify who or what was there, but no, I had run away like a frightened child.

"Owen! Oh my god, Owen, what happened!" Mum cried when she opened the front door and found me dishevelled and bloodied on the porch.

I didn't get a chance to explain. She captured me, and practically threw me into the hallway before grabbing me in a hug that highlighted the pains in my ribs.

"Owen, did someone hurt you!" she shouted into my ear.

I groaned, turning my head away from her noisy face."Mum, there's no need to scream, I'm standing right here by you." I tried to squirm out of her embrace.

"Look at the state of you! What happened?" she exclaimed as she leaned back to take a better look at my face.

"I fell down on the path, that's all. I made a wrong step, and I went flying down the hill," I grumbled, unable to look her in the eye. The truth was I felt stupid and embarrassed, but I didn't want to tell her I had been chased.

"Are you being honest with me? You look like you were attacked." She frowned, and I sighed, shaking my head.

"No, really. I fell, that's all." I sighed again, and moved away from her, lifting my camera strap over my head. She followed me along the hallway, and watched me take my jacket off, and hang it on the coat hooks on the wall. I could tell she didn't believe me.

"Owen, you know if someone hurt you, you can tell me. You don't have to keep it a secret," she told me, her voice quieter than before. She stood with her hands on her hips, her fluffy pink dressing gown pulled tight around her waist, and her teddy bear slippers on her feet. I could tell she had just had a shower because she smelled of rose, and chamomile.

"Really, Mum. I just fell. Look, if someone had hurt me, I would tell you, okay? I just want to go to bed. I'm tired," I murmured as I turned away, and began climbing the stairs.

She stood on the bottom step, and watched me ascend, and I could feel the waves of concern washing out from her towards me.

"We saved some jam pudding for you, it's in the

fridge. There's some custard too. We're going to watch a movie now, if you'd like to join us," she said, and I stopped at the top of the stairs, and looked down at her.

With her red hair damp, and wavy around her plump, heart-shaped face, and her penny-round eyes gazing up at me, I couldn't help, but manage a weak smile. I felt guilty for shrugging her off when she cared about me so.

"Thanks. I'll be down in a minute then, you can start it without me," I replied timidly, and although she smiled, I could tell I hadn't fully reassured her.

"Okay. There's some fresh pyjamas in your drawer." She nodded before shuffling out of view.

Frustrated, I placed my camera on the bed, and turned on my laptop, crossing my fingers that I would be able to retrieve the data from it after the serious damage it had received. Fortunately, I managed to download them all, but the camera itself was useless. The lens was missing, and the camera body was shattered on all corners, cracks, and holes exposing its interior. I didn't have a lot of money; I had no idea how I was going to replace it.

Unlike my camera, my body was something I could repair. Like an old car, it had taken me many years to fix the engine, replace a few of the parts, and repaint the chassis, turning it from scrapheap garbage to something I felt comfortable to drive in public. I cleaned myself up and stuck plasters over my cuts, but the bruises I could do nothing to hide. I was grateful I hadn't broken any bones. With my fresh pyjamas on, I felt much better.

Mum whispered to me that Maredudd was going to stay for a little while, just until he was well enough to travel home. He lived alone, and since he was stubborn as a goat, she knew if he left now, he'd only end up injuring himself further. They were sat in the living room together when I came downstairs, and I silently crept in through the open door, sheepishly aware of my own intrusion, and embarrassed that I might interrupt the movie. Mum gestured to the sofa, and I sank down beside her, allowing her to place the other half of her blanket over my lap. I ate my pudding slowly, cheered by the sweetness of the jam, and the wet sponge, the light from the television screen flashing on our pale faces in the dark.

I looked over at Maredudd, and instinctively he sensed my attention to him, for he looked right at me. I averted my eyes back to my pudding. When I managed to look up again, he made a friendly smile at me, and I watched his hand stroking Jojo's sleeping form. He was sitting in Geraint's armchair, but no, it was his armchair now. I had never seen anyone besides Geraint sit in that chair comfortably. Everyone always perched on the edge, not wanting to get cosy, as though it had pins sewn into the cushions, and yet he sat there like a king on his throne. His energy filled the room and made it his domain. Even the house seemed to feel different, this whole situation so alien, and yet so familiar. It was almost as though Dad was back here with us. That's just how long it had been since Mum and I had sat in the living room together of an evening, like a family should, and it saddened me.

Geraint was a wedge that life had attempted to drive between us.

Three

I found my glasses on the path. Somehow they were still in one piece, and with a little buffing with my sleeve, I was able to rub off what had initially looked like permanent scratches. I had got up early, and walked along the trail in search of them, accompanied by Jojo who jingled ahead of me on her extendable leash. Making sure that the arms weren't crooked, I placed the spectacles back on the bridge of my nose, and turned back towards the house, listening to the chorus of birdsong coming from the woods beyond the wall.

I had struggled to sleep last night, questions, and thoughts humming in the back of my mind, no matter how I tried to switch off, and rest. My body had ached, and ached, and my head had refused to settle. I sat at the window for a while and looked out into the blackness that enveloped the bay, picking out the blinking lights of buoys, and boats on the invisible waves. I realised that the little cottage on the other side of the bay was in darkness when I could usually see a light in one of the windows at this hour. I felt like I was the only person alive on the planet; it always felt that way when I couldn't sleep. Eventually I lay back down and must have drifted off because when I next opened my eyes, it was morning.

When I got home, Mum was getting ready for work,

and she gave me a kiss on the cheek, telling me there was some food scraps in the kitchen for the animals before picking up her bag, and disappearing out the front door. Jojo vibrated on the kitchen floor, standing up and sitting down, over and over again, to get my attention until I went to the cookie jar on the counter, and took out a dental chew for her. I watched her shaking her head, and gnawing at it with her little white teeth, my eyes partially closed, and my chin in my palm. There had been many times in the past where I had wished I could just be a dog, because dogs didn't have any of the worries humans did. The only thing Jojo had to worry about was where her ball might go if she put it down and forgot where she had left it. She didn't care about how people judged her, or whether they wanted to be friends or not. She didn't even know how old she was or how many years she had left to live, she just lived them, lived the days, and enjoyed the present moment. I was trying to teach that to myself—to live in the moment—but it was so difficult. In the late hours before sleep, my brain always brought out its book of awful memories and decided to take me on a sadistic version of This Is Your Life.

I fed the animals, stopping to pet the goats, and baby-talking Roger, who greeted me by pressing his head into my belly to try and elicit scratches. It was another beautiful summer day, but I didn't have much inclination to go out walking after my experience the night before. Maybe it would be best if I stayed in and took a break instead.

I climbed the stairs, yawning into my hand, and grumbling at the aches I felt when I took each step. The guest bedroom was next door to mine, and that's where Maredudd had been when I had last checked. Gingerly, I knocked on the door, and the impact caused it to creak open, so I peeked through the gap, and was surprised to find the room empty. Frowning, I pushed the door ajar.

"Maredudd?" I said, looking from side to side, thinking he might have got up to open the window, but he wasn't there either.

The dolphin-patterned covers on the double bed were crumpled from where he had slept in them, and there were a few dark spots of blood on the sheets, which I hoped would be the last of them. The seal pelt was on the little wooden stool in the corner, so I assumed he hadn't left to return to his own home, wherever that may have been. Humming thoughtfully to myself, I moved back into the pale shadows of the hallway, wondering where a man with a seriously wounded leg could have got himself to. I had passed the bathroom on the way, and I was pretty sure he wasn't in there. That's when I heard Jojo's paws on the floor downstairs. She was bustling, a jaunty little trot she did when she was happy to see someone, so I headed back down the steps, my ears searching.

"Maredudd?" I called.

If he was still here, he was ignoring me. I went through the rear sitting room, a room that was usually utilised for special occasions, family meals, and parties, decorated with kitsch ornaments, and an ancient photograph of one of Geraint's relatives, who stared down at me with glaring eyes as I passed her to the door at the other side. The door was open, which in itself was odd since it led out into the garage, and as I stepped out into the cool, musty air beyond, I saw Maredudd's dark head over the roof of Mum's car. As soon as I appeared, he turned round, and looked over at me. His expression was reserved, but had the sharp alertness of a hunted hare.

"What are you doing out here? How did you get down the stairs by yourself?" I questioned after the awkward moment of silence that had passed between us upon my arrival.

"My leg doesn't feel all that bad," he replied simply.

"I can walk on it unaided."

I looked at him, at his hand resting on the handle of the door he stood in front of. Jojo was beside him, eyes gazing over at me imploringly.

"You can't go in there. That's Geraint's work-room, no one is allowed in there," I told him, resisting the urge to question him about why he was down here. He was showing all the signs of someone up to something they shouldn't be, the mile-long stare, and the tense shoulders, the rigidity in his voice.

"I was just curious, that's all. It's the only door in the house that's locked," he said emotionlessly, excusing himself even though I hadn't asked.

"Yeah, because he'd kick my ass out if I went down there without permission. He doesn't trust anybody, not even Mum, so I think he'd be especially pissed off if he knew you'd been in there while he was away." I was unable to prevent a slight grin from twitching the corner of my mouth.

Maredudd nodded, but he didn't say anything. I got the feeling he was contemplating what I had just said. He released the door handle, and came towards me, rubbing his fingertips together as though there had been a residue on the handle. He walked surprisingly well despite his injury. He still had a limp, but I had expected him to be far more immobile than he was.

"Can I go outside into the garden? Is that allowed, Doctor?" He jested, clapping his hand on my shoulder, and giving it a squeeze.

I chuckled, smiling back at him. I felt slightly embarrassed, perhaps I was babysitting him too closely. "Of course. A bit of sunshine might do you good."

I brought Maredudd a cup of tea as he sat on the stone bench in the garden, the hanging fingers of the willow tree draping either side of him like two curtains while birds whistled and hopped in the hedgerows surrounding us. Jojo ambled about on the lawn, occasionally stopping to bury her snout into a particularly interesting clump of grass. The fire that had burned inside of Maredudd before had shrank to a low flicker, and instead he simmered like a pot of boiling water, warm, but comfortable enough for me to be near him, so I sat down on the bench, and we watched a furry-bodied moth flutter by in front of our feet. I looked at his handsome face and followed the line of his sight towards the goat pen where Roger stood, his chin resting on the fence as he stared back, the pink slug of his tongue emerging to lick his slimy nostrils.

"That's Roger," I answered off-handedly as I lifted my mug to take a sip of tea.

"Roger. That's a good name for a goat." Maredudd made a muffled laugh as he mimicked me, his lips pursing around the rim of his mug. I watched his throat contract as he drank, the sunlight illuminating his eyes, and turning them into polished, precious stones threaded with golden veins.

"It is. He's my favourite goat. Well, I wasn't a huge fan of goats originally, but now I am. A bit the same with chickens too. I became very fond of farm animals after moving here," I said, feeling relaxed enough to ramble on without worrying about making a fool of myself. "I wanted to get some pigs, but Geraint got angry that we'd have to dig up the lawn to make another pen, so that kind of went out the window..."

"I used to have a pet pig." He sighed, seeming wistful for a moment as he looked over at Roger still. I grinned at him curiously, silently urging him to tell me more. He took another sip of tea. "I got her at a farm fair, my dad bought her for me. I must have been ten or eleven years old then. I was looking into a pen full of piglets when I saw this one piglet who was completely black all over, only a pale spot on her forehead. Mooney, I called her."

"Mooney is a very cute name." I saw in his eyes that

he was recalling memories rarely touched upon, especially not in the presence of others.

"Isn't it? Of course, she's long since dead, but she was my only friend besides my dad, for a very long time. Pigs are super intelligent, smarter even than Jojo is, and their ideal shape lends to excellent cuddles. I do have a fondness for pigs." He laughed louder this time, eyes creasing, his smile showing his white teeth. "Mooney always knew when I was feeling sad. I even took her to the beach, she loved swimming in the surf, and going for walks on the sand."

An image filled my head of twelve-year-old Maredudd wandering along the bay in shorts, and a t-shirt, his bronze skin shiny with sweat, and inky hair wet from swimming as a little black pig followed beside him, the two of them leaving a trail of footprints in the sand.

"Do you think you will ever keep another pig?"I asked, and he shook his head.

"Unfortunately, no. Or any pet, for that matter. Pets are like human friends: when they get hurt, you hurt with them. It's easier to go without," he murmured. His eyes closed as he drank from his cup, and I stared, knowing there was some hidden story behind his words, but I wasn't sure he was willing to say more the way he had a moment ago.

Neither of us spoke for several minutes. A band of house sparrows were trilling, and cheeping in the bushes opposite, their fragile brown bodies swaying as they balanced on skinny branches in the gentle breeze. I wanted to speak, to offer something to let him know that I understood how he felt to survive alone, but I couldn't find the words. He had left me hanging on a cliff's edge.

"So, how do you find it living in the bay? Do you like it yere?" He broke the silence suddenly, taking my mind away from many sour memories that I preferred to leave behind.

"It's okay. Everyone is nice enough." I shrugged slightly, unsure of what else to say. I wasn't sure if he knew my secret, although by now I would have been surprised if there was a single person left in the village who didn't know it.

"I see you sometimes, walking around by yourself with your camera," he commented. His voice was neutral, and it made it hard for me to grasp what he meant by it.

"Yeah, well, I guess that won't be happening anymore since I busted it yesterday. I fell over when I was coming down the hill and smashed it to bits." I huffed, all the aches in my body becoming suddenly apparent as though they were trying to remind me of what had happened.

"That explains the bruises," he said, and I nodded. "Your mam mentioned it last night. Shame about your camera, though. I suppose it can't be fixed?"

"Nope. Maybe if I'm lucky, Mum will buy me a new one for Christmas," I grumbled against the edge of my mug before taking a swig of tea.

"That's six months away."

"Don't remind me. I'm already contemplating selling myself to a brothel just to afford one," I grunted, and he chuckled.

"There aren't any of those round yere. I know, I've looked." He smirked, and we both laughed then. I liked the way his eyes glinted, and shone, joy pouring through them, spilling out from his closely-guarded core.

I waited for him to ask me what I photographed, but the question never came. I could see the knowledge was already within, and of course it would be. Everybody knew about the weird young man who went about taking pictures of dead animals, but nobody ever asked me why I did it, they only ever asked how. How could I stand near those bloated sacks of meat that hummed with flies? How did I sleep at night after looking at such horrors? Those were easier questions to answer than the ones I was asked about my gender. I was at least grateful he didn't ask too.

I felt contented sitting in the warmth of the summer sun with Maredudd, surrounded by birdsong, and buzzing bumblebees, and the rich scent coming in off the ocean. There was something about him that made me feel as though I knew him well. We remained in the garden together until Mum came home, and she commandeered his company in the kitchen, saying it was time he earned his keep by peeling the carrots, and potatoes for dinner. He knew her well enough not to refuse.

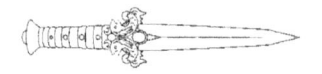

I stood in the shower, letting the hot water run over my face, my ginger hair turned dark copper against the pale skin of my forehead as droplets collected, and fell from the nest of a beard that grew on my chin, and jaw. It felt good to soothe my bruises in the warmth of the downpour, and with a belly full of roast dinner, and my muscles pleasurably tired, I was about ready for bed. For the first time in a long time, I felt happy to have shared such a long conversation with someone other than my own mother, and there was growing an excitable urgency for more, the same sort of urgency I imagined grew inside of Jojo after a brief game of fetch. I wanted to talk more, to find out more about his past.

He dropped hints that he had known my father as a friend, but when I pressed him on it, he became evasive, and almost timid. I had met so few people who knew my dad, and of those few only a couple had known, and remembered him well, so when I came across one I clung to them until I had managed to excavate every scrap of information from their minds. Along with that aspect, it was also refreshing to talk to someone who didn't judge me. At first I had been shy, and apprehensive, but I now felt that Maredudd was open-minded, and gentle despite his rough-and-tough exterior. The salty wind, and harsh sun had not been kind to him, and had aged his good looks by a several years, but in the process they had strengthened him, and behind the fortress of his body there hid a peaceful soul with a mischievous sense of humour.

I thought about him sitting downstairs with Mum, both of them chatting over bottles of beer with the telly on mute. I wished it could be like this forever, for Geraint not to come back, for the house to always be filled with this calm, this friendliness. For the house to be a nest, and a sanctuary, not a prison or a hostel.

I stayed in the shower for much longer than was necessary, just allowing the stream of water to patter upon the top of my head as I leaned against the tiled wall. I still felt down about my camera. I didn't even have a mobile phone or a regular digital camera I could use in its place, so without a replacement it was impossible for me to record the evidence if another attack occurred. Mum still had an ancient analogue camera she had been using since the 80s, but I couldn't afford to buy film or pay for prints. I was totally, and utterly screwed.

The jagged remains of my precious SLR rested on the cabinet near my mirror. I eyed it miserably as I rubbed my hair dry. We had been through a lot, that camera and I. Travelled, and witnessed many things together, its angular weight resting first between small bosoms, then against a tightly bound breast strapped down by a compression vest, and finally, upon a surgically-scarred chest covered with hair. The camera knew my body the way nobody else did. It was like a Yokai from Japanese mythology, carried, and given love until it finally developed a soul of its own, and for that reason, I decided I would hang onto it, because to chuck it in the bin would be every bit akin to throwing Jojo out with the trash.

I stood before the mirror and looked at the chest where my camera would no longer be. The heat from the shower had caused the two white scars there to turn pink, and tiny droplets twinkled in my chest hair. I could walk topless on the beach, and no one would bat an eyelid, something I had fantasised about as a teenager when wearing a bra was like being tangled in some sort of torture apparatus devised by Medieval nuns. To walk beside the sea in nought, but a pair of shorts, feeling the breezes brush against my bare skin, and the sun warming my shoulders. I never thought it would be possible. Yet my self-esteem sometimes took a nosedive, and I found myself too shy and paranoid to do it, instead choosing to keep a vest or t-shirt on, worried that someone would see my scars, and figure out what they meant.

If they had pulled my shorts down, they would know for certain, as my chest was the only part of me I'd had surgery on. I had loathed being in the hospital so much that it outweighed by desire to physical transition any further, and so I had chosen not to go ahead with any further operations. Fortunately, it had borne no effect on acquiring my legal gender as a man. Besides, who could look at me now, and say that it would be appropriate to call me a woman? There was nothing visibly feminine about me, or at least Mum reassured me there wasn't.

That's why it made me so angry when people in the village addressed me with my old name. They had never known me as Cerys. Without knowledge of my transition, they would have only ever seen me as Owen, but instead they chose to be cruel, and spiteful, and I saw the hard pin-pricks of sadistic delight in their staring eyes as they waited for me to rise to the bait. I didn't understand why people enjoyed tormenting others. I wanted to be invisible, a ghost passing by unseen. I didn't want people to take notice of me for what or who I was, I just wanted to live my life, and cause no harm to others. Dad had said people projected their insecurities onto me, because my existence presented difficult questions about themselves that they were uncomfortable about answering, but that was their problem, not mine. It used to make me bitter when I was younger. It was easy for him to say that when he wasn't on the receiving end of the abuse, but I eventually realised that every time I was hurt, he was hurt too. Just like Maredudd had said.

Thinking about Dad brought a pang of longing, as though a dusty box had been opened, and out of it had sprung all the feelings of neediness, and grief I had shut in there following his disappearance. I had always aspired to be like him, right back when I was a gangly little girl with my hair cut short, and grazes on my knees from falling out of trees. Like a cairn carved from an unshakeable mountain, he stood central to my life, providing a sturdy wisdom I could always rely on. Mum was the irrational big-spender, and I had inherited my desire for long intellectual discussion from her, but Dad had been the statue of Buddha, the guide, and the source of my curiosity. He had introduced me to Celtic folk tales, and songs, stories, and myths told by the ancient Britons, and later the religions, and traditions of the Germanic peoples. He held so much historical information inside his clever brain that he always had something new to tell me when we got talking about our shared interest in mythology. When he had vanished from our lives, he had taken all those old tales with him, and in doing so had become a myth himself. He was my folk tale I told myself at night, stories of a man who had once been, like a great, and wise clan chief or an armoured hero, a dragon slayer.

Furiously, I rubbed the tears from my eyes with a grimace of despair. I hated crying. Not because I had been shamed for it by anyone, or because it was humiliating, but because I had never cried in the past, and to do so made me feel weak. I had been bullied, chased, attacked, and woken up from surgery in agony, but I had never shed a tear. But now, even despite the stretch of time that had passed since Dad's false funeral, it was the only thing that made my guts twist, and my eyeballs ache in their sockets.

"Owen—are you okay?" I heard Mum's voice speak from the door, sounding as though she had been about to ask me a different question until she saw me wiping at my face.

"Couldn't you have knocked first?" I mumbled, turning away from her. I didn't want her to see the tears or the redness of my cheeks.

"The door was open," she answered, but she didn't seem annoyed by my complaint. "I was just going to ask if you wanted some hot chocolate. What's the matter?"

"Nothing. I'm fine." I sighed as I went to the cabinet and tugged out one of the drawers. She watched me putting on a shirt whilst struggling to hold my towel around my waist.

"Your camera, is it?" She turned her attention to the damaged device sitting on the cabinet.

"I'm just annoyed about that, I don't know what I'm going to do. I haven't got any money," I murmured as I pulled up my pyjama trousers.

"I can have a chat with Alison, see if there's any work that needs doing?" she suggested, and I managed a grateful smile.

"That'd be great if you could. I don't know if I can wait until Christmas for a new one," I admitted. I folded the damp towel, draping it over my arm.

"Me, and Maredudd were having a look at cameras

on the internet, but I couldn't remember what make yours was. Maybe you can take a look with him, since you're the camera expert." She smiled too, and I grinned sheepishly.

I nodded. "Thanks Mum. I would like some hot chocolate, by the way."

"Oh yeah?" She made a cheeky laugh as she ducked out into the hallway. "Go and put the kettle on then!"

Four

"Is your mammy home?" Rhys threw the question in my face the moment I opened the door.

It was early Friday morning, the sun blazing through the stained-glass windows in the front door, and casting red, and green beams upon my face as I had approached it. He must have been out there banging on the door for at least twenty minutes, but it hadn't been enough to rouse Mum from her hibernation. Still, Maredudd's voice had greeted me when I had scuttled out onto the landing in my pyjamas.

Rhys was standing on the doorstep in grass-stained overalls, wellies on his feet, and a jangle of dog leashes hanging from his utility belt. He was the son of Farmer Jeff, and his wife Mandy, two people I had had the displeasure of meeting only once, although I had seen Farmer Jeff, and his pack of sheepdogs far off in the distance, usually when I was running away from them. Brown-haired, and blue-eyed Rhys had derived a great amount of pleasure from chasing me, with or without the dogs, but his choice of footwear meant he hadn't caught me just yet, always getting his wellies stuck in the mud or slipping on the wet grass. We both knew it was me he pursued, but neither of us spoke of it, he just looked at me with that knowing sneer to let me know he was on my case.

"My mother is asleep." I regarded him as I turned up my nose. I hated it when people called her mammy to my face. It made me feel as though they were trying to belittle me by referring to her with a word reserved for use by small children.

"Go and wake her up, she needs to call Geraint, someone's got to get him to come home sooner." He ignored my correction, and instead moved in to lean against the door frame, forcing me to take a step back. He was taller, and stronger than I was even though I was his senior by six years.

"Why don't you get your mammy to call Geraint?" I glared, disliking how rude he was being.

"Because he haven't taken his mobile with him have he, dipshit. Only your mam have got the hotel number. Now go and wake her up."He waved his hand at me like he was dismissing a servant.

"Can't this wait? It's so rude to go knocking on someone's front door at seven o'clock in the morning, and demanding they get out of bed just because you're too impatient to wait."I motioned to shut the door in his face, but he blocked it with his hand, slamming his palm against the wood, and forcing it ajar again.

"Go, and get her, Cerys!" he shouted at me. "There's been a fucking massacre!"

"Don't call me that!" I shouted back, but just hearing my old name struck me down like a poisoned arrow to Achilles' heel.

An odd sort of quiet settled, and I felt myself choking, trying to lift some kind of insult to toss at him, but instead my words lodged in my throat, and he looked at me at first with uncertainty, but then I saw the amusement on his face, and he knew he had won.

"What's going on down yere!"Mum's voice suddenly exclaimed, startling the both of us as we both hadn't heard her come downstairs, and along the hallway. "Stop that shouting now, the both of you! Fancy making such a racket at the crack of dawn!"

"Sorry, Mrs Vaughn, didn't mean to make such a noise. It was Owen. He wouldn't go and fetch you when I asked of him."Rhys put on his best floor-crawling snivel in a bid to win Mum over, but Mum was smart, and she knew he was a wind-up merchant.

"Now you look yere, young Rhys. I don't care if your mam or dad sent you by yere at the stroke of midnight, you do not come by people's houses banging on the door to wake them, it's plain rude! I know you've been up since five o'clock, but some of us don't have to start work until eleven, and would appreciate a lie-in from time to time, especially since those certain people have to work on weekends as well. Now come on, out with it." Mum frowned at him, hands on her hips as he shrank from a six, and a half feet tall man into a naughty six-year-old.

Rhys couldn't look her in the eye. I saw his hand go to his belt, looking for something to fiddle with. "Well, it's the sheep, see. Dad and me, we went to the field this morning, and most of 'em were dead. All guts taken out all over the place. I've been putting wire traps out on the field edges, but it's doing nothing to stop it. Dad says I'm not doing it properly, wants Geraint to come and take a look. And one of my dogs has gone missing—my old dog Chief."

I was surprised Rhys revealed the well-hidden worry he had concealed from me, I felt how afraid, and upset he was by the disappearance of his dog. That explained why he was carrying the leashes with him, in case he came upon Chief on the road. I knew Chief well, knew the gruff howl of his bark. He was the ringleader of the pack, always the first to bark when strangers came close, setting off a chorus of howling from the other dogs who were often kept outside on chains in the summer months.

"I'll leave Geraint a message, and ask him to call you

back. The thing is, I've been calling him since Monday, and I haven't been able to speak to him directly. He's been so busy. But maybe he will come by sooner if he sees how bad this is getting. All right?"Mum's previously authoritative manner had dissipated into one of pity.

"Thank you, ma'am. I shall tell my dad you said so. If you see Chief, let us know as soon as you can."He nodded gratefully. I couldn't tell if Rhys was just a really good actor when it came to be pretending to be respectful, or if he genuinely felt respect for his elders.

"Of course we will, boyo." She agreed, and he turned, and headed back to the garden gate, giving us a wave as he closed it behind him, and stalked off down the path.

I shuffled off down the hallway, the bitterness of being fecklessly insulted by Rhys on my own doorstep leaving me disheartened, and astounded. Mum shut the door, instantly sensing that something was wrong, and following me into the kitchen where I had already put the kettle on to make some tea.

"I heard what he said to you, Owen," she said as she stopped on the steps in the doorway.

I didn't answer. I turned my back on her, not wanting her to see the look on my face as I screwed my features up. I thought I looked like a squashed cushion when I was going to cry.

"That wasn't very nice of the boy, and I'm surprised he had the nerve to be nasty to you on our porch. I didn't think Rhys was like that," she added when she realised I wasn't going to speak.

"Remember what I said the other day, about how people are different when you're not around? And if you heard what he said, why didn't you stick up for me?" I looked at her over my shoulder. It was so hard not to blame what had happened on her, so hard not feel angry at her instead of Rhys. It didn't make sense, but resisting it was a struggle.

"I did stick up for you," she replied anxiously, folding her arms.

"No, you didn't. You didn't even mention to him what he said. You told him off for shouting. Why didn't you talk to him about it, tell him off for using my old name?" I cried, trying my best not to raise my voice as I couldn't bear the thought of Maredudd seeing or hearing me like this.

"I can't always tell people off for you, Owen! You're an adult, you have to take care of yourself sometimes!" She held out her palms at me, shrugging her shoulders.

"You have never told people off for me. It was always Dad who stood up for me, not you," I whispered, tears forming in the corners of my eyes. "Even when I was bullied at school, Dad sorted it out. Whatever he did for me, he made it stop, and made those people leave me alone. But you always make excuses. Sometimes it feels you think I deserve it! That I've brought it on myself!"

"Owen..." She shook her head slowly, her eyes opening wide with horror at what I was saying. I could tell I had hurt her, and I knew that later, when the anger had subsided, it would be replaced with guilt and humiliation.

"Just—stop. Stop. I don't want to talk about it." I turned back to the kettle on the counter, refusing to look at her.

"Owen, please. You know I've always done my best to look after you..." She tried to reinitiate the conversation, but I ignored her.

I couldn't argue with her because I knew I was wrong. Even with the anger, I knew it. Of course she had always cared about me. Even without Dad here, she always supported me, and listened when I needed a helping hand. The anger rolled over onto me, disappointment in myself for being unable to fight back against Rhys, and against all the other people who teased, and tormented me. Fighting them was already so hard when you were weak from taking many knives in your back before the next battle had yet to begin.

Mum's arms enveloped me, and I felt the warmth of her body through the fluffy fabric of her dressing gown as she rested her chin on my shoulder. Already, I felt terrible.

"The last thing I want is for my precious son to be hurt or angry because of other people's ignorance. If what you need is for me to turn into a gorgon next time anyone even says the old name, then so be it," she whispered to me, her voice close to my ear. "My daughter might have turned into a man, but what you don't know is I can turn into a monster when I feel like it."

"I know that already." I made a snuffling laugh as I rubbed my nose in my sleeve.

"I haven't been doing a good enough job of hiding my snaky hair then, have I?" She giggled, and I laughed with her, both of us rocking together as she held onto me.

"Mum, I'm sorry for what I said, a minute ago."

"It's all right. You've said worse in the past. Let's just put it behind us, okay?" She assured me, and though she was good at pretending, I knew a part of her was still wounded, but I also knew that to keep bringing it up would prevent it from healing. It was the same when Dad disappeared—she found it easier to cope if she didn't speak of it.

The kettle clicked off, and steam billowed from the spout, catching our attention. I hadn't even taken the cups or teabags out of the cupboard.

"Let's get some breakfast ready. I expect Maredudd has been up with the cockerel, and he's probably hungry too." She patted me on the arm as she stepped away, the absence of her body heat leaving my back suddenly cool. "Oh, and one more thing?"

"Hmm?" I glanced at her over my shoulder as I

opened one of the cupboards.

"Please don't go out to the Fairfields' property. If so many sheep were killed as Rhys says, maybe it's for the best that you don't pursue your hobby for now. It's possible that whomever, or whatever is doing this is one day gonna catch *you*. It seems like it's getting worse, and worse with the passing months. I'm scared for you, Owen. Really scared," she answered in a low voice, her eyes only meeting mine at her last sentence. I had never heard my Mum say she was scared before. Worried, yes, plenty of times, but never scared.

"There's no point anyway since I don't have a camera anymore," I told her, withholding the fact that my curiosity urged me to go out there just so I could take a look at the destruction. I kept a written record of everything alongside the photos, in case there were things I couldn't capture in a picture, like sounds, and smells.

Despite my reassurance, her expression didn't change. She simply nodded.

I decided to do as she asked, and not go out to the field, telling my curiosity to give it a rest, and instead trying to sate my desire to witness the evidence with my own eyes by writing down exactly what Rhys had told us. Mum did phone Geraint's hotel, and afterwards she phoned the Fairfields too, chatting with Mandy for a while, letting her know she had done her best to reach Geraint, so hopefully he would get back to them soon. After the call, she came to speak to me about it, as she had managed to glean some additional information she knew I would be interested in. Supposedly, the chain that had connected Chief's collar to the breeze-block wall it was riveted to had been pulled completely free of the concrete, and both the chain, and the dog were nowhere to be found.

On top of that, forty of the sixty sheep that had been kept in the field close to farmhouse had been mauled sometime in the evening, and yet the farmer, and his family hadn't seen or heard anything until late that night when the dogs began crying outside. No one could figure out what sort of animal had attacked them, but Jeff said the only thing he could think might leave similar bite marks was a bear. There were no bears on the loose in the UK, that was for sure.

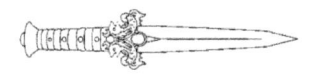

On Saturday morning, Mum went off to work, only for a couple of hours as was customary to freshen up any caravans that needed a little spruce before guests arrived, and that left me to take care of Maredudd. I was surprised she hadn't allowed him to leave yet since he seemed to be doing pretty well, but then again, if the way she threatened to tie me to bed when I had flu, perhaps I should have expected that. Secretly I was glad he was still with us. It gave me more opportunities to spend time with him. Mum gave me some money, and a list alongside it. I got up early with her, anxious to get the shopping out of the way before everybody descended upon the grocery store, meaning I was less likely to bump into people who didn't like me very much.

We walked together down the steep hill, and onto the beach, chatting, and giggling about some shows that had been on the telly last night, and I looked out across the sea, and the expanse of grainy, undulating sand that stretched out towards the gently lapping waves. It was low tide, and clumps of seaweed were strewn across the flat dunes, tiny shells, and bird bones dotted here and there, mirroring the night sky when the stars weren't obscured by clouds. I breathed deeply. The air here tasted good; it was like a salty meal, Mum said.

"Just don't breathe too deep or you'll end up with

the runs."Mum cackled as she slapped my arm, almost losing her footing on the uneven ground. I wasn't sure that breathing the air would give me diarrhoea, but I kept my lungs taut just to be on the safe side.

Laughing, we clung onto each other, and I grinned as she chattered away, that mischievous twinkle in her eye. It was a twinkle I hadn't seen for over a year since Dad's absence, so to be able to witness it again was very reassuring indeed, and I liked to think that perhaps the grief inside her was starting to weather away, like an old rock battered by the winds. Her relationship with Geraint had come about because of the grief, or at least that was what I liked to tell myself.

Mum left me on the other side of the bay, turning to take the long winding road up onto the fields where the caravan park was, and I turned in the opposite direction, climbing the stile, and wandering off down the narrow lane between farmland, and forest towards the cluster of shops that served our small village. The air was a cool relief after yesterday's heat, and I was grateful for the wind that gently lifted my hair and brushed against my bare legs. This was by no means the quickest route to the shops, but I had enjoyed my walk with her, just talking the way we used to do back in Bristol, just walking like we had in the park or up on the Downs.

I banished the grinding sensation of longing for a time past, just the way I did all the other bad feelings, instead focusing on the task at hand. If I was lucky, there would be no one in the shop, and I could get in and out quickly, then walk home and have breakfast with Maredudd. Sometimes I wished we could move further into town, where the shops were large, and no one would notice me as I could just fade into the background, a boring young man in boring clothes, no fuss or bother to anyone.

The shops sat side by side on the main road through

the village, facing outwards towards the bay with several cottages sandwiching them like tacky book-ends. The shops themselves had once been cottages too, but the front exteriors had had large windows put in, and signs installed, and had quickly become essential trade points for everyone who lived here. As I approached, Mrs Bryn was carrying large boxes of fresh vegetables outside, and stacking them. She was a huge woman, built like a Russian bear wrestler with a round face, and rosy cheeks, but her appearance was deceiving as she was sweet, and friendly to everyone, including me. She wore her brown hair in a closely-clipped bob, and her large bosom beneath her work apron was like a pair of footballs tucked down the front of her dress. She cussed when her ankles swelled, making her hobble about, and forcing her to loosen her boot laces.

"Bore da, young Owen, and how be you this fine day?" She greeted me, panting as she tilted back her shoulders, hands on her broad hips.

"Bore da, Mrs Bryn, I'm doing quite well. How are you?" I replied, stopping beside the stack of boxes she had just been handling.

"How many times have I told you, boy, it's Eryl! Call me Eryl!" She clapped a huge hand on my shoulder and gave me a careful shake.

"Sorry, I can't help it." I laughed, and she smiled down at me with her tiny, beady eyes.

"Shopping for yer mam?" she asked, and I nodded. "Good lad. The shelves have all been stocked despite that lazy arse back there. Jamie! Get your arse out of that chair!"

Her voice made my ears ring as she leaned through the doorway, and shouted at her son, who was no doubt hiding away in there somewhere. She patted me on the back, gesturing that I should go in, and then she shuffled into the doorway behind me, her boots thumping on the linoleum floor as she squeezed past me, and went further into the store. I looked around, checking to see if there was anyone else present, but I couldn't see anyone over the racks, and shelves that packed the somewhat claustrophobic space. I often wondered how Mrs Bryn navigated this shop as the aisles were so narrow, and the ceiling so low. It was like being in a cave.

I picked up a basket and pulled the shopping list out of the pocket of my denim shorts and began looking for the items Mum had written down for me. I could hear Mrs Bryn huffing, and grunting in the stock room doorway, and Jamie complaining to her in his squeaky, weaselly voice. But I could hear other voices too. I stopped in the biscuit aisle and listened. There were two people on the other side, talking to each other in a hushed tone as they gossiped. It was Mrs Armitage, and Mrs Bevan, the village's most notorious old wind-bags who knew the ins, and outs of everybody's rears. I pretended to be looking at the shelves in front of me, my eyes skimming over the brightly coloured packets as my ears strained to hear what they were saying.

"Well, I saw Mr Fairfield out looking for the dog..." Mrs Bevan was whispering. "And he told me that late last night, Fred—you know Fred? Dorothy's husband?"

"Oh, Fred! Paul's brother, the one with the..."

"... The big red birth mark on his face," they said in unison.

"I thought he moved up by Aberystwyth?" Mrs Armitage questioned curiously.

"Oh, no, he lives round by Vera..." she continued, and I rolled my eyes.

I wanted to know what they had been saying about Jeff Fairfield, but as usual their conversations never stayed to a single topic, and always went off on a tangent about people they knew.

I glanced down the aisle, noticing Jamie Bryn had come out, his cheeks marked by acne, and his heavily-straightened blonde hair hanging either side of his face, making him look rather like a scarecrow. Unlike his mother, he was thin, and reedy, and walked with a stoop. I didn't mind Jamie so much. Like me, he was shy, but as he was so young, and still at school, I didn't think it would be appropriate to be his friend. He made a breathy "Hi" as he passed me, sleeves rolled up to reveal the studded wristbands he wore. Besides, he was more interested in going to concerts, and spray-painting pentagrams on the nearby churches—we didn't have a lot in common. I turned my attention back to the old ladies once he had left the aisle.

"... Fred was coming along the road over by the Cock Inn, and he swears blind he hadn't been drinking—"

"What time was that?" Mrs Armitage cut her off.

"Oh it was late in the night. He had Teifion come and pick up in the car. He found him laying at the side of the road in a right state! Poor dab was chased all along the lane by a big animal!" Mrs Bevan gasped, her nasally voice difficult to hear over Jamie stacking the crates outside. "Apparently, it was a huge dog or something of the like. A stinking, dirty great thing, and it ran after him all down the hill until he got to the main road..."

"Never! Oh, the poor bugger, and he's had that trouble with his hip since last year, I do hope he's doing all right. You know, I was talking to Jayne last week, and she said her daughter was getting out of a taxi on the circle at the end of the road, and she saw this big black thing running alongside the verge over by the park where the little ones play, you know, near Bishops Road..."

"Oh yes, I think Heath lives up by there, you know where they were going to build that block of flats..."

I turned away, alarmed by what I had heard. Alarmed that someone else had been followed by this creature, and astonished that people had seen it in the village, not out on the fields where few, but the farmers walked. I wanted to question them about it, but they would know I had been eavesdropping, and instead moved about doing my shopping as before, keeping my ear out in case they spoke of the mysterious monster again, but instead they had started talking about someone's baby, and didn't return to the subject.

I picked up some cookies for Maredudd, and the bag of rice Mum had asked for, filling the basket, and then heading to the front of the store where the counter was. Jamie was milling about behind it, gnawing at his badly chewed fingernails, and swinging the swivelling stool from side to side. He stopped as soon as I appeared, and clumsily started checking out each item, his eyes occasionally snatching brief glances at me while I put them into the plastic carrier bag.

"Were you listening to the old ladies a minute ago?" he whispered to me, his voice like an out-of-tune violin. I looked up at him, my eyes wide open.

"Yes, why?" I murmured, worried they would come up behind me, and catch us talking.

"Well, you know what they were saying about... About old Fred being chased, and all that...?" he mumbled, continuing to scan the bar-codes on the packets of food.

"What about it?" I asked, curious to what he was getting at.

"You're taking pictures of the dead animals, right? You know about the monster, right? Well I've seen it." He leaned closer, and whispered to me, his face inches from mine. "I seen it over by the castle ruins. By the witch's cave."

I stepped back slightly, examining his face to check he wasn't winding me up, but his small eyes were darkly serious, and he was biting his braced teeth into his bottom lip.

"You don't believe me, do you."He shook his head

slowly, but I nodded quickly, not wanting to discourage him from telling me.

"I do believe you. What did it look like?" I hissed, trying to keep my voice low. He had finished checking out the shopping, and it was obvious we were deep in conversation to anyone who happened to gaze in our direction.

"A big seal. A big black, and grey seal," he replied, and I stared speechlessly for a moment, unable to believe what he'd said.

"Are you telling me a big seal chased Fred down that lane?" I was unable to stop a frown from creasing my forehead.

"I'm not saying that was what chased him, but I seen a big animal down by the cliffs there, and it wasn't like no seal I've ever seen. Huge it was, and when it seen me, and Nicky coming down the hill, it started humping up the side of the cliff, and was barking at us, so we ran away before it could get us," he told me, seeming slightly embarrassed for a moment. I could tell my disbelief had cowed him somewhat, and he was now reluctant to say anymore. "Don't know where it went after that. But I ain't going back round there any time soon."

I was silent, the little cogs in my head turning rapidly, well-oiled by this new information. He watched me for a minute or two, then pushed some, buttons on the till, and tray shot open as the receipt gradually ejected from the slot.

"Sixteen pounds, and twenty pence, please," he answered glumly, unable to look at me.

"Oh—here, here it is." I stuffed my hand in my pocket and took out some cash. I tried to make eye contact with him as I handed him the money, but it seemed I had upset him. "Jamie, I do believe you, and I'm grateful you told me. If you see or hear anything else, let me know or tell my Mum so she can pass it on to me, and if you have a camera, try and get a picture next time."

He managed an awkward smile and seemed to cheer up a little at my words. "Okay. I said to Nicky you were taking pictures, and all that. Was wondering if you could show us sometime."

"Maybe I will. You'd better have a strong stomach though: they're a bit gross." I chuckled as he handed me my change, and I picked up the carrier bag, and hauled it off the counter. "See you later."

"See you later," he repeated my words back to me as I turned and headed for the door. "And don't worry, we got proper strong stomachs! You got to when you eat mammy's cooking!"

I heard Mrs Bryn's call of disapproval as I set off on my walk back to the house, the coolness in the air already beginning to dissipate as the sun blazed overhead.

When I arrived home, Jojo was in the hallway, and she leapt up against my legs, tail wagging with excitement, and tiny paws slipping about on the polished floor. I bent to greet her, smiling, and attempting to pet her head as she shook her rope toy back and forth in her delicate white jaws, cooing baby talk to her like I usually did. The house was peaceful, and cool, and as I plodded along the hallway, I wiped my hand over the back of my neck, grunting with discomfort as my fingertips fell upon the sunburn that was irritating my skin.

When I reached the kitchen doorway and ascended the steps into the room I found Maredudd was sitting at the table reading the newspaper. The wad of thin paper rustled as he lowered it, and smiled at me over the top, his eyes shining. He looked much more well than he had a day or two ago after he was wounded. I had thought about questioning him again about what had happened when Mum brought him to the house, but I hadn't been able to find the right time to do it, and following my conversation with Jamie about the big seal he had seen, my mind had immediately gone back to the pelt that had accompanied Maredudd to the house. I contemplated broaching the subject again to him while I put the shopping away in the cupboards, and he hummed quietly to himself, his head hidden behind the paper once more.

"I was talking to someone in the shop earlier," I commented thoughtfully, and I heard the paper lower again as he was no doubt looking at my back.

"Hmm?" He sounded curious.

"He said he saw a huge seal down on the cliffs awhile back. Funny since we don't often get seals around here. They congregate more on the islands off the coast further north. Unusual to see one in the bay," I continued with my thinly veiled bait.

He must have picked up on it straight away because he simply chuckled and hummed again. I glanced over my shoulder at him as I put some things away in the cupboards above the counter.

"Have you seen any seals on the beach?" I asked, and he looked up at me with his dazzling green eyes. I couldn't help but feel a sharp twinge of jealousy every time I looked at his face, jealous at how masculine he was, and how beautiful his eyes were. I felt so plain by comparison.

"On occasion, yes. The sea is all connected, so sometimes they do come round yere. Plenty of fish for them to feed on in the bay, no predators either. The only thing stopping them breeding by yere is the tourists." He grinned, flashing his straight, blunt teeth. "I spend a lot of time at the beach so although they are rare, I have seen them about."

"Oh. That's nice, I guess I should visit the beach more often. I spend so much time walking around the woods." I made an awkward smile as I stuffed the carrier bag into one of the drawers under the sink.

"Maybe when my leg is better, we can go for a walk on the beach together? Would be nice to have a bit of company. I'm usually on my own," he suggested amicably.

I couldn't stop a slight blush from creeping into my cheeks, and I tried to fend it off as subtly as possible. "I'd love to. I'm usually on my own too."

He nodded, his smile becoming rueful before he turned his attention to the newspaper, and folded it up, slapping it down on the table top. "Your mam tells me you don't have many friends in the village, and well, I can sympathise with that. Never had a lot of friends either, bit of a lone-wolf you might say, but even we lone-wolves get lonely sometimes."

"Yes, we do."I chuckled.

"I don't know much about your situation, but I've got an open mind for most things, and I can appreciate it must be tough to make friends when you're different. I've always felt like an outcast, especially when I was a kid growing up yere in this tiny village, people talking behind your back, giving you stupid nicknames, and the like. It hardens a man, makes him rough-skinned. You'll know what I mean in twenty years' time," he said cautiously, and carefully, as though he was navigating a mine-field of difficult subjects and wasn't sure how to talk to me about them. It was strange hearing him say things like that, it felt like I was having a heart-to-heart with a long-lost parent. He scratched at his chin and managed a quick look up at my face.

"I guess Mum told you about me, and whatnot... I mean, I assumed you knew already because of what people say."I shrugged, trying to show him that I was comfortable with it.

"No, it was your dad that told me about you." He shook his head slowly, eyes half-closed. "Evan told me all about what was happening."

"Oh..." was all I could manage as I stared, large-eyed, and open-mouthed at him. I didn't think Dad had mentioned it to anyone, especially not here, not even to Geraint.

"Yeah. He did," he continued to nod. He seemed shy all of a sudden, seemed to shrink in size, becoming smaller as his fire died back to a gentle flicker. "He said if anything ever happened, I was to look out for you and your mam. Which I have, from a distance. I just wanted you to know that."

A heavy silence filled the kitchen as we both looked at the tiled ground between us, and I felt my heart twisting up into knots inside me, the aching grief for Dad that would never go away, and the agony it caused to hear someone talk about him, agony that could find no relief, and only made me desire to hear more despite the pain it inflicted on me. When I was close to Mum, I could feel that grief mirrored in her, a vibration that reached out, and joined with my own, as though spectral hands stretched from within us, and clasped together, silently letting the other know we felt the same.

And the strangest thing happened then, because I felt it coming from Maredudd: the hand reaching, the offer of friendship that came without words. I saw, and felt, and heard so much of Dad in him, yet at the same time, I felt that Dad was a loss to him, a piece carved away from his being, exactly the same way it felt with Mum, and even with myself.

"This is going to sound weird, but I feel like Evan is out there somewhere," Maredudd said, the silence still a thick blanket trying to stamp out all sound, and his words cut through it like a knife.

I met his face and saw the sternness in his expression.

"I don't like to talk badly of others, but Geraint was never Evan's friend. I shall say no more in that regard. Geraint can say what he likes about me, I don't care. But if he ever hurts you or Wenda, I want to know about it," he added after a pause. I thought I saw anger this time, strongly suppressed anger that he kept in close check. I couldn't imagine him being violent or aggressive, from how calm, and friendly he had been. "I want you to know, Owen, that I am here for you."

I wanted to ask, why now? Why didn't you speak to me in the years I have spent alone here? But I couldn't bring myself to utter a word. I was so astonished, my mouth opened, and closed, but nothing came out. Jojo, as if sensing that the most serious part of the conversation was over, leapt to her feet, and started to frolic with her rope toy, bounding around in front of us to distract our attention. The stony expression on Maredudd's weather-worn face was quickly replaced with a fond smile, and he leaned forward to take the rope from her mouth, pulling on the end, and getting her to tug o' war with him. I swallowed down my knotted heart, and though my mind was turbulent with the blustering tempest of dozens of questions, I thought better of asking any of them. I needed time to process what had been said.

Maredudd accompanied me in the garden when I went to see to the animals, and he was able to move about quite energetically, one would almost think he had never been injured in the first place. We didn't bring up our previous conversation; we only talked about the animals, about nature, and things we had seen on our walks in the countryside, and on the beach. He told me about how he worked on the farms, helping with the animals, and tending the fields, his experiences with caring for sheep during lambing season, and being chased by territorial bulls.

He much preferred working with the livestock as opposed to using the machinery. I wasn't surprised, especially not after seeing him petting the goats, and sitting in the garden with the chickens on his shoulders, and lap, their round forms cooing contentedly, so quickly accustomed to his presence they had become. One of the smaller hens had even tried to climb onto his head, but his long, silken hair had made it difficult, and her scaly feet gave him scratches on his neck, but he didn't mind.

"One has not lived a full life until one has experienced chicken shit on one's shoulders, as my dad is wont to say."He laughed, blowing a chicken feather from his nose.

"Does your dad live in the village?" I asked, sprinkling some seed on the ground as the hens pecked the grass around my feet. Their heads bobbed, and jerked about, gem-like eyes spying the grains I had put down, and even a little Wren flitted out from the hedge to steal a mouthful.

"Oh, no, he lives on the cliff, on the other side of the bay from yere," he replied as he stroked one of the hens on his lap, her eyes closing in bliss with each passing caress. "He doesn't go into the village anymore."

"Oh, I don't blame him." I smiled, sensing that there was some awkward reason why, and deciding to avoid asking about it. He must have been really old, so perhaps he was infirm, and couldn't manage to walk unaided.

"What about your Mum?" I asked gently, wondering if that would also be a difficult question to ask.

"I've never known my mam. My dad isn't my real dad either. I was adopted."His smile was sad as he beamed at me, the sunshine winking in his eyes when he lifted his head. "My dad found me orphaned as a baby while he was travelling in the Middle East. I'm from Iran originally. He never told me outright, but he always implied that my parents were dead. I never knew them, so I guess there's not a lot for me to feel about it, but I suppose it's quite sad really. Anyway, he's given me so much that I've never wanted for anything."

"Oh, that is sad. So is your dad Welsh?" I asked, rapt with fascination as I realised I knew so little about my new friend.

"No, he's English. Funny, isn't it?" He smirked, tilting his head to the side, and tickling the hen under her chin.

"Funny that I'm Welsh, but I've got an English accent, and you're Iranian, but you've got a Welsh accent." I laughed, moving across the lawn to come, and sit beside him on the bench.

"It has always fascinated me how there are different types of people. On one hand, you've got people whose entire identity is built on where they are from. Their culture, country, language is who they are. On the other hand, you've got people who didn't grow up in their homeland, but the land they grew up in is their identity. And then there are people who only see their identity as where they originated from, never mind where they grew up. I guess I fall into the second category since I'm a Welshman through, and through, never mind the colour of my skin. Do you know what I mean?"His eyes seemed to become more luminous when he was contemplating an interesting thought or looking upon something unusual with curiosity.

"Yes, I think I must be in that category too. Never felt very Welsh, to be honest. But then I don't feel very English either. I'm not sure what I am. Human, I guess."I reasoned with a slight chuckle. "Does it really matter where you came from or grew up?"

"Well, it depends. My dad believes that you should shape your identity with your own hands. He's lived in many different countries, and I think he sees a little bit of every one of them in himself. He told me that if you allow other people to shape your identity for you, you are doing a disservice to yourself," he replied, his expression serious, but there was still a sliver of mischief in his expression. "You'd know about that more than most other people, I expect."

I smiled, almost a sad smile. It was a somewhat cryptic compliment, but a compliment nonetheless. It made me feel strong, and that I was treating myself right despite everything I had been through over the years.

"Your dad sounds like a very wise man."

"Wisdom comes with enlightenment. When your eye is open, you see." He touched the middle of my forehead, a feather drifting from his sleeve, and landing on my shirt.

"Dad used to say stuff like that to me, but I never really understood what he meant. Is it a metaphor for keeping an open mind?" I frowned slightly, finding it odd yet rather interesting that Maredudd seemed to contain a lot of the same knowledge that Dad had.

"Yes, and no. There's duality in everything," he answered, and I thought he would say more, but he stopped.

I looked down at the hen on his lap, Betty her name was, but her eyes were closed, and she was near enough purring with pleasure as he stroked her.

"Even gender?" I asked after a moment of quiet, and he turned to look at me again.

"Yes, of course. Women can't resist a man who is kind, and playful with children. Men can't resist a woman who can give him a run for his own money. There's male and female in all of us," he reasoned, a brief shrug of his shoulder causing the hen to open her eyes a crack.

"Does that mean there's a bit of female in you, as well?" I nudged him with my elbow jokingly, and he made a gruff, refuting laugh.

"I'm man enough to say yes." He nudged me back, his mouth breaking into a broad grin. "I've been told I'm the most romantic chap round yere."

I tried to prevent myself from blushing, but I

couldn't help it, and I wasn't sure if he noticed my demeanour change because he didn't point it out. When his eyes looked into mine, it felt like our gazes were two mirrors reflecting the same light back and forth between us, and it made it difficult for me to hide my embarrassment. Aggression I couldn't imagine, but romance, yes, that seemed so incredibly natural for him. For a moment I was madly jealous that I wasn't the chicken sitting on his lap. The strangest thing about Maredudd was how I felt as though he was reading my mind, innately aware of all the feelings I tried to disguise, feelings I had learned to conceal so well from others, even from Mum. Or perhaps I wasn't as good an actor as I first thought.

When Mum came home in time for lunch, I had already prepared some hot cheese, and tomato toasties for her, and the three of us sat in the garden munching on them, in between sips of cold orange juice. I realised this would be the last day that Maredudd was going to spend with us as Geraint was returning home tomorrow morning, and Mum said he wouldn't be happy to see Maredudd had been staying here with us. I wondered as I watched them chatting over bowls of jelly, and ice cream, whether something had happened between them before. Mum's eyes got that soft, fuzzy look about them when she was face-to-face with him, and she laughed in that high-pitched giggle she used to use when Dad was fooling around.

Surely they had never had an affair? I looked at Maredudd, watched him banging his hand on the table top, and doing an impression of someone in the village, jigging his shoulders from side to side, pointing his finger as he pretended to tell Mum off. There was an old friendship there that had been evident from the moment I first saw them interacting, and I knew there was much more going on here than they were willing to tell me. I told myself I was being stupid, that my jealousy, which had been so freely applied to a chicken of all things, was now attempting to release itself on my own mother, and I needed to stop right there before I let my imagination run wild.

In the afternoon, the bright sun became obscured by darkening clouds, and we all fled indoors when thunder, and lightning banished the summer warmth, rain beginning to froth in the air. Mum brought out a load of old photo albums as we sat in the living room, the television blessedly switched off, while I cringed, and begged them to skip over any photos of me when I was younger. Before we knew it, four hours had passed, and it was approaching seven o'clock at night.

"Owen, is it alright if you give Maredudd a lift home in the car?" Mum asked as I brought out the dirty cutlery from the living room. She was standing at the sink doing the washing up, pink rubber gloves pulled over her hands, and her round cheeks rosy from where she had been laughing so much that she'd cried.

"Oh, I guess I could..." I hesitated. It had been a few months since I had last driven Mum's little matchbox car, and I was worried I was too rusty.

"Go on, boyo. I've got a mountain of washing up to do. Unless you wanna swap?" she suggested, but I shook my head quickly.

"No, it's all right! I can manage," I chirped as I placed the mugs, and plates on the counter.

There was no way I was going to swap spending time with Maredudd in the car for standing to the sink cleaning dishes. He was still wearing some of my pyjamas, and I had expected him to borrow some shoes, but he said he was perfectly fine to go barefoot, and so once I had pulled on a raincoat, and boots, I took Mum's keys, and we went out into the garage where the small, box-shaped car was waiting for us. He climbed into the passenger seat with such ease, I was surprised as I had expected him to need help manoeuvring into the tight space, but it was almost as though his leg was completely healed. I used the remote on the keyring to open the garage door, and then reversed out onto the road, the downpour gradually consuming the entire vehicle as we emerged from beneath the shelter. With the garage closed once more, I went to turn the car, and ended up stalling it by accident, both of us laughing as I fought to correct my mistake.

"It's been awhile. Hopefully I don't crash, don't think that'd be a great ending to the day." I joked as we drove along the winding lane that led out towards the main road.

"Ideally I'd like to make it home with just the one dodgy leg, not two." He smirked. It was so dark now that it was difficult for me to see him in the shadows. The seal pelt folded on his lap glistened occasionally when light passed over it, distracting my peripheral vision.

"How is your leg doing now?" I asked, my eyes focused on the dark road, hedges lit up either side by the headlights of the car.

"Very well. I think I should be back to work on Monday."

"Oh, that's good. It looked really bad though. Are you sure you weren't attacked by a shark?" I asked with slight amusement. He had somehow skirted around talking about his injury the entire time he'd spent at our house, able to distract me with other topics when we were talking.

"No, I was swimming over by the cliffs, and a wave washed me onto the rocks, tore up my clothes really badly, and ripped a hole in my leg. I crawled onto the shore just in time to see your mam passing, and she helped me up," he explained, sounding completely relaxed about the matter. "I suppose I can tell people I was bitten. It would make a pretty impressive story to brag about."

"I'm not sure if it would be a good idea to go telling people like Mrs Bevan about it. You'll soon enough have the whole village too scared to go in the water, thinking Jaws is gonna come out of the deep, and swallow them whole." I giggled, enjoying imagining the old wind-bag swimming away from a dorsal fin cutting through the waves towards her.

"Well, at least I'd have the whole beach to myself so perhaps it wouldn't be such a bad idea after all." He laughed with amusement.

"Then no one would see you turn into a seal." I feigned innocence by attempting to disguise my words with jest.

At first he seemed confused, but then he laughed too, suddenly remembering the seal pelt on his lap. "Oh! You had me there then, Owen. Course I wouldn't want anyone seeing me transform, would be quite an embarrassing sight."

"Are you a Selkie or something?" I questioned light-heartedly, even though I felt as though I was beginning to interrogate him, and it made me guilty. I glanced at him, trying to make out his features in the dark.

"You don't believe in stories like that, do you?" He chuckled incredulously, and I was grateful the dim light hid my blush of shame.

"Well... I don't know..." I murmured, regretting that I had ever asked.

There was an awkward silence, only the rumble of the engine, and the hiss of the tires moving over wet asphalt as the rain hammered on the roof of the car. We had made it onto the main road, and pretty soon I would need his directions.

"I like that you put a lot of stock in old folk tales. Evan was like that too. There's a lot to be said for myths, and legends. Like they say, there's a shred of truth in every rumour." He broke the silence, his voice soft, and friendly. "That said, I'm no mythical creature. I may be exotic, but I'm not that exotic."

When the glow from the streetlights flashed through the window, I saw that he was smiling broadly, and I smiled back, feeling foolish. We fell silent again, and as we came to a crossroad, he told me which turn to take, before the quiet took over once more. I didn't quite know what to say, and it was taking a lot of concentration to focus on the road in the dark with the rain gushing down the windows, interrupted only by the windscreen wipers.

"Have you visited the little church up on the hill by you?" he asked suddenly. I got the feeling that he wanted to raise my spirits, not leave me feeling like I'd been shamed for what I had asked him.

"Which one?" I replied quietly.

"St. Illtyd's, the little chapel tucked away at the edge of the forest," he said, and I nodded, remembering the small, ancient structure surrounded by its miniscule graveyard, almost completely absorbed by the encroaching trees. "Have you heard the tale of the Ceffyl Dwr?"

"The water horse? Yes!" I grinned excitedly, quickly rousing with enthusiasm as he touched upon a subject I knew well.

"Ah, but have you heard the tale of St. Illtyd's Ceffyl Dwr?" He leaned close, nudged me with his elbow. "The ghostly horse that lived in the well?"

"I'm not sure...Go on, tell me then! I like hearing stories," I prompted cheerily, like a child awaiting a puppet show.

I listened to Maredudd's purring voice, the drama, and suspense he laid on thick with each sentence, at first making me laugh, and then making me nervous as the tale progressed, my eyes desiring only to look at him as I forced them to remain upon the road. He talked of how the equestrian apparition had been seen drifting through the graveyard of the medieval chapel, how it was believed to have been an archaic Celtic god, an elemental energy that protected, and oversaw the well that was dug in the churchyard. At night, it's shining, ethereal body flew soundlessly through the air once it had leaped clear out of the well, and into the night, appearing before lonely, night-time travellers. As the years passed, the site of worship fell into Christian hands, and with it, the future of the Ceffyl Dwr itself. Visitors to the churchyard on winter evenings were so afraid of the spectral creature that the priest was asked to banish it from the churchyard, and so he did, sending the horse vanishing down into the darkness of the well, where it was never to be seen again. With the Ceffyl Dwr gone, the water disappeared with it, and the well has been dry ever since.

Maredudd's talent for storytelling made me believe he'd be an excellent baby-sitter. I could imagine him surrounded by children, all of them craning their necks with their mouths open in fascination. Dad had been the same, able to hold an audience from beginning to end. I had been so rapt with attention that I hadn't realised how far we had driven to the other side of the bay. I could make out the dark void of the ocean over the hedges, and fences as we drove by, the winking dots of ships floating on its colourless surface the only clue as to what I looked at.

"Turn left at the bottom by yere, and then straight up the lane, and you'll come to my house," he told me as he pointed through the window at the road.

I followed his instruction, turning the car down a bumpy, gravel lane that led up between two round hillocks, long grass waving in the breeze either side of us, small stones crunching under the tires. Towards the top, the white shape of a cottage came into view, and suddenly I felt as if I recognised this place. I pulled up at the end of the path where it was cut off sharply by a cluster of boulders, and to the left there ran a series of stone steps that were dug into the knoll, leading to a gravel walkway that meandered towards the cottage door.

"I know this place—I can see your house from my window!" I exclaimed, turning in my seat to look around at what was illuminated by the car headlights.

"Yes, and I can see yours." He beamed at me. "Small world we're living in, huh."

"Sure is." I agreed, feeling somehow comforted that all this time I had been looking at his light in the window, his sign that he was home. "Do you need any help getting up the steps?"

"Nah, I'll be alright. Might get a bit wet, but I'll be fine. Fortunately, I didn't lose my house key." He took a keyring out of his trouser pocket and wiggled it at me. "Anyway, it was nice staying with you and your mam for a few days. It's been awhile since I got to spend time with Wenda, and it was great to meet you in person finally. You're welcome to come by any time, now you know where I am."

"Thanks, that'd be lovely..." I trailed off sheepishly, wondering if I would ever be brave enough to just knock on his door.

"Take care of yourself, Owen." He patted me on the shoulder, giving it a brief squeeze before he opened the car door, the pattering of the rain a sudden crescendo as he turned in his seat, and climbed out. There was no wind, only a ceaseless shower that soaked him right away.

I sat and watched him climb the steep steps towards the cottage, not even caring to shield himself from the rain, instead walking as though he was taking a leisurely stroll in the sunshine. I didn't drive off until he had gone inside, lighting up the front of the house with the headlamps so that he could see where he was going, and he turned, and waved to me before he stepped into the dark rectangle of his front door, and vanished from sight. Part of me wanted to get out of the car, and run to the door, to bang on it, and beg him to let me stay with him. Geraint would be home soon, and the holiday I had so enjoyed was now at an end, a holiday I wished could be an every-day. I realised I had forgot to ask him for his phone number, or even his email address, so I could contact him, but it was too late for that now.

I had to verbally command myself to leave, otherwise I would have sat there all night in the rain, hoping he would come outside, and beckon me in. Instead, I turned the car around, and began the journey home, my mind buzzing with so many memories, questions, thoughts of the time we'd spent together.

For the first time in my entire life, my heart ached in a way so alien to me, not the crushing ache of grief I felt for Dad or the joyful ache of friendship I felt for Mum, or even the ache of hatred, and disgust I had for Geraint. It was different, harder, hotter. Like a heavy iron kettle simmering away in my chest, wobbling with the pressure of the bubbling water, and ejecting gouts of steam from its spout. It was painful and pleasurable at the same time, and I had never felt that way about anyone before.

Trying to keep myself under control, I turned the radio on, the car filling with the sound of Elvis's crooning voice as he sang *Can't Help Falling In Love*, and frustrated by the CD Mum had left in the player, I turned it off abruptly. I half-expected to drive past a billboard advertising romantic meals for couples, or a pair of newly-weds kissing on their doorstep. I was grateful there was only darkness, and the rain streaming in rivulets down the windows. A few minutes passed in silence as I thought about my current situation, then I leaned forward, and turned Elvis back on. Maybe it was a sign or something, but I suddenly felt like I needed to listen to the song. Somehow it made me feel better.

Five

It took me a long time to fall asleep that night. I lay awake beside the window, staring out at the blackness of the bay, and on the other side, the light glowing in Maredudd's window. All I could think about was whether he was lying awake too, thinking of me. I knew I was being silly, that no good would come from this, but my heart was arrogant, and did what it wanted. There was no way it would listen to my sensible, logical brain.

Along with that, I was feeling rather unnerved by my journey back in the dark. A short distance from Maredudd's house, I had slowed at a set of traffic lights, which was absurd since there were no other cars on the road for me to let pass, and as I was waiting there, I saw a pale shape on the roadside ahead. Even though I had my fog lights on, the density of the rain dulled them, and it took me awhile to make out the black, and white collie standing there on the grass verge, its shaggy fur drenched with water, and its eyes glowing, reflecting the headlights back towards me. Trailing from its neck onto the closely-trimmed grass was a long, steel chain.

Sound sank away from me, silence causing my ears to ring as I gazed across the way at the dog, at first mesmerised, and then frightened as I realised it was Chief. I could recognise that old bastard anywhere because he was missing part of his left ear and had one black sock on his front leg. The lights turned green, and I should have pulled away and driven off, but I couldn't move. I could get out of the car, and try and call him to me, but something inside was telling me that was a very bad idea. I didn't have a mobile phone to call anyone for help, either. A minute passed, and still neither of us moved, and I swallowed deep, my throat dry, and a chill creeping over me, causing every hair on my body to prickle.

Why wasn't the dog moving? I reached to the glove compartment, opening the door to an avalanche of A-Z handbooks, and an assortment of junk, searching for the powerful LED torch Mum kept in there for emergencies, and when my hand seized the metal shaft, and I pulled it from its resting place, I went to open the car door. That's when I saw that the dog had disappeared. I bent, and peered through the windows on all sides, wondering if perhaps he had come towards the car, but I couldn't see or hear anything, not even the dragging of the chain on the asphalt. He must have gone back down the grass verge, under the hedgerow, and into the field beyond because there was nowhere else he could have gone that meant I wouldn't have heard the clatter of the chain.

Suddenly, I heard the blaring of a car horn, the startling noise frightening me so much that I accidentally chucked the torch down into the foot-well and threw myself back against the door of the car, bumping my head on the ceiling. A van had pulled up behind me at the junction, and the driver was thumping his palm on the horn, frustrated that I wasn't moving anywhere, but I was so bewildered by the sudden shock that I couldn't compose myself quick enough, so he swerved around me, and sped off down the road. After that, I drove home as quickly as I could with the radio on full blast, determined that this time I would stop for nothing, and no one until I had reached the garage.

I noted my sighting of Chief in my record book as soon as I shut the door to my bedroom, thankful that Mum was in the shower, and wasn't there to ask why I was white as a sheet. I planned to tell her about it tomorrow; she could pass on the message to the Fairfields because I sure as hell wasn't going to tell Rhys myself. With some fresh pyjamas on, and my duvet pulled right up to my chin, I soon managed to let go of the ordeal, and instead my mind drifted back to Maredudd. Jojo had come to lay on the bed with me, and her snout was buried in the duvet, causing her to make a muffled snoring sound as she slept peacefully beside me. Her eyes opened wide when I rested my hand on her back, before relaxing once more when she noticed it was just me, her tail giving a little wag of approval as she closed her eyes again.

I had put Mum's CD into my laptop, and Elvis's voice warbled quietly close behind me, while I gazed over the bay towards the source of this aching inside me, my hand slowly stroking Jojo's smooth fur. That was what was happening to me: I was falling in love, and I was frustrated with myself for it. Like Cerberus of Hades, it seemed the only way to make this beast sleep was to play it music, and that's when the frustration subsided, leaving me in a dreamy, glittery-eyed state.

Now I felt myself longing for Maredudd, and missing my father too, and it was doing nothing for my mental health. I was grateful when sleep finally took me. It was the only time I was able to shirk the thoughts going round in my head.

I woke the following morning to find that Jojo had abandoned me, no doubt scuttling off to the kitchen to await her breakfast, and so I was laying on my side hugging a pillow and feeling quite sorry for myself. I squinted into the watery light that was struggling through the window, noting upon the gloomy sky, and the sooty clouds that were floating in it. Wind shook the trees, and hedges outside, and they danced as though taking part in a silent party, waving their limbs back and forth to a beat I couldn't hear. The bay was damp and muggy with fog, and I could no longer see Maredudd's cottage for the thick layer of mist that had been blown in off the ocean, bringing with it more rain. I closed my eyes once more as there came a voice I had been dreading to hear. Geraint was home already, and it sounded like he was angry about something, which wasn't so much of a surprise really.

"Someone's been yere! Don't lie to me!" he shouted, and I heard something clang in the kitchen sink.

"It's none of your business what friends I have! I'm an adult!" Mum's voice shrieked back at him, and then the kitchen door was slammed shut, their voices becoming a murmured symphony through the walls of the house.

I had never seen Mum argue with someone until we had moved here. Of course she had had the occasional disagreement with Dad, but not to the extent where she was screaming, and abusing the furniture. It wasn't that she fought with Geraint often, on the contrary they got on well the majority of the time, but it seemed that when they did fight, it was like throwing kerosene on a fire. It was better to stay out of their way until they had run out of fuel than to show my face, and somehow end up getting dragged into it too. That's when I heard the tapping of Jojo's claws on the floor, and she squeezed through the gap in the door, her head lifting as she sought my shape under the duvet before she jumped up beside me.

"I suppose you thought better of it, huh?" I asked, turning to smile at her while she spun in a circle a few times to get the spot of a satisfactory comfort before she collapsed on it.

If Jojo had chosen to evacuate herself from the ground floor then it must have been a particularly incendiary slanging match going on down there. I decided to wait a bit longer than usual before getting up to fetch breakfast. In the kitchen, Mum was furiously stirring a raw casserole in the slow-cooker, her eyes pointing into nowhere with a hard, fixated stare. She was still wearing her nightie, and her faced was wiped of make-up. Approaching cautiously, I placed my hands on her shoulders, and she near enough jumped out of her skin with a gasp of surprise, the wooden spoon poised to attack me.

"Oh—Owen! What a fright you gave me!" she exclaimed, slapping me on the chest, and following with a giggle of relief.

"Sorry. I was just wondering if you were all right," I replied imploringly as I watched her turn back to the pot, putting the lid on, and twisting it until it locked in place.

"Did our fight wake you up?" she asked, but it sounded more like a statement. I nodded in agreement, standing there awkwardly while she scooped the vegetable peels into the recycling bin. She glanced at me over her shoulder, rolling her eyes. "He comes home, and the man is absolutely tamping! I think he thinks I'm having an affair or something!"

"You're not having an affair, are you?" I frowned slightly, and she scoffed.

"Don't be ridiculous! I'm here because I want to be! With the mouth he's got, believe me, if I wanted out, we'd be gone in a flash. You know me, I don't hang around, and I don't believe in any of that cheating nonsense." She huffed and grunted. Leaning against the edge of the counter, she suddenly seemed so tired. "It's best if you don't mention Maredudd. Let's just pretend it never happened."

"I wasn't planning on having *a* conversation with him, let alone one about Maredudd," I commented amusedly, deciding now would be a good time to get some breakfast in case Geraint came back and the argument started up again.

"By the way, Geraint says he heard you playing music all night, so there's a heads up before he starts getting chopsy at you," she muttered. I could tell she was stressed out. Sometimes it was hard to tell because her face was red most of the time, but she looked especially flustered today.

"Oh, joy..." I grumbled, watching the corn flakes tumbling into my cereal bowl. I had that to look forward to, then.

That's when I heard the garage door thumping, and boots thundering down the hallway towards us before Geraint appeared in the doorway, the keys to his van jangling in his pocket. It was a pity he was so unattractive on the inside because he might have otherwise been considered slightly handsome, and by handsome, I mean he looked like he could be the ugly cousin of one of Mum's favourite celebrities. He had a big, pointed nose, and small, squinting eyes that regularly shot daggers in my direction, and his dark brown hair was usually slicked back from his deeply lined face, turning grey at the temples with odd silvery hairs dotted here and there. His tall frame was slender but belied an uncanny strength. I had seen him pull fence posts clear out the ground single-handedly, and he liked to show off by biting chunks out of empty beer cans.

As was usual, he was dressed in his forest green oilskin coat, a red, and black chequered shirt beneath, and mud-spattered jeans tucked into his hiking boots. His hands were so scaly from the chemicals he used for his taxidermy that Mum used to say they were like chicken feet, and the big scar that had healed unevenly on his bottom lip gave him a permanent slight sneer. He often chewed, and bit at it when the rusty cogs began to turn inside his head.

"You, playing Elvis all fuckin' night. This ain't a student dorm, and when I come home in the small hours, I expect this house to be silent." He pointed a gnarled finger at me.

"It was so quiet though. Mum didn't have any trouble sleeping." I glared at him, knowing he was just bringing this up because he wanted to pick a fight with me, just the way he had with Mum earlier.

"You do as you're told, kid. This is my house, and if I want silence, I'll bloody have it. Don't let me catch you doing it again." He dismissed me, apparently uninterested in hearing any excuses. "And which one of you has been down in my work room?"

"Neither of us has been inside that stinking, filthy room the entire time you were away!" Mum struggled not to raise her voice at him. "It's the only room in this building that hasn't had a vacuum round it in donkey's years!"

"I'm telling you now, someone has been in there! I'm not blind!" he responded with an equally strained voice, and suddenly I found myself in the centre of the war-zone I had wanted to avoid.

"We haven't been by there. The door was locked anyway! As if we'd break in. If we did, we might catch a disease!" Mum wasn't about to back down, her voice so loud that it hurt my ear on one side.

"Somebody has been rummaging through my tool box! One of my knives has gone missing! I bet it was you, wasn't it!" he shouted at me, seeming to lose any desire to fight with Mum again, and instead choosing me as an adequate target.

"You leave him alone. He hasn't been anywhere near your tool box." She stepped around me, blocking me from his verbal onslaught.

I sighed irritably, and picked up my bowl of cereal, navigating around Mum, and brushing past Geraint as he hovered by the steps, his hands on his hips. He swivelled on his heels to face me as I moved by, turning his nose up at me.

"That's it, run away like the little fuckin' coward you are," he muttered after me as I tried to stop myself from fleeing as quickly as possible, instead walking at a steady pace towards the stairs.

His comment must have got Mum fuming because as I reached the top of the stairs I heard an almighty slap, and then she started disciplining him for insulting her precious son. The problem with Geraint was that fighting fire with fire didn't work. He wanted attention, especially negative attention, so my greatest weapon was to simply ignore him when he tried to bait me into arguing. Mum on the other hand, being that she had the passion of her Welsh blood inside her, blew up like a bonfire the moment he started trying it on, and nothing would put out the blaze until she was convinced that Geraint was good, and sorry for what he'd said.

After breakfast, I dressed for the weather, and clipped on Jojo's leash, both of us anxious to get out of the house, and away from the uncomfortable atmosphere that now filled it. The fresh, placid atmosphere that had been created by Maredudd when he'd been there had been taken over by Geraint, as though the man exuded a foul stench, and it was now wafting through every room, making them unbearable to sit in. Despite the fog in the air, the coolness of the rain was bracing, and relieving, reassuring me that coming out for a walk had been a wise idea after all, and even Jojo seemed to agree as she was in a particularly jolly mood.

We made our way down the steep coastal path in the direction of the beach, where through the mist I could see that the tide was out, and the sand held an otherworldly, milky sheen under the pale sunlight. I thought about trekking to the other side of the bay and climbing the mountainous hillsides until I reached

Maredudd's house, but I was too shy to go knocking on his door when I had only seen him just yesterday. Instead, I let Jojo off her lead, and we walked through the fog, both of us pausing on odd occasions to investigate something interesting on the shore. It was completely silent, and the tide was far off in the distance, so not even the rhythmic flow of the water coming onto the sand was audible, and I felt suddenly so alone.

"Let's run away, and seek sanctuary at Maredudd's house..." I whispered to Jojo as I sat down on the ground, knees drawn up to my chest while I poked at the sand with a twig. She watched me do so, tail wiggling, as she no doubt expected me to throw it for her.

"Maybe if I put on a collar, he'll think I'm a dog, and want to keep me." I sighed, throwing the stick, and sending the little white dog darting into the mist, and out of sight. She soon came trotting back with the branch in her jaws, seeming remarkably pleased with herself.

Eventually, the tide would start to come in, and I'd have to leave the beach, and not long after it would start to get dark, which meant I would have no choice, but to return to the house. I only hoped that when I did, everything might have calmed down.

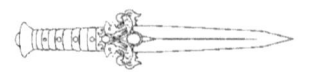

"Did you hear about that Indian chap working for Mr Phillips? You know, the one with the long hair?" I heard one of the women whispering on the other side of the waiting room.

"I thought he was from Iraq?" the other woman replied, both of them wearing expressions of confusion as they strained their brains to think where he might have come from.

I had seen these two ladies a few times before because they also worked at the caravan site with Mum, but I had never had the pleasure of actually working with them myself. The curly-haired one who was like a large scale model of a pumpkin, was Sue, and the skinny blonde one with the long neck that reminded me of a vulture, was one of several women named Sian that lived in the village. They were relatively friendly, and when I had walked into the doctor's surgery, they had both greeted me with a cheerful, "Bore da, Owen!", but I knew they were terrible gossips, so the most I ever said to them was a greeting in return.

Another bad habit they shared was to talk loudly in public, so anyone standing within ten metres of their conversation had no choice, but to listen to every word that came out of their mouths. Today was no exception, and as I sat waiting for my appointment with the nurse with my head hidden behind a magazine, I could hear what they were saying perfectly well. There was another woman sat several seats away from me watching her small son playing with the building blocks in the play area, and even she was getting a good earful. Usually I didn't bother eavesdropping unless people had something interesting to say. There were times where I silently thought replies to their discussions and wanted so badly to chime in with my opinion, often to the point where I had to bite my lip to stay quiet.

"Nooo, he's not from Iraq. Well, you know the one I mean? Evidently, he got his leg bit off by a shark when he was swimming in the bay last week," Sue continued, her eyes bulging as she stared at Sian, nodding with approval at her friend's horrified expression.

"Never! See, I was just telling Marcus the other day there are sharks round by yere in the summer time, and he wouldn't have it!" Sian was shaking her head now, and they looked like a pair of nodding dogs sitting on a dashboard. "How is he managing with his work then?"

"Well, evidently, he's gone back to working for John Phillips even so," Sue told her in amazement. "I saw him climbing into a tractor on Tuesday, but I didn't get a good look at his leg. He did have a bit of a limp, mind."

I tried my best to stifle a chuckle, but it managed to escape through my teeth, and they both looked across at me, so I pretended to be giggling at something I was reading, though whether they fell for it or not, I couldn't tell.

"Maybe he's got one of those wooden legs on," Sian suggested thoughtfully.

"I don't think so. I don't think they make them out of wood anymore."Sue was equally contemplative, and they both stared at the floor for a minute or two. Watching them both thinking felt just as painful as it probably was for them to physically do the act of making their brains function. Mum said that if they were any slower, they'd be going backwards.

"Ooh he is handsome, though, that Indian fellow. Saw him topless cutting the hedges once, well, I got such a hot flush, Marcus said I was on the change!" Sian leaned forward, squeezing her friend's forearm as she crowed with laughter, and they both shrieked, and slapped each other as they were both thoroughly entertained at this point.

The door to the reception opened, and another lady came in, and who should it be, but Mrs Bevan herself. She walked with a stoop and was even more vulture-like in appearance than Sian was, except she wore her white hair back in a tightly knotted bun and liked to dress in as many shades of cerise as was physically possible, which served to make her stand out like a big, purple, and pink thumb when she was walking down the road. The other two greeted her as she approached the counter, and once she had signed in for her appointment, she went, and sat down beside them where Sue recounted the tale of Maredudd *evidently* having been partially eaten by a shark.

In the meantime, I sat there smiling to myself as I thought of what Maredudd would think when he found out this hilarious story was now doing the rounds, just like we'd said it would. I half-wondered if he had intentionally told someone with the knowledge that it would very rapidly start spreading about, and soon enough find its way back to me. I couldn't help feeling like this was a message from him, to let me know that he was thinking about the conversations we'd had, and the jokes we'd shared.

"I did say to the minister last Sunday gone by that if we had any sharks biting people in the bay that we'd have to close the beach," Mrs Bevan declared in a voice that sounded rather like a creaky door. "We can't be having any fatalities of that nature."

I wondered which nature of fatalities were permissible to Mrs Bevan. I could see her enjoying a thrilling jousting match or encouraging a good old-fashioned public hanging. My amusement was short-lived though. It felt so empty without Maredudd sitting beside me to share in my jokes and shoot me back one of his own. How was it that I had known him for less than a week, and yet it already felt like there was a gaping hole that he needed to fill with his presence? It had been a few days since I had last seen him, but it felt like it had been a century, and every night I found myself looking out my window with my binoculars, hoping that I might catch a glimpse of his leaving his front door or pegging his washing on the line.

The weather had been terrible all week, which meant I had stayed mostly indoors. Just as well really, since it seemed the attacks on the local livestock had come to a momentary pause. Perhaps the weather had placated the unknown monster for the time being, and it had gone to hide away in a lair somewhere to stay dry? I figured I would go, and take a look at my record, and see if there was a pattern linked to the weather. It might turn out to be a temporary solution if it meant the farmers could protect their flocks by bringing them into sheds when it rained overnight. An even better outcome would be for me to camp out somewhere, and hopefully catch a glimpse of it myself.

"Hello there, Owen. How have you been doing?" The nurse smiled at me as I entered the nurse's surgery room. She was a small, grey-haired lady with glasses, and even though she was tasked with piercing my backside with a needle the size of a dart one might use to tranquilise a rhino, she was always very caring, and supportive.

"Hello Lynne! I'm very well, thank you."I smiled back as I closed the door behind me. "And you?"

"Oh you know how it is round yere, one can't complain. Anyway, I'm looking forward to having a holiday next week so it's not all bad."She tittered, standing by with her wrinkled hands on her broad hips while I rifled through my rucksack.

"That's nice, I wish I could go away for a week or two. Any chance you could squeeze me into your suitcase? I promise I won't be any trouble." I chuckled as I procured the small white box, and she accepted it from me gently.

"I don't know if you'd like it very much where I'm going. We're going on a shopping trip to Vegas. Not a lot of countryside by there," she replied merrily as she went to the counter and took the tiny glass vial out of the box.

"Hmm, on second thoughts, maybe I'd do best to stay here then. Besides, who knows what might happen while I was gone." I yawned into my hand as I sat down on the chair beside her cluttered desk.

"Oh, the animal attacks, is it?"she asked, and I nodded, watching as she put on some surgical gloves, and unwrapped a sterile syringe from its packaging. "I suppose you've heard about the gentleman who was bitten by a shark?"

"Yes! Maredudd, he's... He's my friend."I beamed, unable to stop my face from lighting up with joy, and she seemed to pick up on how happy I was just as the mention of his name. Telling her he was my friend caused a shameful warmth to flare up inside my chest, shameful because I wasn't completely sure if it was too soon to say he was my friend, warm because just the thought of him made me go red in the cheeks.

"Then you'll know as good as I that it were no shark that attacked him, and he most certainly does not have a false leg."She feigned a stern expression that soon cracked into a wicked smirk.

I started to laugh, and she chuckled too, her small eyes shining, and her crow's feet turning to deep crinkles at the corners of her eyelids.

"No, he doesn't have a false leg, wooden or otherwise." I shook my head, my jaw aching from smiling so broadly.

"What happened to him, do you know?" she asked with genuine curiosity as she began to withdraw the liquid in the vial into the small syringe. "I'd like to dispel some of the nonsense going about, is all."

"He cut his leg on some rocks when he was swimming by the cliffs," I told her. "My Mum found him on the beach, and she bandaged him up. He's all right, he was walking perfectly fine a few days later."

"I've said it before: your mam would make a fine nurse."She winked at me before glancing back at the syringe. "Sorry this is taking so long, you know how thick this stuff is. Like trying to suck treacle through a straw!"

After my injection, I said goodbye to Lynne for another three months, and hobbled out of the surgery, my buttock feeling as though a giant bumblebee had stuck its venomous stinger into it. There was a bench that had been built upon a slight cliff that jutted out over a steep drop overlooking the beach, and I always went to sit there to rest after my appointment. A three-foot stone wall constructed at the edge was a rather unsafe barrier, but few people tended to sit here as they could just as well see the view from their own houses, and so I had never seen anyone, but the occasional visit from the old folk's as they took a break from walking up the hill. The rain had stopped, but the fog still thickened the air, tasting moist, and watery in my mouth, and leaving a damp residue on my face as I zipped up my raincoat to my chin.

The wooden bench was somewhat slimy, but I didn't much care. It creaked under my weight as I sat down, and looked out over the bay, seeing my home on one side to the right, but unable to see Maredudd's to the left because of the outcrop jutting from the cliff's surface that was clustered with unkempt trees, and bushes. Some of the fog had cleared, so the beach was visible, but the ocean was lurking beneath its swirling white duvet. I had never seen weather like this when we lived in England. It changed whenever it pleased, and it was usually quite pointless to refer to weather forecasts on the news because they often turned out to be inaccurate.

Grunting with discomfort, I pressed my hand to the injection site and huffed, wishing the pain would subside enough for me to walk home. I wouldn't make the mistake of walking now. When I had done that before, some of the liquid had leaked out, and made the plaster fall off.

In the beginning, I had found receiving the treatment to be a struggle. Intra-muscular injections were never fun, but they got easier to cope with as time went on, and I learned how to care for my body afterwards through trial, and error. On top of that, there came the symptoms of change: the hair loss, the hair growth, the squeaky voice before it dropped, and the acne. Second puberty turned out not to be a lot of fun either, so I was glad when it started to clear off, and the spots went away, and my hairline seemed to be maintaining a regular shape, at least for the meantime. I hoped that my hair was more like Dad's because he had never gone thin on top, but if it turned out that I did start to go bald, then I had come to accept that that was a necessary sacrifice to be a man.

Flecks of moisture had developed on my glasses, so I took them off, and gave them a wipe. This view was one of the best in the bay, and I figured that whoever had put this old bench here must have shared the same love for it that I did. I wondered if Maredudd had ever sat here. From talking to him, I knew he enjoyed views of the countryside too, especially views of the beach, a place he seemed to have a great affinity for. I imagined bringing him here on a hot summer's evening so we could watch the sun setting. We could have a few bottles of ice cold cider, and share a picnic of cheese sandwiches, and crisps, followed by some chocolate, buttons. Maybe he'd let me sit close to him. Maybe.

Silently, I scolded myself.

I had reached the point where I was fantasising about us going on dates together, albeit the kind of dates most people would probably consider to be rather boring or childish, but I couldn't imagine him wanting to go to a posh restaurant or the cinema to see a cheesy chick flick. That's what I liked about him though, he was like me, he liked the simple things in life, and appreciated nature the way I did. Knowing my luck though, he probably wasn't even remotely gay, and even if he was, he would probably think dating the child of his dead friend was too weird, and creepy, which was a pity considering he didn't seem to have any problem with the complexity of my gender situation. Then again, maybe I was wrong, and things would work out for us, but I wasn't overly optimistic on that front. All the times in the past where I had thought someone liked me, it had gone horribly and dramatically wrong, and I was left seriously regretting ever saying anything. I was only fortunate that back then I hadn't really liked those people, not the way I liked Maredudd. This was so different, and that's what frightened me, because it meant if he turned around, and shot me down, the fall would be so much more painful, and humiliating.

The pain in my backside had dulled somewhat, so stiffly I got to my feet, and took one last look at the view before shuffling out onto the pavement, and beginning the journey home along the main road, hoping that it wouldn't hammer down before I got back.

As the afternoon drew on, with it came the rain again, bringing the rumble of thunder, and the alarming shocks of lightning that still managed to flash through the gaps in the curtains. I sat in my bedroom with my laptop on my knees, spooning some chocolate cereal into my mouth between taking notes on a lined notepad to my right. Jojo was curled up between a giant leopard bean toy, and one of my pillows, her snore the only sound besides the tapping of my keyboard, and the rain blustering, and hissing against the window pane. As I scrolled through the spreadsheet I had made, marking off all the dates on a calendar, I checked the weather I had written down for each day, keeping a tally of how many times the attacks correlated with whether it was raining or not. As far as I could tell, there didn't seem to be a lot of connections between the two. Some horses had been slaughtered during one of the worst downpours the village had seen in years, and many of the other attacks had taken place when it had been tipping down out on the hills. Surely the attacks weren't entirely random. They seemed to occur for a week at a time before pausing for another week or two, but what was causing the hiatus? There were very rarely any attacks that happened as one-offs, and the killer was becoming more, and more indiscriminate about the victims it chose.

In the beginning, it had been only sheep, then cows, and horses, and the list soon began to include things like pigs, chickens, goats, and even dogs. Chief wasn't the only man's best friend that had gone missing during the last year. Although, I was completely certain that Chief hadn't been dismembered because I had seen him, so his escape seemed to be more on the fault of the Fairfields for not keeping his chain secure.

At the dinner table I was silent, my brain chugging this information like a pint of water, absorbing it to be processed into something useful. Mum sat to my left, and on the other side of the table, Geraint was scoffing his food noisily between swigs of beer direct from the bottle. His pale blue eyes kept flicking between us, looking at me for a minute, then looking at Mum, then back again, as if he wanted to say something, but wasn't sure how to broach the subject. Mum was cutting up her food neatly with her knife, and fork, her eyes gazing up at the ceiling or towards the window, anywhere, but Geraint. He stabbed his fork into a chunk of chicken and began tearing at it with his teeth like a hyena, his eyes trained on me. He got a perverse enjoyment from eating meat in front of me while I sat there tucking into my soya burgers or vegetable patties. Mum eating meat didn't bother me because she didn't sit there waving it in my face the whole time, but he was always looking for ways to antagonise people, studying them until he had figured out what got them riled up, before using it to entice them into doing battle. For a long while I didn't even notice he was looking at me because I was far away with my spreadsheets, and records, contemplating everything I had noted down earlier, and this seemed to annoy him a great deal.

"Still haven't found that knife," he commented, looking down at his plate as he selected which piece of flesh to consume next. He licked the gravy from his fork, awaiting a response.

"It's just a knife, Geraint. You can buy another one," Mum murmured once she had swallowed a mouthful of carrot.

"Other things are missing, not just the knife. I couldn't give a damn about the knife, it's the other things that I'm pissed off about."He grunted, curling his lip to show his teeth like a growling dog. "I'm telling you now, someone has moved my stuff around. When I locked that door, I knew exactly where I had left everything, and when I got back, it was different."

"Sign of old age, that."Mum made a snorting laugh as she nudged me with her elbow, and I managed an awkward smile.

He glowered, clearly frustrated with how silly Mum was behaving. Just like him, she knew how to get his back up too, and being silly was something he truly hated.

"I don't want any liars living under this roof," he answered, and though he didn't look at me, I knew I was the target of that remark.

"Nobody's lying, will you please stop it with this moany attitude you've come back with? Frankly, it's driving me up the wall, and I'm seriously considering just getting in the car and going on a world tour until you decide to stop being such a massive prick."Mum lowered her knife, and fork, and leaned forward in her seat. "All you've done since you got home is blow hot air, it's like you're on your bloody period or something."

"Well, I wouldn't have to be if people weren't breaking into my private work room and stealing from me!" he exclaimed through a mouthful of chicken.

"Don't talk with your mouth full!" Mum snapped back.

"What have you done with my things, Cerys?" He ignored her and turned on me. I had sat there the whole time this conversation was progressing wondering when he was going to start having a go at me, and so it had begun.

"My name is Owen," I muttered, looking up at him through my eyelashes.

"The only one who's stayed quiet is you. Why are you being so quiet, huh? Is it because you know you're in the wrong?" He pointed his knife at me. I hated how he did that all the time, pointing his finger or whatever happened to be in his hand at the time, at the person he was addressing.

"You know it's rude to point at people?" I disregarded his accusations, and Mum snorted again as she cut up her roast potatoes.

"The boy's been so busy doing chores for me, as if he'd have time to go breaking into your stinking animal den," she scoffed in an undertone.

"Stop lying to me, Cerys. I can tell when you're lying," he continued to jab his knife in the air that separated us over the table top.

"Stop calling me Cerys, for fuck's sake! That's not my name!" I shouted, surprising myself with the volume of my own voice. It was getting harder, and harder to control myself, and this time I wasn't going to walk away while being accused of being a thief.

"It's the name on your birth certificate," he sneered, and I slammed my hands on the table.

"My old birth certificate. It says Owen now—Owen Evan Vaughn! So stop fucking calling me Cerys! And I'm not a thief!" I yelled at him and rose to my feet. "Unlike you! I've seen you tucking newspapers inside each other at Mrs Bryn's shop!"

"But you're not man enough to go and grass on me, are you?" His sneer turned into a cruel smirk as he tilted himself back in his chair, still chewing a piece of chicken in his cheek.

"I didn't want to bring shame on Mum for dating

such a horrible asshole."I breathed, the adrenaline in my chest starting to swell, and tighten into a hard lump surrounding my heart, squashing my lungs against my rib cage.

"Will you two stop arguing at the dinner table?" Mum answered, but we both ignored her. It was a sentence she had spoken many times, and we'd grown so used to, it hardly had any effect nowadays.

"Complaining about my relationship with your mammy isn't going to bring your tada back. It's real pathetic how you keep taking it out on me all the time, Cerys. Nothing is gonna stop me seeing your mammy, not even you." He smiled, a dark, grim smile of pleasure as he watched the tears seething in my eyes, and the way my bottom lip wobbled when he spoke of Dad.

"I hate you." I tried to push out the shouting voice I had somehow let go of earlier, but all that emerged was a whimper.

"Good, maybe it'll convince you to get a job, and stop free-loading off your mam and me! Nothing would please me more than to see the back of you!" He rested his jaw in his palm as he spat a wad of chewy gristle on the table top. "I'm tired of you using my electric, and gas, eating my food, and sleeping in my house, walking in on my privacy! If you were a real man, you'd be out there ploughing the fields with the other jacks in the village, but instead you go about with a camera stuck to your face, looking at corpses!"

The tears were coming out so fast that no matter how I wiped at them, they continued to run in rivers down my cheeks. I tried to find the words to say to make him see he was being unfair, but nothing would come out.

"If I didn't care so much for your mam's feelings, I would have kicked you out on your ear a month after you'd come yere. She's the only reason I put up with having you round yere, and now I see you're stealing from me on top of being a sponge, I can't see any good reason not to kick you out now," he answered, pretending to sound like he was disappointed.

"I'm not a thief. I didn't steal from you." I choked, realising I had squeezed my hands into fists so tightly that my fingernails were biting into the flesh of my palm.

"But you *are* a sponge, Cerys," he repeated calmly. He could see that he had driven me to my very limit now, and he was beginning to gloat, wallowing in the misery he inflicted.

"Stop it." I whimpered. I looked down at Mum, silently begging her to help me, but she was looking down at the table top, her face obscured by her auburn hair. Why wasn't she saying anything? Why was she sitting there, and pretending she couldn't hear what he was saying?

"This is my house, and I will say whatever I want."He raised his eyebrows.

I breathed deeply to try and steel my nerves, but all it did was push more tears out. "I will fight you, Geraint. I will fight you until you realise you can't tell me what to do."

I only realised my mistake when he suddenly pushed back his chair, and rose to his feet, standing a whole head taller than me, his plaid shirt tucked into his washed out jeans.

"What's that? You want to fight with me?" He prompted with a tilt of his head, his eyes opening wide, penetrating like the threat-stare of a wolf. "Come on then, show me how much of a man you are! Come, and fight me, Cerys!"

The moment he had stood up, Jojo had lifted her head, and was watching us from her bed in the corner, and I pleaded with her in my head, pleaded for her to come to my aid when Mum wouldn't. Her lip curled this time, whiskers bristling, and ears folded back as she let out a low, rattling growl that Geraint appeared not to hear.

"See what I mean! The second you're face to face with a real man, you turn into a blubbering little girl!" He laughed, a booming laugh that filled the room in a shockwave of sound.

"Stop it! If you hadn't gone around telling everyone that I was trans then maybe I would have had a chance! It's not my fault they take one look at the 'village tranny' and tell me to get lost! You shot yourself in the foot just to bully me!" I howled, and that's when Jojo leapt from her station.

Her compact, muscular body shot across the floor in a blur of white, jaws agape, and teeth flashing, her clawed feet a clattering musical note on the wooden flooring. Geraint only noticed she had moved when her teeth sank into his leg, and he cried out, flinging the chair out of the way, and staggering against the chimney breast behind him, the tiny terrier snarling, and foaming as she locked her mouth upon his ankle. Mum jumped up, shrieking at Jojo to stop, but I didn't stay to find out whether the dog listened.

I turned, and fled out of the kitchen, running up the steps as the tears burst free at last, and I heard myself sobbing and hiccupping. I didn't even stop to grab my coat; it was fortunate that I was still wearing my boots after having been out to see to the goats, because otherwise I would have found myself running along the road bare foot. I slammed open the front door, and darted out into the heavy shower beyond, water drenching me, and plastering my hair to my forehead as I ran down the path towards the open gate. Seconds later I heard the front door banging, and Mum's voice screaming at me down the garden.

"Owen! Owen! Stop!" Her words cried after me, but they became a distance siren through the loud pattering of the storm on the trees, and concrete.

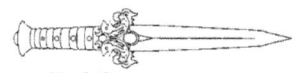

My breath puffed from my open mouth in white clouds that vanished in the wind, and my tears ran with the rain, disappearing in the presence of their watery brethren that were pelting from the black sky above. The swelling that had puffed up into my chest burst like a balloon, and I staggered to the side of the lane, bending to empty my stomach contents on the gravel-strewn earth, my belly contracting, and with every clench, there came a sob of despair. The rage filled me, swimming through my blood to every fibre of my being, and making it throb with an unbearable fury, a fury I had somehow managed to keep sedated over the years. Its petals unfurled, and it bloomed in me at last, having grown from a tiny seed planted in my youth, watered by bullying, stunned by the death of Dad, and finally coaxed to its adult form by Geraint's poison. A flower that spewed hatred and sank its thorny roots into my heart where it twisted, gouging, leaving wounds that took so long to heal.

I hated confrontations, hated fighting, hated arguing. I wanted to live peacefully, and be polite, and civil with everyone I met, but Geraint wasn't satisfied with that. He wanted this flower to reproduce, sprouting more, and more Hydra-like heads until finally, it consumed me completely. Because he too was consumed by the exact same thing, a wound that never healed, and that he was too proud to bandage or nurse.

I sat down on one of the boulders that created a border around the edge of a field. It wasn't totally dark just yet, but the sky was inky, and the sea was a churning mass like the bristling back of a disgruntled beast. Wind tore at the leaves of every plant in sight, and the torrents throbbed in waves, blasting their droplets upon every surface. My clothes were soaked through, and I shivered, not just from the cold, but from the intolerable, unnameable emotion that flooded me. I put my head in my hands and cried. It was the first time in a long time that I had really wept this way, and it seemed I was making up for it, having saved up so many numbers of tears that had never found their way out. Now they came, relentless, and hot, surging from my crushed eyelids.

Why couldn't things just be easy for once? Why couldn't there be peace and friendship?

The need for Dad to be here clawed and slashed at my heart like the paws of a badger digging into the earth, scratching away until there was nothing, but a hole, and my throat ached, but still the sobbing wouldn't stop. My body rocked back and forth, my arms holding my torso in a meagre embrace. Maybe I had made a mistake. Maybe I shouldn't have changed my gender, maybe I should have gone through life pretending to be something I wasn't, like a fish that cloaked itself to hide amongst the anemones, disguised from predators. I chose to throw back that camouflage, becoming a beacon for everybody to come towards, and offload their self-hatred, like a public bin in the centre of a London station overflowing with trash. My home had been a sanctuary from the cruel world, but now I didn't even have that. I could handle being kicked, and punched, getting lighters sparked on my clothes or lit matches thrown on me, even being held to the ground, and urinated on, because I forgave those people for the abuse when I saw how they went home to houses devoid of love, and support, parents who didn't care about them, and left them to fend for themselves. No toys for their birthday, no hugs or bedtime stories. Those were things I did have, so I was grateful. But now, those things I had were gone.

For a long time I sat there, not moving. The violent shudders had gradually calmed, and instead I trembled, and sniffed, wondering if the tears would come back at any moment, and leave me incapacitated once more. I got up and started walking. The ground was pitted with puddles, but it didn't matter. I was wet already, and they made no difference. I had never felt so lost in my entire life, I didn't know where I was going or what was going to happen to me when the sun rose again. The ground passed beneath my boots, and soon I was walking through a field, mud squelching under my grip soles, passing between rows upon rows of cabbages whose leaves fluttered, and twinkled under the moonlight.

If I didn't think the morning would come, I don't think I would have ever stopped walking. I would have walked right into my grave. My belly ached with hunger or sickness, I couldn't tell which, and I heard myself gasping, wheezing in the chill air, fighting to climb the steep hill to the top. As I reached the peak, I turned and looked down at the bay, this place I had grown to love, and had become my territory regardless of the walls, and fences that divided it up into property. I knew that I loved this place, even more than I had loved England, and it wasn't the fault of this land that I was suffering. I could find no concrete reason to loathe the village, either.

There, across the water at the edge of the cliff, the glow of lights within the white-walled cottage— Maredudd was home. Suddenly, hope showed herself to me, and I saw that I wasn't alone, that I had someone to run to now, someone who wouldn't close the door in my face when I needed them most. It would be a long journey on foot, but what other choice did I have? I heard Jojo growling in the back of my mind, bit my lip when I thought of her loyalty, and the company she had given me. I should have brought her with me, but there was nothing I could do now. I could only move forward.

I lurched onward, arms clutching my shivering body as the rain gushed down my back and turned my shoes into spongy prisons on my feet. Even without a well-trodden path or the light of streetlamps to guide me, I knew where I was going, and as I made my way across the field, I was careful not to tramp over the farmer's vegetables. Gales battered me from one side, the south wind sweeping over the field, and sending the rainfall almost horizontal so that it flew into my face and tried to seek refuge in my ear canal. Time seemed to disappear as I travelled. Without a watch on my wrist, I had no idea just how long I was walking, but that was of no consequence.

Even as I rounded the bay, I kept as far upon the hills as I could, steering clear of the coastal path where Mum was likely to look for me, but also so that I could see Maredudd in the distance, beckoning me on. All of the fields I cut through were empty, no livestock huddling in the storm, no people walking the lanes, because everyone knew it wouldn't be wise to go wandering on a night like this. With every footstep, the flower that Geraint had caused to blossom was starting to die back, shrinking into a withered weed in the bottom of my belly, retracting into the shadows where it belonged. The crying started again, but this time it was something else. I thought of the relief of being out of that house, and of having warm, dry arms around me, squeezing me tightly, of hot cocoa in front of the fire, a comfortable bed, and a kind face. A friend. Companionship.

Finally, I made it to a paved street, and I waited until a car had moved by slowly, its headlights catching me briefly, and causing the driver to lean sideways in his seat to get a better look at me, his eyes wide as if he thought he had seen a ghost. He didn't stop to offer me a lift, and I didn't blame him. My face was screwed up and red from weeping, and my clothes were dripping. I was more trouble than I was worth. I crossed the road to the other side, and took a shortcut through a churchyard, navigating the slippery path between the rows of headstones. Funny how we grew vegetables in rows, and then buried people in the exact same fashion. Life often seemed to mirror death in its rituals, and nuances. On the other side of the churchyard was another field, this time only grass. If I continued along the hilltop, I would come towards the old castle ruins, but I had no intention of going through there at this time of night, so I headed down off the hill towards the coastal path once more.

I was filled with an urgency that carried me on despite the aching in my legs, and feet, and the discomfort of my wet clothes. I needed to get there at any cost, and if that meant walking in the storm then that was what I would do. I looked out to sea. There were no ships out there tonight, only the blinking of buoys thrown about on the heaving waves. If I looked to my left up the hill in the day time, I would have been able to see the crumbling tower of the castle, but the darkness enveloped it, and hid it from my eyes. Even the path was hard to see in this low light, and occasionally my ankle went askew as I placed my foot on a large stone or an uneven patch of ground.

There were a few lights nearby, people's homes where families were probably cuddled up in front of the telly with snacks and smiles on their faces. Eventually, I came to the road where I had seen Chief, but I was too reckless to be afraid, and if the damned dog came towards me I would have grabbed him by his chain and taken him with me. My boots pounded the pavement, and I marched on, until finally I came to the lane that lead to Maredudd's home. I stopped suddenly, as if I had made impact with a barrier that would let me go no further, and I stared up the slope surrounded by swishing grass, knowing that I was nearly there, and just when I thought I would go on, my nerve had deflated, leaving me hesitant and ashamed.

He had told me I could come round anytime I wanted. The invitation was there, so what did I have to be afraid of? If I wanted to be friends with Maredudd, I had to trust him first, which meant trusting that he wouldn't ignore me when I knocked on the door. I wiped at my face, but it did nothing to cover how red, and puffy my eyes were or how sore my nose was from where I had rubbed it in my sleeve. Besides, it was obvious something was wrong for me to turn up in the dark without my raincoat. I took a deep breath, and started making my way along the lane, stones crunching underfoot, and the grass hissing, swaying as it was barraged by the gale. Thunder pealed somewhere beyond the hills after the cliff was momentarily lit by a blaze of milky lightning that splashed its pale light over every leaf, and stone in sight.

I could see the roof of the cottage growing closer, and the yellow light that warmed the curtains closed to the night, soft, and encouraging. Somehow time seemed to slow down, and while the walk I had made across the bay had seemed like little more than a few minutes on foot, this small hill now felt like I was climbing a mountain. Exhaustion began to rob me of my strength, and I panted through clenched teeth. On and on I pushed myself, until finally the road came to an end. I hauled myself up the near-vertical steps to the path of the cottage.

I could almost feel the warmth from within bathing upon my face, and chest. I stumbled the final few steps towards the door, and reaching weakly, my hand fell upon the iron knocker that depicted a coiled ammonite.

Tap, tap. Silence.

Six

Finally, the door opened. The light from inside beamed out onto my face, and my eyes hurt from its brightness, so accustomed to the dark they had become as I had walked through the tempest. A silhouette appeared in the centre of the light, rays radiating from behind the shape of its head, and then my pupils shrank, and I was able to squint into his eyes as he peered out at me. Maredudd was standing there in loose-fitting cotton pyjamas, his bare feet on the bristly mat, a pair of silver spectacles balanced on the bridge of his triangular nose. He seemed astonished to see me there, shivering, and soaked from the rain, my bloodshot eyes begging wordlessly for help.

"Owen...! What—what on earth has happened?" he stammered, pulling the door ajar and reaching for me. His big, warm hand grabbed me by the arm, and I felt the heat of it through my shirt as though a hot iron had suddenly been pressed to my skin. I was dragged forward, and then I found myself standing on the mat, droplets falling all around me.

"Owen! Talk to me!" He bent slightly so that we were eye to eye, and I saw the worry there. "Has something happened? Are you okay?"

"M—Maredudd..." I breathed. I couldn't believe I had made it. Here he was, right in front of me, and how handsome, and perfect he was.

Sensing that he wasn't going to get anything intelligent out of me, he shut the door on the rain.

"I'll get you a towel, so stay yere. I'll be back now in a minute."He gave my shoulder a squeeze before turning and jogging off up the stairs.

It was so tiny inside. I was standing in the living room, which had a floor space no bigger than two car-parking spots, and to my right a flight of creaky wooden stairs lead up to the next floor. In front was a small doorway, the frame of which was so low that I imagined he had to duck to pass through it, and I guess that must have been the kitchen beyond. The living room was crammed to the low ceiling with stuff, shelves, and cabinets pushed against the walls meaning it was hard to tell what colour exactly they were painted, and a big slouchy sofa faced towards the front window.

The air smelled sweet, and fragrant with incense, and candles clustered on the squat sideboard that was beneath the window, the light, and heat from the flames warming, and illuminating the small room. Statues, and ornaments of what looked like different mythological gods stood on a few shelves above the fireplace, the flickering flames below changing the shadows upon their familiar faces as I picked out the delicate features of Shiva, and the rearing shape of Kali. A Buddha lovingly adorned with flower wreaths sat amongst them in the Lotus position, hands folded in his lap, and his pretty, feminine face bearing a serene smile. I realised there was no television. At the most, there was a modest CD player in the corner hidden amongst piles of incense boxes, and a vase stuffed with feathers. It was cosy, and curious at the same time.

I looked down at the puddle I had created on the wooden floor. My mind was clearing, and I figured it must have been the heat defrosting my brain because I was becoming more alert. His feet descended the stairs, and he appeared again, a pile of towels under one arm, and his glasses pushed atop his head, causing strands of shiny hair to fall either side of his face.

"Looks like it's my turn to let you borrow some of my pyjamas." He smiled jestingly as he came towards me and offered me a towel.

"I'm sorry... I..." I stumbled over my words, unsure of what to say.

"Don't worry about it, you weren't interrupting anything. I'm glad to see you, I'm just concerned you've been walking round yere in the dark, and you're completely soaking." He helped me to wrap a towel round my shoulders. It was warm, and soft, and smelled of him.

"I had an argument with Geraint..." I breathed, struggling to explain myself as my hands clutched the towel to my chest. "And Jojo attacked him...and I ran away, like I always do..."

"Animals run away too, it's how they protect themselves without sacrificing their safety in a fight," he answered gently, and I smiled. How did he always know what to say? How did he always make it intelligent, and kind at the same time?

"Are you saying I'm an animal?" My face ached when I smiled at him.

"Well, you certainly eat like one." He grinned back, and I found myself laughing, a sound which seemed so alien, and I couldn't understand why.

"Here, you can wear these. I'm sorry I haven't washed the ones you let me borrow. I know it's been a week already," he answered as he pushed the folded clothing into my hands. "The bathroom is just through there if you'd like to get changed in private. I'll put some milk on the hob."

"Thanks," I replied, and although I hesitated, and the movement was jerky, I reached for him, and took hold of his hand, bringing it to my chest. "I'm so glad you're here. I've missed you."

He nodded slowly, and for a moment, I thought I saw my own emotions reflected back in his expression as he gazed at me. "I've missed you too, and I'm glad you came to me."

He gestured I should follow him, and he took me out into the miniscule kitchen, which barely had room for two people to stand in. I saw that he had most of the modern amenities like a cooker, and a washing machine, but he only had the functional, practical things—there were no radios or televisions in sight. It looked like he had only just finished having his dinner because a dirty plate, and fork were on the washboard, and a pan was soaking in the washing up bowl. Through the kitchen there was another door, and he pushed it open, revealing the surprisingly spacious bathroom within, which had probably been a larder of some sort in years gone by.

He left me to see to myself, and I sat on the edge of the bath, breathing in the delicious scent of vanilla coming from the sticks on the narrow window sill, my eyes drawn to the large photo of Maredudd standing with a group of people in front of the Egyptian Pyramids. He looked young, his face absent of creases, and wrinkles, his hair cut short, and his smile filled with innocence. I couldn't imagine him being naïve.

Drying myself was a chore as my body had already decided it was time to rest now that I had reached my destination. I hung my wet clothes on the rail above the bath so they could drip dry and turned my boots upside down on top of the radiator before rubbing myself all over with one of the towels. As I was doing so, I looked at the photo one more time, and that's when I noticed that Mum and Dad were in the photo too, and I stopped, moving closer to get a better look.

Geraint was standing at the back of the group as they all squeezed together to fit in the frame, their faces smiling with excitement. Mum's cheeks were red as usual, but so were Dad's. One of his arms was round Mum's shoulders, and strangely, the other was round Geraint's, and he was hugging Dad back. Geraint looked different somehow, and not just because he was young. I couldn't quite put my finger on it, but I thought perhaps it was because he was smiling differently. It was a hopeful smile, one of positivity, and joy, not the sneer or smirk that I usually saw. I felt sad to see him there, sad because nobody was inherently mean. He had been innocent too, once.

I focused on Dad. He looked so boyish, and naughty, puckish like Peter Pan with his bright red hair, freckled cheeks, and slightly upturned nose. I smiled back at him, telling him that I missed him so. It was a lovely photograph.

Maredudd was standing in the kitchen when I scuttled out in his cornflower blue pyjamas, the legs sagging around my feet as the trousers were so long, and the sleeves hanging down over my hands, but the, buttons round the middle feeling tight against my belly. He chuckled when he saw me as he stood to the cooker, stirring a pan of milk on the gas ring.

"So, am I right in understanding that you walked yere on foot?" He asked as I dragged myself up onto the stool by the back door.

"Yes, I did, and I know it was stupid, you don't have to tell me." I wiped my damp hair back from my face. "I wasn't thinking straight; I just ran away."

"Are you okay?" he asked me again. The way he was staring at me told me that he knew that I had been sobbing my guts out, but his stare was a careful, beseeching one.

"I'm okay." I nodded, before sighing. "I'm hurt, very hurt. But I'll manage."

He just watched me for a moment, only the scraping of the spoon in the pan filling the quiet between us until he spoke again. "What did Geraint say to you?"

I shrugged, feeling stressed just remembering the words that had been exchanged.

"He accused me of breaking into his work room and stealing things from him when I've done no such thing. I'm not a thief, and I wouldn't want any of his junk anyway. Then he started calling me by the old name, and saying I was basically using him for money, and board. I mean, it was a horrible argument anyway, but it's not the first we've had. The worst part was that Mum didn't even step in when he started asking me to fight him." I hung my head, unable to make eye contact with him. "I just feel so... Betrayed. She wouldn't even acknowledge that I was there. I don't know why she did that..."

Maredudd nodded, his lime-green eyes half-closed, and thoughtful.

"I feel like a waste of space," I mumbled, trying to sniff back the tears, but here they were again, urgent, and fast-flowing. "I just feel like I should walk into the sea and disappear."

"You're not a waste of space. Your dad wouldn't want to hear you say that." He reasoned as he took the pan off the heat. I expected him to pour the milk into the cups, but he left it on the hob, and suddenly he was there in front of me, and his arms were moving around me.

I whimpered as he captured me in a determined embrace that was going to have me whether I resisted or not. My head fell upon his chest, and he crushed me like a dried flower, my resolve crumbling to dust, my hands gripping the fabric of his shirt tightly.

"If you will walk into the sea, I will walk with you," he whispered against my ear.

"I'm sorry! I don't know what else to do! I don't know where to go, I'm a disappointment to my family, and Dad... Dad's not here..." I choked as my tears covered my cheeks in a sheen of moisture like dewdrops on a spring-time field. I buried my face into his shoulder, blocking out the entire world, until all I could hear was his heart beating.

For a long time he just held me, the only part of him moving was his chest as he breathed, like a statue that had come to life for just long enough to put his arms around me, and I held onto him too, forgetting that I might be digging my fingertips into his back, not caring that my tears left a wet patch on his shirt. He was strong, and nothing I did would cause him harm. He smelled of welcoming things, sandalwood, and sage incense, hot milk, and his own natural scent that was unique to him. I breathed it in the way Dad used to breathe in the forest air, like it would clear my lungs, and rejuvenate me.

Like Jojo, he didn't judge me; like Mum, he comforted me;, and like Dad, he was wise. He was all three of the people I loved most rolled into one, and they were the only people that had ever seen me cry, so it felt acceptable to allow him to witness how weak, and damaged I was on the inside. I didn't feel embarrassed or humiliated, and it didn't matter that I was ugly-crying, my face screwed up, and my cries coming out in noisy bursts, my agonised voice muffled by his clothing. Soon, the worst of my weeping began to dissipate, and I was left drained, my body rapidly losing its energy. If he had let go of me suddenly, I would have collapsed to the floor like a discarded puppet.

"If ever, and I mean ever, you feel like you need to run away or you need someone to protect you, please come yere. It doesn't matter what time in the day, or whether I'm home or not. The back door is always unlocked, just let yourself in," he said against my ear, his voice becoming everything, absorbing, and destroying the despair that had ravaged me. "I promised Evan I would. I'm only sorry I waited so long, but I was weak, and needed to grow. I'm weak no more. I won't let

Geraint hurt you. You may not have known this, but Evan was like a lion tamer, and Geraint was the lion. Now it's my turn to tame him. If you're willing for us to be trusting with each other, there is much I can tell you, and much I can teach you. But you have to trust me."

"I trust you," I breathed, exhausted. I needed to sleep.

"And I trust you, Owen. Tonight you need to rest, okay? I will be here beside you." He leaned back in my arms and smiled at me reassuringly. His eyes were glittering, his thick eyelashes in spikes as they soaked up his tears.

"Okay..." I mumbled, managing a tired smile in return. "I'm sorry for crying so much. I haven't cried in a while..."

"Never apologise for crying, it's healthy to cry. You'd make your mind sick if you never let it out." He stroked my head, raking my wavy hair from my eyes, and cupping my cheek in his palm. His rough skin didn't feel so much like sandpaper now. "Tomorrow, I'll tell you some things you'll be amazed to hear, but it will empower you. And if my dad is comfortable with it, I'd like to take you to meet him."

"But... Haven't you got to work tomorrow?" I was confused, and he chuckled.

"Work? I think you've got it a bit mixed up. They pay me for my time, which I offer if the price is right. They serve me, not the other way around, and right now, no price is worth more than this time with you." He grinned, the mischief creeping back into his expression, his fire rekindled, and burning after the dampening of my tears.

"Wow... I wish it was like that for me." I sighed ruefully, secretly jealous of how graceful, and free he was, and how little it seemed he needed to fight to live.

"You will have a job soon, don't worry. Then you will understand what I mean." He rubbed his hands up and down my arms to warm me, as though he had just brought me in from a blizzard. "Are you alright to sit by yere while I finish making cocoa?"

"I'll cope." I joked, and he laughed as he released me from his embrace. I turned my head, and watched him move to the cooker, sparking the gas, and adjusting the heat until the blue flames hissed at an adequate heat before he put the pan back on.

"I saw that big photo in the bathroom," I said slowly, unsure of how to approach the subject. "The one with the Pyramids? I've never seen that picture before."

"Well, you wouldn't have. I'm the only one with a copy." He smiled cheekily as he glanced over at me. "Anyway, I don't think Geraint would want you knowing about their relationship."

"Their relationship?"

"Sure. Geraint, Evan, and Wenda," he replied simply, like it was the most obvious thing, and I hadn't noticed it.

"What are you talking about?" I frowned slightly, unsure if I knew what he was getting at, and unsure if I actually wanted to know.

"Before you were born, there were two young Welshmen who fell for a red-haired beauty. She chose one, the dashing, and brilliant Evan, and that left dark-haired, brooding Geraint alone and bitter. But Evan was fond of Geraint, and together with Wenda, they invited him to be a third member of their relationship, but Geraint refused," he said, telling the story as if it was some sort of old fairy tale. "Wenda and Evan moved away to have a child, and Geraint realised he had made a serious mistake, but he was a victim of his pride, and his ego wouldn't allow him to say he was wrong. Jealous and lonely, he began to loathe the two people whom he adored, and in their absence he became a twisted version of himself. The story ends with the jealous knave doing battle with the heroic prince. No one knows what became of the prince, but we know the princess pitied the knave and recalled her former love for him soon welcomed him into her arms."

"Stop right there—you're saying... Wait a second..." I stuttered, holding my hand to my forehead as my brain became jumbled, and disoriented with all this new information.

He eyed me with a small smile turning the corners of his mouth as he stirred the spoon around the pan. Before I said another word, he turned off the gas, and began pouring the bubbling milk into the two mugs on the counter.

"I can't believe any of this. You're saying that Mum and Dad were in a relationship with Geraint? All three of them, together?" I gasped, baffled, and amazed by the words that were coming out of my mouth. "That's so... weird."

"What's weird about it?" He chuffed as he stirred some spoonfuls of cocoa into the mugs.

"Well... What's *not* weird about it?"

"You don't have to imagine them in bed together, even I have to admit that's probably a terrifying sight, but what I'm saying is, do you understand now why your mam is with Geraint?" he asked.

A steaming mug of hot chocolate was presented to me, and I accepted it gratefully, bringing it to my lips to take a sip. It was like molten lava with a sprinkle of sugar. I licked it from my bottom lip, humming with delight.

"Come on, let's sit in the front room." He waved his hand towards the door, and I got up shakily, following him through into the next room.

I sank into the sofa with a sigh of relief. It moulded around my backside, and I felt as if I might disappear into it if I stayed sat there too long, which was quite different to the angular, merciless perch of the stool. Maredudd sat beside me and rested his feet on the little coffee table. I looked at them, thinking how even his feet were attractive. I imagined them walking across sand, waves washing up around his ankles, and leaving them bejewelled with pale droplets of water.

"I won't tell you too much tonight. You're tired enough as it is. Take this time to contemplate what I've told you. It might illuminate you when you look back at certain things with this new knowledge," he answered over the top of his mug.

"I think it's going to take more than one night for me to comprehend this story," I murmured, my eyes glassy as I tried to envision Dad and Geraint being friendly, or romantic. The image was too gross, and I wrinkled my nose.

"That's okay. Whenever you're ready, we'll come by the next lesson..." He chuckled, blowing the steam from his mug. "So, what do you think of my little house? Cute, huh?"

"Isn't it just? It's so cosy, like a candle-lit grotto." I beamed, my spirits lifting again. Seeing him sat there, glasses propped atop his head, his hair falling around his shoulders in wavy reams, his rough, unshaven face smiling back at me, it felt so right. I felt like I belonged here.

"I know it's small, but I have a spare bedroom... I mean, you can stay there anytime you like." He hesitated. He seemed embarrassed for a moment, and I wanted to question him about what had gone through his head, the shy little blush on his cheeks catching my curiosity.

"I wanted to come and see you, during the week. I thought about climbing the hill, and knocking on your door, but I was worried you would be annoyed," I confessed, hoping that by admitting my own sheepishness, it would make him feel better.

"I wouldn't have been annoyed." He shook his head slowly.

"No, it was stupid. I wish I had come sooner." I bit my lip, finding something interesting to look at in my hot cocoa rather than making eye contact with him.

"You know when you brought me back in the car, and you were outside, after I went in…?"

"Oh yeah, I was kinda—I needed a rest, and…" I tried to find an excuse for why I had stayed outside for so long.

"I thought you were going to come and knock then. I hoped you would. I was going to open the door, and ask you to come in. But then you drove away," he murmured, and he too had noticed something fascinating floating in his mug.

Neither of us spoke, and I felt my cheeks burning.

"Did you have a safe journey back?" he asked.

I nodded, but again, there was silence. I glanced over at the fireplace as the log fire spat and crackled cheerily. The candle flames bobbed and danced.

My eyes darted to the side when his hand was placed on top of mine, and I froze like a frightened fox as he lifted it out of my sight. I couldn't look at him, my face was on fire, and I was tingling all over from both excitement, and nervousness, my heart beginning to pound madly in my chest when I felt his lips gently kissing my knuckles. I didn't know what to do or what to say. I had gone rigid like a fox that had just had a close call with a car bumper, and now I was glued to the spot on the kerb as I waited for shock to set in. He turned my hand, and placed my palm against his cheek, the spiky hair of his stubble surprisingly springy to touch, and his skin deceptively soft. Slowly I turned my head, and found he wasn't looking at me. His eyes were closed, and he had an expression of adoration on his face as he leaned into my touch.

My beating heart was palpitating so frantically that I was worried I was going to go into cardiac arrest. I checked that I wasn't getting any pains in my arm. No, I was doing all right, but my cheeks were starting to hurt with how hard they were blushing. I wanted to move closer, to put aside my mug, and touch him with my other hand, but I felt too clumsy, and awkward, and what then? What would happen next? I had never even kissed another person in a romantic way. I was so inexperienced; it was embarrassing, especially for someone my age.

His eyes opened, and mine darted away, too afraid to make contact. I had never been in a situation like this before. Why had no one ever said how hard it was? Romance movies always made it look so easy, how the characters in the films would just fall into each other's arms, and that would be that. Instead, I felt like I was leaping over hurdles, one long, and terrifying steeplechase, each jump with a pit into oblivion on the other side, waiting to swallow me up if I couldn't make it to safety. His hand slipped away, and my arm supported itself as he waited for me to move forward, or backward, and my hand began to tremble as I couldn't decide what to do.

I was surprised when he chose for me by taking hold of my wrist and lowering my arm so that my hand was resting in his lap, and after putting his mug on the table, he enclosed it in both of his, stroking it soothingly like he was petting an anxious kitten. I swallowed down the hard lump that had accumulated in the back of my throat. I was being ridiculous, and awkward when this was my chance to show him that I liked him, and instead I was sitting there like I was playing musical statues, waiting for the music to start again.

"I'm sorry... I didn't mean to scare you like that..." he whispered, his voice barely audible over the snapping of the fireplace. He sounded like he was talking to himself, and not to me.

"You—you didn't. I'm not... Scared." I struggled to get the words out, stalling over, and over like a trainee driver.

"I can see it in your eyes. I can feel it in your energy, fear. I'm sorry, it was too forward of me." He apologised again, but he didn't let go of my hand. "I won't do it again."

"N—no! I mean, no! I mean, please don't not do it again." I sat bolt upright, desperate for him to hear me, and believe me. "I'm not scared of you. I'm just, well, shy. I'm very shy."

He smiled fondly at me, and I wanted so badly to jump onto him the way a dog jumps into a pile of autumn leaves, joyous, and hysterical with abandon. If only I could do all the things I imagined in my head, perhaps things would be better? Even though my heart was close to exploding, and even though my lungs were on fire, and my skin felt like I was humming with static, I managed to shuffle nearer to him, urging myself to move, talking myself down from the cliff. He observed me silently, and I saw how he was nibbling at his bottom lip. Was he nervous too? It was so hard to tell when he appeared so confident all the time, so being given a momentary glimpse of his delicate core was both thrilling, and endearing. As I moved closer, I felt his body heat suddenly merging with my own, and I tingled all over, feeling so naked in these thin pyjamas. Our thighs touched, and we were side by side then, looking sideways at each other.

"I like you very much, Maredudd." I breathed. His hands enclosing mine were like a live socket docking a plug, providing it with power, and I was becoming so sensitive to his touch that it was almost unbearable.

He smiled down at me, and I knew the feeling was mutual. For a long time we just sat there in silence as though communicating telepathically, gradually sinking back into the softness of the sofa as we listened to each other breathing. My head sank towards him, eventually falling to rest against his shoulder, and my eyes became heavy, refusing to stay open to the point where only toothpicks would hold them up. I could have stayed there in that moment forever.

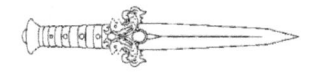

I could hear waves. Water rushing, lifting, rising, a brief quiet before it fell, crashing upon rocks, and sand, bubbles exploding into a head of froth that dissipated between the gaps in the jagged boulders, draining back into sea. Quiet, and then came the rushing again. Rhythmic ebbing and flowing that left me feeling like I was being cradled and rocked gently. Seagulls cawed throatily in the sky, followed by the distant horn of a ship out on the smoothly undulating waves, each lift, and fall of the current sparking a new stripe of yellow on its surface as the sun beamed down upon it.

I lay on my side gazing out at the horizon, my head sunk into a warm, feather-down pillow, and my body nested beneath a duvet. It was cold, for now. The storm had passed over night and left in its wake a dazzling sunrise that turned the sky pink, and red throughout its ascent. I didn't remember finding my way to this bed, but here I was, and I had no intention of moving. I had been so exhausted that I must have fallen asleep on the sofa beside Maredudd, which meant he must have carried me upstairs to this bedroom. I felt embarrassed, but also relieved that he hadn't shaken me awake. It was sweet that he had brought me up here.

My smile was frozen on my face, eyelids half-open as I watched a black-headed gull nosedive over the edge of the cliff, wings tucked into its body as it let gravity guide it towards the water. The misery of the night before was gone. I closed my hand, recalling the sensation of Maredudd's fingers in my grasp, the callouses on his palm, and the thickness of his bony knuckles. My hand felt so empty now, and my body felt so cold without his beside it, yearning for his warmth. Finally, I turned onto my back and stared up at the ceiling. I was disappointed in myself that I had been so shy, but everything in my life took baby steps. I was used to waiting. Undergoing transition had taught me to be patient. I at least had that on my side. My patience wavered when I thought of how he had hugged me the night before, guarding me, his heart beating under my ear, and his hands on my back. I wanted more.

My eyes fell to the statue of Shiva on the cabinet opposite, his own eyes closed in meditation, hands held out palms-up on his knees. I took a deep breath, reminding myself to be calm as he was, and to focus, not to let my heart go running away again, and leaving me stranded with no map like it had yesterday. It had been awhile since I had last meditated. I had been so busy running around, dealing with emotions, and dead animals that I had completely forgotten how liberating it felt to pause, and just breathe. It was hard to pause when my mind was raring to go, a muzzled greyhound watching the motorised bunny zoom off when the cage had yet to spring open.

Yawning, I crawled from the bed.

Downstairs, the sun splashing through the windows lit up every room with a yellow aura. I crept down each step cautiously, wondering where Maredudd was, and listening for any sounds. It was quiet here, only the sound of the waves, the birds twittering outside, and water dripping in a drain somewhere. All of the candles that had been burning last night were now cold, black wicks tiny specks on the white, waxy heads, and the logs in the fireplace like a heap of sleeping bears in their den. I moved through the living room and peered into the kitchen where I saw the back door was open, so padding across the tiles, I leaned out of the doorway into the fresh morning air. The garden, if I could really call it that, since it had no fences, and was nothing more than a grassy hillside, was green, and lush; clean clothing was flapping like a row of flags on the washing line. Maredudd was sitting on a bench near the wall, and when I noticed him I found him staring back at me. His pyjama top was missing, and I saw his muscular hair-covered chest, those strong arms I wanted to hold me again bare to the summer morning. The hair trailed down his belly and disappeared beneath the waistband of his loose grey trousers.

"Hi," I mumbled, suddenly feeling silly, and childlike.

"Hi," was all he said in return. His smile caused his eyes to twinkle as the breeze fluttered his hair about his face.

"So..." I began slowly. For Christ's sake, it's not even like we had sex, and here I was acting like we'd made love passionately on the beach, and I didn't know what to do next. We weren't a couple. All we did was hold hands.

"Would you like some breakfast?" he asked, saving me the embarrassment of trying to stutter out a nonsense question.

"Sure, that'd be great."I agreed.

The silence between us was intolerable as I watched him pouring hot water into two mugs, and munched on a mouthful of cereal, the noise in my head seeming much louder than it really was. We kept looking at each other and saying nothing. He kept smiling at me, and I kept staring back with the expression of a rabbit in the headlights of a car. He looked so beautiful in the morning sunlight, and I wanted to compliment him, but I didn't know how to say it, and when I did open my mouth, I ended up spluttering some rubbish that didn't make a lot of sense.

I felt conflicted because I wanted him so badly to be close to me, but that meant he might eventually see my scars, the physical, and the mental ones, and even worse than that was the thought of him seeing me naked. The parts I had down there were... Not right. Incorrect. Female. Did he know? Or did he think I had the same parts as he did, whether they were surgically created or biological? I hated my body for being so difficult. I had never had the chance to come this far, where I thought I might actually have to be naked in front of someone who wasn't a doctor, so this new fear was an unconquered foe I had yet to tackle. I was the hunchback that belonged in the tower, too ugly, and strange for love.

"There are some things I want to talk about today," he commented as he picked up the two mugs of tea and nodded towards the back door. "Let's sit outside while it's still cool."

Outside on the bench, he passed me a cup, and I put it on the flagstones that encircled the cottage while I ate the rest of my breakfast.

"First of all, your mam called," he said, waiting for my response, which never came. I didn't know how to react, but I did look round at him. He continued. "She's hysterical. I told her you were safe, and with me, but just so you know to expect her screaming, and jumping on you as soon as she sees you. I told her you would go home today."

"Okay..." I murmured, feeling downcast that he was sending me away.

"Running away from Geraint won't make things better." He leaned closer to me, and I smiled weakly as he stroked my cheek. "Besides, your mam and Jojo need you there."

"Can I come back here?" I asked, trying not to sound so needy, but it was obvious.

"Of course you can. This is not the last day we will see each other." He grinned. "Secondly, I want to help you protect yourself from Geraint."

"How am I supposed to do that?" I made a little frown as I bent to pick up my tea.

He let out a deep breath, his lips pressed firmly into a thin line as he gazed down the garden towards the ocean. "Do you believe in magic?"

"Magic? Well... I can't say I don't believe it." I stared at him over my cup of tea as I blew the wisps of steam from the rim. "I guess unless I see evidence in front of my eyes, I'm more inclined not to believe it, but part of me never gives up hope that the supernatural is real."

He nodded, seeming pleased with my response. "Well, imagine how people a hundred years ago would respond to seeing a mobile phone? To them it would look like magic, but it's what we know as science. Do you think perhaps that magic is a science we have yet to fully understand?"

"That would be cool. But I don't know if this would ever happen," I murmured pensively, warming my hands around my mug. "What has this got to do with Geraint?"

"I can teach you some things to protect yourself against him. I was gonna take you to meet Dad, but he's not in the mood for visitors today, so I'm going to show you myself," he explained, and I couldn't help, but look at him as if he was crazy. He smirked. "I know you must think I'm nuts but hear me out."

"So first my parents were in a threesome with Satan's little helper, and now you're telling me you can perform magic?"

"Just hear me out, Owen. I thought you were open-minded?" He raised his brows at me, and to that there was no excuse.

"Okay." I nodded slowly, but I had to admit that I was curious. "I'm sorry. Teach me how."

He reached into his pocket, taking out a thick piece of glossy brown string, and holding it out in front of me. "Here, this is your weapon. Hold out your hands."

"This? A piece of thread?" I chuckled as I let him place it in my palm, and it curled in a circle like a tiny, woven snake.

"It's weaved from Geraint's hair," he told me, and, horrified, I flung it to the ground in disgust.

Expecting him to be annoyed with me, I apologised, and bent to pick it up, but when I looked at his face he was grinning. He started to laugh, slapping me on the back and causing droplets of tea to leap from my mug."You sounded just like Wenda then!" he exclaimed. "It ain't gonna hurt you! Here, let me show you what to do."

He shuffled closer, and I became instantly aware of how near to me he was, soft strands of his hair falling upon my shoulder, and his warmth reaching towards me again. Unable to stop myself from blushing, I looked down at the thread as he straightened it out on my palm.

"Take this thread, and protect it at all costs from Geraint's eyes, do not let him see it. When you are close by, call out his name until he responds, and as soon as you hear his voice, tie a knot in the thread, starting at the end yere." He pointed to one end of the string. "You will need nine knots in total. When you tie it, imagine whatever you would like for him to do. You could imagine him leaving you alone, or ignoring you, or even being kind to you. As you tie more knots, you will notice his behaviour change. When the final knot is tied, go into his bedroom, and place it under the mattress where he sleeps. If that's not possible, put it somewhere where he will have to step over it, like beneath a floorboard, or you can even hide it in the underside of his van."

"Is this really made of his hair? How did you get it?" I stared, mesmerised by what he was telling me. Folklore fascinated me anyway, and this was some genuine witch's spell he was teaching me, something I'd read about in the books I'd shared with my father, so he captured my attention with very little drama required.

"You don't want to know. You must follow my instructions to the dot, do you understand? If he sees what you are doing, you will be in danger." He lowered his voice, and his luminous eyes became serious as they gazed into mine, seeking confirmation.

"I—I will. Of course I will." I nodded quickly.

"Geraint is very powerful, and you are not. Your strength lies in the fact that he does not know that you can do this spell on him. Once he finds out, it's game over. I will have to step in then. We can do this together, but I need you to be stealth, and because you have access to his house, we will be more successful," he explained carefully, his hands holding onto my wrists as I clutched the oily thread tightly. "You can go places I can't get to. I need you to be my eyes, and ears, and to follow my instructions."

"I don't understand... Why are you doing this? Why do you need to do spells on him?" I shook my head, confused by what was happening. I understood each word, but I didn't understand them when they were put together into the sentences he was saying. I felt like I was missing something.

"It's better if you don't know right now. I'm saying this for your own good, not to punish you. I will tell you everything soon enough," he promised.

I looked down at our hands entwined, my eyes half-closing, and my expression becoming downcast, and sullen. I knew it, something was very wrong. I knew it, from the day the police decided Dad wasn't worth searching for anymore, that something was happening that was out of my control. Why had I never noticed before? Had I really been wandering around blindfolded this whole time? The sternness in Maredudd's eyes told me this wasn't a joke. He wasn't telling me how to tie knots in string just for fun, and he genuinely believed in this spell. If it weren't for the way he was looking at me,

I would have thought it was just a bunch of superstitious hogwash, but Maredudd wasn't a liar, and I had promised myself I would trust him.

"There's kind of a problem. I don't usually talk to Geraint, so if I started calling to him all the time, wouldn't he get suspicious?" I asked awkwardly. If I was going to do it right, I needed to figure out how I was going to avoid these kinds of obstacles.

"Does your mam call to him often?"

"All the time." I giggled, and he smiled at me, the corners of his eyes creasing.

"Perfect. Just make sure you are present when your mam calls to him. And another thing: it's probably best if Wenda doesn't see what you're doing either. I don't think she'd be best pleased about it," he admitted sheepishly. "Oh, and once you've decided what you want the thread to do, stick with it. Don't go changing your mind when you've already tied a knot in it, because it will fail. It needs solid, repetitive visualisation of a single goal."

"Okay. Does this spell have a name?" I asked curiously, a grin soon returning to my mouth.

"It's called a Witch's Ladder. It's one of the oldest and simplest forms of cursing. There are many different types, but this is the one my dad taught to me." His smile became hopeful, and he gave my wrists a gentle squeeze.

He looked so adorable then with the wind blowing his hair about, the bright green eyes that had been so stern, and serious moments ago softening, growing friendly, and fond again, and that gentle smile that somehow made him appear younger than his years. The smile faltered though, and he looked down, his brow creasing, and his eyes hidden from me as he wiped his hand across his face, tugging a strand of hair from his lips. I thought he was about to cry, and I leaned closer, my hand instinctively going to his shoulder in a bid to comfort him.

"I don't want anything to happen to you or Wenda. I'm sorry I'm sending you off to do this. I really am," he whispered.

"I'll be alright, I promise," I told him, but I wasn't very convincing.

I had no idea what I was getting myself into.

Seven

"Owen! Oh gosh, Owen! My precious boy!" Mum shrieked when she opened the door and saw me standing outside. I was given several seconds before she launched at me, and I was squashed against her bosom, her arms nearly cracking a rib as they wound around me like an anaconda from which there was no escape.

"Mum!" I wheezed, and she released her grip just enough to let me breathe.

"Don't you ever do that that again, you hear me! You had me pulling my hair out at the root!" she shouted at me, and now she was shaking me back and forth, her fingernails pinching into my shoulders. "Owen! You nearly gave me a fuckin' heart attack! You shouldn't have run off like that!"

I shook my head, unsure of what to say to her. It was so hard to stay angry at her when I loved her so. "I was upset... I didn't know what else to do."

"Oh Owen, I'm so sorry!" Her anger suddenly switched to tears, and she started to cry loudly, not caring at all that anyone might see or hear her in such a state.

"Mum, let's go inside." I gently urged her towards the door, and she allowed me to lead her into the cool shade of the hallway, closing the door behind us.

"Owen, I'm so sorry, I really am. I'm sorry I didn't protect you, it's all my fault." She wept, and now it was my turn to hug her. I put my arms around her, resting my chin on her shoulder, and she clung onto me, her soft body so different to hugging Maredudd.

"It's not your fault, Mum... Like you said, I've got to stand up for myself sometimes..." I trailed off, realising I didn't really know how to explain what I had done. Maredudd's explanation seemed the most logical. "I ran away to protect myself. I didn't do it to punish you."

"No, darling, I know you didn't. I'm not mad at you. I was tamping after you left, but no, I should have said something before it escalated," she whined into my neck. "I should have said something. It's my fault."

"Mum, I'm okay. There's nothing to worry about so stop saying that. I forgive you, and I love you," I reminded her with a small chuckle as I held onto her. It wasn't the first time I had comforted her, but for some reason this time it was different. Being with Maredudd had made me stronger somehow, and I couldn't figure it out.

Sniffing, and snorting, she leaned back in my arms, and wiped at her eyes with the apron she was wearing. Her face, which was normally a blushing shade of scarlet was now glowing like Rudolph's nose at Christmas time.

"Darling, I won't let him say those wicked, wicked things to you again," she told me firmly.

"Is he home right now?" I asked, turning to glance over my shoulder in the direction of the garage where he was most likely to be lurking.

"No, he's gone round Farmer Thomas's fields setting traps." She peered after me as though we both expected him to fly out of the shadows at us. "Oh you should have seen him after you left, I wiped the floor with the bugger. Turned him into a right sorry drip."

"Do you know when he's coming back?" I looked round at her, and she frowned.

"You're not gonna run away again, are you?" She

clutched at my arm as though she thought I might run out of the door at any moment.

"No. I just think I should, you know. Talk to him. Or something." I shrugged.

"I will keep you company if that's what you want to do. Come, come into the kitchen, I've got something for you." She took hold of my hand, and pulled me along the hallway.

Something wasn't right. Where was a certain little dog? I looked around, listening for her paws on the floor that I was so accustomed to.

"Mum, where's Jojo?" I questioned nervously, and she giggled as we stepped down into the kitchen together.

"She's in the garden. Why, you didn't think he'd hurt her, did you?" She let go of me, depositing me beside the kitchen table as she opened the back door, and whistled. "Geraint would never hurt my second baby, even if she tried to bite his bollocks off."

The bouncing terrier came scooting up the steps, and flew in through the door, skidding across the tiles towards me, her face a picture of excitement. I bent to greet her, baby-talking her as I stroked her all over, and she spun in circles to ensure both sides of her furry body were thoroughly petted. Mum looked on fondly, hands on hips as she watched us together.

"She's been pining for you the whole time you were gone," she said as I picked Jojo up into my arms, and cuddled her, her tiny paws on my shoulders as she grinned from ear to ear.

"Aww, did you miss me, Jojo!" I laughed when she started licking my beard, her pink tongue flapping out from between her black lips.

"Put the dog down now, I got a present for you by yere."Mum fussed, taking the dog out of my arms, and placing her on the ground. She picked up a carrier bag off the table, and thrust it into my hands, seeming surprisingly shy about it. "It's not much, but it's the best I could do on my budget. I know how upset you were about your camera, so..."

Curiously, I peered into the bag. It contained dozens of small boxes, and so I gave it a shake to turn them, revealing the gold writing on some of the sides. They were all different brands of analogue film, but most of them were the same ISO, and some were black, and white, and infra-red.

"I got them for you the other day at the car-boot sale. I only popped past on the way home, I wasn't meaning to buy anything, but the man was selling the whole lot for a bargain, and I thought of you and your camera." She reasoned as she eyed me tentatively, hoping she had made the right choice. "You can use my old camera, start taking pictures again..."

"Oh Mum, that's so sweet of you."I sighed, grabbing her in a bear-hug with the bag still in my hand, so it bumped against her back and swished when we moved. "What would I do without you...?"

"A bloody shit-ton of washing up, most likely," she wise-cracked, and we both laughed.

Now that I had film, and a camera to shoot it with, I was back in action. Sure, it was likely I would have to wait months before developing the film rolls, but a treasure trove of spent film was better than no photographs at all, especially when it meant I might capture the beast in a photo. I knew Mum hadn't bought the film with the intention of encouraging me to go out walking the woods at night again, and because of that, I decided it would be best not to tell her that I was planning to head out as soon as possible. She was already feeling sensitive about my running away the night before; I really didn't want to stress her out further.

In the meantime, we sat together in the living room, and watched some chat shows, laughing at the people screaming at each other, and getting separated by bald-headed bouncers. Every time I looked at her, all I could think about was what Maredudd had said the night before, and it made me feel so baffled to imagine her, and Dad with Geraint. I wanted to ask her about it, but would she deny it? Would she be angry that Maredudd had told me things she had silently kept from me? What if the story was false, and I made myself look like a complete idiot? Still, it was the only genuine reason I could think of that would explain why Mum had fallen so quickly into a relationship with him.

It's not like he was the sweetest, kindest man in town, or that he was particularly good-looking, or even that he had a lot of money. Perhaps one of those qualities alone would have explained it, but he had none of those things. He was old, and scruffy, belligerent, and aggressive, and didn't have a penny to scratch his arse with. The complete opposite of Dad, perhaps with the exception of the money aspect, since Dad wasn't exactly rolling in it either. But he more than made up for it in the other two departments.

"Mum, I was talking to Maredudd, and he said some things to me, and I just want to know..." I began slowly, giving her time to try and guess what I might say next. Her eyes focused on me, and she looked at my expression like she was doing an eye-sight test at the opticians, squinting to make out the small letters.

"What did he say?" She prompted.

"He said umm, that a long time ago, you, Dad, and Geraint were, you know... Like that." I poked the fingertips of both hands together awkwardly, waiting for her to guess what I meant, and when it didn't happen, I made a loop with my thumb, and forefinger, and started poking my index finger through it with an apprehensive expression.

Mum's eyes grew large, squinted again, and then opened wide once more when she realised what I was saying. Her chin wobbled, and she looked at the telly as if for guidance, but all that appeared on the screen was a pair of teenagers squabbling.

"It's okay, you know, if that's what happened. I'm not angry about it, it's just really weird, and kind of gross to imagine Dad being close to Geraint in that way..." I felt myself becoming speechless. "I mean, it's gross that you're with him right now, without Dad."

We both sat in silence for a moment, and it was a minute or two before Mum finally looked at me again. I couldn't tell if she was annoyed or shocked, or a combination of both.

"W—well, your dad and me, our parents were hippies. I was nearly named Starshine, before your bampa decided he thought Wenda was more work-friendly," she said, still looking rather shell-shocked towards the television screen. "Not—not that that excuses it, but. We were already liberated in that respect, before we met Geraint, and Maredudd, and Morcant."

"Who is Morcant?" I frowned, tilting my head. It was a name I had never heard her or Dad mention before.

"Maredudd's father," she murmured, taking a sip from the teacup she had been holding in her lap.

An awkward silence followed, and I began to wish I had never said anything.

"Clever man, he is. Or was. I don't know if he's still alive. But Maredudd is right: me, y—your dad, and Geraint did, were, in like a love triangle. You know, like that film with the vampires, and werewolves." She shrugged a shoulder, her face still completely serious, but I wanted to laugh because I had never seen her act so uncomfortable before. "I guess I chose the vampire over the werewolf, when really I wanted both of them. And your dad, he wanted Geraint too."

"Oh god, stop right there, I don't think I want to

hear any more of that." I pretended to throw up, making vomiting noises into my hand.

Finally, she laughed too, and the air between us seemed to clear, becoming relaxed again as it had before. She seemed relieved that this information was out in the open now.

"Geraint wasn't always like this. I hope one day you two can be friends and see the good in one another. Inside he's got a kind heart. Sort of in the way a murderous stalker has a kind heart," she began, sounding sincere, but then she erupted into a snorting chuckle. "But you don't see that, of course you don't, because all he shows you is the wall he puts up around himself. The Geraint I see is incredibly protective, loving, and passionate."

"Well, maybe one day I will get to see what's over the wall," I murmured, but I wasn't really sure if that would happen, or whether I wanted it to.

The atmosphere was strained when Geraint did come home, late in the evening when it was getting dark, and Mum and I had already had our dinner, while his was left in the oven to stay warm for when he arrived. I had kept the thread that Maredudd gave me in my trouser pocket. It was strange; when I rubbed it between my fingertips, I felt like Geraint was there. It gave me an unsettling feeling that he might be right behind me, and I fought the desire to look over my shoulder, because of course he wasn't present. I got my chance to tie the first knot within the first hour of him arriving home, when Mum asked me to go, and ask him if he wanted his dinner put in the microwave, so I stood in the hallway, and called out his name.

"Geraint!" I shouted up the stairs, as I knew he was up there getting changed out of his muddy work-clothes.

"What!" he yelled back.

As fast as I could, I fumbled to tie the knot in the string. What had at first seemed like a relatively easy task now became complicated, and nerve-wracking as I tried to tie the thread, visualise what I wanted from him, and make sure Mum didn't see what I was doing. I envisaged him being friendly towards me, being kind to me, and Mum, not being a total jerk like usual. I startled when I heard him coming along the upstairs landing, shoving the knotted thread into my pocket just as he appeared on the top step, his glaring, beady eyes peering down the stairs at me. He had put on a pair of scruffy jogging bottoms, and was holding a football t-shirt in both hands, his top half clad in a discoloured vest. I was worried he had seen what I was doing.

"Mum wants to know if you want your dinner reheated," I asked quickly, and he huffed.

"Yeah, go on then," he grunted before turning and moving off again.

I let go of the breath I hadn't realised I had been holding. He hadn't seen me. If he had, I knew for certain that he would have said something.

Sitting in the living room while he ate his food from a tray on his lap, things felt kind of odd. Mum was doing her crochet, and had spread out all of her balls of yarn on the sofa, leaving a small gap for me to curl up in while I watched the telly, occasionally bringing a corn chip to my mouth as my eyes attempted to glance at Geraint covertly. He was eating like a pig as usual, but something seemed different. He wasn't staring at me like he often did. I waited and waited for him to start saying something, to start moaning and complaining, attempting to get an argument brewing, but instead he just shovelled his cheese and tuna bake into his mouth, eyes moving between his plate and the television screen like he needed the information from the game show it was displaying in order to correctly eat his food. I must have been staring too much because he finally noticed me, eyes as cool, and colourless as winter frost focusing on me momentarily as he chewed a big mouthful of pasta, but then he looked away. My hand fell upon my trouser pocket, and I fiddled with the little knot through the fabric that covered it. Maybe this was just a coincidence, and he was giving it a rest because Mum had told him off.

"Finished pitching the traps by Mr Thomas's farm," he remarked a few minutes later when the adverts had come on. "Still a lot to do though. I was wondering..."

"Hmm?"Mum looked over at him as if she hadn't heard a single word he was saying.

"I was wondering..." he repeated, seeming to have forgotten what he was about to say next. "I wondered if Owen could come and help out."

Mum's head turned towards me sharply. She was as astonished as I was. She turned back to Geraint. "Well, why don't you ask the boy yourself?"

I stared at the floor, my lips parted, and another corn chip in my hand, poised to be eaten, but going nowhere. I couldn't look at him. I kept telling myself it was because of Mum, not the thread that this was happening. She had wiped the floor with him, and he wanted to get back into her good books by being nice to me.

"Owen. I... I was wondering if you would come and help me at work tomorrow," Geraint said to me. I heard his words, but I didn't see him. I saw only the carpet on the floor between us.

"Please," Mum added tartly.

"Please," he tacked on quickly, sounding surprisingly tentative. It almost didn't sound like Geraint talking at all. If I didn't know any better, and had heard these words from behind a screen, I would have thought it was somebody else.

Somehow, I managed to clench the muscles in my neck to tilt my head up, and I found them both peering at me expectantly, awaiting an answer. When I didn't speak, he put his knife, and fork down, clawing his hair back from his forehead with his badly-chewed fingertips.

"I'd pay you for it. The same wage as an apprentice. Cash in hand," he said, his sentences short, and almost robotic. "Eight until five. I'll give you a lift as well."

I could feel that Mum was practically vibrating on the sofa next to me, waves of urgency crashing against my right-hand side as she so desperately wanted me to say yes. When I hazarded a glance at her, I saw the pleading in her eyes. She wanted us to get along, and if this was Geraint's way of burying the hatchet then perhaps I should run with it.

"Okay. Sure," I finally agreed.

I nearly found it physically painful to see him smile. It was so unnatural. His eyes relaxed, opening wide, and his mouth turned at the corners into a crooked grin that showed his teeth. I felt like I had lobotomised him, and this was the effect, him being nice to me, and acting like there was a sliver of kindness in his black soul. I wasn't sure which version of Geraint I preferred. At least when he was an asshole he was behaving as I expected. Whatever the case, I had to finish tying the Witch's Ladder, and I was given another opportunity that evening when Mum called to him to make a pot of tea. After that, I hid away upstairs in my bedroom, staring with amazement at the thick piece of string in my hands.

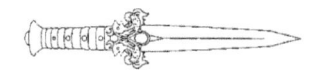

Being outside in the sunshine, surrounded by birdsong and fresh air, I actually started to enjoy myself as I followed Geraint through the woodland that surrounded the edge of the Fairfields' property, carrying a crate of clunking metal objects as he looked at the ground under our feet, searching ideal spots to plant a hidden spring-trap. Early that morning, he had knocked on my bedroom door to get me up, but I was already awake and eating my breakfast as I sat by the window, fully dressed and prepared for the day ahead. At first he seemed grumpy, and I felt very awkward and out of place as I sat in the passenger seat of his transit van, watching his frowning face in the reflection of the window while he drove down the narrow, winding lanes that mapped the area we lived in. He was chewing a great big wad of something, and he wound down the window, and spat it out into the wind. When we pulled up at a junction, he stopped just long enough to take out his tobacco tin, and offer some to me, but I shook my head and politely declined. He looked so funny, dorky even, when he grinned at me, his teeth all black, and sticky from the tobacco. I almost, almost, was starting to like this version of Geraint.

When we arrived at Fairfield Farm, Rhys was outside grooming the dogs, his overalls covered in a thick smattering of shed fur, and one of the collies tied to a stake in the ground so that it couldn't escape while he worked. He stood upright, and looked down the sloping yard towards us, picking a clump of fluff from the long-tooth comb. I realised I had forgotten to tell Mum about Chief. Now would be a great time to tell Rhys myself, but after the way he had spoken to me at the front door, I wasn't sure he deserved to know. Then again, I thought about Jojo, and how upset I would be if she went missing. Rhys had grown up with Chief, that dog had been his best friend from childhood, and although they had a number of sheepdogs on the farm, Chief had been his favourite. Geraint pulled the van up on the driveway of the farmhouse, and climbed out, telling me to wait as he went to speak to Rhys's father. I sat in the passenger seat awhile, watching Rhys combing the panting sheepdog. It wasn't right for me to keep it a secret.

"Hiya, Owen," he answered when he saw me approaching in my black cargo shorts, and green vest, my freckled skin thoroughly covered in sub-block.

"Rhys—I just wanted to say that—well, last week..." I stuttered, too nervous now that I was standing right in front of him.

"I know, I'm sorry about what I said to you. It weren't right," he said before I could finish my sentence.

"Oh—umm." I was speechless. His voice sounded genuine, and he had a serious look in his eye before he leaned forward to continue combing the dog. I opened my mouth, forcing myself to speak. "Thanks. I mean, it's fine, I'm not pissed off about it. I actually came over because I wanted to speak to you about something else..."

He stopped again, and stood upright, plucking a knot of downy fur from his lips, and spitting. "What's that then?"

"The other day, I was driving late in the evening, when the storm was going on, and I stopped at a junction and saw Chief..." I hurried to get the words out otherwise they would never be said. "He still had his chain attached to his collar, and he was standing by the road in the rain. I stopped the car, but he ran away before I could get to him."

"Chief!" He gasped, and I flinched when he moved towards me, his free hand grabbing my shoulder, and depositing strands of dog hair on my sleeve. "When did you see him? Was he all right?"

"It—it was on Saturday night. He looked fine, just very wet," I explained, recognising the desperate hope in his eyes, and instantly feeling bad that I hadn't told him sooner.

"And where was that?"

"The T-junction on the hill, by the castle," I told him. He let go of me abruptly, and without another word, ran down the slope towards the house, vanishing from sight. The sheepdog he had left standing there looked up at me expectantly, tongue lolling from its open mouth, so I reached down, and stroked its soft, silken head.

Soon after, Geraint reappeared, and told me to get back in the van—we were going somewhere. He drove up the dirt track between the fields, heading to the far edges of the property where the fences were almost fully integrated with the trees. This was where we were going to lay the traps. Although Geraint seemed grouchy, he was polite to me, helping to carry the equipment, and asking me if I was all right as we walked through the trees, butterflies scattering around our legs, and birds taking flight as we passed. Cows were grazing in the neighbouring field, and every now, and again, I heard one mooing, the horn-like noise carrying through despite the density of the woodland.

Geraint clearly knew exactly what he was doing, I deferred to him for every decision, and he showed me how to put the trap together, hammering a stake into the ground to which a chain was attached, and then carefully pinning open the jaws of the leg-hold device. I stood back after successfully setting my first one alone, and turned to look at him standing there, hands on his hips.

"Good job." He spat a gob of brown liquid into the leaf litter.

"Are these even legal nowadays? They're really old-fashioned," I asked, half-jokingly. The other half of me was concerned that an innocent animal, like a fox or a badger, would get captured by it, and end up injured or dead.

"Legality hasn't got a lot to do with the peace of mind of our farmers, Owen. This is the only thing that keeps the attacks from happening yere," he replied, and I was amazed at how calm he was behaving. Normally, I would have expected some kind of insulting remark for asking such a question.

"But what happens if you catch a fox or something?"

"It ends up at auction, stuffed, and mounted." He made a gruff, cackling laugh, and turned, picking up the bag of jangling chains, still chuckling to himself as he continued to walk down towards the stream. I hauled the crate into my arms and followed silently.

"The fact is, kid, the farmers don't like foxes either. Or badgers, or weasels. They're all vermin to us. The only place we like them to be seen is on the cabinet in our living rooms as an ornament, or on the telly, filmed in some distant land where they don't bother us," he said as I caught up, waiting for him to cross the tinkling brook first before joining him on the other side, my boots sinking in the mud. "We've got no care for the natural world anymore. In days gone past, there was respect for the wild. Maybe this thing that keeps mutilating the cattle is a sign."

I was quiet, my eyes focused on the uneven ground as I walked alongside him. This was the most Geraint had ever spoken to me in one go. For the first time ever, he was actually saying something I agreed with, and because of that, I was utterly astounded.

"Do you think we deserve it? Do you think the cows, and sheep deserve it?" I asked hesitantly after a few minutes.

"Life doesn't work like that. You get what you work for, not what you deserve. Deserving implies entitlement," he grunted, sounding as though he didn't want to talk about this anymore. He didn't even answer my question, so I decided to let that topic go.

Being able to spend time out here with him gave me all of the opportunities I needed to finish tying the knots, and by the end of the day, I had all nine of them. The string sat in my pocket, feeling warm, and heavy like a pebble heated in a fire-pit, giving off an energy all of its own. I was comfortably tired, and hungry, looking forward to having dinner when we got home, and Geraint stopped by at the farmhouse before we left.

"Here ya go, mun. You're worth every penny, I swear it," Jeff Fairfield brayed as he slapped a wad of cash in Geraint's waiting hand. Big, round-bellied Mr Fairfield looked nothing like his lithe son, who I assumed must take after his mother, but perhaps it was the copious amount of locally brewed ale that made him so rotund and caused the pattern of burst blood vessels in his nose, and cheeks. He smelled like a pub too.

"Cheers Jeff, I won't insult you by counting it by yere, I'll wait until I hop in the van." Geraint laughed, and the two men guffawed, and clapped each other's backs.

"You cheeky git! You know I recommend you to every chap with a bit of land round yere, 'tis only your traps what keeps this thing off our turf. I tried that weaselly little grease-monkey from in town, but bugger it, barely did a thing." Jeff continued to kiss Geraint's ass, and I rolled my eyes as I looked through the van window at them.

I turned and looked over the darkening fields towards the pink sunset, their conversation becoming a dull hum behind me as I rested my feet. There was dirt under my fingernails, so I began to scrape it out with the nail of my thumb, and as I sat there doing so, I contemplated what Jeff Fairfield had said only moments ago. I thought of Maredudd, of what he had told me about magic, and I was teetering on the very edge of believing that it was real. The knotted string in my pocket told me that it might be true, but I needed more convincing to be sure just yet. Still, I couldn't help wondering if it had something to do with Geraint's traps. So the farmer had tried other trappers, but to no avail? And only Geraint's traps seemed to keep the beast at bay? It was easy to put two and two together. Maybe it was possible that Geraint was doing something else to prevent the thing from coming onto the land, a spell of some kind? If that was the case, then...

That meant Geraint wasn't all that bad after all. It meant he wasn't as much of a villain as I had thought he was, but that didn't explain why Maredudd was so set on infiltrating Geraint's fortress. The story he had told me that night had been playing on my mind, and I realised that in a not-so subtle way he had implied that Geraint was responsible for Dad's death. Geraint was an asshole, there was no skirting around that, but in no way did he make me believe he could be a killer. Perhaps I needed to tell Maredudd that he had got it all wrong.

As we drove home in the van, the setting sun sent rays of radiant yellow, and orange upon our drowsy faces. I closed my eyes from time to time, and listened to the radio's tinny chatter, which was occasionally drowned out by the roar of the engine when we sped uphill. The narrow lanes caused the close-standing bushes, and reaching branches to scratch, and scrape the windows, and the sides of the vehicle, adding their own touches to the already marred paintwork of his vehicle. I could tell he was tired, and not much in the mood for talking so I remained quiet, but I did catch a glimpse of him every now, and again. His features had softened slightly, and he looked kinder, younger. His eyes weren't squinting the way they usually did, and I think that was it, he wasn't frowning or scowling, so his eyes opened up and became clear, catching the light and flashing. For that moment in time, I could see the man that Mum loved, and I forgave her for it.

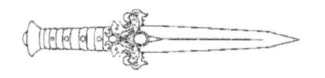

Over the week that followed, work with Geraint kept me very busy indeed, and I was afforded very little time to myself, except in the evenings after we got home. As promised, Geraint paid me for my work, and I was thrilled to have some money for myself, so I tucked it away somewhere safe with the intention of using some of it to process my film, and the rest of it to save for a new camera. Late at night, I looked across the bay with my binoculars, and yearned for Maredudd. Mum gave me his phone number, but when I sat beside the landline, and brought the receiver to my ear, my confidence faltered, and I couldn't bring myself to dial the numbers, eventually running away to chew my fingernails, and worry my head to aching.

I missed him, missed him to the point where my every waking thought began to be consumed by his image, his face, and his eyes gazing at me. I remembered all the words we had spoken to each other, and it warmed me to know that he liked me too, and maybe, if I was really lucky, we might end up together. I hadn't told Mum about the tiny little seed of our relationship that I was trying to nurture into a precious, green shoot. I didn't know what she would think if she knew, and that scared me. Knowing her, I didn't think she would have a problem, but after all the things I had learned about it recently, I saw that there was a whole other side to her that was a stranger to me.

That weekend, she drove off on a shopping trip in town, and Geraint went out to the pub for a darts competition, leaving the house to me, and Jojo. She followed me outside, investigating every inch of the lawn with her fruit pastel nose as I fed the other animals, stopping occasionally to look round at me when I banged the gate or sprinkled feed on the ground. Roger lipped at my t-shirt as I inspected Mary's eyes to make sure she didn't have an infection, and I turned, telling him off with a hopeless chuckle as he tried to chew the material into a wad in his mouth. Every time I turned my back, he would start again, so I tucked it into my shorts, but that made little difference as he started on those instead.

"Stop that! Naughty boy!" I laughed as I tugged the flap of my pocket from between his teeth, and he raised his head, observing me through his big glassy eyes. "It's bad for you! Now don't look at me like that. There's plenty of food there for you so there's no need to eat my clothing."

He blinked, his head tilting slightly as he stared. Sometimes it felt like there was a human inside there trying to communicate with me, the way he looked at things as though trying to solve a puzzle. Jojo did that too, especially when she was trying to get treats out of a rubber chew toy, and it was always fascinating to watch. I sighed, reaching to stroke the tuft of hair between his horns.

"Silly Roger." I smiled, but then he plodded closer, and started mouthing at my pocket once more. I moved away, worried that he would take the string from my pocket, and eat it, thus undoing all of my hard work.

He stood there staring at me as I stepped out of the pen, and closed the gate, making sure it was secure before I went back into the house, leaving the back door open so that Jojo could come, and go as she pleased. I washed my hands at the sink, the white shape of the telephone on the wall just within my peripheral vision, taunting me until I turned my head to look at it. No one was here to listen to me if I chose to make a call, which was also one of the major reasons that had put me off calling before. The thought of mumbling sweet nothings down the phone while Mum or Geraint were listening made me want to puke. It was now or never, and I didn't know when I would be getting another chance to be alone here. I picked up the receiver and leaned against the counter as I peered down at Mum's address book, dialling the number quickly before I had a chance to change my mind, then the dial tone started to beep as the call went through. My heart began to pound, and I felt my body starting to sweat with anxiety. On, and on it went. I could put the phone down now, and he would never know I had tried to contact him. But what if it went to an answer-machine? I bit down on my lip, my fist clenching at my side. This was so horrible!

You can put the phone down, I told myself. Put it down, he's not home...

"Hello?" he suddenly said, and my mind went blank. My mouth opened, but no sound coming out.

"Hello? Who is it?" he asked, waiting for a response.

"Maredudd... It's me," I stammered. Hearing his voice in my ear caused a nerve to shoot down my neck, straight into my heart like Cupid's arrow, and all of a sudden I was red-faced, and nervous like before. Even my hands were shaking.

"Owen," he breathed. It was the most beautiful sound. I realised I was biting my tongue.

"I—I just want to call, and... and tell you that I finished the Witch's Ladder," I chirped, trying to keep my voice level. Reminding myself that he couldn't see me blushing, and trembling.

"That's great. Is it working?"

"Yes, I think so." I was grinning so broadly that my jaw was aching. The joy I had initially felt though was gradually dissolving into neediness, and my heart was hurting for him, hurting so uncontrollably that nothing would make it stop.

"Have you put it somewhere hidden yet?" he asked, and I slapped my forehead, realising I had forgotten the final step of the spell.

"No... I will now, though. He's not home. I'm going to put it under the floorboard outside his work room. Do you think that's a good idea?"

"It's perfect. I knew you could do it. Just like your dad." He chuckled, and the sound of him breathing was like the rushing of waves on a sundown beach.

"I miss you," I blurted, not knowing how else to get my feelings across.

"Don't worry, Owen. I'm working this weekend, but maybe we can meet up during the week?" he suggested thoughtfully.

"Oh... I can't at the moment... I've been working a lot, and I've been pretty tired out..." I mumbled, disheartened. Suddenly, the idea of having to go to work with Geraint again filled me with dread.

"Oh... Well, how about next weekend? I'll keep it free for you," he mused, and although it was a logical solution, it wasn't good enough for me. I didn't want to make a fuss though, so I agreed. It was the best I was going to get for now.

He told me he had to go as he was about to head out when I called, so we said goodbye, and he put the phone down. I leaned against the wall, hating this overwhelming yet unrecognisable emotion that was welling up inside me. It was like what I had felt after Dad died, that clawing, gnawing need to see him again, only this was different, because it was a different kind of love. I had come to admit to myself that I was falling in love, but actually coping with it was proving difficult. Did I fall in love too quickly? Is that why I couldn't handle it? But more importantly, was he in love with me? I covered my eyes with my hand, unable to even entertain the thought that he might not be. If he was looking for a casual hook-up then he had chosen the wrong person. There was no way I was going to just put out on the second date, so he could dump me off when he was satisfied.

"Stop it," I muttered to myself, sighing.

I was being ridiculous, and blaming him when he wasn't here, hating him because he wasn't with me so that I could see how handsome, and wonderful he was, and remember why I had started feeling this way in the first place. I shouldn't have even thought those things about him. Maredudd wasn't like that at all. He was kind, gentle, sensitive, and considerate, not a womaniser, or whatever the gay equivalent was, I had no idea. Besides, it was near enough impossible to have a one-night-stand in this village without Mrs Bevan, and the Village Gossip Committee finding out about it. If Maredudd was doing something like that, I would have heard already.

I took a claw hammer out of the utility cupboard under the stairs, and went down into the back room, opening the door into the dull air of the garage. The floor of the garage was concrete, but fortunately there were some wooden floorboards along the side where the work room was, and I knelt in front of the locked door, using the hammer to wrench one up. I picked the one closest to the door that was impossible for him to avoid. Underneath, the cavity was full of cobwebs, and a big spider scuttled away to avoid the light, making me startle, and jump back. I had wrapped the thread in some tissue, and I gently placed it down amongst the cobwebs; it was almost tempting to tuck it in like a babe at bed-time. Then, I replaced the floorboard, and hammered it back down. There. It wasn't likely he would notice anything different.

I then went to sit upstairs, and fiddle with Mum's camera, figuring out how to use it by eyes alone since the manual that had come with it was long since lost, probably back in the 90s when she first took it to Glastonbury Festival. It was an SLR like my old camera, and fortunately a self-winding one too, so with a little attention I got it to wind on a new film before taking the lens off, and giving it a good clean, wiping away the dust, and smears from the glass. I wondered if Maredudd would let me take a picture of him. Probably.

I sat facing the window, the spirit within me reaching for his cottage on the hillside. Why did love make me feel so sad? Wasn't it meant to be uplifting?

Instead I felt so forlorn and empty, all desire to do the things I usually did were draining out of me, dripping from my feet into nothingness as I fought to re-absorb it. But doing so was pointless. It had been easier when I was just alone. I thought that was difficult, that nothing could be worse than the loneliness, but how wrong I was. This was worse. I was alone, and I was pining too. I drew my knees up under my chin and closed my eyes.

My mind took me back to that night at his house, the two of us sitting side by side on the sofa, the warmth of his body close to me, his hand enclosed in mine, our breathing synchronised. The crackle of the fire and the fragrance of the candles. The rain beating at the windows, unable to get in, and the darkness outside making me believe we were the only two people in the world. I wanted to go back to that moment in time and stay there.

I must have fallen asleep. The sun that had warmed my face had faded, and now I lay on my side, a chill creeping over my skin. The hazy sky, lilac and a tepid shade of blue, stretched over the ocean towards me, offering handfuls of wispy clouds here and there, no wind to shift them from their chosen positions. It didn't matter how much time had passed. The feeling hadn't gone away, and I lay there unmoving, looking down at the peaceful twinkling of the waves below. If the wind had been blowing towards the house then I would have been able to hear the water on the beach, lulling me to sleep again. My ears were alerted to the front door opening, and Mum's shuffling footfalls entered the house, the crinkle of plastic carrier bags accompanying on her journey down the hallway to the kitchen. It must have been late if she had returned.

"Whatever's the matter with you?"Mum remarked as I hung in the kitchen doorway and watched her putting a flagon of milk in the fridge.

"Oh—nothing." I rubbed at my eyes, unsure of what

I looked like. A wreck, probably.

"Did you feed the dog?" she questioned, bending at the waist to chuck a bag of onions in the bottom cupboard.

Yawning into my hand, I realised I hadn't. "No... I'll do it now."

I turned into the hallway, wondering where she might have got to, calling her name, and waiting for the familiar clatter of claws on the flooring, but none came. She must have still been in the garden, then. I squeezed past Mum as she bent suddenly to put something else away, heading to the back door, and squinting down into the garden to see if I could spot her.

"Jojo!" I called.

Usually by now she would have come hurtling up the steps towards me, tongue flying out of her mouth with that crazed expression she always wore when she knew food was waiting for her. I tiptoed bare foot into the garden, and called to her again, turning this way, and that as my eyes sought her little white form. Roger raised his head over the fence, and watched me pass, chewing a mouthful of food, and grass combined. The chickens startled when I appeared outside their coop, squawking, and bustling manically to get away until they realised it was me, followed by a shrill gobbling from the turkeys who jerked upright to face the sudden foe. They quieted down as I stopped next to the wire pen, frowning. It wasn't like Jojo not to come when called, and even less like Jojo to escape from the garden. We could leave the gate wide open, and she wouldn't walk through it without permission. I rushed back to the house.

Jojo had never gone missing before, and Mum was in a state when she realised I wasn't joking around. We took a bag of dog treats, and left the garden, wading through waist-high grass in the fields around the house as we called for her, whistling, and shouting, hoping to hear her coming, bustling, through the undergrowth. Pheasants, and other hidden birds took flight, screeching in fear as we moved past them. We covered the nearest fields, and then moved onto the ones just beyond that. Pretty soon, the sky darkened as night set in, and I had to take Mum by the arm, and tell her we needed to stop, and go back to the house.

"I can't, Owen! She's lost out yere somewhere, all alone!" Mum was distraught, big tears bubbling from her eyes as she dabbed at them with her fingertips.

"It's getting late, we'll never find her in the dark," I told her, holding onto her wrist to stop her from pulling away from me. "Geraint is probably wondering where we've got to."

Mum sniffled and nodded slowly. She knew I was talking sense, but her instinct was to go on looking. I sighed, unable to believe that Jojo had intentionally climbed over the garden fence knowing full well that that was naughty, especially after all the years she had been well-behaved. Maybe she had been following a scent, maybe a fox had dug beneath the fencing, and she had followed it, her nose to the ground, only to discover that she had accidentally wandered too far, and found herself lost? I linked arms with Mum and pattered her hand.

"We'll find her, don't worry. Come on, let's go back and have a cup of tea," I said. "You never know, she might find her own way back. You know how smart she is."

"You're always so optimistic, Owen. I wish I could be like that sometimes," she mumbled as she allowed me to turn her around in the direction of the house.

From up on the hill, I could see the house beyond the trees, and the lights were on, which could only mean that Geraint was home. We found him in the kitchen, sitting to the table with a bag of fish and chips to himself, stuffing his face, and slurping a can of beer. He looked round as we came in through the back door, surprised.

"Where have you been, then?" he grumbled as I shut the door on the night.

"Jojo's gone missing. We've been searching for her," Mum told him. She sat down at the table, and took a chip from his meal, nibbling the end of it.

"The dog's gone," he repeated.

Neither of us answered. I leaned against the counter, dumping the plastic packet of chocolate bones atop it.

"I'll put up some posters tomorrow. Someone's bound to find her," he said unprompted, scooping up a chunk of fish and slathering it with ketchup.

I was surprised when he reached towards Mum and put his hand on her arm, giving it an abrupt rub. Her eyes shifted towards him, and they smiled at each other.

I decided I would leave them alone for the evening. I had run out of energy, so it was probably best if I left him to comfort her. As I was leaving the kitchen, a strange smell caught my nostrils, and I paused in the hallway. It was foul, like a mixture of liquorice, and rotting vegetation, and it burned my nasal canals. Mum and Geraint talked softly close by. It wasn't worth disrupting them just to point it out, so I sniffed about to try and figure out where it was coming from, but being that I didn't have Jojo's scenting skills, it was impossible to pin down. It smelled familiar somehow, and I wasn't sure why. Frowning, I climbed the stairs, and headed to my room for the night.

Eight

Geraint knocked on my bedroom door as I scooped the last mouthful of cornflakes onto my spoon. It was Tuesday morning, and I had woken up late, leaving me rushing to get ready for work. When I looked round at him, I had milk in my beard, but since his table manners were far worse than my own, I didn't much care. I was surprised to see him standing there, peering through the crack at me as he was still in his pyjamas, slippers on his feet.

"Got a call. No work today or tomorrow. I'm going out to Bridgend for a market, hopefully gonna sell some of my taxidermy. You wanna come?" He offered, his eyes glancing down at the carpet, scratching at his jaw with his fingernail.

I was starting to get used to him being civil towards me, but I warned myself not to get too comfortable, to just enjoy it while it lasted. For all I knew, the spell could wear off, and he would soon enough go back to the way he was before, and all of this would have been for nothing. I would have gone with him—shocking, right?—but I knew Maredudd wasn't working today. That was the first thought that had popped into my head.

"Oh... Sorry, I've got some things I need to take care of, but thanks for offering, though, maybe next time I'll come," I replied, hoping I sounded as apologetic as I felt.

"Never mind. I'm taking your mam out with me, so we won't be back until late this evening," he told me, shuffling his feet, and examining the paint peeling from the door frame.

He left to go, and shower, and sort out his van in time so that he could pick Mum up as she was leaving work. I had got the feeling that he was disappointed that I didn't want to come, but maybe I was just projecting what I wanted onto him. To be fair though, yesterday we finished work early so that we could go into town, and print off a stack of missing posters, and then he drove me, and Mum around the village, stopping the van at the roadside while we taped them to lamp-posts, and pinned them to fences, and trees, all in the hope that someone might have found her. The sad thing was I saw posters with Chief's picture on too, all of them hand-written in marker pen, as Rhys had been so anxious to find his dog again, he had written upon dozens of sheets, and then put them about. After I had spoken to him, he had walked over to the area surrounding the castle ruin, and his father had to drive out there, and persuade him to get in the car at nightfall because he had spent the entire day trekking through fields, calling out for Chief to come home.

It was very strange, and empty with Jojo gone. The house felt desolate, stagnant. I kept looking down, expecting her to be there, or expecting to hear her running along the hallway, but no, there was only silence. I was so worried about her, worried that the thing was lurking out there somewhere, and might have caught her, and eaten her, or worse, that she had become tangled in one of Geraint's traps in the middle of nowhere. Maybe we'd find her, and she'd be all right. We could rush her to a vet, she'd heal, and Mum would tell Geraint he had to use different methods for his work.

It wasn't that Mum didn't like what he did. On the contrary, she was very fond of taxidermy, and had a little stuffed duckling on her bedside cabinet. It was that she didn't agree with how Geraint seemed to think animals didn't have feelings, and that included pain, and fear. Perhaps that was why he didn't display any of his mounts inside the house, because Mum would look at them, and end up going on at him about it. The only place we could see them was in the work room, but that was a rare occurrence since he always kept the room locked, and guests out.

I slowed down, swallowing my cornflakes with a gulp, and rubbing my damp beard in my wrist. I had no need to rush now, but I was still in emergency mode. If I hurried now, I could get the next bus to the other side of the bay and be at Maredudd's house in twenty minutes instead of an hour. I leapt off the bed, swiping my backpack containing my laptop, and other useful items, and Mum's camera from the bedside table, and headed for the door, my boots clunking on the floor, and thundering down the stairs. Geraint leaned out of the living room as I ran towards the porch, a bowl held to his face while he ate his breakfast, and he grunted in response when I said goodbye, and flung myself out into the vibrant summer sun.

Riding on the bus was a luxury. I didn't get to do it often as I didn't usually have any money to pay for fare, and I felt very privileged indeed to be able to sit beside the window and admire the scenery without being out of breath or sun-burned. The bus passed by a group of ramblers with their sun-hats and walking sticks, and I looked down on them like they were peasants before chuckling to myself light-heartedly. The bus wasn't exactly first class travel, but that morning I was feeling rather pleased with myself to have earned some cash, and to finally have a working camera. The bus stop was a five-minute walk from the lane that lead up to

Maredudd's cottage.

I said thank you to the driver, and stepped out into the fresh, ocean breeze that was sweeping up over the cliffs, and bringing with it the brackish scent of drying sea-weed washed upon the shore. Birds of all kinds were singing their hearts out in the trees, and bushes, a flock of cormorants passing overhead, their honking calls becoming lost in the wind as they went by. I saw the distinctive shape of a Red Kite darting over the neighbouring field as it tracked its prey far below, the predator little more than a black V moving across the sky. I climbed the hill towards the cottage, sweat beading on my forehead. It was incredibly warm today, grasshoppers ticking in the undergrowth, butterflies unsteadily navigating from shrub to shrub as flies buzzed about.

When I knocked on the door, my heart was already palpitating, and it wasn't from the walk uphill. My nerves had started to go wobbly now that I was here. I was starting to get used to the knowledge that this happened every time I knew Maredudd was going to be with me, but that didn't make it any easier. I waited, vibrating on the spot, but there was no answer. Perhaps he didn't hear me? I knocked again, but as before, the door didn't open. He told me he always left the back door unlocked, so I thought I would go inside, and wait for him. He might have gone out to the shops to pick up some essentials, or he might be visiting his dad, and would be back soon.

The cool fragrance of the cottage greeted me as I stepped into the empty kitchen, glancing this way, and that to see if he was hiding somewhere, but there was nobody. It was strange being in someone else's house when they weren't there. I felt like I was an intruder, invading Maredudd's private territory. I was tempted to have a nose around, to go exploring, and take a closer look at his ornaments, and pictures, but that would be rude. With a sigh of relief, I slipped my backpack off my shoulders, and placed it on the kitchen counter, laying it down gently so that my laptop wouldn't get knocked, before placing the camera beside it. They could stay there for the meantime. Maybe I could go for a walk on the hills since he wasn't here, and he would know I had been because he would see my belongings waiting there. I stood before the sink and splashed some water on my face to cool myself. My skin was getting that hot tingling sensation that warned of sun-burn, so I topped up my sun-block before I stepped outside again.

I moved away from the cottage, facing out to sea, and taking in the view as the wind blustered against the front of my body. It always made me breathless, even more so knowing I was standing right near the edge of the cliff. I saw a figure on the beach below waving, so I stepped near to the fence at the very edge, and peered down at it, my squinting eyes unable to make out a lot of detail despite the assistance of my spectacles. That's when I realised it was Maredudd. He must have been walking on the sand and seen me at the top of the cliff. I waved back, grinning stupidly.

Behind the cottage was a treacherous path that went winding round towards the bottom, and if I edged along a narrow ledge I would have been able to squeeze into the Witch's Cave below. The wind blew sand in my eyes, and I knew it had been wise to leave my stuff in his kitchen before making my way down, because knowing my luck I might slip, and smash them on the rocks. My boots gripped the lumpy, chipped surface of the cliff, and I had to cling onto whatever available jutting stone I could reach in order to keep balanced, but the view of the beach from here was stunning. If there had been somewhere cosy to sit, it would have been a lovely place to watch the birds and see the sun rise.

Maredudd was waiting for me at the bottom; his hair was loose, tossed about in the sea winds, and tangling round his ears, wavy tendrils emanating from his head like he was underwater. He was dressed in a tight-fitting white t-shirt, and a pair of khaki shorts, his feet bare on the sand. As I approached him, my heart went into overdrive, and I breathed deeply in a meagre attempt to calm myself down, but it simply wouldn't work. My whole body started to shiver, and if I had had a tail, it would have been wagging madly.

"Fancy seeing you yere," he greeted merrily.

"I've got today, and tomorrow off, so I thought I would come, and see you. I do have more important things to do, but I figured I would grace you with my presence." I jested, stopping right before him, the wind making my shorts flap around my legs.

"I was going to say, perhaps I should do a lottery ticket since I must be lucky today." He laughed, his eyelids pressing together. "Good thing I spotted you by there, otherwise you might have been sat on the sofa a fair few hours waiting for me. Come on, let's go for a walk."

He extended his hand, and I looked down at it, thinking at first that he was just gesturing for me to follow, but when I glanced up at his face, and saw that he nodded encouragingly, I realised that he meant for me to take it. An electric spark shot up my arm as soon as I touched him, like two live wires crossing, creating an explosive shock to start a fire burning. His coaxing smile soon became one of fondness, and, turning, he started to lead me down towards the water. I was so nervous that someone would see us walking together, that they would see us holding hands in public, and soon enough the whole village would be talking about us, and it would escalate into something much worse, and then Mrs Bevan would be saying we were doing it doggy-style in the surf while dog-walkers, and families drifted by, horrified expressions on their faces.

Maredudd rubbed my knuckles with his other hand.

"Relax. There's nothing to worry about."

"But what if someone sees?"

"Sees what?" he asked, his smile morphing into a mischievous grin. I stared at him, exasperated.

"You know... Sees us holding hands..." I whispered, even though there was no one around to hear our conversation.

"So what if they do? We're not breaking the law. I like holding your hand. Nobody is going to stop me from doing that, especially if you like holding mine in return." He raised his eyebrows at me, and I couldn't very well argue with that.

"I do like holding your hand," I mumbled, feeling stupid. We had stopped at the bottom of the beach, and the tide was lapping at the sand, gushing up to meet our toes. I contemplated taking my boots off.

When I turned to look at him, he had moved closer, and I drew in a sharp breath, aware that he was now right against my side. I could feel the front of his hard torso touching my arm, his body heat comfortable, and gentle despite the blazing sun overheard. His eyes, like green lanterns that seemed to give off light of their own no matter the shadow upon his face, peered right into my own, and I was so astonished, frozen to the spot, when I should have known what would come next. He lowered his head, brushed his nose against mine as though asking permission. My chest was rising, and falling heavily, heart throbbing, lungs puffing, my throat contracting as I swallowed.

I wanted it desperately, but I couldn't lead when I was so shy, and untouched, afraid of embarrassing myself, and anxious that someone would see us out here. His eyes half-closed, and I thought he would move away. My hand immediately gripped onto his tightly, squeezing it in my grasp in a silent bid to tell him not to. The whole world began to slide and melt out of my consciousness, and we were the only people left, isolated except for the soundless surf that flowed towards us rhythmically. Finally, I felt his lips pressing to mine, and that electricity that had crackled earlier suddenly became a shower of lightning. Like a developing storm, the clouds rolling, and thunder tolling, I let go of my emotions, abandoning the fear I was clutching at moments before.

It didn't matter that this was untrodden territory. I felt his tongue, tasted it, goosebumps prickling first my arms, and scalp, travelling downwards until it had taken all of me. His free hand slipped to the back of my neck, holding me close. The other soon moved to my waist, but I hadn't even noticed that I had released it seconds before, instead reaching to cling to the front of his shirt, my hands balled into fists against his chest. The undulating mass of his hair blew around my face, flicking about my ears, catching on the curls of my beard. This kiss, the first I had ever had, was unlike anything I could have ever imagined. It broke suddenly, and I came up for air, gasping, eyes rolling into the back of my head as he stopped me from falling, the heat of his mouth behind my ear, and upon my throat causing an unbearable need to grow within me.

"Forgive me," he whispered to me, his voice sending shock-waves of tingling, and trembling to go through me as he breathed close to my ear. He was breathless too, his body heat becoming intense under my fists.

I turned my head, pressing my forehead to his, and smiling. I felt tears in my eyes, and I tried to force them back. "There's nothing to forgive."

His muscular arms enclosed me in a gentle embrace, and I lay my head against his shoulder, unable to believe that this wasn't just a dream. Through sleepy eyes, I watched the water, soothed by his rocking motion, and the calm roar, and hiss of the tide. Gingerly, I slipped my arms round him, laying my palms flat so that I could secretly explore the knots of muscle that created his elegant body, sliding them down slowly towards his hips where I felt the waistband of his shorts. When we were close like this, I could feel my own energy culminating within, and radiating towards him, and the best part was how I felt his return, a blue, and silver aura that consumed me, and left me feeling protected, and at peace.

A strand of his hair clung to my lips, but I didn't move to pull it away. More were catching upon my eyelashes and tumbling across my cheeks with the changing direction of the wind. I was so preoccupied with touching him that I didn't notice how he was doing the same to me. His fingertips raked through my short, ginger hair, and he stroked my back firmly, checking if he could sense any nervousness or shaking. I wasn't shaking anymore, the trembles gone, only the occasional shiver when I felt his breath on my neck. I wondered if this was what it would feel like to wake up beside him, completely entangled in each other.

Would that ever be possible? For us to lay naked together under the moonlight, bathed in its silver glow. Our noses touching, my hand on his chest. I was overwhelmed with happiness, so much so that I had to swallow back tears, stuffing them back down within. The crushing sadness I had felt the other day after spending so many days away from him was forgotten on the wayside. It was this polarised joy that outweighed it, made it so worth it. I understood now.

We curled together for another feverish kiss. The wind blustered between our joined faces, cool upon our reddening cheeks, unable to fill our lungs as we shared each other's air as though giving life between us. The kiss became deeper; I felt giddy and aroused. I didn't know how much more of this I could handle, but what would happen when we both reached our limits? Would we move onto something further? I wanted to. But I was excited, and afraid all at once.

I felt warm, and secure in his arms, even when I saw Fred, and Teifion walking along the beach with their fishing gear. Both short, and squat with thick necks, father, and son in matching green clothing, Fred with his birth-marked face, and Teifion with his big glasses askew. They had obviously passed us from behind, and I hadn't noticed until I saw them moving away, both heads turned as they stared at us over their shoulders. I smirked. There was no point in trying to hide it; people would find out eventually, anyway. It didn't matter, really. After enduring the confusion and disgust about my gender, the village finding out about Maredudd and me kissing on the beach was a piece of cake. He had been right not to care, I wished I could be as carefree as he was. Maybe I would be in time.

The tide was starting to come in, and fishermen were setting up their lines in preparation for it, so we decided to climb back up onto the cliffs and go for a walk in the fields. I picked up my camera on the way, and we stopped from time to time so that I could attempt to capture birds, and insects on film. Maredudd allowed me to take his picture. I was thrilled. I would keep it with me always. As we walked hand in hand through the long grass that grew wild around the ruins, he leaned close to kiss me again, and again, seemingly unable to stop himself, and every time it startled me. I wasn't used to having someone within my personal boundary, so distant to everyone I usually was, but this was a welcome intrusion. My cheeks, and jaw ached as I was smiling so much.

We talked, and laughed, and swapped stories. My previous memory of the night at his house was easily conquered by this new one, a whole day of being beside him, kissing, and hugging, being able to touch him, to feel that he was real. It didn't matter how much I held his hand or touched his shoulder or face, there was always a slight hesitance, for fear that my hand would go straight through him, and I'd find him a ghost, or the fantasy would shatter, and I would find myself lying in bed, alone in the dark.

Away from the beach, in the seclusion of the surrounding forest, I saw something else lurking in his eyes, something much more personal than fondness. I had to look away when I saw it, because it made me so breathless that I couldn't bear it for more than a second. Only a fool would think that his interest in me was purely innocent. I didn't want innocence, anyway. I was an adult; I wanted adult things. I didn't want to be like Buffy, and Angel. Kissing was wonderful, but it would eventually become unfulfilling. I wondered how long we would be this way until he taught me something new.

We sat on the slope overlooking the estuary, my head resting against his shoulder, my hand in his lap cradling between his. I wanted to ask him if we were, well, boyfriends now. Boyfriends. Such a silly word, because we were boys that were friends even before this had happened. Lovers. That was a nicer word. I wanted to know if we were lovers. It seemed silly to ask, though. I felt like a stuttering teen again, like a fish out of water, staggering clumsily over obstacles because I didn't know any better as I tried to find my own feet, learning these lessons I should have learned years ago. Better late than never, I suppose.

"What's that over by there?" he said suddenly, and I sat up slothfully, my dreamy expression changing as I focused in the direction he pointed.

"What? I don't see anything," I mumbled, shading my eyes from the sun.

Maredudd managed to find a way to cross the river. An enormous tree must have fallen in the storm, and it bridged the flowing water diagonally, wide enough to walk safely across. He crossed in front of me, and I held onto his wrist so that I wouldn't be left behind. On the other side, he helped me down onto the marshy ground, and we waded through reeds, and tall grass, surrounded by the chirping of crickets while dragonflies darted over the water's surface. As we got closer, the smell grew stronger. I knew what it was before we stumbled upon it. Once you had smelled it, it was a stench that stayed with you forever, the pungent reek of rotting flesh, a scent strong enough to turn your stomach. He kept me behind him protectively, checking the ground with his walking boots to ensure it wasn't harbouring a hidden puddle. Finally, he stopped, and I peered over his shoulder.

A rippling cloud of flies hummed above the form that lay there, its putrid body liquids spreading out into the surrounding earth, and causing the grasses to wilt back, creating a small clearing around it. The long graceful neck was thrown back, displaying the gaping bite-wound to the throat, its legs rearing as though it had fallen mid-leap. The torso was an empty cavity, and the pale spines of ribs were jutting through the soggy, maggot-infested flesh that normally enveloped them. Something, probably a fox, had torn at the animal's anus, unravelling the ribbons of intestine through the hole, and most of it was partially chewed, clods of undigested hay in heaps around its rear. I noticed that the dapple-grey horse was still wearing a bridle, but I was loath to go near and retrieve it.

"Good thing you brought your camera."Maredudd managed an apprehensive smirk as he looked down at me.

"I know this horse," I replied, pinching my nose between thumb, and finger. "It was reported missing last week by the riding school. Vanished while out grazing on the field."

"It looks like whatever attacked it ate most of it," he remarked, moving cautiously around the edge of the clearing to get a better look.

"Maredudd—don't go too close." I warned him,

worried that he might slip, and fall onto it.

"Look." He pointed, pushing aside the grass. "There's a track."

"What do you mean?"

"Whatever killed it had been coming back and forth to feed from it," he told me, so I stepped carefully around the kill-site to where he was standing.

"Are you sure they aren't fox tracks?" I questioned, pushing back the grass to get a better look.

"Does that look like a fox track to you?" He stepped around the track, and bent, holding his hand beside a print in the mud.

I breathed in sharply when I saw what he meant. The print was as big as his hand, four toes, and a paw pad, small pinholes where the claws had gone into the blood-soaked mud. I fumbled for my camera, tugging off the lens-cover, and panicking with urgency, and excitement to photograph this new evidence. Never before had I seen a paw-print like this at the scenes of the crimes. There had been hoof prints before, but I thought they had been made by the cows, and horses, not the attacker. This proved that whatever was attacking was not an ungulate. It was probably canine. I took several shots, then Maredudd held me steady so that I could photograph the horse.

It was as I was adjusting the zoom that I spotted a clump of hair caught in the horse's teeth, as though the poor creature had attempted to bite its assailant back, and in the process ripped out some of its fur. The beast was stalking prey closer, and closer to the village where evidence could be stumbled upon by ramblers, far away from the secluded land of the farms, and pastures. A fly buzzed in my face as I crouched to collect the fur. I shuddered in abhorrence.

"Let me see?" Maredudd requested as I returned to his side.

"It's yellow, sandy-coloured." I placed it in his hand

so that he could examine it. "Do you think it could be an escaped exotic pet?"

"Like a lion, or some other kind of big cat?" He asked, and I nodded. "But that foot-print looks like a wolf or a big dog. Cats retract there claws; this isn't consistent with that. What are those puncture wounds in the horse's side? They look like they were made by horns."

"Believe me, this is a problem I've been having in trying to identify this thing. It seems like no matter how much I examine the bodies, it's as if it's being done by something different every time. I can't tell what kind of animal this is." I sighed as I wiped the sweat from my forehead and pushed my glasses back onto the bridge of my nose. "Maybe there is more than one killer?"

"A motley crew of odd animal predators banding together to kill?" He chuckled, and I realised how silly that sounded.

"Okay, I admit defeat."

"Let's get away from this stinking corpse. I don't know about you, but the smell is making it hard to think." He patted me on the shoulder and gestured back the way we had come.

I wrapped the hair up in a tissue to keep it safe, and we crossed back over the river, as far away from the foul stench as possible.

"It seems like it's getting worse," Maredudd commented as we walked side by side along the bank. "Someone has to make it stop, before it puts humans on the menu."

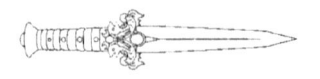

"Hi Mum, it's me," I said into the phone as I leaned against Maredudd's kitchen wall. "I'm going to stay at Maredudd's tonight. I just wanted to let you know."

"Oh, well that has come as a surprise." She sounded genuinely shocked. I don't think she was aware that I had been visiting him, or even that I had been lusting after him since we had first met.

"Well, I visited him today, and neither of us are doing anything tomorrow, so I thought it would be nice." I made the sweetest smile I could muster in the hopes that it translated into my tone of voice. I could hear that she was thinking on the other end of the line.

"He's a bit old for you, isn't he?" she asked suddenly.

"What are you talking about?" I startled, at first not realising what she meant, but then the information sank in. She knew me too well.

"You know what I'm talking about. I've heard the way you talk about him, and that little twinkle in your eye when you hear his name. I ain't stupid, boyo."

"Mum, please." I huffed, trying to maintain the facade, but it wasn't working. She hummed, letting me know that she wasn't going to fall for it, and I sighed. "Okay, we're friends. Good friends. Really good friends."

"Mm-hmm. Okay. Well, just make sure you use a condom," she replied.

"Mum!" I gasped in horror, turning towards the kitchen doorway to make sure Maredudd wasn't eavesdropping. I lowered my voice to a whisper before I spoke again. "I can't get pregnant, you know that."

"I wasn't talking about that. He might have some diseases. I can't vouch for his private affairs," she retorted in a matter-of-fact manner. "Anyway, he's old enough to be your dad! Now I think it's really cheeky how you acted about my love triangle. You're a fine one to talk."

"Mum, he is not old enough to be my dad." I wrinkled my nose. I hadn't even thought about his age. All I had seen was his handsome face and gentle personality. Age was of no importance.

"Huh, well, hmm, my math is rusty, but if I'm

correct, he was fifteen years old when you were born. Fifteen! I can still remember what he looked like before he had a single facial hair. Really Owen, I find this quite disturbing," she declared, but I could hear the slight wobble of a restrained giggle in her voice, and I knew she was winding me up.

"Oh, stop it. It's none of your business, and he's very nice, so that's all I care about."

She made a wicked laugh. "Well, I wouldn't complain if he was my toy-boy anyway. Not sure what Geraint would think about that. But I'm happy for you, Owen."

"Thanks." I smiled sadly, clutching the receiver with both hands.

"If your father was yere, he'd give you his blessing, I'm sure. I must admit, I found the whole transgender thing a bit confusing in the beginning, but somehow this just seems to make a lot of sense in my head right off the bat. Maybe that's a sign that you two are right for each other," she said contemplatively, and I heard her nibble her fingernail. "Besides, Maredudd is an old friend of mine. I know him well, have done since he was a child. You could have picked worse, put it that way."

"I'll take that as a compliment."I grinned. "Just don't go embarrassing me by pointing it out next time you see him otherwise I might just drop dead on the spot."

"I'll be a good girl, I promise. Oh, before I go, I just wanted to ask if you wanted to come to work with me tomorrow? I know you were planning to spend the day with Maredudd, but it's only a couple of hours, and I could really do with some help," she asked pleadingly, and I couldn't say no. I would have felt too cruel to turn her down.

"Oh, okay. What time? I hope you don't expect me to get up too early."I joked.

"I'll meet you over by the pub at say eleven o'clock?"

"Alright then! See you tomorrow." I beamed, even though she couldn't see me smile.

After saying goodbye to Mum, I put the phone down, and when I turned, I found Maredudd standing in the kitchen doorway. I wasn't sure how much of our conversation he had heard, but I wasn't about to ask. I watched, my heart fluttering as he came towards me, and he leaned against the wall right beside me, bowing his head so that he could nuzzle my ear with his nose.

"You're not leaving me, are you?" he said. His words sounded like a challenge, as though I was disobeying him, and it made me shiver with excitement.

"No, but I'm going to meet Mum for work tomorrow at eleven," I replied timidly, aware that my cheeks had responded with a vivid blush.

"That's all right then. I was worried I might have to tie you up and hold you hostage," he whispered, his hand stroking my chest through my shirt.

My brain had gone into overdrive to try and form a reply, but my heart was pumping madly, and he always managed to shut me down into a speechless wreck while saying so little himself. I knew he could feel my rapid heartbeat against his palm, see the glittering in my eyes.

"It's so cute how red your face goes when I'm near you," he said, and somehow my blush darkened.

"I—if you didn't say such suggestive things then maybe it wouldn't," I stuttered.

He chuckled, nuzzling my ear again, and kissing my hair-covered jaw. "I'm going to graze on your beard like a goat on grass until you're completely bald."

"You wally, stop that." I nudged him with my elbow as he nibbled at my hair, and he moved away, laughing.

"Come on, let's go, and take a look at this computer of yours. I've been waiting to see some of your pictures." He backed towards the living room, his bare feet padding on the hard floor.

I brought my bag into the next room, and took my

laptop out of it, and perching on the edge of the sofa, I folded it open, and switched it on. He looked upon it like it was some sort of alien machinery that had fallen to Earth on a meteor, and when I offered to let him use it, he flatly declined. He sank back into the corner, leaning against the arm of the sofa with his own arm propped up along the back, inviting me to come, and sit beside him, so I shuffled closer awkwardly until I was leaning against his chest. Now that I was in range, he leaned his head close, and started to nestle his face in my hair, his breath tickling me, and covering me in goosebumps. I liked that he couldn't seem to keep his hands off me. It made me feel wanted, attractive even. I might have felt different without my clothes on, though.

"I've organised all my pictures by years. Although I've only been taking pictures of the attacks for two years, and inside, the months, then inside again, the weeks, and the photos are numbered by the date," I explained as I clicked on the folders, and entered them, rows of thumbnails popping up in the window. "Here are the first photos I ever took."

I showed him the pictures of the eviscerated sheep, his eyes glancing between me, and the screen.

"Okay, and they're all like that?"

"Well, yes. But some have different bite wounds or stab wounds. Like I said, I can't figure out what type of animal it is," I replied, scrolling through the dozens, and dozens of thumbnails. "Today is the first time I've seen a paw-print. Before that, there have only been hoof prints. But do you want to know something? Awhile ago, when I broke my camera, I fell on the hill because I was being chased by a big animal in the woods. The noise it made was sort of like a horse, and the footfalls were almost like hoof-falls. But I didn't see it."

"A horse? I've never heard of a horse eating the meat of other animals. I know deer do sometimes, if they come across another dead animal, they may scavenge.

Perhaps it's a large stag? There were puncture marks in the horse we saw. Could have been antlers," he suggested, and for the first time, a lightbulb went on in my head.

"A stag? I didn't think of that. Deer do live in the area, so that's not all that strange. But the noise this thing made, I've never heard anything like it. It wasn't the sound a deer makes. That also doesn't explain the large paw-print," I explained, although I was quite impressed with the conclusion he had come to.

"The paw-print does throw a spanner in the works. But perhaps it was another wild animal coming to scavenge from the carcass and wasn't what caused the death," he reasoned, and I had to admit, it made sense.

"So, we're looking for a giant, carnivorous stag, and some sort of sandy-furred wolf creature." I frowned, thinking how stupid it sounded. "I'm not sure anyone's going to believe that."

"They don't have to. But they know something is out there, killing. They can't deny that."

"But they have, when they've told me to stop photographing the evidence. The village wants to sweep it under the carpet. I've tried to get people to listen by showing them my pictures, but they aren't interested," I mumbled disappointedly. "The farmers are angry at me because of it. They don't want reporters, and journalists coming here, and disturbing the peace... Even when there isn't peace, because this thing is out there, picking livestock off one by one."

Maredudd was quiet. When he spoke, he sounded defeated. "I think someone is controlling this creature, or creatures. I don't think it's a natural occurrence, but rather, a supernatural one."

"Really? Like, someone else is using magic on these animals?" I tilted my head to look at him, finding it hard to understand why someone would want to do that. They didn't gain anything from it, nobody did.

"Sure. I saw a movie once where a man used a trained lion to kill people, and everyone thought it was a werewolf, because the biggest predator they had in France was the wolf. So perhaps this animal isn't native to the countryside, and is under the control of someone, though I couldn't think why they would go to the trouble," he told me, seeming a bit more hopeful than he had a moment ago.

"Do you think Geraint has something to do with this?" I asked outright. I felt as though he was skirting around saying it, but I wasn't sure why.

"No. But I think Geraint had something to do with Evan's disappearance. I just need to prove it," he responded flatly.

"I don't think Geraint could kill anyone. He's a jerk, but that doesn't automatically make someone a killer. Anyway, I think Geraint is helping to keep the beast away from people, because wherever he puts his traps, it won't attack. I thought he might be a witch or whatever, like you are." I was hesitant to explain myself because I wasn't sure if 'witch' was a derogatory term, but I didn't know how else to describe him. "Maybe he's putting spells or something, around the edges of people's farms, and it keeps it away."

Maredudd pondered, his eyes half-closed as he gazed across at the orange glow of the setting sun that was illuminating the far wall.

"You're right about Geraint being a witch," he finally murmured. "But he gave up doing the work years ago, just like Wenda, and Evan did. I suppose there's a chance he still hangs onto the old ways, but he swore it off after your parents moved away, stopped talking to me, and my dad. When I say he swore it off, I mean it seriously. For me, it feels unlikely that he would still be doing it in secret, but one can't be sure."

"Why did he stop?" I asked curiously.

"Your mam, and dad left the circle, which meant

there was only me, and Geraint to fulfil the four elements alone. We couldn't sit a circle with only two elements, and neither Geraint nor I are skilled enough to handle bearing two elements each, not that he would have wanted to. It wasn't worth keeping the circle together because he was so bitter, and grieving, and he eventually cut off all contact with us anyway. My dad works alone, and I assist him. It's harder to work alone, but not impossible. Possible because he's highly skilled. Harder because it means a lesser worker might make mistakes without the guidance of a more experienced witch," he explained, rubbing his hand over the stubble growing on his chin.

"My dad is ancient, and very knowledgeable," he continued after a moment. "There are many things I wouldn't even consider trying without his guidance. Things that can corrupt, and damage you in ways you don't realise until it's too late. So, Geraint being the wily fox that he is, would rather preserve himself than dabble in magic that is too dangerous for his own good. Because there's only one person Geraint puts first, and that's Geraint."

"Aren't there any other witches around?" I asked.

"Not that we're aware of in South Wales. My dad is good friends with a few others in Scotland, and the West Country. There are people who say they are witches... But all they do is Morris Dance, and pour whiskey on effigies. There is so much more to witchcraft than saying the right words or mixing the right herbs." He sounded deflated, and I got the feeling he'd had more than his fair share of disappointments in the past.

"Will you teach me how to be a real witch?" I grinned, reaching up and stroking his cheek gently, which seemed to coax a smile back to his face.

"Of course. But it won't be easy." He winked.

"In return, I'll teach you how to use a computer. I saw the way you looked at my laptop. You're not computer literate, are you?" I asked with a knowing smirk, and now it was his turn to blush for a change. He glanced at me through his eyelashes.

"No. But that's not my fault. Computers are a fairly recent thing, whereas magic is eternal." He made the excuse, which only served to make me laugh amusedly.

"Now who's the one with the red face?" I teased, enjoying seeing him go shy. It didn't happen often, so I had to make the most of it while I had the chance.

In the evening, I sat on the stool by the counter while Maredudd cooked dinner, both of us chatting away with barely a breath between sentences. We never seemed to run out of things to talk about. I watched his deft, thickly veined hands stirring the frying pan on the hob as he stir-fried some vegetables, admiring how angular, and rough they were, before gazing upon his strong, hairy arms, scars dotted here and there from where he had had accidents while working. They were my most favourite arms in the world, I realised. It was stupid, I know, but I tended to have these nonsensical thoughts whenever I thought about him. A favourite pair of arms? A favourite chest? A favourite pair of ears? Every part of him was my favourite; he was my favourite past-time. He noticed the dreamy look in my eyes, acknowledging it with an equally fond smile. I could be like this forever, and never grow tired of it.

We only stopped talking when we were eating, and even then we gazed at each other, our eyes constantly connecting, transferring little packets of data like a phone-line bridging the space between us. I was impressed that he was vegetarian like I was too. He told me that his dad's diet was even stricter, and that eating the flesh of a living being that was killed unnaturally brought with it a negative energy that rotted you inside. I talked to him about Jojo, allowing this close familiarity we now had to voice my worries for her disappearance, and just as I had expected, he tried to reassure me that she would return.

I was fascinated by all the things he had to say, he knew so many things, like Dad had, only they were different things. Maybe Dad might have eventually told me these things himself, but he didn't get the chance. I realised my grief for Dad was starting to go away lately, I thought it was because I was with Maredudd, his presence banishing my negative thoughts. I didn't want to go home, ever. It wasn't my home anyway—it was Geraint's home. I had no home anymore, I was a stray, and I wanted to settle here, for Maredudd to take me in like a lost dog found wandering the streets. I thought before that it would be fine because Jojo would keep Mum company, but now she was gone, there was an edge of guilt to my desire. But I couldn't live at home forever for my mother's sake. I needed to move out. Or, maybe I was getting ahead of myself. Maybe it would never happen.

The hour grew late, and Maredudd blew out the candles. We decided to retire to bed, and after I had used the bathroom, and changed into the clean pyjamas I had originally let him borrow, I found him waiting on the landing, half-peering through the door of his bedroom. I stopped at the top of the stairs, my clothes bunched under my arm, and my hand on the rail.

"Do... Do you... Would you like to sleep in here, instead?" He hesitated, scratching behind his ear slowly as if to distract himself from the embarrassment of the situation.

"Really?" I perked up, my eyes becoming wide with amazement.

"I—I wouldn't do anything to you. Just so you know. I know I'm bad, and I touch you so much. But I—I'd be good. I'd behave." He tripped over his words as he tried to explain himself. "I don't want you to be afraid of me... I won't hurt you, ever..."

"I'm not afraid of you. I told you that." I made a sad

smile.

"No, but I feel it, when you're close. I feel your fear and—and I understand it, I know, I know why, and it's okay. I just wanted you to know, that's all." He wouldn't look at me now, his voice falling to a murmur. "We've all got scars, just different kinds. I feel you more than I see you. So don't worry."

I understood what he was trying to say. How did he guess that I was anxious about him seeing my body? Was I that obvious?

I moved along the landing towards him and pushed the door wider so that I could reach up and kiss the corner of his mouth.

"That's one of the kindest things anyone has ever said to me. So thank you. Besides, maybe I want you to do bad things to me." I smirked cheekily, and he managed to smile then, his eyes finally looking up at me, sparkly, shining like wet pebbles.

I had never slept next to another man before. I say slept, but I didn't sleep at first. I lay awake in the dark, the partially-open window letting in the sound of the rolling waves below the cliff, and Maredudd's breath slow, and steady beside me. I was lying on my back, and when I squinted in the shadows, I saw he was too. His head turned towards me, I quickly closed my eyes, pretending to be asleep. My heart was pounding. How was I ever going to sleep when it was racing like this? I sucked in a sharp breath through my teeth when his hand was placed upon my chest, and I tried not to flinch as I hadn't been expecting it. He rubbed my belly gently like he was petting a friendly dog, then I felt him shuffling closer, and his head on the pillow next to me.

I couldn't sleep. He was too close, too present. It was putting thoughts in my head that I couldn't control, and that wouldn't allow me to rest. I knew that it wouldn't be like this forever, that I would be able to get used to it gradually, but I hadn't expected to be so alert, and aware that he was there. Normally, I would switch off like a light, even with Jojo padding about on the duvet to find a comfy spot. I sighed to try and discharge some of my anxiety.

"You're awake," he whispered to me in the dark.

"So are you," I whispered back.

Silence.

"I can't help it," he replied. "It feels like I should stay awake to confirm that you're really there."

I looked at him, but I could only make out his black silhouette. He couldn't see me either, but I was smiling.

"Me too," I confessed timidly. "I think I'm in love with you."

"Snap."

NINE

Mum waited outside the pub on the main road, a floppy sun-hat keeping the light off her shoulders, and her eyes disguised behind her sunglasses. She reminded me of Shirley Valentine in summer-time, mainly because I could imagine her running away from Geraint to the Mediterranean and finding herself a handsome Greek floozy. The pub landlord had given her a bottle of lemonade, which she was drinking when I finally made it to the bench she was sitting on, and she let me have a sip through the straw before we started walking on our way to the caravan site. I was early, fortunately, and only because Maredudd had woken me with breakfast, and a hot cup of tea. We sat outside, admiring the beautiful cloudless sky, neither of us speaking at all, but just enjoying being in each other's company. When it was time to go, I gave him a kiss, and promised I'd be back as soon as I could. It felt so lovely to know he would be waiting at home for me.

"So, have a nice day yesterday, then?" Mum asked as she watched me sipping some lemonade, the cold liquid giving me brain freeze.

"Mmm—yeah, I had a lovely day yesterday. Maredudd and me found a rotting horse out in the fields behind the ruin," I answered, licking my lips.

"Ach-y-fie, Owen! That's not what I meant by 'nice.'" she rolled her eyes in disgust. "Don't tell me you've got old Maredudd admiring corpses too, now?"

"He was the one that found it." I grinned, holding the bottle against my chest as we paused before crossing the road. "And I got some concrete evidence too."

"I was talking about you two, not the dead animals," she reminded me before giggling, and shaking her head.

My grin turned sheepish as I glanced at her, unable to stop my expression from giving it away. "Well, we did kiss, and that was lovely."

"Soon you'll be getting married." She took hold of my arm, and gave it a pat, using me to stay balanced as we stepped over a leaking drain, water bubbling out through the grating, and flooding the gutter.

"Mum, this isn't the 16th century." I laughed, and she patted my arm again.

"No, but you know, Maredudd isn't exactly a spring chicken," she remarked. "You really don't care about his age, do you?"

"The only one that cares is you." I stuck my tongue out.

"I don't care, I'm just surprised. I thought you liked girls, but how wrong am I?"

"I'm just full of surprises." I chuckled, handing her the bottle back so that she could drink some more. "Anyway, I quite like how old he is. Makes him rugged, you know, rough, and ready. But his long hair, and when he wears his reading glasses, makes him look so intellectual. I like how he can do both looks. I don't understand how someone as smart as he is goes to work as a farm labourer."

"I think he does it because it suits his lifestyle. I don't think Maredudd would cope with a career. He's too spontaneous," she told me, lifting up the bouncing brim of her hat so she could see me. "Can you imagine if he was a doctor or a lawyer or something, saying he couldn't come into work that day because his chakras weren't aligned, or whatever?"

I laughed, picturing it in my head.

"Hang on, what's happening by yere?" Mum stopped me as we came to the next turning.

We were faced by a cluster of police cars, and they had sectioned off the road we normally took with strips of stripy tape. The road was fringed by woods on one side, facing a line of small houses that were usually used for holiday-goers, and it led towards the western side of the caravan park. We could cut through the woods to get there if need be, but it looked as though they had secured that area too. A policeman was standing on the other side of the road-mouth, and Mum looked at me knowingly. I knew what she meant to do.

"Good morning, kind sir. What's occurring by yere then?"Mum asked in her sweetest, most subtly-flirty voice as we approached the young man.

He was sweating like a pig, small droplets running down his forehead as the hot sun turned his entire head, and forearms bright red. He must have been roasting slowly in that protective vest, and those black trousers. He unfolded his arms, wiping at his forehead, his brown hair in damp tufts.

"Sorry ma'am, you can't go by there today, there's been a murder," he told her in his equally most subtly-flirty voice, apparently flattered to be called 'sir' by a member of the public.

"A murder?"Mum looked round at me, wide-eyed.

"I can't tell you more than that, I'm afraid," he answered apologetically. "Only that the body of a man was found on the path this morning by one of the families staying in these cottages. Other than that, I can't tell you a thing."

"Well, you've pretty much told us darn near everything we needed to know. Maybe you can show us a picture or two as well."Mum teased with her usual cheeky grin, which quickly embarrassed the poor policeman whose brain was probably half-boiled by now.

"Was it a local man?" I asked, craning my neck to try and see over the group of police cars.

The policeman bit his tongue, and stuck out his chin, trying to keep quiet. I took that as a yes. He wasn't very good at keeping secrets, but then when everyone knew everyone around here, it wasn't much of a surprise. He was probably distantly linked to Mum through a friend of a friend anyway.

"I suppose my son and I will have to take the long way round. Thank you, officer."Mum steered me back in the direction we had come.

We didn't speak until we were out of earshot.

"I've got a sneaking suspicion it might have been Fred," she said in a hush, her expression becoming serious. "He walks home from work on the footpath through there. I do hope the old dab is all right, not that I'm wishing it on someone else, but... You know what I mean."

"I heard that he was chased by an animal a few weeks ago," I told her, taking a deep swallow. Suddenly my throat was dry, but we'd run out of lemonade.

We fell silent again. Neither of us were really sure what to say. What could we say? We both knew that the death had probably been caused by whatever was slaughtering the livestock. The same creature that had chased me too. I was fortunate that I had escaped, and not ended up like whoever had been found lying on the path. I waited for Mum to bring up my macabre photography, but she didn't. Maybe she thought the death of a human this time would make me think twice, but something like that wouldn't deter me.

"Any sign of Jojo?" I asked as we approached the camp-site, but she shook her head.

"None at all. I think she's gone the way of Chief. Vanished without a trace, even though young Rhys combed the fields for him, and Jojo, well, that was so unlike her to run away like that. It makes me think she was taken. But what can we do? It's like looking for a needle in a hay-stack." She sighed, her mood dampening. "I could walk the hills day, and night searching for her, but in all likelihood... She's not coming back."

"I'm sorry, Mum." I put my arm around her shoulders and gave her a squeeze. "I loved Jojo. She was a good friend. I will go and look for her. You never know."

"I'd rather you didn't, boyo. I've lost the dog, I don't want to lose you too." She managed a meagre smile. "If all she's done is got herself lost then she might find her way back. Anyway, she can run much faster than you can."

I nodded in agreement, but I don't think she believed me.

While I worked, my mind drifted back to Jojo, imagining her running free through the fields. I thought she would have found her way back by now, followed the scent trail all the way home, her white paws covered in dirt, and prickly burrs stuck in her short fur, but she still hadn't materialised. Mum didn't have the time or energy to look for her, and no one had called after seeing the missing posters. What if she was out there, wandering around, lost, and starving? I bit my lip as I vacuumed the carpet in the caravan. I could go out there and look, camp out in the woods overnight, and maybe she would smell me, and coming running to me. It was a long-shot, but it was better than sitting around waiting to find out if we'd ever see her again.

I planned to ask Maredudd if he would come with me. I thought he would, since I didn't expect he would much like the idea of me being out there on my own, even without prior knowledge of the murder that had taken place. I decided that's what I would do as I carried the sack of rubbish out of the caravan door, and down the steps, the door-keys in my pocket jangling on my way to the bin store. As far as the weather looked to be going, we were expecting a few days of hot sunshine, and no rain, but one could never tell. I had a small tent that I could take, small enough for two people if they cwtched in together. I didn't think Maredudd would mind too much about that.

After work, I went home with Mum on the pretence that I needed to pick up some clothes, and other essentials because I didn't have any fresh at Maredudd's, and that seemed to appease her, although I saw from the way she looked at me that she suspected I was up to something. She had to pop out for some shopping, which gave me the opportune moment to escape the house with my rucksack rammed full of stuff, and the heavy weight of the bagged-up tent on the other shoulder. Perhaps if I had told her what I intended to do, I could have left it at the house, and collected it later when we returned to the area to set up camp, but I couldn't risk Mum knowing because she would throw a fit and try to stop me. I hoped that the bus wouldn't pull up alongside her car at a traffic light, and she would look up and see me sitting there with the tent propped beside me, because knowing her, she'd follow me all the way to my bus-stop and prevent me from escaping until the tent was firmly in her grasp. She did it to protect me, because she had my best interests at heart, but it was still frustrating.

Maredudd was sitting on the front step when I came struggling up the hill towards the cottage. He jogged down to meet me, lifting the weight off my back.

"What's this?" he asked as he walked alongside me back towards the house.

"It's my tent. We're going camping tonight." I grinned, and he grinned back with an equal measure of bafflement.

"Whatever for?"

"I want to try and find Jojo. She still hasn't come home, so I figured I would camp out in the woods near Geraint's house, and maybe she'd find her way to us. I kinda hoped you would come with me," I said as we reached the steps leading up to the front path. "Will you?"

"Of course. I wouldn't want to leave you on your own," he replied jovially, and I got the feeling he hadn't heard about the death the police were investigating. He didn't have a television, and he never listened to the radio even though his CD player had a tuner. I wondered how he coped whilst being so out of the loop.

He told me he didn't plan to go to work tomorrow, anyway. In the beginning, I had wondered how he could get away with being so flaky all the time—how did he pay his bills without wages? But on numerous occasions, when we were out walking or just sitting somewhere, he would randomly discover money laying on the ground. One time the wind blew a fifty pound note right into his face, and it got tangled in his hair.

Another time we sat down on a bench, and he found a handful of pound coins on the ground beneath our feet. It was as though he was magnetised to attract money, and it came flying in his general direction whenever he stepped out of the house. He didn't seem shocked by it either. He simply chuckled and put the money in his pocket without a word, leaving me at his side with an expression of amazement, and confusion on my face. Whatever this magic was he used to make this happen, it was certainly a spell I could do with using too. It did make me wonder why he didn't just quit working altogether and cast magic on the lottery so that he could become a millionaire, but then I thought perhaps he wasn't comfortable with that. He enjoyed living simply, and there was nothing simple about managing large sums of cash. He'd probably end up giving it all to charity.

Maredudd put together a bag of food and drinks to take with us on our camping trip, and I had also swiped a can of dog food from the cupboard, which I planned to use to entice Jojo to our camp, although in all likelihood I would just end up attracting hedgehogs and foxes. We got the bus to the other side of the bay in the late afternoon. The bus driver that had brought me to Maredudd's in the first place was surprised to see me again, this time with more luggage, and a companion, and he greeted me amusedly as I paid for my fare. Maredudd sat next to me on the bus, and during the journey I noticed how other people were looking at us.

Some of the faces I could put names too, and I knew that the gossip about us on the beach was no doubt doing the rounds, swapped from mouth to mouth like toddlers sharing dummies, but I didn't care. I don't know what was different in me, but something had definitely changed. I felt proud to have Maredudd next to me, almost to the point of wanting to show him off like a trophy. I didn't have the nerve to kiss him there, and then, but I would have if I didn't think it would be rubbing it in too much. People disliked me enough as it was without giving them more ammo to shoot with. Maredudd on the other hand was none the wiser, and his head was turned towards the window as he watched the fields dotted with animals swooping past in a blur.

The place I planned to set up camp was not far from the lights of home. In fact, from on the hill, we'd probably be able to see the house, and hopefully Mum would keep the curtains closed when she got changed into her nightie, otherwise we'd see something much more frightening than any monster. We carried our luggage up the hill, walking along the tree-line as we figured out where to set up for the night.

"This is a good spot," Maredudd declared as he stood beneath a huge oak tree that seemed to be crawling its way out of the woods to stand alone.

"It's a bit close to the house though." I stopped to see where he was pointing.

"It's sheltered, and if we need help, we're close to home. If we get really stuck, we can pop in and ask Wenda for some toilet paper." He joked with an entertained grin.

I rolled my eyes before laughing as I trudged over to where he was waiting for me. The ground was flat, which was a plus, so I could see no reason not to stay here. We set up the tent together after dumping our bags, and while he went to collect some twigs to build a little fire, I went off into the woods with my tin of dog food. I whistled Jojo's name as I walked, depositing scoops of jelly and meat here and there.

"Jojo! Here, Jojo!" I called out to her in between shrill wolf-whistles.

But I got the strange sensation that I really should have tread softly, pausing beneath the boughs of some intermingled sycamores, my shoes crunching on the blanket of dried leaves, and seeds they had littered around the bases of their trunks. There was a weird atmosphere here, a heavy one that coated everything like dust, and smoke. When I opened my mouth to call out, I got the overwhelming desire to stay quiet, and make a swift exit. I had been here many times in the past on walks with Jojo, and it was easy to get lost if you didn't know the paths well, but it had never felt so eerie before. Deciding it would be wise to return to the camp, I emptied the rest of the can, and began walking back, the whole time desiring to look over my shoulder, but resisting the urge to panic. I knew I was just being a wimp. When I got to the edge of the woods, I found Maredudd sitting before a tiny camp-fire, poking at it with a long branch to shift the smouldering twigs about as the orange flames hummed gently.

"Ta-da." He suddenly revealed a packet of jumbo marshmallows from behind his back, waving them at me excitedly.

Night began to descend upon the hills as we sat with marshmallows bubbling over the fire. We held the sticks attentively, occasionally glancing at each other or into the shadows whilst hearing the shriek of a barn owl or the rustle of an unknown nocturnal animal. There was the shuffle bustle of a badger grunting in the undergrowth, and the scraping of a hedgehog, and the flutter of wings as a bird sought to hide itself away in the shadows of the densely leafed branches. It wasn't cold, but after the heat of the day it began to feel rather chilly, so we budged closer together. We decided to take a walk before the darkness fully settled over the forest, and fortunately we had brought some warm clothes with us, and a powerful torch to light the way.

It was quite spooky stepping between the trees in the dim light, but I felt safe with Maredudd beside me, letting me hold onto his arm as I shone the torch about, and called for Jojo. We even thought that she might be coming towards us as we heard paws moving across the ground, but then suddenly a startled fox popped its head out of the bushes, the torch turning its eyes into glowing lanterns before it fled from us in terror. I felt sorry for Jojo, being stuck out here alone. I knew she could hunt for herself, since she was an excellent ratter, and had been trained thus, but she was used to the comforts of a human home and might have been lonely by herself. Eventually it became so dark that we had no choice, but to turn back. I hoped that she might have heard me calling and would follow our scent back to the campsite.

We had some lunch of sandwiches, and crisps, followed by a few bottles of cider, and soon I began to feel sleepy. It was calm, and quiet here, much more so than when we had first arrived. Maredudd kept his back to me while I discreetly put some pyjamas on before crawling into my sleeping bag, and we chatted for a little while, the firelight pasting a creamy glow on one side of his face as he turned to peer into the tent at me. Soon, I fell asleep.

I startled awake, my eyes opening to darkness. For a moment I didn't move, my ears alert as I felt so disoriented, and my body protested at having rested upon the hard ground. I remembered where I was then, and reached into the space beside me, searching for Maredudd's body. He had put his sleeping bag down and appeared to have at least slept in it for a while since it was all crumpled, but the fabric was stone cold. Trying to squint in the low light, I searched blindly for my torch, and turned it on.

As I suspected, the tent was empty besides me. I thought he must have got up to go to the toilet in the woods, so I nestled back down, and punched my pillow into a more pleasing shape, resting the torch on my chest, and shining it up at the ceiling of the tent. My eyelids sagged, and I could feel myself drifting off again. I woke again, blinking, realising I had sank back into my dreams with the torch back on, but Maredudd still hadn't materialised. I started to feel worried. Maybe he had gone down to the house for some reason? I had the feeling he might have. Was he alright? The worry gnawed away at me inside my head, making me restless and anxious. Bones creaking, I dragged myself to my knees, and crawled out of the tent, pausing only to put my boots on. I shined the torch about, first finding the burned out fireplace, then noticing that his boots were still there next to the tent, which meant he had wandered off bare foot.

The ground around the camp-site was mostly bare mud, and I spotted his footprints heading away down the hill, towards the house. Confused, and beginning to feel rather afraid, I decided to follow them. I tried to keep as quiet as I could, which was hard when I was wearing these clunky shoes, and in the dark every tiny sound seemed a thousand times louder than it really was. I could see the lights of the house close by, so I switched the torch off as I knew just where I was going. His footprints had finished where the grass started, but unless he had suddenly changed direction, he must have headed straight for the back gate into Geraint's house.

I knew there was another way to access the garden round the side, deciding not to open the gate, and risk waking Geraint, who might run down the stairs with his double-barrelled shotgun thinking he had an intruder. The fence was low here, usually hidden away behind the large bushes that engulfed them, but there was a gap where Geraint had fallen through the hedge while trying to repair the roof of the chicken coop. Before I had a chance to climb over though, I heard a faint sound coming from the other side of the garden.

The moon was providing a minimum of visible light that with a bit of straining allowed me to see the bare shapes that populated the garden, making out the goat shed, and paddock. Mum must have left the hallway light on upstairs as a yellow glow was shining through the landing window, and that helped somewhat. I could just about see a figure by the back door, and as I fought to make it out in the shadows, I realised it was Maredudd. He was crouched down, his back towards me, his arms moving hastily in a methodical, mechanical fashion. There was something on the ground next to him, but I couldn't tell what it was. He was digging into the earth below the garden step with his bare hands, but why?

I was so unnerved by what I was seeing that I couldn't bring myself to utter a sound. He stopped suddenly, his head turning to listen for any noises, and I held my breath, restraining the irrational fear that was creeping inside me. Deciding that nothing was amiss, he continued until a satisfactory depth had been achieved, then he took whatever object it was he had brought with him, and put it in the hole, using his palms to push the earth back into the hole. For a while he simply flattened, and squashed the mud back into place, standing up and giving it a good stamp with his bare feet. Then he turned and walked off through the garden. I heard him climbing over the back gate, then his footfalls on the grass moving away.

I swallowed down the lump in my throat, unable to move an inch from the spot. Maredudd would get back to the tent, and find I had disappeared, but why did I have to explain myself? He was the one that had walked off in the dark, burying things in people's gardens. If he was up to something, why didn't he tell me? Why did he wait until I had gone to sleep?

I felt slightly betrayed, but also incredibly curious. I climbed the fence into the garden, and crept across the grass, stopping only to pull Mum's trowel out of the flower-pot she kept it in, and then I knelt at the stop he had been digging at. Sweating profusely, and with shaking hands, I put the torch down, and began to dig. The hole he had unearthed must have been quite deep as I was there for a while until I finally struck something hard below. I switched the torch on and shone it into the hole. Glass glittered under the dazzling light. I reached in, and wrapped my hand around the object, lifting it out onto my lap, and discovering he had buried a jar down there. It was heavy, full of liquid, and other objects that clinked against the glass when I turned it. I stood upright, and shined the torch into the jar, tipping it this way, and that as I tried to figure out what was inside.

All of a sudden, the back door opened, and something long, and cold was shoved under my chin.

"What are you doing in my garden!" Geraint's furious voice shouted down at me from the back door. I was absolutely petrified, frozen to the spot with terror as he was pointing his rifle at my throat, and before I had a chance to compose myself, the jar, and the torch fell from my hands. My whole body was so stiff with fear that I didn't even make to catch them.

Crash! The glass bottle exploded on the angular concrete of the back step. The torch went clattering onto the grass, its white beam shining across the lawn, and highlighting the far trees. As the jar burst into a thousand pieces of glass, the contents erupted out of it, splashing across my pyjama trousers, and raining upon Geraint's boxer shorts, and bare legs, both of us crying out in horror, and disgust at the repugnant smell. I flew back as soon as the liquid touched me, landing on my rear as the scene unfolded in slow motion, Geraint gasping, his gun bashing against the door frame as he too almost slipped over on the tiled kitchen floor, but managed to save himself from hitting the ground. The metallic ping of nails, and screws were like odd musical notes as they struck the backdoor steps, accompanied by the wet slap of the other unidentified objects. Panting, I shielded my eyes from the light as the kitchen light turned on, and Mum came thundering through the kitchen in her nightgown.

"What in God's name are you two doing down here!" she shrieked, and when she smelled the horrid stench, she covered her face with her hand. "Ach-y-fie! What's that nasty stink!"

Geraint looked down at me, glaring, and I looked at them both blank-faced. I got the feeling I was in a lot of trouble.

"What's this! Owen! What have you been doing!"Mum was completely livid as she stepped around Geraint and peered down at the mess before me.

"It wasn't me! I didn't do it, I don't even know what

this is!" I exclaimed, forcing down the gagging sensation in my throat. It smelled like a mix of sea water and stale urine, perhaps a little drop of vomit, and a liberal dash of dog shit. There was a huge clump of wet hair, a sliced open lemon, and some other unidentifiable things, surrounded by a ring of scattered nails, and screws, all of them rusting to pieces as some had broken on the floor.

Geraint's threat-stare remained unchanged. I felt it penetrating me like a knife, seeking my soft innards. His leg hairs were shedding droplets of the stinking liquid onto the back-door mat.

"I don't know what you're playing at young man, but if this is your idea of a practical joke, it's not funny!" Mum shouted at me. I felt like I was playing a character in a children's television show, being accused of something that wasn't my fault.

I was surprised that Geraint had so little to say on the matter. He instead shuffled off to go, and clean himself, while Mum helped me pick up the glass, and other items, both of us wearing rubber gloves. I was so embarrassed. I should have just left it alone, not gone over, and sated my curiosity. Mum didn't utter a word to me as we worked, her mouth pressed into a thin line, and her usually cheerful eyes frowning down at the task at hand. I wondered why she was so mad. Did she know what this jar was for? I knew it would be unwise to ask.

She didn't even speak to me when we were finished, ignoring me as I went upstairs to change my pyjama trousers, and give myself a wash, and when I emerged from the bathroom, I saw Geraint standing in the door of his bedroom, staring at me still as I went to the stairs. The fact alone that he was just looking at me, and not speaking was making me feel very frightened. His eyes seemed to be separating, looking in opposite directions around me instead of focusing right at me, like I was standing between the two lasers of his vision.

Shuddering, I went back downstairs to avoid him.

"Mum, it wasn't me that put it there. I saw... Someone digging in the garden, so I went to investigate—" I began as I stepped into the kitchen, but Mum cut me off.

"It's not about the jar, Owen. It's the fact that it's two o'clock in the morning, and you're wandering about in the dark by yourself! You know about the murder! I wasn't wrong: it was Fred who was killed! You know, and you're still out there endangering yourself," Mum exclaimed as she leaned against the kitchen counter. "I thought, I won't nag him, I won't keep going on at him about it. I thought you would try to be safer."

I clasped my hands together, and bowed my head, feeling very guilty indeed. She observed my expression, tears of worried stress forming at the corners of her eyes.

"Yere we are, having this conversation again. I don't like being angry at you, Owen, but I am because I love you, and I want you to be safe," she said, the fury in her voice softening when she saw how ashamed I was. "I've done nothing, but worry about you, ever since these killings began. Sometimes I can't sleep at night, worried where you are, even more so now you've been going to stay with Maredudd. I'm sure he's been taking care of you, but I can't help it."

I nodded, unable to look up at her. It had been foolish, I should have stayed in the tent, and waited for Maredudd to come back.

"I'm sorry, Mum," I mumbled weakly.

"I know you're an adult. But to me, you're my baby, and it's my instinct to protect you." She sighed, stepping forward, and putting her arms around me. "Hmm, I'm glad you smell better now too. It was honking by yere a moment ago."

"Yeah, I don't know what that was, but it was nasty." I managed a tentative chuckle.

"Now, tell me what you were doing round yere? I thought you were at Maredudd's house?" she questioned, leaning back so she could see my face.

"We're camping up on the hill by the woods together. He's waiting for me," I told her, leaving out the part where I had followed him to the house. She could already tell I had been up to some funny business, but she chose not to pursue it.

"Okay. Shall I walk you back to him?" she suggested, but I shook my head.

"No, it's fine. It's not far, and I have my torch."

She eyed me closely for a moment, silently urging me to let her come too, but then she would just have to walk back alone anyway. I was surprised that she allowed me to go, standing by the back door, and watching me exit through the gate, turning to wave to her before making the slow walk up the hill again. I hoped Maredudd wouldn't notice that I was wearing different trousers than the ones I had worn to bed. Then I began to wonder how I was going to talk to him about what I had seen... and what had happened after.

I found him sitting outside the tent when I arrived, his hand moving to block the torch beam as I shined it on his form.

"Where have you been?" he asked, like I was the one behaving strangely.

"I was looking for you. Where have you been?" I turned the question back to him.

"Nowhere. I went for a pee by yere." He gestured to the woods behind us. I couldn't believe he was lying to my face.

I looked down at the ground, anywhere, but him. I didn't know what to say.

"Are you alright?" he asked, getting to his feet, and coming towards me. I saw that his hands were clean, not covered in soil like they had been when he'd escaped from the garden.

"I saw you in Geraint's garden," I blurted the words out before my nervous mind could stop them, and he paused before me, his hands stopped in the air either side of my body.

"What do you mean?"

"I saw you digging in Geraint's garden," I repeated, this time my voice hardening. "I saw you burying that jar, and I dug it up."

His eyes closed briefly, and when they opened again, he was looking skyward. He sighed.

"Oh, Owen..." he murmured.

"Geraint nearly shot my bloody head off when he caught me too!" I exclaimed, becoming frustrated with his silence. "I dropped it; it smashed everywhere. Just so you know."

Maredudd nodded slowly, his half-closed eyes staring down at the earthy ground beneath us. His hands had moved to his own hips, and he was biting his lip. He didn't look angry, rather, he seemed disappointed. I expected him to put his hand on his forehead, but he didn't move.

"Why didn't you tell me what you were up to? Why did you just sneak off like that? And what the hell was that thing for anyway? It was disgusting," I continued, trying to coax some explanation out of him before I really lost my temper.

"You dug up my curse jar," he said emotionlessly. "I was putting it there to curse Geraint. I didn't tell you because I didn't want to endanger you. I didn't want him to think that you had put it there. I thought you were asleep, so I thought what you didn't know couldn't hurt you."

"Why do you need to curse him when I've worked so hard on the spell you gave me? You could have told me what you were doing. I would have stayed away. Don't you trust me? Do you think I'm stupid or something?" I questioned, my words sharp like firecrackers.

"No, I don't think you're stupid." He frowned, finally making eye contact with me, but still avoiding my questions.

"But you don't trust me?" I asked. "Otherwise you would have told me."

"It's not that I don't trust you. I didn't want you to be in danger," he persisted, but I was too hurt to hear his excuses.

"You're just like Mum. You think I'm a child still, because I'm not six-foot-tall, and I don't own my own home or car, because I don't have my own children or a steady job. You still think I'm a child," I snapped, unconsciously stepping back away from him.

"No, Owen. I do not think you're a child." He moved towards me, but I stepped further away.

"Yes, you do. Everyone is always talking about how they have to protect me and look after me like I'm a baby who can't look after himself. If you had just told me, I wouldn't have dug it up or smashed it." I refused to let him near me, holding the torch out between us like a weapon. "You could have told me."

"Owen, please don't say those things. I'm sorry I didn't tell you, and I don't think you're a child. You're more than able to care for yourself. I was just scared for your safety," he told me, his hands held out palm-up, trying to reason with me.

"I'm real tired of hearing people say that," I muttered. "I feel like you don't trust me enough to make intelligent decisions. I feel like it was a waste of time agreeing to trust you when you obviously don't trust me. Now I've made a fool of myself in front of Mum and Geraint, and even worse, they think *I* was the one burying the jar there."

He nodded slowly, ashamedly. He went to move closer, but I threw the torch down at his feet, and turned away, walking off down the hill.

"Owen, where are you going?" he called after me,

confused.

"Home. I'm going home," I answered back bluntly. "I don't want to talk right now. See you later."

He didn't pick up the torch, but I knew he stood and watched me go until I merged with the shadows, out of sight. I wasn't angry anymore; I was disappointed. Mum was sitting by the back door with a mug of cocoa when I turned up at the back gate, and she was astonished to see me there. It was only when I was lying on my bed, the curtains closed to block out the view of the bay, that the disappointment drained away, and left me with feelings of embarrassment. I wanted to run back to the tent and apologise, but I had already made a fool of myself once this night. On top of that, Jojo was still nowhere to be seen, and now Maredudd thought I was angry at him, and that I believed he didn't trust me.

I was still somewhat bitter about that. I knew it was silly of me to think that he wouldn't behave autonomously, that he wouldn't be doing these activities without my knowledge of them, but I didn't understand why he hadn't told me he was going to do it. I felt like such an idiot. I wanted to crawl into a hole in the ground and be buried myself.

Somehow I managed to get some sleep that night, but when I woke in the morning, my head was aching, and my mood was no better. Mum asked me if I wanted to come to work with her, so I did. I was glad that Geraint had gone out early though, so I didn't have to see him when I went down for breakfast. Mum didn't bring up what had happened, though her eyes looked at me searchingly. I could tell she knew some altercation must have occurred between Maredudd and I because I wouldn't talk about him. When we got to the caravan-site, I worked myself into a frenzy. Anything to take my mind off of it.

The bedroom was dark. I lay down after spending the day working, as I had done for the last couple of days, taking on some extra over-time to keep myself busy. The thought of going back to my bedroom, a room that didn't have Jojo or Maredudd in it, was intolerable. I helped Mum do chores around the house, helped her to cook dinner, helped her to feed the other animals. Maredudd supposedly came around, bringing with him my tent, and other belongings, asking to see me, but Mum told him I was out somewhere, so he left. I wanted to see him, but I didn't know what I would say. I felt so tired, my whole body aching and devoid of vital energy, as with flu, and my mind was empty, and cold. I felt ill.

The more I worked, the worse I felt, but it was the only thing that seemed to make the feelings inside me shrink back into the corners, at least for a little while. I felt so down, more down than I had felt for a long time. All I wanted to do was curl up in a ball beneath my duvet and hide from the sun. When night came, I sank into a deep, thoughtless sleep, but the desolate pool of my solitude was interrupted abruptly as soon as I relaxed. Nightmares, violent images of people I cared for, flashed through my mind. I was gripped by my shoulders and pinned down as these terrible dreams were pumped into my brain, and I was forced to witness them all. No matter how I struggled, I couldn't make myself wake. When morning finally came, I was a trembling wreck, tangled in damp bed-sheets, and coated in sweat.

The first night they began, I dreamed of Jojo. She was trapped in a tiny box with air-holes cut in it, and then a dark figure began to submerse it in water, and I was to one side, screaming, screaming for them to stop until my voice cracked into a breathless groan. The images were so vivid, and so horrifying that when I woke, I felt traumatised as though it had truly happened. There were more, worse visions. Mum tied down to a table, and the dark figure took up a scalpel, and began to cut off her skin while she was still alive, and I was powerless to stop it. Dad was put in a sack and thrown down stone steps into a basement where the figure beat him endlessly with a stick. And lastly, Maredudd, swimming, alone in churning waters, fighting to stay above the surface as an unknown creature beneath tore at his legs, trying to drag him down to his death. All the while, I was left on the sidelines awaiting my own fate, struggling against the invisible chains that kept me in my place as I cried for mercy.

The nightmares soon chose me as the victim, and I found myself on an empty beach at midnight, fighting the urge to walk towards the water. Screaming at myself, begging myself not to go into the water, and drown. I felt I was being guided by someone else, a shadow luring me towards the waves where I would sink beneath and vanish. Just like Dad.

Tiredness swiftly turned into exhaustion. There were dark rings under my eyes, and come the weekend, I could do nothing except lay on the sofa, dazedly staring in the general direction of the telly as I ate lethargically from a bowl of popcorn. Mum noticed the nosedive my health had taken, and started to fuss over me, making me sip energy drinks, and pop pain-killers. My mood was black, cold, and vacant. It was like the grief I had felt after Dad's funeral: it had no name, and no face, no shape or sound, only emptiness, an emotional vacuum filled only by snippets of suicidal thought. I felt something was seriously wrong with me, but I couldn't put my finger on it.

The nightmares finally came to a climax. The house was quiet. Mum and Geraint were sleeping in their room, and I was laying in my bed, toying with the idea of staying awake just to make the nightmares leave me alone. I could feel myself drifting in, and out of consciousness as I fought to stay awake, only my body allowing itself to get some rest, my aching eyes throbbing in their sockets as I stared up at the ceiling. I suddenly became aware of a presence in the corner of the room. It exerted a palpable pressure, as though compressing every atom in the air between us into a wall that began to squash me to the bed, creating a heavy weight on my chest, like a breeze-block had been placed on my ribs, forcing me to fight for air. I tried to turn my head to look at it, to figure out who was there, but only my eyes would move. My whole body had gone rigid, my muscles seizing up as though cramping, even my fingers twisted into claws at my sides. The shadows swirled and plumed like smoke. A shape began to emerge, first a snout, then a head topped with pointed ears. Shaggy fur, a chain. Chief.

"No...!" I wheezed. "No...! No...!"

I opened my mouth, and tried to scream, but no sound would come out. The dog was staring at me with glowing blue eyes that only served to darken the space around it. I panicked, breath puffing, and panting, body shaking with dread, sweat forming tiny twinkling spots on my forehead. My whole body was frozen stiff. I became faint.

A deep, muffled voice moaned close by, the floor rumbling, and quaking, but none of the furniture moved, even as the voice dropped away into a bass noise so loud that it was as if stadium speakers were discharging the sound right beneath my floorboards. The voice returned, booming, uttering indistinguishable words. The dog began to move closer, and as it took another step it began to change, cloaking in tendrils of black steam that amassed into the form of a human who stopped beside my bed. I looked up at the faceless head, my mouth open, and my throat dry. A black arm was lifted, and a hand covered my mouth as the thing climbed up onto the mattress, and sat atop me, its weight as heavy as if it were made of lead, the smoking of its flesh slipping into my nostrils, and choking me. My lungs burned, every fibre of the deflated sacks on fire with the need for oxygen, my head spinning, the room going round, and round like a carousel. My ribs made a wet, crushing sound as they started to snap under the knees of the stranger. Crack, crack. They split apart like brittle twigs, shards of bone squashed into my torso like I was made of sponge. My eyes rolled back into my head.

"Owen! Owen!" a voice was calling to me in the distance.

It distracted me, drawing me away from the desire to give in, to allow myself to be killed. It was a voice I recognised. Maredudd. He was calling to me. I called back with my mind's voice.

A blinding light appeared in the room, another glowing figure so bright that it hurt to look into its aura, and it filled the space with its presence, sucking in the pressure that pinned me down. Coughing, oxygen began to seep back into my lungs as the darkness released its grip on me.

Daylight.

When had I opened my eyes? When had I opened the curtains? The ocean winds were blowing in, flapping the curtains about the open window, birdsong performed in the garden below by the usual winged orchestra. The cover was wet beneath me, and my whole body shivered in an icy fever. I drew in a deep breath, finally. It felt so good to taste the fresh air, and as I sat up to look out at the bay, I realised I didn't feel as bad as I had yesterday. Still aching, still sleepy, but better somehow. I shuffled up to the window sill and had to shield my gaze from the sunshine that was beaming down on the eastern wall of the house.

Suddenly, I heard the humming of rapidly-beating wings, and I ducked back slightly as a small shape navigated the air around the window. It came closer, wings gracefully keeping it aloft until it landed on the window sill right before me, and I saw that it was a small starling, its oily feathers flecked with pale spots. I was so alarmed to see a wild bird perched there that I was too nervous to move in case I frightened it off. It regarded me, head twitching to the side, then it beat its wings, and was off, darting down into the garden below. It had left something there for me. The Witch's Ladder.

I stared at the curled piece of yarn, my throat contracting to attempt to swallow, my brain slow to react to what I was seeing. For a long time, I didn't move. I only swiped it up and hid it in the pocket of my pyjama trousers when I heard Mum knocking on my door, and I turned just in time to see her opening it, her cautious face looking in at me.

"How are you feeling today, Owen? I brought you some ox tail soup," Mum asked softly when she saw me kneeling there.

"Oh—I—I'm much better," I stuttered, trying to banish the nervousness that gripped me. "Oh, umm, I'm—never mind."

She smiled at me fondly as she came into the room with the tray and put it on the bed beside me. I was about to tell her I wouldn't eat ox tail soup because I was vegetarian, but she had gone to the trouble of making it for me, so I accepted it, and said thank you. She often got mixed up when it came to soups, because by her reasoning it didn't have any meat in it, but then she hadn't taken into consideration that it was made from severed cow tails. She sat on the edge of the bed and watched me dip my toast into my bowl.

"You were making a lot of noise last night," she said, her eyes following the bread to my mouth where I took a bite. "I popped in to check on you. You were red hot, so I opened the window, and let some air in."

"Thanks. I was having another nightmare, but it soon went away. I feel a lot better today, not sure why," I made a muted smile as I swallowed a spoonful of the salty liquid. It was almost too salty for my palate after going so long without eating beef.

"I'm glad. Geraint didn't have a very good night either, poor dab. Sent him off to Cardiff with a flask of soup as well. That's home-made you know," she pointed out proudly, and I grinned.

"Oh—it's lovely. Thank you." I let her stroke down the tufts of my messy hair, which were sticking up in all directions.

"Maredudd called again. He's very worried about you after I told him you were unwell, and kept having bad dreams," she answered, inspecting behind my ear before continuing to rake her fingernails against my scalp. "And you'll never guess what. I went out to the shop earlier, and I saw up on the hill, all of the sheep are dead. Every single one killed."

"What?" I lowered my spoon, my eyes wide open.

"First time I've seen it myself by yere, but it was a nasty sight. Along the main road by the grocery store. Go, and take a look if you're up for it. They've already started clearing it up," she told me, and I jumped out of bed with my spoon in my hand. She watched me eat the soup as I struggled out of my pyjamas. "Well at least finish your breakfast before you go running out there!"

"Sorry," I collapsed back down on the bed topless, bending to quickly scoff down the rest of my food while she looked on disapprovingly.

"You'll give yourself heartburn," she reminded me. "And don't forget to wear plenty of sun-block."

Ten

I told Mum I would pop round to Maredudd's house. She knew something had happened between us, and I told her that we'd had an argument, but I didn't say what it was about, only that I had walked off, and left him, which was why he had dropped my stuff to the house. She seemed relieved that I was going to pay him a visit. Even though she'd kept bringing up his age, and how she was surprised that I liked him, I could tell she was disappointed that it appeared we weren't seeing each other for the time being. I had to admit to myself that I was disappointed too.

I had missed him while we were apart. I would have gone out to see him sooner if I hadn't been so unwell. I hoped that he would forgive me for walking away the other night. I had come to the conclusion that he kept the secret from me with the sole intention of protecting me, and it was stupid of me to hold that against him the way I often held it against Mum. He knew more about magic than I did; I couldn't expect him to tell me things that might end with me getting hurt, and I knew him well enough by now to know that he wasn't spiteful the way Geraint was. There was wisdom in Maredudd, and I should have respected that.

I thought of him as I walked along the road, camera bouncing on my chest, food in my backpack, along with some fresh clothes, and some money. On the way to the kill-site, I popped into the grocery store where Mrs Bryn was sitting behind the counter, and she greeted me when I stepped through the door.

"Bore da, Owen." She smiled with a nod, and I nodded back.

"Hello there, Mrs Bryn," I replied, knowing full well that she'd correct me like she always did, so I was especially surprised when she didn't.

"I've been waiting for you to come by yere, actually. Come yere, I'd like to have a chat." She gestured to the counter, so I approached curiously, wondering what she wanted to talk about. When I stood right before her, she continued. "As you will know, Jamie is starting college in September, and he wants to go to one in town. His dad has offered for him to stay by there with him while he studies. But that leaves me with no staff to help me out in the store."

"Oh... That's nice that Jamie has been accepted into the college he wanted." I smiled reassuringly, before realising the point she was trying to make had gone straight over my head.

"Owen! You drip, what I'm trying to say is, I've got a job vacancy to fill. D'ya think you'd be interested?" She leaned over the counter, and gave me a clap on my arm, making me jump back laughing.

"Really?" I was so flattered that I couldn't stop my cheeks from blushing, and my eyes from glittering. She nodded and sat back on the stool.

"You're a good lad despite what other mouthy cows might say. Never mind about this rumour going about with you and that Iranian chap," she remarked.

"Maredudd is—he's just my friend..." I trailed off, but she waved her hand at me, shaking her head dismissively.

"I won't be having none of these fibs when you're working for me. If the chap is your boyfriend, then that's good for you. 'Tis a shame that people would be so jealous of another's love as to talk badly of it," she pointed a finger at me, her expression serious. "Besides, I know of Maredudd's kind deeds, and he's a good lad too. But I'll have no canoodling in my shop, understand?"

I chuckled, and her stony expression turned to a mutual grin.

"Of course, Mrs Bryn. I'd never skive on the job. I'm a good worker," I promised, and she seemed to agree with me.

"I was talking to Alison over by the caravan site. She told me you've been working hard there, and your mam had nought, but good to say about you," she told me sincerely. "So if you can wait a month for Jamie to finish, I'd be glad to have you yere with me."

"Thank you, Mrs Bryn! Thank you so much!" I took her hand and shook it enthusiastically.

"And that's another thing! It's Eryl! Eryl!" She finally corrected me, and we both laughed then.

I was so disoriented by the conversation with her that I almost walked out and forgot to pick something up for Maredudd. Mrs Bryn asked me where I was off to for the day, and I told her I was going to see the field where the sheep had been killed before heading to Maredudd's house. She told me that a large animal had been seen running across the hill by the field late in the night, but no one had been able to identify it, and she warned me to be careful. I picked up a bottle of Maredudd's favourite cider, and some lunch for me while I was out walking, then I said goodbye, and started off on my journey.

As I walked, I started to think about how things were when I first came to live here. I used to think everybody hated me, but perhaps I was wrong. My lack of self-esteem was projected onto others, just the way they projected theirs onto me, creating an endless circle of bad energy that never cleared. No one was inherently bad or evil, perhaps not even Geraint. It gave me hope for the future, hope that one day I wouldn't be afraid of speaking to new people or making new friends, and now that I had Maredudd, I wouldn't be so lonely anymore. I couldn't tell if my renewed self-esteem came from having Maredudd, or whether he had come about because of it. A bit of a chicken-and-the-egg situation, I suppose. It wasn't far from the grocery store, and as I walked, I whistled a tune, and enjoyed the cool breeze that was sweeping over the bay.

As I got closer, I could smell the scent of iron in the air, mingling with the salt of the sea so that it smelled embarrassingly similar to the soup Mum had given me for breakfast. But there was another smell accompanying it: fear, a distinct scent given off by animals in distress that made my guts tangle up. I could hear machines working, and as I came alongside the fields, Tractors were forming a heap of the bodies, scooping them all up and taking them to the neighbouring field where it was harder to see the destruction. Not many of the bodies remained, which was going to make it difficult to get some photos. I saw Farmer Thomas standing at the gate further down the road, his arms folded as he watched the commotion with an expression of listlessness. As I approached, he turned to look round at me, and I saw the face of a man who had near enough given up.

"Good morning to ye, Owen," he grumbled as I got closer.

"Hello, Mr Thomas," I replied cautiously, unsure of what mood the old fellow was in.

He observed me a moment before we both looked back at the field, littered with the dismembered corpses of his entire herd.

"Not a single one spared," he eventually murmured. "Even the lambs were rent to pieces. I don't know what to do anymore. All of my stock is gone."

I opened my mouth to speak, to ask him about Geraint's traps, or to offer some words of false hope, but there was nothing I could say to change his mood.

"This injustice will go unpunished, I'm afraid to say," he continued slowly. He was not a man to shed tears, but he looked pretty close to it, and I saw the rings of worry under his eyes from sleepless nights, and long work hours. He had been a farmer in this area since he was a boy, as had his father, and his father before him, and so on.

"Mr Thomas, I've been investigating these massacres thoroughly since they began. I've got an archive of data on them. I want to contact one of the universities, in the hopes of getting some people down here to see what's going on, and maybe solve the mystery. It's the sole reason I've been documenting this, because I can't bear to see it continue," I told him hurriedly before he could say anything more, urging myself that now was the time to explain, hoping that he would see hope too. "If you would be so kind, I'd like to photograph this evidence before you dispose of the bodies. I want to see this animal captured so that this doesn't have to happen anymore."

Farmer Thomas looked at me, his chin moving as he chewed the air, and his rheumy eyes examining my honest expression. He stroked his moustache thoughtfully, looking again at the field where his livestock lay covered in flies.

"Alright. You may do so, and when you contact these academics, I want them to know that they can come, and speak to me about it too. Something needs to be done about this. We've already lost one of our village members, let alone all the animals that have been killed for nothing," he finally declared, and relief filled me instantly. "I will talk to the other farmers. Everyone by yere has lost stock because of this, and even now the traps seem to be doing no good at all. I will try and rally everyone."

"That would be great, and—and if there's any information you would like me to provide, records, photos, I can do that for you." I nodded quickly. It was such a pity that it had to come to him losing everything before he would want to team up with me, but better late than never.

"Thank you, sir," he replied with a blunt nod, and I knew then that the conversation was over.

"Thank you, Mr Thomas," I replied as I opened the gate, and entered the field.

He watched me silently as I crossed it, heading towards the remaining bodies that were strewn alongside the far hedgerows. I had to be careful not to use too much film as I had forgot to pick up an extra roll when I left the house, so I chose my frames wisely. More than once, I stepped back to focus the camera, and found myself standing on a severed leg or some kind internal organ. It seemed that whatever was doing this was no longer eating. It was just killing, and killing, as though for fun, and now it was choosing more, and more audacious spots to commit its crimes. This field was right by the road, and anyone driving by could have seen it, which explains why it had been spotted running away.

I knew the direction it had gone in because I discovered bloody hoof-prints in the earth, but what was also baffling was that there were paw-prints present too. I took pictures of the tracks, unable to make heads or tails of them. What it seemed to my eyes was that the animal had both hooves, and paws. Hooves at the back, paws on the front legs, or perhaps I was wrong. I followed them, going round in circles until finally I discovered where it had fled the field by leaping through a hole in the fencing onto the marshy ground beyond. Mr Thomas was busy talking to one of the farm workers by the gate. Neither of them saw me slip through into the next field.

I held my camera tightly to my chest as I squinted into the grass, occasionally pausing to push my glasses up my nose as my skin was damp, and they kept slipping. The creature's confidence in the fact that it had so far gone unnoticed was increasing, confident enough to leave a visible track like this that even I could follow with my poor eyesight. The yellowed grass bowed to either side of the path it had followed, giving me a clear-cut direction to head in. I was convinced now that it had both hooves, and feet, but that meant it was unlike any animal that existed on the planet, or at least that I knew of anyway.

On, and on it went, zig-zagging when it darted off in another direction to investigate something interesting. It was taking me in the direction of the ruins, closer, and closer to Maredudd's house, only to back away again, and take another route, entering the woods, and trampling the mud there. I stopped following only to have something to eat, and when I checked my watch, I realised I had been walking for over two hours. I told myself I would stop soon and go to Maredudd's cottage. The sun was getting hot on my neck, and my ankles were aching.

Huge white clouds rolled in the azure sky above the cool shade of the woods as I stepped over tree-roots, and sent birds escaping from my presence, pausing occasionally to make sure I hadn't lost sight of the tracks. I was determined to follow to their source... But I hadn't thought about what I would do when I got there. I had no way of contacting anyone. I didn't actually think I would find anything. The clouds departed, and the sky began to dim. It was now approaching six o'clock, and the sky was purple, and striped with pale wisps. The wind had died back, and the sun's heat was cooling to a comfortable warmth. I was splattered with mud, etched with grass stains, and soaked in sweat. The tracks had taken me round in circles, or perhaps I had become confused by the trail, and ended up following it round as it overlapped.

Exhausted, I stopped walking, and fell to lean my weight against the closest tree as I looked either side of myself into the woods. I knew vaguely where I was. That was something, at least. Maredudd's house wasn't far from here, I could get there by nightfall. But first, a rest was in order. I sank to the ground, tugging my water bottle from my pocket so that I could take a swig of tepid liquid. It was pointless. I had wasted the day following a path that lead me nowhere. But on the plus side, I had photos of Farmer Thomas's field, and of the tracks themselves. When I checked my camera, I found I had one shot left. Probably one that would be spent on me taking a goofy self-portrait. I stretched my legs out with a sigh and wiped at my wet forehead.

The woods were strangely quiet. Usually there were birds singing at this time, taking part in the last tweeting match of the day before bedding down for the night. Instead there was only silence, the only movement being that of the occasional leaf that floated to the ground from the boughs above. Maybe the heat had exhausted their tiny bodies, and they were relaxing in the branches already. I rested awhile, thinking of what I would say to Maredudd when I knocked on the door.

That's when I heard heavy footfalls somewhere close by.

I opened my eyes, my hand immediately falling upon my camera. Something big was coming this way. My breath tightened in my chest, and I drew my legs in slowly in a pointless bid to hide myself, my ears alert to the clumping footsteps of something walking, then the wet puff of it sucking in a deep breath. It was sniffing the air, taking in my scent. It knew I was here.

Oh God, I thought to myself. *God help me...*

Suddenly, I changed my mind. I didn't want to find the monster. I wanted to be at Maredudd's house, none the wiser. But now was my chance to get a photo, when I had failed to do so the last time we had met. I could hear it breathing. It was getting closer, and closer. I estimated its size from sound alone to be as big as a bull, if not bigger. Leaves, and twigs crunched under it as it moved, and not a single thing in the forest moved, everything, including myself, staying still as statues with baited breath. The temptation to look round, to peer round the side of the tree, and catch a glimpse of it was overwhelming.

Slowly, I raised my camera. Closer, closer still. My hands were shaking as I moved the camera to the edge of the tree trunk. My finger was moist with sweat, and was slipping over the shutter, button. All it would take was a simple movement of my digit to fire the shutter and capture this animal. Finally, it was so close that I could smell its foul stench. It was the bitter, stinking herbal scent I had smelled before, and it made my nostrils burn so profusely that my eyes began to water. It was now or never. I pressed the shutter.

The sound was so loud in the desolate silence of the forest. Suddenly, my camera began to wind on the film, and I shook it, panicking, desperate to make it shut up as it whirred, and hummed noisily. The creature snorted, sucking in my smell, hoofs kicking the earth. I got up, I ran. The forest became a labyrinth of roots, and branches, my boots like heavy weights on my feet as I dodged them, and leaped over fallen tree trunks, the thudding of the monster close behind me, its stench dogging my footsteps. I swerved sharply like a fleeing hare, changing direction to the left, and catching a brief glance of its enormous shaggy body before the trees enveloped it, its feet skidding in the mud to turn, and follow. Its sheer size made it hard to turn as quickly as I could.

One of my boots was coming loose. I darted behind a large tree, and pressed hard against the trunk, my breath burning in my lungs, and my legs aching with tiredness. I bent, and fumbled madly with my laces, eyes shifting this way, and that as I heard it galloping somewhere behind me. I managed to kick off my shoes just as it gained on me, forcing me to abandon my hiding place bare foot, my socks taking up bits of leaf litter as they hit the earthy ground. The camera thumped on my chest, matching my rapid heartbeat, the contents of my backpack jingling loudly, giving it a certain beacon to hone in on as it ploughed through the long grass after me.

I broke free of the trees, running as fast as I could through the chest-high grass, over a small clearing, and into the shadows of the forest on the other side. My trousers were soaked in marsh water, and I think, perhaps, I might have wet myself slightly out of fright. The stodgy ground slowed the beast somewhat as I heard it falling behind, but I didn't stop to look back. The woods sloped up onto a hill, and I shouted at myself to urge my sore feet on, my heart palpitating, my pulse racing. Its footfalls entered the woods behind me, but it had yet to catch up with me. Up, up I climbed, the slope becoming so steep that I was almost running on all-fours.

Suddenly, the ground beneath my feet disappeared, and I was falling, rolling, and tumbling down a hole in the earth. Rippling, buzzing masses of black flies puffed up around me. The air became thick with the smell of death. I fell free, hitting a soft landing at the very bottom, liquid bursting out under the impact of my body, and my head banging on something hard. Sudden quiet, except for the hum of the flies. I felt moisture seeping into my clothing, and an unfamiliar pulsating under my hands as I lay there, momentarily stunned. A wound was throbbing in my forehead, and blood poured down into my eye-socket to pool there, unable to be blinked away. The horrific smell made me gag, and vomit reared up in my throat, choking me. The footfalls were coming to the top of the hill.

The shrill roar of the beast startled me alert, and I sat up, finding my clothes covered in a stinking brownish-red slime, and glued all over my clothes were the white wriggling bodies of hundreds of maggots. The terror was absolute; it cut off my ability to scream. A strangled whimper escaped through my clenched teeth when I realised I was surrounded by corpses, all of them in varying degrees of putrefaction, legs, and heads rising out of the heap. I looked up, seeing the dark shape of the beast toeing the edge of the trench, debating how it would climb down here towards me, until deciding there was a quicker way down, both of us turning to face the steep slope that led down opposite.

Panting, and spitting, I struggled to my feet, my soles sinking in the bloated flesh of the sheep, and cows that lay there, a shudder of repulsion shaking my entire body each time I felt something pop or squish between my toes. The beast was navigating down the slope. I could hear it skidding, and tripping as it tried to keep its balance. I ran as quickly as I could through the mess of bodies, my belly contracting, forcing my gorge up until I bent to throw up, but I didn't stop running. There was another way out on the other side. I jumped onto it, landing on my chest, and struggling out of the pit, aware of the squelching noise of the beast's feet trampling its old victims, my legs kicking to pull myself out on the other side.

My skin itched with the crawling sensation of the maggots, and my throat stung from the vomit. With my fingertips, I clawed my way out onto the grass above, but just as I was about to pull myself out, I felt something clamp down on my leg. The pain didn't arrive at my brain until seconds later when I turned my head and looked down into the staring eyes of Chief. His mouth was on my limb, his teeth sunk into the flesh of my calf. His head, so tiny, and disproportionate to his grotesque body, the torso of a sandy coloured cow, the legs of a horse, the forepaws of a dog of some kind, and from its head there grew antlers. It was like a nightmarish creation stitched together by Frankenstein himself.

The astonishment was so much that I didn't make a sound. But then the instinct for survival kicked in, and I drew up my leg, sending my foot hammering down upon the creature's snout. The impact struck its nose, blood spewing from its nostrils, and in a flash, I was free, forgetting the pain, forgetting the fear, seeking only to escape, to get away before it had another chance to sink its fangs into me. My chest was thick with adrenaline; my fingers, and toes felt numb. I didn't even know where I was going anymore.

Suddenly, the chill embrace of water surrounded me. I found myself sinking down into fast-flowing currents, being spun round, and round, my exhausted body fighting to reach the surface where I could snatch a gasp of air. The roar of the water blocked out all other sounds except for a loud splash that rung out further upstream as the creature dove in after me. My hands clawed through the water. My camera strap tangled around my throat. Every scream invited a mouthful of fresh water, leaving me spluttering before I was submerged again. The current turned me over with its powerful hand, sending me on a course I had no choice, but to flow with, and I began to feel faint. The wound in my head was making it hard to form conscious thought. Suddenly, I felt the currents slowing, and the depth of the water beneath me decreased, the flavour gradually becoming salty. Finally, hard ground beneath me.

Exhausted, I allowed the tide to wash me up on a tiny stretch of sandy rock beneath the cliff. My whole body hurt. I was drenched from head to toe, and I was bleeding and bruised. My arms trembled violently as I dragged myself out of the water, sandy grit sticking to my clothes, and chin. My injured leg throbbed madly when I brought it up onto the sand-bank. I had to verbally coach myself into turning over so that I could sit against the rock and look out to sea. I was in the estuary, and the tide was in. It would be impossible for me to walk round the base of the cliff until it had gone out again, but how long would that take? I closed my eyes and sucked in breath after deep breath.

The important thing was that I had escaped.

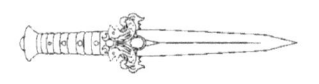

The night was freezing. I curled up against the rock, the water lapping at my toes as I struggled to stay warm, teeth chattering, and shivers wracking my body until I genuinely believed I was going to die there. Blood drenched my trouser leg. I had tried to bind it with a piece of cloth from my t-shirt, and some spare shoelaces I kept in my bag, but it did nothing to help with the pain. Blood stained my face down one side, and the hole there felt so big that I half-expected to hear the wind whistle through it. I had thrown a large pebble into the water, and watched it sink out of sight. The water was deep, and although I was a strong swimmer, I was in too much agony to make it to the beach on the other side, especially not when the waves were crashing upon the jagged boulders, disguising their treacherous claws under the surf. It would be a swim to my death if I chose to do that.

Instead, I brought my knees to my chest, and chose to remain on the sand-bank. The only good thing to come out of this was that my camera seemed to be okay. It had gotten wet, but it was still functioning, and the film roll was waterproof anyway. I held it in my lap, anxious not to drop it in the water again. Darkness quickly consumed everything in sight, and I saw the blinking of the buoys beyond, much closer to them than I had ever been at this hour. It was so quiet, so peaceful.

Finally, I dozed off.

The rhythmic slapping of the water roused me from a dreamless sleep. My eyelids were glued together, and I rubbed at them with my wrist until I was able to part my lids to the sunlight that was now creeping over the bay as the morning floated in. My body ached in ways I didn't know it could. The tide was starting to go out. I could see the sand beginning to emerge, and soon a pathway would rise out of the water, allowing me to walk round the bottom of the cliff.

I lay there, head resting against the granite, my sore tongue licking at my cracked lips. I had no water left to drink. There was Maredudd's cider, but I had bought it for him, and I couldn't bring myself to drink it, not when I owed him an apology. I watched the waves rising, and falling, thinking how beautiful, and endless they were in their shapes, and forms. Maybe it was the exhaustion talking, but I began to have conversations with myself in my head, and before long I realised I was saying the words out loud.

"Not doing this again," I muttered to myself. "The last time you're going out in the woods alone. You damn near got yourself killed."

I startled when I saw something bob up from beneath the ebbing waters. It ducked down again with a plop, resurfacing closer. The sunlight glinted on its large round eyes, and I realised it was a big seal, its dome-shaped head glistening with seawater as it stayed afloat before me. I smiled gently. It was the first time I had seen a seal in this area, and it cheered me considerably to see its sweet face keeping me company. It dove down again, out of sight. I was alone once more.

I closed my eyes, the last remnants of spare liquid in my body accumulating into solitary tears in the corners of my crusty eyelids. I was so stupid. Why did I do this to myself? Maybe Mum and Maredudd were right, and I needed to be protected. Stupid Owen.

Suddenly, I noticed something dark moving through the water towards me, and I thought it must have been the seal. But it wasn't the seal. The shape began to look distinctly human. I breathed in sharply, preparing to run, but unable to summon the energy to get up, so I just stared at it dumbly, my mouth open, and eyes dazed. A head rose up out of the water, black tendrils of hair sticking to its every contour, running down like a mass of ink strokes onto bare shoulders, and a hair-smattered chest. Veiny arms pulled it up onto the sand, one hand tossing a folded wad of rubbery leather at my feet, before the strong, muscular torso followed, and then the knees knelt upon the sand.

I couldn't move, only my throat clenched as I attempted to swallow. Slowly, the stranger rose, and I saw his brown skin, droplets of seawater showering from his black body hair, the pink scarring on his lower leg starkly pale against his swarthy complexion. I was so dumbfounded by what I was seeing that I didn't even register it as Maredudd until he had parted the soaked curtains of his hair to reveal his face. His green eyes looked down at me, his face wearing an expression of alarm, apparently unconcerned with his obvious nudity. My eyes dropped to the organ that began where his groin ended. Typical, I felt a blush heating my cheeks.

"Owen," he breathed, and dropped to his knees before me, his eyes large, and questioning, his hands reaching to cup my face.

"M—Maredudd..." I stammered, looking up at him like he was a god just descended from the heavens to rescue me. I looked down at the pelt he was kneeling on. A seal pelt.

"What are you doing by yere? What's happened? You're bleeding!" he cried when he noticed my injuries. I groaned when he prodded at the gash in my head.

"I fell into the water. I've been here all night." I whimpered, relieved when he leaned back to look into my eyes again.

"We need to get you to safety. Do you think you can swim?" he asked, but I shook my head. He bit his lip, gnawing on it as he looked around helplessly for a clue. "All right then, I'll swim, and you hold onto me."

"Are you sure?"My cheeks coloured further at the thought of putting my arms around his naked body. Fortunately, he was thinking more of my wellbeing and not about sexy things like I was. Amazing how I even managed after the night I'd had.

"Yes. Come on." He urged, taking my arm and trying to get me to rise.

"Wait—wait a second." I stopped him, and he relaxed his grip on my wrist. I reached towards him, placing my hand on his stubbled cheek. My heart was starting to race again, but this time not from fear, and I wasn't sure I was making much sense when I started to speak. "I'm really sorry for how I acted the other night. I was a jerk. I didn't mean what I said... I've missed you so much, and I should have told Mum to let you in. Please don't be angry at me."

"I was never angry." He made a small, wry smile. His hand closed over mine, and he leaned his head into my touch, his eyes half-closing. "I understand why it upset you, and I know I should have trusted you enough to tell you what I was doing. I won't do that anymore, I promise."

I smiled optimistically, my heart filled with hope again.

"I'm very much in love with you, Owen. There are times when I'm alone, and it becomes unbearable to know you are on the other side of the bay, within reach of me, but I can't be with you. I can't think or focus on anything when I'm working. I can't even meditate without losing control of my thoughts, and finding you filling my head," he whispered, his eyes closed, perhaps because he was too shy to look at me. "I don't want to work or go anywhere or see anyone. Only you. I only want to be with you."

"Maredudd... That's so sweet." I grinned, those tears that had initially formed in my eyes suddenly multiplying to the point where I felt them bubbling over and trying to get free. I pulled him towards me by the hand, reaching to put my arms around his neck and hugging him so tightly that my arms hurt. His hard body was moist with seawater, but I didn't care.

I had almost forgotten he was naked too. Was he a Selkie after all?

The swim back to the beach was difficult and frightening, and I was panicking the whole time whilst trying to keep my mouth shut should a wave suddenly wash into it and gag me. The current was choppy, and sent us bobbing up and down, but Maredudd was strong, and determined. I was terrified that we would be swept up onto the rocks. I tried to keep my camera from getting submerged again, to little avail. When the beach was in sight, I calmed somewhat, and then the new struggle began when he dragged me up onto the sand, and took hold of my hands, pulling me to my feet with an effortful grunt. I couldn't put my weight on my leg, agony shooting up into my knee from the source of the pain, and I had no idea how I was going to make either the long walk to the other end of the beach or the steep path up to Maredudd's cottage. Once he had tied the seal pelt around his waist, he urged me towards the cliff path, my arm round his neck so that he could keep me balanced, and every time I put pressure on my injury, I cried out in agony.

"No—no, Maredudd. I'm not gonna make it up the

cliff, it's too far." I tried to stop him from leading me up there.

"We're not going to the cliff. We're going to the cave, it's just by yere, not far at all," he told me, pausing only to look me in the eyes.

"What for?" I stared confusedly.

"We're going to see my dad," he replied simply before urging me on again.

"Your dad lives in the *cave*?" I was aghast, but he didn't reply as we reached the bottom of the path, and began climbing the steep, winding track up the side of the cliff.

Looking over the edge whilst knowing that losing my footing could easily result in my falling over to the rocks below made me very anxious indeed, and I clung to Maredudd tightly, trying not to focus on the pain, and instead watching where I was putting my feet. The ledge towards the mouth of the cage was the difficult part. He edged across first, and reached for me, taking me by the hands, and helping me to limp over to the other side. I found myself standing beneath the roof of the cave entrance, droplets of water ran-off from the cliffs above dripping into a small pool by my feet. It was dark within, but the ceiling was high enough to be able to walk upright, a pale layer of soft sand covering the ground. I had never been in here before, and if I wasn't feeling so awful, I might have been excited to explore it. Maredudd took my arm and put it round his shoulders again.

"Not far now. I will warn you, my dad can look a little... alarming, at first. But don't be afraid of him. He's very kind," he said in a hush as we entered the cave tunnel.

"What do you mean, alarming?" I whispered, unsure of what to think. Was he disfigured in some way? Mum hadn't said anything about that when she spoke of him before. I was expecting a crooked old man with a hunchback and an eye-patch to come hobbling out round the corner.

"He looks different to you or I," he answered simply.

I frowned, bewildered, as the tunnel came to a junction, and he chose the right-hand turning, moving us further away from the sunlight beaming down into the hole. The air became distinctly cooler, and no longer smelled of seaweed, and salt. Instead, there drifted a lingering scent of old incense, and burned wood, and close by I saw a flickering orange light. A creaky iron lantern was hanging from a stalagmite that had long since dried out, turning into a white unicorn horn jutting from the rocky ground, and the lamp gave off a timid glow in the shadows of the tunnel.

"Maredudd?" I said, my voice falling to a whisper. I don't know why I felt like I couldn't speak at a normal volume. It was so quiet here except for the occasional sound of dripping echoing in the dark.

"Hmm?" he grunted in response.

"The seal I saw in the water. That was you, wasn't it," I asked.

He didn't reply. I looked up at his face, at his thick eyelashes partially obscuring his eyes from me. Finally, he spoke."Yes, that was me. I was surprised you figured it out in the beginning," he confessed, seeming slightly embarrassed that he had been revealed for what he was.

"So are you a Selkie, then?"

"No, not by the standards of the old folk tales. I'm only a witch, and a witch may turn into whatever animal they are capable of getting their hands on," he replied.

I contemplated his words, my brain coming alive with all the possibilities. I wondered if one day he would teach me to turn into an animal too.

"How do you do it?" I eventually questioned.

He chuckled, apparently having expected me to ask such a thing. "With a salve, and the pelt of the animal you wish to become. The salve is made from several ingredients, including water from the footprint of the animal. The transformation is temporary, but can last several nights if you stay dry. It has been used for centuries by witches to turn into birds for fast travel."

"That's amazing," I murmured to myself.

"We're almost there. Dad's home is just in this chamber yere." He gestured ahead of us to where I could see the tunnel opening up into a much larger room. Light was bouncing down the lumpy, pockmarked surface of the rock walls, shining on our faces. I was grateful the ground was so flat so that it was easier for me to walk.

The smell of incense became much stronger as we neared the doorway, and when we stepped through, I discovered the quaint, cluttered home that was hidden away. An array of different household items lined the natural shelf in the rock-face, burning candles melted into upright positions all along the edge, their bobbing light illuminating what would have otherwise been in total darkness. The room was rectangular in shape, odd horns of rock jutting up out of the ground in some corners, which had been utilised for hanging things up, the one nearest me was being used to drape clothes over. There was a tiny copper stove against the wall, its chimney pipe threaded up through a hole in the ceiling, and embers glowed within its grated belly, emitting a comfortable warmth across the floor.

There was no sand here, the stony ground dry, and smooth underfoot, a woven rug spread out in the middle of the room that was threadbare with many years of feet walking across it. Facing the stove was a bed that had been built out of discarded factory pallets, heaped to overflowing with duvets, coverlets, and cushions, an old-fashioned nightcap laid out neatly on the little wooden cabinet beside it, accompanied by a pair of spectacles, and a small, tatty-looking handbook. Bunches of herbs were hung from string in various places to dry out, and I accidentally bumped my head on a bouquet of lavender as Maredudd helped me towards the bed. I was apprehensive about sitting down on his dad's bed in my damp, filthy clothes, so he pulled a holey towel out of the large wooden trunk at the end of the nest and laid it out for me to sit on.

"I think he's gone round by the other side, probably meditating or something. I'll go and find him. I'm afraid my skills in first aid are lacking," he admitted with an awkward grin.

"No, no, don't leave me." I clutched at his wrist. To be honest, I was quite afraid about being here. It was gloomy and strange, like something out of a creepy fantasy movie.

"It's fine, don't worry. I'll be back now in a minute, and Dad will take a look at your injuries," he reassured me, bending to plant a kiss on my forehead that instantly silenced me. He stroked my hair, and leaned closer still, kissing my ear, and my jaw before finally capturing my mouth, coaxing a compliant whimper from my throat. When he spoke, his voice was husky. "I wouldn't leave you here if I thought you'd come to harm. Now don't move, I'll be back."

"Okay," I mumbled, aware that my cheeks had become hot.

I watched him walk off through the other narrow doorway that adjoined the chamber, his padding footfalls disappearing into the darkness. He looked like a wild-man with the pelt wrapped round his waist, his attractive torso dominating my thoughts as I sat there warming my toes before the stove. It was cosy here, at least. Minutes passed by. I heard the metallic ticking of a wind-up clock somewhere, but I couldn't see it. The shelf above the stove was crammed full of jars, many of them without any labels on. I wondered how he figured out which ingredient to use, and if he ever got them mixed up in his cooking. I chuckled to myself, but it soon turned to a sigh.

Suddenly, I heard voices nearby. Maredudd was talking to his dad. I heard their feet striking the ground, and the dragging of something soft over the rocks. The other voice was smooth, as silken, and rich as milk chocolate. I could imagine him speaking on some kind of posh food advert. It wasn't the kind of voice I had expected to hear, as he didn't sound very old at all, perhaps around the same age as Maredudd was, and his accent was distinctly English, but with an edge of other accents blended in, and a slight sliver of upper-class articulation. Their voices echoed, bounding off the uneven walls, making it difficult to understand what they were saying to each other until they reached the entrance to the room where I waited. Maredudd reappeared, and my smile lit up once more as he beamed at me, coming over to the bed, and kneeling at my side, his hand cupping the bottom of my back and the other on my wrist. A dark figure emerged from the shadows of the tunnel, and I stared, wide-eyed as it came closer.

He was tall, but stooped, his entire form draped in a long grey cloak that covered him from head to toe, and as he stepped closer, I caught glimpses of black feet beneath the hem of the fabric. They didn't look human at all. I stared, not even realising that I wasn't blinking. The feet looked reptilian in appearance, the skin rough and scaly. Long, curled claws, as black and shiny as obsidian, grew from the toes. Behind him, the dragging sound I had heard moments ago was coming from a tapered tail, the end of which occasionally lifted up from the ground as he moved. Only when he had come into the corona of candlelight was I able to see the head tucked beneath the hood of the cloak, and when I witnessed his face, I was unable to restrain an astonished gasp.

What had first looked like a mask turned out to be

his true visage. His skin was white as parchment, without blemish or bump, beautiful, and masculine as a Greek statue with almond-shaped eyes, a large aquiline nose, and perfectly shaped lips. He really did look like a statue that had come to life. Either side of his face there tumbled wavy strands of ebony hair, some of it tucked inside the cloak, and the rest of it falling out onto his chest. His eyes appeared to give off a glow all their own as I was able to see them within the shadow cast by the hood, the royal blue irises enclosing his strange, oval pupils that were remarkably similar in shape to that of a goat. A gnarled, taloned hand was lifted from beneath the cloak, and I let out a cry, flinching when the rough thumb, and index finger touched my damaged forehead.

"It's okay, don't be afraid," Maredudd whispered to me, nuzzling my ear with his lips.

"The wound is shallow. You are fortunate indeed," the stranger answered in his calm, sleek voice as he turned away, and moved over to the cluster of cabinets on the other side of the room.

"His leg is injured too, a bite wound," Maredudd told him.

"If you'd be so kind as to remove his trousers, we will do well," the cloaked man replied coolly.

Maredudd looked up at me, and I shook my head quickly. I had never seen such a bizarre-looking man before. Was he even human? Was it just a disguise, like Maredudd wearing the seal pelt?

"I'm going to help you take your trousers off, okay?" he said to me gently, but I shook my head again, and he smiled. "It's okay, he's going to make your injuries better. I promise it won't hurt. Now would I bring you yere if I thought it was going to make you suffer?"

I looked him in the eyes and saw his sincerity. Where were my manners? I was being so rude acting like this in front of his father, someone he had brought me to meet because he trusted that I would be open-minded. I took a deep breath.

"Okay, I can do it myself," I mumbled weakly.

Maredudd got up and stepped away, allowing me space to inch my trousers down my legs, whimpering pleadingly as I peeled the fabric away from the oozing bite in my calf. The fabric I had tied around it was drenched with blood and had glued itself to the inside of my clothes overnight, making removing it frustratingly painful. Maredudd returned to my side having pulled on a vest, and shorts, and he sat down beside me, leaning forward to help me shirk the dirty trousers from my ankles, and pulling off my socks with it. I flinched again when his dad appeared in front of me, a huge dark shape blocking out the light from the candles. His pale face peered down at me from beneath the hood, and I stared back, petrified.

"My name is Morcant, by the way. I believe we haven't had the pleasure of an introduction just yet. You must be Owen," he said, holding out one of his clawed hands. I looked down at it, at the thick knuckles, the rough, scaly flesh, the sickle-shaped nails. It was like a black crocodile's paw.

"Y—yes, my name's Owen. I—I'm M—Maredudd's friend." I was unable to stop my teeth from chattering as I lifted my hand, and took hold of his, surprised by how warm it was in my grip.

"He has spoken of you many times. One almost feels as though one knows you already through my son's cheerful tales. It's wonderful to meet you in person finally. I apologise for not meeting sooner. Rather, I was concerned that my ghoulish countenance would frighten you off," he confessed, his handsome face cracking into a friendly smile as he patted my hand gently before releasing it.

"Here, Dad. I've brought your stool," Maredudd said, having risen from his spot and fetched a wooden chair from beside the wall.

"Oh, thank you dearly," he replied as he perched on it. He placed a wooden box on the towel beside me.

I felt very bare sitting before him trouser-less, my face glowing with embarrassment. His voice was so sweet and gentlemanly, completely different to whatever body was swathed in the fabric he wore to hide himself. It was almost sad that someone so kind had to live hidden away in a cave.

"Why do you look... the way you do?" I hesitated to ask for fear that I would offend him.

Maredudd looked at us over his shoulder as he placed a pan of water on the stove to heat it up, an amused smirk on his face. Morcant chuckled, lifting my injured leg, and resting my ankle upon his knee. His tail slapped the ground in search of a more comfortable position.

"I did not always look this way. I was human once," he replied, reaching for his spectacles and sliding them upon his nose. I stared, fixated, as he pushed back his hood to reveal long, glistening hair, the two points of his small ears poking out the sides.

"Did somebody put a curse on you?" I asked cautiously, his unusual face doing well to distract me as he examined my wound.

"It is both a curse and a blessing." He smiled at me, squinting slightly through his gold-rimmed glasses that served to make him look strangely like Maredudd did. "The Goddess gave me this body. Bodies are transient vehicles designed to navigate this world. The soul is immortal. I do not mind looking this way, because it is my soul that is eternal. An ugly soul is an eternity of ugliness. I like to think mine is quite beautiful."

"Ah!" I jerked away from him when his claws parted the split in my flesh. I was horrified when he lifted a tiny white speck, and when I peered closer, I saw the milky body of a maggot.

"You are very fortunate indeed. Though one does

have to ask how you managed to acquire a maggot within a clean wound?" he asked me as he turned and deposited the creature in the flames of the stove. "In fact, one does have to ask how you acquired these wounds in the first place?"

"I was chased by the beast. It bit me as I was escaping, and I fell into the estuary," I confessed, feeling like an idiot. "There was a big hole in the ground full of dead animals... I landed in them. I was covered in maggots."

"Mm-hmm." He hummed in acknowledgement.

I watched his surprisingly precise hands working, checking the wound closely for any debris, and anymore rogue maggots that might have hidden in there. Maredudd brought me a cup of herbal tea after I had watched him brew it on the stove, wringing out some strips of what looked like wood bark, then adding a scoop of a greyish powder, and a drop of honey before handing it to me. I drank it even though the flavour left much to be desired. I started to feel a bit woozy, becoming more, and more lightheaded, and relaxed as I reached the bottom of the tin mug. Maredudd came to perch beside me with another pan of hot water, holding it steady for his father while he cleaned the wounds thoroughly.

"Lay back, it's better if you don't look," Maredudd told me, guiding me to lay down as he took the empty mug from my hand.

I gazed up at the dancing shadows on the ceiling, my vision becoming cloudy, and my head filling with fog. There was a tingling sensation of numbness in my fingers, and toes. Maredudd's hand stroked my forehead soothingly, coaxing me into a dreamlike state, almost like sleep, except my eyes were open, and I could hear their voices talking softly beside me. Time disappeared. My breath became deep, my heartbeat slowed, and the tingling sensation moved to my lips, and tongue, even my eyelids, making blinking feel very funny indeed. I wondered how long they were going to take to fix me up—an hour? Two hours? It didn't feel like they were doing much down there. I struggled to lift my head, and when I did, I saw Maredudd sitting on the stool, and Morcant in a rocking chair by the stove, both of them talking mutedly over mugs of tea.

I didn't recall them having moved me, but somehow I had been laid out the correct way upon the bed, a soft cover placed gently over my body, and when I looked down, I saw that my leg had been firmly bandaged. A bandage was wrapped around my head too, as I discovered when I raised my hand to search for the wound. I didn't remember them even touching my head. I closed my eyes. It had seemed like minutes I had been laying there waiting for them to start sorting me out. Suddenly, I felt very disoriented, and I calmed myself to the gentle murmurings they made as they chuckled and whispered to each other. The pain-relieving properties of the tea were still swimming in my blood stream, and I allowed it to transport me to a deep, relaxing sleep.

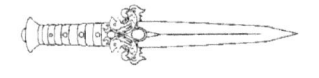

It was impossible for me to tell how much time had passed or whether it was day or night. I opened my eyes to the same welcoming glow of the candlelight, feeling all the better for my nap. My wounds were throbbing somewhat uncomfortably, but not painfully, so that was a plus. I opened my eyes, and yawned, turning my head to see where the other two had gone. Maredudd had departed the scene for as far as I could see, but Morcant was still sitting in his rocking chair, smoking a pipe as he gazed into the flames that danced within the stove. He had removed the cloak, and instead I was able to see that he wore the clothes of a Victorian gentleman, a dark green waistcoat over white shirt, and brown trousers, the chain of a pocket watch glinting in the candlelight. His body looked thick, and hard, clearly made of solid muscle, thighs strong enough to crush a watermelon, and his clawed hands, and feet were now properly visible to my eyes. I saw how the smooth whiteness of his face began at his jawline and went right up to his hairline. The rest of his skin was the colour of coal. His head turned slowly to look at me as I groaned, lifting my body upright, and shuffling back on the bed so that I could sit up aided by the many cushions. His pale pink lips curved into a smile, and I saw his white teeth as he removed the end of his pipe, smoke curling from his nostrils.

"How are you feeling?" he asked softly. His voice made me want to go back to sleep, how peaceful, and lustrous it was.

"Much better, thank you," I replied, rubbing the sleep from my eyes with my knuckle. "I'm sorry for how I acted earlier. I didn't mean to. I hope I didn't offend you."

"No offense taken, my friend." He sucked on the pipe, smoke pluming from the corners of his mouth as he rocked in his chair. "I'm used to that sort of response. Compared to others, I found it a rather muted affair. I hope that you will see, I am not a barbarian."

"Oh—I—I don't think you look like a barbarian at all. You just look... strange." I tried to choose my words carefully. I wasn't afraid of him now, but instead I was sensitive to his looks, and didn't want to say something stupid, especially when Maredudd wasn't here to defend me.

His chuckle was deep, fluid. He said nothing.

"I'm not gonna turn into a werewolf am I? From the bite? I won't turn into a beast too?" I asked, something that had been on my mind since the attack had occurred.

"I do not think so. If that were the case, we would have two creatures on our hands, and that would be rather a difficult situation."

I watched him rocking back and forth slowly, his eyes half-mast, gazing up at the ceiling momentarily before he looked at me again. It seemed he was waiting for me to talk again, choosing his words wisely.

"There is something in your bag that has been catching my attention since you arrived here. But it would be rude of me to look through your personal belongings. I would be thrilled if you could show me what it is," he eventually answered.

"There's nothing important in my bag. Only hiking stuff. Oh, and a bottle of cider for Maredudd," I replied, trying to think what would be so interesting to him. "My camera, perhaps?"

"No, it is much smaller than a camera." He breathed.

"Can... Can you get my bag for me, please? I will look for you," I asked.

He rose gracefully from the chair and shuffled over to where Maredudd had placed my bag atop the trunk, lifting it, and bringing it over to me. He placed it on my lap, before perching on the edge of the bed. My eyes were drawn to his long tail as it unfurled, and lay twitching from side to side on the duvet while I opened my bag, and started going through it, lifting out different things so that he could see them, but he only shook his head.

"That! That is it," he exclaimed suddenly, pressing a claw upon my house key as I took it out of the bag pocket. "May I examine it?"

"Sure...?" I was confused as I held it out for him to take.

He enveloped the small, bronze key in his palm, and brought it to his chest, his eyes closing for a moment. He breathed deeply, smiling.

"Yes. It's as I thought. Wanda's work." He made an amused laugh, and offered it back to me, his open hand before my face. "Your mother has blessed this for you. It is functioning as an amulet of protection. I recommend that you wear it at your throat where it will be safe from loss."

"Oh..." was all I could manage as I took the key and looked at it. To my eyes it just looked like a regular house key... But then I thought of all the times I had felt it in my pocket, seeming to radiate a warmth all of its own.

"Oh, and this..." Morcant peered into my backpack, and reached in. He took out the Witch's Ladder, and I looked upon it with a defeated expression.

"Yeah, I guess it didn't work, after all."

"No, I'm rather sure that it did. But I would like to hang onto it, if that is all right with you?" he asked in a tone that made me believe he wouldn't take no for an answer.

"Sure, it's not like I'm gonna use it for anything." I shrugged, watching as he tucked it away in one of his pockets whilst he rose, and turned from the bed.

"Hmm. You know, I do miss Wenda. It's been a long time. I would be overjoyed to see her again. Perhaps you could persuade her to visit," he suggested as he went over to the stove, picking up a large bottle of water, and pouring some into the tin mug for me. "I always did have fond eyes for Wenda. She was kind, and caring, and made sure Maredudd got to school on time..."

"Mum used to take Maredudd to school?" I smirked, trying to imagine what they must have looked like back then.

"Oh yes. Somebody had to. I couldn't very well turn up at the school gates looking the way I do," he replied, holding the mug hovering before me until I accepted it.

"What about Dad—I mean, Evan? You knew Evan too, didn't you?" I asked with a grin, beginning to feel excited at the prospect of this unusual man having known both my parents.

"Evan was my fourth student." He nodded, returning to pour himself a cup of water before he sat back down in his rocking chair. "Maredudd was my first, and in between were Wenda and Geraint."

"You taught Geraint to be a witch too?" I peered at him over the mug as I sipped some of the lukewarm water. It had an odd taste, slightly flowery.

"Yes..." He sighed, licking his lips before drawing on his pipe once more. "I took Geraint in when he was a young man. Overflowing with intelligence, yet troubled with an inconsolable anger. I tried my best for him."

I stared, listening to him speak with fascination. All of these things Mum had never told me, things from their past I might never have found out about if I had never come here.

"Geraint's father left when he was a babe. His mother died young with a tumour in her throat. The village did little to help him when he found himself homeless. I found him while walking, late one night, shivering, and half-dead on the beach after trying to drown himself," he continued, his eyes glancing at me as he sensed my interest in the topic. "Clothes folded neatly on the shore, and not a penny in his wallet. The Goddess demands that I care for those who need me. To say no would be to disobey her desires. She has made a father of me many times. Geraint was one of those times."

I let what he had said sink in awhile, trying to imagine young Geraint filled with despair, despair enough that he would try to kill himself. Geraint was a dark pool whose bottom I could not fathom, and I was unable to see beyond the very surface, or at least just below it. There had to be a reason why he was how he was, and perhaps this was it.

"Who is this Goddess you keep mentioning? What's

her name?" I changed subject, sensing that Morcant's mood was becoming dampened by it.

"She has many names. Ostara, Isis, Mary, to name a few. Many incarnations, many faces. The only face that has been consistent is the face of the moon, for she is the Goddess of the moon," he explained, not seeming at all annoyed that I had asked.

"What do you call her by?"

"Ostara," he replied with a slightly sheepish smile as though he was naming his secret girlfriend.

"But I thought Ostara was the goddess of the dawn, and spring-time?" I was baffled by the name he had chosen.

"As I said, she has many faces. As in Hindu mythology, the gods wear avatars. In my experience, there are but four gods, all of them primarily genderless, but often taking the form of males, and females, and all of them assuming many forms in different cultures. Ostara is the name I called her in the beginning, when I was young and foolish. She simply tolerates it these days." He chuckled, the glow in his eyes flashing brighter for a moment. The way he talked about her was like a man speaking of a wife with which he had shared a home for many years, both of them putting up with each other's quirks.

"So who are the other gods then?" I grinned, tilting my head. Everything he was telling me flew in the face of what I had studied in books, and essays.

"They are the four elements, of course," he said like it was the most obvious answer. "My mistress is the element of Air, the moon. There is Enki, also commonly known as the Leviathan, of the element Water. Lucifer, or Prometheus, the light-bearer, who is the element of Fire. And lastly, Cernunnos, of the Earth. All have many names, and forms. Many occultists worship the elements as they are, Earth, Air, Fire, and Water, without these embellishments. But my Goddess has become fond of the frilly approach I tend to her with, and so it remains."

My grin turned into a lazy smile as I listened to him talk. "Is she easy to please?"

He made a scoffing laugh under his breath, and looked away from me, his shyness surprising me, which only made me all the more curious.

"Yes, sometimes," he eventually murmured before sipping some water.

"Is she why you aren't married? Do you have a partner or something?" I questioned gently, worried I might touch on a sore nerve.

"I have no lovers. Not anymore. I was arranged to marry once, but alas, it never happened. It has been many years since I lay with another mortal," he whispered, the firelight flickering in his eyes as he looked at the stove.

"How many?" I pressed, surprised that he was willing to share this with me.

He glanced across at me blank-faced for a moment before he smirked again and shook his head slowly. "Decades. Many, many decades. More than the sum of your days, and Maredudd's combined."

I stared at him dumbfounded, my eyes near to bulging with amazement. This appeared to entertain him because he laughed and slapped a taloned hand upon his knee.

"I bid you, name a woman willing to lay with a body such as this." He gestured to his strange form jokingly, but I sensed an edge of sadness to his voice. "There are no such females for me. Besides, the company of a handsome woman would distract me from my work. My Goddess might be displeased."

"Am I distracting Maredudd from his work?" I mumbled, worried that I was getting the way of his studies in witchcraft.

Morcant shook his head, smiling. "Not at all.

Maredudd will not live this life. He needs the warmth of a soul mate. He would not fare taking in nought, but dirt, seawater, oxygen, and sunlight. He has much love to offer, and I think it is better for him that he has you. I have seen the way he looks when he speaks your name."

My cheeks warmed as I smiled back at him, eyes twinkling with joy. Mum had said a similar thing about me. The way we looked when we talked about each other. Was it really noticeable? How many people had noticed it? I felt suddenly embarrassed.

"I love him," I whispered, looking down at my hand clasping the tin cup. "I love him very much."

"Then do not trouble yourself worrying that he does not feel the same," he told me sincerely. "I am certain he does you also."

Eleven

"Here." I offered Maredudd the somewhat tatty-looking bottle of cider. The label had become water-damaged after my foray in the estuary, and the glass was covered in scratches, and scrapes. He accepted it with a bemused grin, his eyes glancing up at me once it was in his hand.

"What's this for?" he asked.

We were standing in his kitchen, the evening sunshine glowing red through the windows. We had spent the day talking to Morcant in his hidden lair, after Maredudd had returned with two bags full of Chinese takeaway. I was surprised that Morcant had somewhat of a penchant for takeaway food. He had sat there scoffing it, and apologising for his bad manners the entire time, scooping it down his throat like he hadn't eaten in days, and not even stopping to wipe his chin. Apparently, he was also unashamedly addicted to marshmallow teacakes. I never would have guessed it to look at him, although he did say he would have to pay for this sinful meal in other ways later, most likely by fasting.

Maredudd said he often went days eating only grass, and soil, and drinking the seawater from the beach. The rest of his sustenance came from the sunlight, and wind. I thought he was like some sort of exotic plant. His life seemed complicated, and difficult despite his simplistic living arrangements. I had forgotten about the cider in my bag until we had made it back to the cottage and realised the clinking noise I had heard on the long trek up the cliff path was actually the bottle rocking around amongst my other belongings.

"It's an apology. I'm sorry I couldn't get it to you in a better condition, but I just wanted to say sorry for the way I acted the other night." I scratched at the back of my head shyly.

"Don't be silly. There was nothing to be sorry for. You apologised to me earlier. That was plenty enough." He shook his head at me as he moved closer and bent to my eye level so that he could kiss my cheek. "We'll share the bottle between us."

And so we did.

We had a light evening meal, and Maredudd invited me out onto the lawn overlooking the beach, putting down a blanket so that we could both sit, and meditate. There was a calm breeze, enough to keep the birds airborne as they seemed not to move very much over the horizon, and a few wind-surfers were taking their chances on the lethargic waves. I collapsed down onto my backside like an uncouth child while he slunk down into a perfect cross-legged position, and when I looked at his flowing hair, and peaceful smile, I was reminded of the Shiva statue in the guest bedroom. The sunlight on his handsome features, the wind turning his wavy hair about his shoulders as he closed his eyes, his expression softening. It was hard for me to close my own eyes and empty my mind with him sitting there looking like that. I tried to focus for a time, taking a deep breath, and sending my thoughts towards every inch of my body, but then I started thinking about every inch of his, and ended up opening my eyes again. When I glanced towards him, his eyes opened, and he looked at me, the both of us laughing. It seemed doing such a mental exercise was proving difficult when we were in close company. We ended up laying side by side, gazing up at the lilac clouds floating overhead, then on our sides face to face, gazing at each other, my fingers twirling strands of his hair into curls. Night began to drift in, and the sky darkened. We retired indoors.

This time, I managed to fall asleep lying beside him. My injuries gave me some pain, but nothing substantial, and not enough to make me restless. Whatever tea Morcant kept giving me throughout the day had done a lot to restore my energy. I was feeling rather well despite the difficult week I had had, and for a long time I lay awake staring out at the stars through the open window. This house felt so different to Geraint's house. It was still, placid. I didn't feel like an intruder. My heart was given a chance to settle into a nest where it felt it belonged. I wondered if Maredudd would allow me to live here with him, and if he did, when? Was I moving too fast? Yes, probably. But I couldn't help fantasising.

I woke hazily, my eyelids fluttering. It was still dark, and when I glanced at the clock on the bedside cabinet I realised I had only been asleep for a couple of hours. I didn't feel tired though. I turned onto my side, and found Maredudd facing me, eyes closed, and lips slightly parted as he dreamed. I wished I had my camera to take a photo of him.

"Are you okay?" he whispered suddenly, causing me to startle.

"Oh—I'm fine, I'm just not sleepy," I whispered back, feeling silly. He probably didn't appreciate me laying there, staring at him.

He didn't open his eyes. I felt movement under the cover, shivering when I felt his hand slip up onto my hip, his fingertips inching under my pyjama shirt. I decided to be brave, and shuffled closer to him, resting my head in the crook of his outstretched arm so that I could brush my nose against his. His hand moved to my back, stroking me slowly, his rough fingertips feeling my skin, and raking through my body hair. I closed my eyes, breathing a deep sigh. Taking this as a sign that I was relaxed, his hand moved down toward my backside. I nestled closer still, shyly tilting back my head so that I could kiss his mouth like a timid devotee worshipping a stone idol. I felt the warmth coming from his cheeks, and yet his breath was cool. Only when he kissed me back did I feel the heat of his tongue.

I wanted to give him permission to touch me, but I didn't know how to without saying it. What if I tried to touch him? Would that give him the right idea? My hands were hesitant, clenching into fists before opening again. I needed to. More than anything, I needed to. Not just because I wanted to communicate with him, but because I had spent so long staring at him longingly when he was right here in front of me. His eyes opened when he felt me unbuttoning his pyjama shirt. I flinched, letting out a nervous whimper.

"It's okay." He leaned in to kiss me again, and helped me unbutton the shirt. I stared, eyes wide, as I watched him shrug it off and throw it to the floor before he returned to me, his hard, bare chest rising, and falling deeply under my hands.

"Sorry," I mumbled, suddenly afraid of making a fool of myself.

"Come here." He tugged at my shirt, and I allowed him to pull it off over my head, the chill air making me shiver until I was back in his arms.

"You can say no any time," he reassured me, his voice a delicate murmur in my ear. "Just tell me."

"I don't want to say no. I want to say yes," I replied, unable to make eye contact with him.

"I'll be gentle," he promised.

"I know. You don't have to worry about hurting me."

His hand stroked over my chest, fingertips searching out the scars there, but I didn't care. I wanted him to recognise the injuries I had healed from, the wounds that had shaped me. I could feel his scars too, even on his torso, old wounds that had damaged him in his youth. He gripped my hips firmly, and pulled me against him, his kiss banishing any questions or words that may have attempted to rise from my throat. All that emerged was a breathless cry of urgency. His thumbs curled round the waistband of my trousers and slid them down my backside so that he could grip my exposed buttocks tightly, and I thought I would lose my mind right there and then.

He turned onto his back and, struggling out of my trousers, I climbed atop him, pressing him into the bed, my fingers tangled in the mass of his wild hair, my bare skin sensing every point of contact with his, and only when he finally wriggled free of his own trousers did I pull him down upon me, offering myself to him, a sacrificial virgin. He was a powerful god, but a merciful one. My nails scored lines in the knotted muscle of his back, and his lips left warm, damp kisses on my throat as we merged into a single entity. At first there was no sound, or perhaps I was deaf to it? But soon I became aware of the ragged moans of hysteria I was making, and the long sighs of abandon he whispered into my crying mouth.

The warmth I had felt before, of our energies reaching for each other, had become much more than the meeting of two candlewicks. It had burst into a roaring fire, an unimaginable heat that sweltered, and simmered between us. I knew after this that I would never be the same. I couldn't imagine a life after this without him inside me. I would give up everything to be with him this way, again and again, first, last, and always.

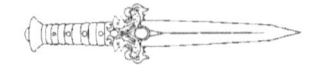

"Thank you very much, have a nice day both." The lady behind the counter smiled at me, and Maredudd as I picked up the wallet of fresh photo prints from the counter. The paper was warm in my hands, and I clutched them to my chest as I followed at Maredudd's shoulder to the door of the store and stepped out into the high-ceilinged coolness of the shopping centre.

"Let's find somewhere to sit, and we'll take a look," he suggested, hands in the pockets of his khaki trousers. He looked so smart in his black polo shirt, his long hair pulled back in a high ponytail, and his glasses sitting on the bridge of his nose. I felt so undeserving of his company when he looked the way he did.

"I could do with some coffee. I'm nervous that the last snap didn't catch anything. I can't even remember if the flash went off," I mumbled as I looked this way, and that at the people passing by with their shopping bags, and prams.

We had caught a bus into town and gone into the nearest store capable of developing my film, before going for a little meander as we waited an hour for them to be processed. Maredudd took me to a stall in the market where he liked to buy incense, and candles, and I bought him a big red apple from the vegetable stall because he was feeling hungry. I didn't come here often, usually only in winter because Mum liked visiting the Christmas stalls that set up around the high street. It was strange for me to be here in summer time. The heat did nothing to keep the shoppers home though, and it was fairly busy, or at least as busy as a small town was likely to get.

"Better to take in something cool to ease your brain. All that caffeine won't do you any good," he remarked as he offered his arm for me to take.

We picked a small Italian café just outside the quadrant and opted to take a seat inside the shop where the sun was less likely to turn me into a cooked lobster. I took the prints out of the card wallet, and flicked through them while Maredudd sat beside me, stirring his straw around in a rather large glass of chocolate milkshake, his green eyes glancing down at the pictures with curiosity. Most of the photos I had taken had come out fairly decent. The analogue was very different to the digital camera I was used to, so a few of the earlier photos I had taken had come out quite blurry. I flipped to the last photograph, and my eyes opened wide as I found myself staring back at the snarling face of the creature that had attacked me, and biting my lip, I slipped it across the table-top towards Maredudd. He leaned forward slightly, observing the photograph with great interest, his tongue licking his lips, and the corners of his mouth.

"Chief," he said, and I nodded.

"Chief's head. Only the head. The rest of the body as you can see, well... It's hard to tell, but..." I ran my fingertip over the blurred shape that emerged from the shadows behind the black, and white collie head. "That part was mostly cow. You can't see in the picture, but its front feet were canine. But see here? It's got horse legs, they're brown, not sandy."

Maredudd's eyes glanced sideways at me for a brief moment then he looked at the picture again.

"It looks like a fantasy creature a taxidermist might create," he commented in an undertone. He said nothing more, only pulled his straw into his mouth again for another sip, and I looked down at the photo, knowing exactly what he meant.

"Is it possible that Geraint created this thing?" I whispered hesitantly.

"Sure."

"So, does that mean Chief is dead?" I felt suddenly sad for Rhys, who had tried so hard to find the missing dog. "But I saw Chief on the road. How did Geraint catch him?"

"Maybe the dog was taken from the farm long ago, and maybe that night Geraint was using the dog as a sentinel," he suggested with a slight shrug of the shoulder. "At least we know where those puncture marks came from. I suppose it wasn't a carnivorous stag after all."

"You sound disappointed by this," I answered with an amused grin.

"Only a little." He chuckled, his eyes twinkling elfishly. "But, I'm now wondering where on earth Geraint is hiding this thing."

"Is it really possible to make a creature out of other animal parts?" I asked, fascinated.

"Yes, but I couldn't tell you how. Dad will know. Everything Geraint knows was learned from him. I've never had the desire to try myself, to be honest. My real question now is not how, but why?" He raised his eyebrows at me, and I nodded.

"I haven't figured that out either. Geraint seems to get on so well with everybody in the village." I reasoned, thinking of all the times I had seen him slapping backs with the farmers, and being invited out to the pub for a pint, and a game of darts.

"Have you ever been in that work room of his?" he questioned, and I nodded again.

"Once or twice, but unless there's more to it than what I saw, it wouldn't be possible to keep a large creature in there without me or Mum hearing it." I picked up my glass of orange juice, and finally tasted it.

"He's got to be keeping it somewhere. There's no way this thing is wandering around day, and night— people would see it. It must have a hiding place somewhere, perhaps a cave or a den, from which he summons it." He contemplated, resting his chin in the palm of his hand.

"What if... What if Geraint took Jojo too?" I suddenly realised, a pang of worry coupled with a sharp stab of fear spreading out from the thought.

"Jojo is too small for him to use as a part of his creature. Besides, I don't think he'd touch Jojo. He knows how much your mam loves her," he replied gently, and I felt his hand fall upon my thigh under the table, at first sending a jolt of goosebumps to cover me, closely followed by reassurance.

"But Jojo bit him, that night we argued..."

"Owen, I think Jojo is fine. Sometimes I get these feelings, these images, and flashes of sound, and smell in my mind. I just know she's okay." He leaned close and kissed my forehead.

"Do you think you could use those flashes to figure out where she is?"

"Maybe, if we sat a circle, and I had your help." He smiled, leaning his elbow on the table, and lifting his straw again. "Anyway, I think Dad needs to see this photograph. I think it's plenty of evidence for us to justify attacking Geraint."

"I thought you said you didn't think he was responsible for the animal attacks?" I said as I rubbed the cold glass against my damp forehead. The ice in the orange juice was chill enough to give me brain freeze.

"Do you know of any other taxidermist witches living round yere?" He grinned that wicked grin he always made, and I gave him a disciplinary slap on the arm.

"Stop it."

"There aren't any, though. Geraint is the only viable suspect. Might also explain why he won't allow anybody in that work room of his," he answered, his grin fading to an expression of seriousness.

I hummed thoughtfully and swallowed a mouthful of orange juice. "I have to ask though, was it you that stole the things from his work room?"

He grunted, and I saw that little guilty smirk he made, like a dog caught stealing food from the counter, his eyes looking down at the ugly photograph instead of at me.

"It was, wasn't it? I knew it. What did you take?" I prodded him further, wondering how he had managed to get inside a locked room without the key.

"Some of his ceremonial items. Most of them, actually. Most importantly, his athame," he confessed, his half-closed eyes regarding me, searching for anger, but finding only curiosity.

"What's an athame?" I frowned.

"A knife used for magickal means. It's deeply important to a witch for casting protective circles and opening ceremonies. Without it, he's probably been finding it a struggle. Probably tried to get acquainted with a new one, but that takes time," he explained. "It's also from that room I took his hair thread, along with a couple of other things. Things we can use against him."

"So Geraint is doing magic inside the house?" I was surprised Mum hadn't found out.

"Once a witch, always a witch, even if it's only in small ways. Like your mam. She's wandered from the path, but she still rubbed love, and luck into that little key you've got." He smiled fondly as he thought of Mum's care for me.

My hand instinctively went to my throat where the key was hanging from a piece of string, the metal warm against my skin. Maredudd had tied it there for me. The string was woven from his own hair, and having it close to me along with the key made me feel protected, and safe. I wanted to give something to him in returned, but my hair was cut so short that I couldn't imagine how he would make thread out of it. Still, Geraint's hair was short, and yet there had been plenty to make up the Witch's Ladder.

"I think we should visit the trench you found. I've got a feeling the beast's lair could be by there. Why else would it dump the bodies there? Perhaps what you crawled through was actually the beast's pantry." He winked, his lips pursed around the straw as he held the glass to his face.

"Okay then. When should we go?" I asked, although the thought of returning there made me feel very apprehensive indeed.

"Today. While it's still sunny." He decided.

"We'd better hurry up and drink this, then. The next bus leaves in twenty minutes."

The forest near the estuary was alive with birdsong. After we jumped off the bus, and made our way up the hill, it wasn't a long walk from the ruins or Maredudd's house, but my wounded leg protested sharply at the exercise. The entire area felt so different compared to the day I had been attacked, and with Maredudd beside me, I almost didn't feel afraid at all. It took some searching to find the trench full of bodies, which mainly comprised of me returning to the spot where I had been chased and retracing my steps from there.

Maredudd listened intensely as I recounted the story to him with as much drama as I could muster, because if there was one thing he had taught me, it was that a story wasn't worth hearing if it was poorly told. The bright sun, and the singing birds made me feel as though we were in a completely different patch of land. The thought of a monster wandering about in this summery vale was alarming, and unbelievable. Maredudd held onto my hand as we climbed the steep slope I had clawed my way up in a bid to escape, and I felt him grip me tightly. When I looked at his face, he seemed strangely pale, and his eyes were glassy, and dull, as though he was suffering with seasickness.

"Are you okay?" I asked, concerned that he wasn't feeling well.

"I'm fine, don't worry." He dismissed my worry as we approached the top of the incline. I eyed him cautiously, aware that he was trying to be brave for me.

The hill seemed so tall. It had felt like barely a few metres when I had been pursued up it, but now in the bright sunshine, and the heat of the day, my injured leg was aching as we made it to the top.

"This is where I fell, down—down here..." I trailed off as we both looked over the edge.

Maredudd looked at me, and I looked at him. The trench was empty.

"There's nothing yere," he murmured. "But it still stinks. Looks like someone came and cleared it up after you left."

"But—but it was full of dead animals," I stammered, a frown of frustration making my brows meet as I looked down at the muddy ditch below. Flies were still hanging about, and the earth was burgundy with old blood, but the corpses were gone. Even my footprints had been churned up and erased, as though the evidence was intentionally destroyed.

"I need to get down from yere." Maredudd suddenly grasped hold of my shoulder to steady himself, and I turned, holding onto his arms as he wobbled on his feet. He had become paler all of a sudden, his chest rising, and falling deeply.

"What's wrong? Maredudd, what's wrong?" I pleaded with him as he turned and began stumbling back down the slope.

"I—I feel... I feel..." he mumbled, pressing his hand to his forehead.

I ran alongside him, holding onto his arm in the hopes of keeping him upright, but as we got to the bottom, he tumbled to the ground, and I cried out, shocked by how much heavier he was than I had expected.

"Maredudd! Are you okay!" I exclaimed, kneeling at his side, and trying to lift him. I started to panic. I had never seen him so weak before.

"It's here... Somewhere..." he whispered, groaning as

I managed to roll him onto his side. His eyes were hazy, and stared into a far-off space, his ashen face looking so drained, and ill.

"What's here? The beast is here?" I prompted, cradling his head in my lap, and stroking his hair back from his forehead.

"No..."

"What are you talking about?" I pressed him further, terrified that we would be attacked when he was lying here this way.

He grumbled as he managed to struggle to his hands, and knees, and I fussed around him, wiping dried leaves, and bits of grass from his clothes.

"Maredudd, you're scaring me. Please, let's go. I don't want to be here. It's making you unwell," I pleaded with him as I knelt at his side. Sweat was creating a shiny sheen on his face, and tears were forming in the corners of his eyes as he panted.

"Follow me." He breathed. He lurched forward, and I fell back onto my rear as he began to crawl across the small clearing towards the trees.

My heart was galloping a mile a minute as I followed Maredudd through the woods, my eyes flicking about nervously, waiting for the monster to come leaping out at us from the shadows. I had no idea where he was leading me, and I was beginning to think I didn't want to find out. The forest began to bend in on itself, and I realised I didn't know this place, as though a whole second area of woods was creeping out from another dimension to populate a secret space that I might have walked on by without noticing. Finally, I saw light between the tree trunks, and realised we were heading towards another clearing. Maredudd was looking worse for wear, and at the edge of the clearing, I cried out when he collapsed to the grassy ground with an exhausted huff, his spectacles falling from his face. I rushed to his side and took up his glasses before they could get damaged.

"Maredudd, please. I want to go home. You're not well." I begged as I held onto his head, terrified that something was seriously wrong with him.

His eyes opened, and he looked up at me, and I craned my neck to glance over my shoulder as he lifted his arm and pointed ahead of us into the clearing. I gazed across the sunlit ground, realising the birdsong had died back, and we were surrounded by an oppressive silence.

"Look for me. I can't do it." He breathed.

"Look? Where? What am I looking for?" I was apprehensive as I glanced over my shoulder at the clearing.

"On the ground... the stones." He blinked, squeezing his eyelids together, and shuddering.

"What if the beast attacks us?"

"I'd never send you anywhere dangerous." He made a wry grin. I took hold of his hand and rubbed it briskly between my own.

"Okay, I'll look. But then we're going home, okay?" I told him, and he nodded awkwardly.

I rose to my feet, patting bits of dried-out twig, and crusty leaves from my trousers before turning towards the clearing. As I stepped closer, I felt a strange humming begin to run through me, as though I had stepped onto a densely vibrating floor, the tremors shooting through the soles of my feet, and flowing through my body, making walking uncomfortable, and difficult. My lungs tightened, and my rapid heartbeat became erratic. The grass became shorter, and shorter as I moved to the centre, as though the ground here was regularly trodden on, preventing the grass from sprouting up to the wild lengths seen elsewhere in the woodland. I stopped at the edge of the sparse yellow circle upon which the radiant sun was beaming, my eyes squinting in the bright light, picking out the grey shapes dotted here and there on the ground. There were large stones, nearly a hundred of them, laid out in a pattern on the forest floor to form some sort of letter, but it was no symbol I had ever seen before. Standing right beside it, the vibration had become intolerable.

"The sigil," Maredudd said behind me, and I looked over my shoulder to find him kneeling, his hands flat on the ground to support him. "He's been hiding here... Hiding the creature here... a sigil to camouflage this place."

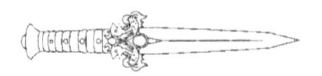

Maredudd was feeling well enough to stand after we moved away from the area, but he was still shaky on his feet, and seemed quite disorientated from it, so I held onto his arm, and kept him steady on the walk back to the cliffs. I was terrified that he would lose balance and fall as we made our way down the path to the cave where his father lived. It had been a struggle making it there. He had to keep stopping for a rest, and his skin was damp with a cold sweat. I was deeply concerned that whatever that symbol on the ground was, it had inflicted upon him a feverish illness.

We found Morcant sitting in his rocking chair again, this time cradling a young seagull wrapped up in a knotted sheet of calico to keep its delicate wings tucked in and restrained. He was surprised to see us, embarrassed even, that I had witnessed what he got up to in the privacy of his own home, and rushed to explain to me that he had found the poor creature crashed on the cliffs with a broken leg, so had taken it in for the time being until it was healed. The seagull wasn't overly thrilled to see us, and it squawked, and chirruped noisily as he placed it down on his rocking chair, one of its legs bandaged firmly to a splint, which caused it to stick out to one angle, and look very funny indeed.

I helped Maredudd across the chamber where he collapsed on the bed, and I hovered at his side as Morcant pressed a reptilian hand upon his clammy forehead. Maredudd's eyes opened, eyelashes fluttering briefly before they closed once more, his face scrunching slightly in discomfort.

"He will be fine, there is no need to fret." Morcant smiled at me reassuringly, but I felt little relief. "I believe the sigil was placed there specifically to ward off Maredudd, and generally to bewilder, and confuse passers-by, which may explain why you are perfectly healthy. Whoever laid it there doesn't see you as a threat."

"Has it hurt him?" I gnawed at my lip anxiously, perching on the bed, and holding onto Maredudd's limp hand in my lap. His skin felt cold to touch, and every now, and again, a little trembling shiver would run through him, my fingers gripping tightly to assure him that I was near.

"The energy has entered him and is playing havoc with his immune system. If it was allowed to roam freely, and feed upon his own energy, it would slowly kill him as a virus would. As I said, though, he will be fine. He just requires a little care from a wise hand. You did good to bring him here," Morcant replied with his purring words as he shuffled away. I watched him as he sorted through a cabinet overflowing with jars, and pots, taking items out, and placing them on the bedside table.

"I was so worried. He collapsed suddenly and could barely walk. There were these stones on the ground, they were laid out in a sort of symmetrical symbol with a big circle in the centre..." I tried to describe what I had seen, and Morcant nodded in understanding.

"Sigils are like that. It was not meant to be seen by your eyes. Sometimes they can lose their power if such is the case. As you are unaffected, it may be that I will require your help to dismantle it," he replied quietly as he opened a small silver censer and began filling it with scoops of dried incense. "For now, I can only dispel the harm that has been done to my son."

I watched him mutedly as he lit a match in the stove, and used it to light the incense, plumes of silvery smoke whisping through the slits in the censor as he lifted it by its fragile chain.

"Breathe deeply, son," Morcant said as he brought the smoking object close to the bed. The incense smelled good, and I sniffed it curiously, trying to identify what he was burning, but my knowledge of incense was quite limited to what Mum normally used to make the house smell nice.

"Geraint... Geraint placed the sigil..." Maredudd mumbled weakly, his whole body flinching slightly as his father's hand touched his forehead again.

"Yes, as suspected. Can you tell me how you came upon it?"

I waited for Maredudd to answer his question, but when I looked up I saw Morcant's caprine eyes were staring straight at me.

"Oh—we, well, I took Maredudd out there to show him where I was attacked, and to find the trench where I had fallen. It was full of dead animals. But when we got there, they were all gone, and that's when Maredudd said he knew there was something close by," I explained, stroking Maredudd's knuckles with my fingertips. "He crawled to a clearing in the woods, and I found the stones. That's about it. Oh, and I've got a photograph to show you. It's in my bag."

"A photograph?" Morcant purred interestedly.

I slipped my bag off my shoulders, and took out the wallet, his strange eyes opening wider as I presented the photo to him. He accepted it daintily, the censor rocking back and forth on its chain from his other hand as he brought the picture to his face.

"Hmm." He grunted after a moment of silence before offering the photo back.

I looked down at it wearily, feeling suddenly very tired. Morcant set the incense burner on the small shelf above the bed, shifting a pile of books slightly so there was room to put it down. He then brought a stool over, and sat beside the bed, rolling up his shirt sleeves to reveal his coal-coloured, muscular arms. I wasn't sure what else to do except sit there in silence as he stretched in some rather unorthodox ways, causing a number of bones to click quite loudly, before flexing his big hands, and placing them on Maredudd's torso.

My head jerked up when I heard him say something, but I soon realised he wasn't speaking to me. His lips were moving as he uttered under his breath, the words so quiet I couldn't make them out. I heard Maredudd whisper too, as though they were having some sort of conversation I wasn't privy to.

"Bring Wenda to me," he suddenly answered, the volume of his voice startling me as I hadn't expected it.

"Here?" I asked, and he grunted, still whispering, his eyes now closed.

"And one more thing..." he murmured. "Put a pan of water on the stove for me. I will have a few more instructions to follow, but please do that for me first."

"Oh—okay." I hesitated, dumping my bag, and going over to the stove. My hands shook slightly as I picked up one of the small pans sitting on the rock ledge, and after struggling with the cork on one of the tall bottles of water, I poured some into it. The stove hissed and spluttered as I placed the pan atop it.

"In my cabinet there... I need you to take a clove of garlic, and put it in the pan," he told me, sensing that I was done without needing to turn, and see.

I peered into the open cabinet cautiously, searching for what he asked, and discovering a jar filled to the brim with unpeeled garlic bulbs, so I took one, and snapped a clove from the bulb. The rich scent of garlic began to rise from the water as the clove sank to the bottom of the pan.

"On the ledge there are some spoons. Take up the tablespoon. One spoon of rock salt," he instructed emotionlessly.

I began to panic as I looked through all the tiny bottles of herbs, and other ingredients. Many of the labels were so ancient they had turned brown, and flaky or had been scribbled over so many times they were unreadable. I picked out a bottle full of chunky white grains, hoping I had got the right one, but he didn't turn to check whether I had. I pulled the cork out and tipped some into the spoon before adding it to the pan.

"Two teaspoons of tea tree oil," Morcant continued slowly, pausing in between as he waited for me to do as he wanted. "And two of clove oil."

It took me awhile as I had to sniff every individual bottle until I had found the right ones, and I began to get the feeling that he was testing me. I was so careful to get it right because if I did it wrong, I was worried that I would end up doing harm to Maredudd, and it seemed Morcant knew this, and used it to pressure me. Despite his gentlemanly nature, Morcant might have been a cruel teacher for all I knew. He gave me several more instructions, each time waiting in silence, occasionally reaching to touch Maredudd's face as I fumbled with the bottles, and jars.

"And lastly, you will see many crystals in the glass case there," he said, a slight edge of amusement to his voice this time. "Take out the biggest chunk of quartz and put that in too."

I was sweating by the time I dropped the fist-sized piece of stone into the pan, swirls of herbs floating on the surface as the liquid gave off a pungent scent.

"Well done, Owen. I am very impressed that you did

not complain of my harsh treatment of you," he remarked, sounding even more amused now, and I saw that he was smiling as I moved to stand beside him. "I will teach you properly when we are not in emergency circumstances. I can tell you are a fast learner. I believe you will make an excellent student."

"Thanks..." I murmured, feeling both embarrassed, and flattered at the same time.

"Fetch me the knife over there, but please wrap the silk sheet around your hand before handling it. Not because I think you will dirty it, but because it is attuned only to me, and I wouldn't wish for it to hurt you," he requested, his smile fading to sternness once more.

I had never seen a ritual athame before, and as I stepped up to the isolated shelf upon which it lay, I was amazed by how plain, and simple it was. Two well-used candles were melted to the surface either side of it, their wicks shrivelled by flame, and beneath the knife there was a black silk covering draped, hanging from the edges of the wooden shelf. The blade itself was single-sided and looked to be made of silver because of the odd little blackened marks in the finely polished exterior, and the handle was wood, possibly yew, wrapped neatly in strips of leather, discoloured, and oiled by repeated use.

I lifted the edges of the silk and folded it over the knife so that I could pick it up. Even with the material wrapped around it, I felt a bizarre sensation instantly seep into my palm as I took it in my hand. I expected to pull back the fabric, and find a small creature hiding within, so strong was the sensation of it being alive. I brought it to Morcant, handling it delicately as though it was a precious antique, and he gestured that I should place it on the bed beside Maredudd's leg.

"You may go now. Try to catch Wenda and bring her here. We need her here, tonight." His eyes opened at last, and when he looked up at me, I saw how bloodshot they had become. "Walk safely, Owen. I am with you."

It was difficult to tear myself away, but I knew if I stayed any longer, I wouldn't be able to catch Mum before she left work, and then I would have to run along the beach in search of her. Morcant smiled patiently as I bent to kiss Maredudd's cool cheek, but his eyes were closed, and he seemed not to register that I was there. I trusted Morcant would care for him. He knew far more than I did, and there was very little I could do to make him better again.

The seagull turned its grey head and observed me with its beady yellow eye as I ran off alone. I jogged along the path down towards the village, hurrying along the roadside as cars passed, and a group of people on bicycles darted by in flashes of primary colour, the sun was still high despite the hour. By the time I reached the caravan park, my lungs were burning, and my freckled cheeks were coloured with breathlessness. Fortunately I had made it just in time.

I stumbled to a halt at the gate, groups of holiday-goers wandering by, children with buckets, and spades, parents holding hands with their toddlers, grandparents in white, and beige carrying picnic baskets. People were still heading down to the beach even though it was mid-afternoon. I patted my chest, and coughed, ridding myself of the annoying wheeze there. All I could do was wait for Mum to appear.

Waiting was the worst part. When I finally saw her familiar shape heading towards me, I hurried through into the park, my boots thudding on the asphalt, and an alarmed expression appearing on her face as she saw me approaching. She was still wearing her blue tabard, and her handbag was dangling from one arm. She smelled of cleaning chemicals too.

"Owen! What are you doing yere?" she exclaimed, her eyes staring at me questioningly.

"Mum, you've got to come with me to see Morcant."

I held onto her arm as though she might suddenly escape. "We need you to help us. Maredudd is sick, and—and I saw the beast, and—"

"Wait just a second, young man. I can't understand what you're saying." She took hold of my hand, and stopped walking, forcing me to stop too. "What's this about the beast? What's this about Morcant?"

"Morcant needs your help, and Maredudd is sick, and I took a picture of the beast, and we think Geraint is in control of it," I blurted out all in one go, not caring that the people walking around us might overhear our conversation.

"You saw the beast?" She gasped.

"Mum, you have to come, and see Morcant. Please, it's really important. We need your help." I pulled at her arm again, but she refused to budge.

"No, Owen. No. Absolutely not." She shook her head quickly, her brows frowning.

"Please Mum. We need your help." I begged, but she just kept shaking her head as she began walking again, forcing me to walk alongside her. "Why not? Why won't you help us?"

"I don't believe what I'm hearing. Geraint, responsible for these attacks? Never." She sounded disappointed, but I couldn't tell if it was disappointment in me or something else. She started walking, giving me no choice, but to follow her out of the gate, and down the path. "Just when you two seemed to be getting along so well..."

"Mum, Maredudd said that Geraint killed Dad." I stepped in front of her, preventing her from going any further, and forcing her to confront me.

"Can you hear yourself, Owen! Can you hear what you're saying to me by yere? It's madness." She tutted, her hands moving to her hips defensively.

"Can we at least go somewhere so I can explain this to you?" I leaned closer, aware that people were staring as they passed us.

"I'm going home. You can talk to me there."

"No—Mum, I can't go back to the house." I stopped her from stepping off again. "Mum, the other night I was attacked, and the monster bit me. But I managed to take a photo of it. I've got proof, now. Proof that it really is a monster, and not just some escaped lion or tiger."

"You were attacked!" She was aghast, her hands grabbed me by the arms as she looked me up and down. "Oh my god, are you all right?!"

"I'm fine, really. It's okay." I promised.

"I told you not to go out there—" she began, but I cut her off before she could start ranting at me about safety again.

"This is why you need to come to see Morcant with me. It's not safe anymore, for any of us. Please Mum. We need your help," I urged, feeling hopeful that she was now quiet instead of outright refusing.

She sighed. "Owen, I don't do that sort of thing anymore. I gave it all up with your dad."

"But what about the key you gave me? Morcant told me what it was for," I questioned, knowing that I had struck something inside her because I saw the little glint in her eye.

For a second she just huffed, and stuttered, unsure of what to say, but then she regained her composure. "Well that was just a one-off. I'm not doing it anymore."

"But you need to do it now, for Dad's sake. Dad would want you to. Morcant wants to try and find him, but we can't do it without you. We think Geraint is responsible for his disappearance, but we can't find out how unless you come, and help us." I reasoned, hoping that she would understand, hoping that she would listen.

"I don't think Geraint would ever hurt your dad," she said, her eyes looking down at the ground between us. She said the words, but she didn't seem overly convinced herself.

"Then let's at least find out, and maybe we can figure out if he's innocent." I placed my hand on her shoulder comfortingly.

"No, Owen, you don't understand." She felt at her forehead, shielding her eyes from me.

"What? What don't I understand?" I tilted my head to try and make eye contact with her, but she turned slightly, obscuring her eyes further.

"Please, let's get off the path. I don't want to talk about this by yere." She moved away, and I followed her through the wooden gate into the lane that led between the adjoining fields. People didn't come this way often as it led further into the countryside, away from the beach where they tended to head. Once we were far from the path, Mum stopped again, and I saw how she was struggling to find the words to say to me. I held onto her arm, unsure of whether I wanted to know. The face she was making was causing me to feel afraid, and apprehensive.

"About your father," she answered, her voice barely a whisper. The blowing wind made her words almost inaudible, and I had to strain to hear them. "There were some things I didn't tell you... back then. Because I thought it would hurt you too much."

"What things?" I was astounded.

She licked her lips, and lowered her hand, allowing me to see her eyes. They were glittering with unspent tears, and I saw her bottom lip tremble slightly.

"I didn't tell you, because I knew it would hurt you bad. But when the police were looking for him... They found his clothes on the beach near Geraint's house. Folded up neat in a nice pile. Shoes on top. Wallet tucked inside one of them," she whispered, her throat contracting as she swallowed hard. "That's why they stopped searching... Because they said he had walked into the sea and drowned. They couldn't recover his body, so... There was nothing else they could do."

I stared. A hard lump formed in my chest, and rose slowly, lodging itself in my throat where it began to choke me, and I felt pressure behind my eyes, the pressure of tears threatening to come out. I forced them down, breathing slowly through my nose as I fought to stay composed. I didn't know what to say; I was completely speechless. Why had she kept this from me all this time?

"Can you remember, not long before he disappeared, he came home, and he was... Different. All the joy, and light had been sucked out of him. He had lost his job, and we couldn't pay the mortgage," she continued, her hand reaching for mine, and squeezing it tightly, anchoring me in reality. "We planned to move back yere, to stay with Geraint. Your dad was stubborn; he didn't want to. But not long before he disappeared, he decided it'd be a good idea. Sell the house, come back yere again. But something wasn't right with him. I saw it, and then he never came home."

She looked into my eyes, recognised my silence as hurt, and stroked my cheek gently with her free hand, her handbag hanging from her elbow.

"You can't blame Geraint for Evan's death. None of us are responsible. We did everything we could to help him." She cupped my face in her palms, thumbs stroking my cheeks. "I'm sorry I didn't tell you this before, but you were distraught. I couldn't very well pile this on top as well. I was already terrified of losing you in the middle of your transition—things were hard enough."

"Mum..." I sniffed, allowing her to bend me into a hug. She wrapped her arms round me, patting my back as I wrestled with my tears.

It was several minutes before I was able to compose myself, and she allowed me to stand upright, my eyes puffy, and my nose running, so I wiped it in my wrist.

"I'm sorry," I mumbled, feeling stupid for doing this to her.

"It's okay, sweetie." She nodded, patting the middle of my chest. "You didn't know, and I don't suppose Maredudd putting all these wild thoughts in your head are doing much good either."

Suddenly, there was the beating of small wings, and she startled as something dark flew down from the overhanging trees, and fluttered about us, our heads turning towards the source of the sound. I gasped as a small bird hovered close to me, wings ploughing the air, its tail turning this way, and that to manoeuvre as it sought to land on me. I watched, awestruck, as the starling found purchase on my shoulder, its tiny feet burying its claws into my shirt, and its tail bobbing as it kept balanced. Mum's mouth was open with surprise, and she looked between me, and the bird.

"I don't believe it," she said, lifting her hand, and tentatively moving it closer to the bird, who cocked its head, and stared at her approaching digit. It allowed her to gently stroke its back, puffing out its neck feathers, and reorganising its wing feathers to a more comfortable position.

"It's Morcant's starling," she said, her amazement turning to a grin.

"How do you know?" I questioned, hesitant to look down at the tiny thing for fear of frightening it away.

"This white spot on its forehead," she replied.

I glanced down, and the bird looked up at me quickly, feathers fluffing up again. "Has it brought a message or something?"

"Yes. Well, I guess I will come then. Provided there's a cup of tea, and something to eat on offer," Mum declared reluctantly.

I thought she was talking to me, but I soon realised she had been talking to the bird because as soon as she had spoken, the weightless little thing darted off, its triangular wings taking it high into the sky before it disappeared down over the hill.

"Come on then, before I change my mind." She gestured with her chin as she took hold of my arm and guided me back along the path.

Twelve

Maredudd was sitting up on the bed when we arrived at Morcant's cave. His eyes lit up when I stepped through the doorway, lifting his hand from the copper mug he was cradling to give me a little wave, alarming the snoozing seagull that had been moved from the chair to sit beside him. Mum followed behind me cautiously, her eyes looking all around us, and when she spotted Morcant standing at the stove, her mouth opened in astonishment.

"Wenda," he greeted as she moved around me, and rushed towards him. He let out a muffled cry of surprise when she jumped upon him in an inescapable bear hug, Mum making a squealing shriek as she grabbed him.

"You old bastard!" she screeched. "Have you been by yere all these years, and you didn't think to come by for a cuppa?"

I grinned, watching my small red-haired mother being embraced by tall, dark Morcant, his clawed hands resting on her back timidly. While Mum questioned him about why he seemed to think he wasn't welcome to come for Sunday dinner, I navigated to the bed where my handsome man was waiting for me. His ponytail had been undone, and his wavy hair was falling all over his shoulders, tucked haphazardly behind his ears. His eyes closed as I reached for his face, and cupped it in my palm, leaning towards him to give him a gentle kiss.

"How are you feeling?" I asked as I sat down, the seagull snapping its beak. Maredudd placed his hand upon its packaged body to calm it.

"Much better. I apologise that I must stink like an incense gift-box at present." He chuckled, grinning as I kissed his bearded jaw, and cheek.

"You've smelled worse." I teased, and he pretended to slap my face, my hands grabbing his wrist as we both laughed mutedly.

"Owen, have you explained to your mother what has happened?" Morcant interrupted us, and we turned our heads to find he and Mum were looking at us.

"Yes, I told her on the way here." I nodded.

"I don't understand though, why do you want to do this tonight? What's the point of it?" Mum questioned as she sat down in Morcant's rocking chair and placed her bag on the ground.

"We are going to seek the location of Evan's body," he told her blankly.

"I already told Owen what happened. His body won't be found, you're wasting your time." Mum shook her head.

"We don't think Evan just vanished," Maredudd said firmly, which surprised Mum as she looked at him nearly accusingly, like she thought he was calling her a liar.

"Wenda, sweetheart." Morcant stepped between her, and Maredudd, forcing her to look up at him instead. "It is my belief that Geraint is committing obscene crimes, and one of those crimes is Evan's dubious disappearance. If indeed his disappearance is due to his suicide, the Goddess will tell us. But please allow us to try. If Geraint is innocent, he will be eliminated from our suspicions. No harm done."

She sighed, frowning as she looked down at her clasped hands. We waited quietly, hoping she would agree to go through with it. There was nothing to lose after all.

"All right. But I want a cup of tea, and some cake if you have it. I'm bloody starving," she finally answered, much to our relief. "The starling agreed to this, so you'd better not go back on it."

"You drive a hard bargain, woman." Morcant smiled, placing his hand on her shoulder.

She grumbled, and slapped his hand away, but it did nothing to remove his smile as when he turned away from her, he winked at us both, and moved to put some water on the stove. While Mum scoffed a huge slice of fruit cake, and Maredudd enjoyed his third cup of tea of the afternoon, Morcant acquired my assistance as he gathered the things we would need for the ritual. He took me down a narrow tunnel from the chamber, so narrow that I had to turn on my side, and squeeze through after him, the light from his lamp rocking about, and flashing up the sides of the rock walls as we went deeper into the cliff.

"There are many tunnels down here," he commented as we walked side by side. "I have used many of them myself. A few of the chambers have been used by others previously, but I have found no use for them just yet."

"Others? Are there other people living here?" I breathed, again feeling as though I couldn't talk at normal volume in this place.

"In years gone by, but not anymore. I suspect you have heard the old tale of the witch that haunts these caves?"he asked, and I nodded worriedly. "It is, but a myth. But, these caves have been used as residence by witches since pre-Medieval times. You will see, as we go deeper, the veins of magnetic ore creeping through the granite. It is a centre of ancient Earth energy."

"Like ley-lines?"

"Like that, yes. The life essence of Cernunnos exudes from these tunnels as though we walk through the bowels of the God himself," Morcant replied softly.

"Well, that's a rather unpleasant thought," I murmured, unable to stop a slight smirk from quirking the corner of my mouth.

"Your childish humour is quite reminiscent of Evan's schoolboy remarks," he said, and when I looked up at him, I saw him smile sadly. "Do not prohibit yourself from saying such remarks in front of me. One as old as I can appreciate a good joke when he hears one. In fact, you may find I lay out bait for such humour. I would be so disappointed if you didn't take it."

"How old are you?" I asked, since it was hard to tell from looking at his appearance.

"I was born in 1884. You may do the subtraction." He chuckled.

I stared at him in amazement, and he looked down at me with a jovial smile. That made him over a hundred years old, and yet he walked, and talked with a kind of ageless youth that was impossible to put a number on.

"How—how are you still alive?" I stammered.

"The Goddess is kind to me. Should you choose to pledge your life to the Magnum Opus, you could find yourself walking these tunnels in a hundred years' time too," he told me, the moving shadows turning his eye sockets into black holes lit only by the glow from his eyes.

"No thanks. Besides, I planned to write it into my will that I want my monument painted day-glow yellow. I don't think I could give up on that." I grinned, and he laughed, the silken sound echoing down the tunnel.

He took me into a tiny room deep beneath the rock where the air was so cold that my breath plumed in clouds of steam. The space was filled with boxes, crates, and cabinets, a few draped with cotton sheets. I stood by awkwardly while he opened a cupboard and took out one of several huge bottles of white liquid, and handed it to me, the chilly glass freezing my fingertips. It was heavy, and slippery, and I had to be careful not to drop it. He took up two wooden boxes, one of which was full of metal objects that clattered about as he walked, and together we returned to his bedchamber.

Mum was sipping her tea, and rocking back and forth, chatting quietly to Maredudd as he petted the seagull, and fed it small bits of bread, but they stopped when we reappeared. I put the bottle by the stove to warm it. Morcant said it was full fat milk from the local dairy, kept purely for ritual use as he didn't consume animal products, and took his tea black. He then thrust a broom into my hands and took me to another chamber. This one opened out to the side of the cliff, and from there I could see right out to sea, but we were sufficiently shielded from the wind by the jutted rock around the mouth of the cave. He instructed me to sweep the space thoroughly, so I set to work at clearing away abandoned seabird nests, twigs, and dried grass, and the occasional lump of stone. In the middle of the floor there was a large scorch-mark that looked as if it had been the place of many of camp-fires. I then stood back and watched as Morcant drew an enormous circle with salt crystals, and then a symbol where the scorch-mark was.

"This cave will become our protective work-space. I have used it many times alone, but with the three of you accompanying me, it will become much more than that," he told me as he gestured I come with him once more. "I will teach you the basic ritual of protection that must be fulfilled before we begin our work. You must not be open to attack, not just from Geraint, but from other entities that will sense your presence the second you open yourself to magic workings."

"Are you sure this is, you know... Safe? I mean, I've never done this before," I asked as I hurried at his side through the tunnel with the broom in my hand.

"A chain is as strong as its weakest link." He made a

wry grin that did nothing to reassure me. "Follow my instructions. We have no room for error, here. But, should anything go wrong, we will support you."

I grunted, unsure if this was going to be such a good idea after all. There was a lot to do to prepare for this, and when Morcant presented a bottle of liquid to me, and told me to go, and wash myself with it, I simply stared at it reluctantly.

"Come with me, I'll show you what to do." Maredudd hauled himself to his feet and took the glass bottle from his father's hand.

"No funny business with my boy, you understand!"Mum called after him jokingly as Maredudd took me by my arm and pulled me from the chamber.

He took me through the dark, following the tunnel with his bare feet as though he had walked these trails a thousand times, and knew them by heart. He brought me to another open cave overlooking the sea, but this one was much smaller, and the window to the outside was no bigger than a doorway. The sun was shining right into the hole, and the stone felt warm under my touch as I leaned against the rock wall to squeeze through the tight gap, and step inside. Maredudd wriggled through beside me, and put the bottle on the ground, the glass clinking against the rocks. I startled when his hands took me from behind, and I giggled when his mouth kissed my neck, his breath hot on my cool skin.

"Hey, I'm pretty sure this isn't what your dad meant," I complained jestingly.

"It's not. But you do have to take your clothes off," he purred, his precise fingertips undoing the, buttons of my polo shirt.

"You're having me on."

"I'm not. Yere, I'll show you myself then." He let go of me, and I turned, leaning back against the wall as he pulled his t-shirt off over his head. His chest hair was ruffled into curls by the movement of the fabric, and when he began to pull his shorts down, I had to look away as the embarrassment was overwhelming. It didn't matter that we'd made love, that we had lain naked together in bed, and kissed, and held each other as lovers did. It would be awhile before I got used to seeing him nude.

"What's the matter with your face? You look like you've been slapped." He grinned at me as he bent to pick up the bottle.

"Shut up, I can't help it." I pouted. When I glanced up at him, I saw his dark, firm body, and my heart began to thump erratically, pounding faster, and faster when I tried to prevent my eyes from falling on his private parts.

"You will have to get used to being naked if you want to be a witch." He raised his eyebrows at me, his smile disappearing. He took the lid off the bottle and poured some of the oily liquid into his hand, the herbal scent reaching me from across the small cave.

"It's not about me being naked—it's about you being naked." I chewed at my bottom lip, trying to focus on his face, and not let my lustful eyes drift below his shoulders.

He tittered under his breath as he began to rake the liquid through his hair, starting at the very top, and working down while I stood there silently, trying to calm my racing heart.

"Why don't you come, and help me," he suggested.

"Stop teasing me." I waved a hand at him dismissively, and he outright laughed then. I flinched when his wet hand took my wrist and lifted my arm so that he could press my hand to his slippery face. He smelled strongly of basil, and rosemary.

"You smell like a chicken dinner." I smirked as I wiped some droplets from the end of his nose.

"I'm gonna wash it off after, silly. Did you think that's what we were building a fire for, to roast me on it?" He stuck his tongue out at me, and I gasped with laughter as I imagined him on a spit.

"To be honest, I'm struggling to draw a line between your dad being a witch, and a rather eccentric chef," I grinned.

"I'll give you a clue: he's a terrible chef," he whispered, giggling, as he leaned close to me, and I wrestled with him as he attempted to pull my top off.

After persuading me out of my clothes, Maredudd helped me rub the powerful-smelling salve into my skin. I had to start with the top of my head, and work down, otherwise it would attract energy rather than reflect it. I felt a little sheepish being nude in front of him, especially as he kept trying to kiss me, his eyes twinkling with mischief like they usually did. It took even more effort for him to persuade me to leave my clothes behind as he took me down a steep tunnel below, to a cave where the sea was rushing in from a gap under the rock, creating a shallow pool.

We helped each other bathe in the salt water, and by then I wasn't feeling so shy anymore. I kind of wished we could just go back to the cottage on the cliff and spend the night alone rather than sitting round a fire with Mum and Morcant. We sat on the rocky floor of the cave, and dried naturally, whispering to each other, and sharing kisses until we were ready to put our clothes back on, and by the time we returned, Mum and Morcant were cussing impatiently.

I warmed my hands round a mug of hot tea, smiling curiously as I stroked the seagull's chin with a tentative finger. We were waiting while Mum and Morcant readied themselves, and Maredudd seemed to pick up on my desire to run off with him alone because he kept gazing at me longingly, and bending to kiss my ear, and jaw. When I did the same back, I managed to make him blush too. I still wasn't accustomed to the idea that I was allowed to fawn over him too, nor to the idea that he found me attractive when I still felt so ugly compared to him.

We waited until darkness covered the bay. Mum and Maredudd piled dry wood in the centre of the salt circle while Morcant explained to me in the simplest way possible what I needed to do when the ritual began, which only served to leave me feeling anxious, like a first-time actor waiting to go on stage in front of a huge audience. The cave soon began to warm with the fire lit, filling the space with orange light; it was a clean fire, and there was no smoke to choke us.

Morcant poured the bottle of milk into a large copper pan, and placed it atop the crackling fire, arranging his little wooden boxes around the hearth of the flames with some unlit candles, and dusting off his knees as he rose. He had lit more incense, and with his silver censer, he blew wafts of sage smoke around each of us, encouraging us to breathe it in, and even to behave as though we were washing in it by waving it into our hair, and under our clothes. It was difficult to stop myself from coughing, and Mum laughed at me. I thought the occasion was meant to be a solemn one, but we weren't even chanting in Latin or wearing robes like I'd seen in so many Hammer Horror movies.

"You will take Evan's place as Fire." Morcant addressed me, and I looked down at the object that was resting upon his open hands. "This wand you will use to fulfil the instructions I have given you. Do you remember everything I taught you?"

"Yes, I think so." I nodded quickly, my hands hesitating to take the long piece of polished wood from him.

He scrutinized me for a moment. "You only think so?"

"I mean, yes. I do remember everything." I hurried

to respond out of fear that he would think I was unprepared.

"Take the wand," he murmured. "Treat it with respect."

I stared down at it as my hand reached, and carefully took hold. The wand was warm from being beside the fire, and when my skin made contact with it, a spark of pins, and needles shot up my arm, causing me to flinch sharply.

"Don't be afraid of it, child." His stern face cracked into an entertained grin. "And try not to wave it around too much. That would be quite inappropriate. We'll have none of that nonsense here."

"You were meant to say *you're a wizard, Owen*." I made a face at him as he turned away from me, but he seemed not to hear me as he approached Mum instead.

Mum was given a carved talisman made of beautiful, honey-coloured gold. It was thick, and heavy, and I imagined was probably worth quite a lot of money. She clutched it to her bosom as though comforting it like a child while she crouched to stir the milk in the pan with a long wooden spoon. Maredudd was given a cup made out of the horn of a ram, the surface of which was so finely polished that the firelight reflected from it in glittering winks when it swapped hands. Morcant's silver athame was reserved for him, and he laid it out on the floor where he intended to stand. I waited on the other side of the fire in the spot I had been designated to, waiting until the others had moved to their places. The air was foggy with incense, and the milk in the pan was starting to give off a rich, creamy scent that made my mouth water. Morcant cleared his throat, and bent, picking up his knife, and holding it in both hands, then he glanced at each of us.

"Before us, Ostara, Goddess of the Moon, offers her wisdom, and kindness." He spoke calmly as he pointed the athame into the air before him, slowly drawing the shape of a pentacle. We all did the same, imitating his movements without making a sound. The heat from the fire was beginning to make me sweat, and the shiny surface of the wand felt slippery in my grasp.

I almost tripped when I turned to step to my left, all of us trading places clockwise. It was my turn next, and I was panicking, my nerves frayed with the fear that I would mess up.

"Behind us, Lucifer, the burning Light of the Sun, offers her knowledge, and—and bravery." I panted as I struggled to speak the words, cringing at the sound of my own voice when I stuttered at the very end. It was hard to remember the line and draw the pentacle with the wand at the same time when I had so little time to practice. When I looked across the fire, I met Morcant's intense stare, but then he smiled, and we traded places again. I felt much better knowing my moment as the centre of attention was over.

"To our left, Leviathan, Father of the Deep, offers his power, and determination," Maredudd answered, his eyes glancing across at me over his hands holding up the horn cup. He continued to gaze at me encouragingly as we moved again, and I found myself standing in the spot Morcant had been in moments ago.

"To our right, Cernunnos, Stag of the Earth, offers his spirit, and fertility," Mum declared, sounding the most dramatic of the four of us as she used the talisman to ascribe the air.

"Above us shines the six-pointed star, around us the Elements offer protection, and below us burns the circle of fire," we all said in unison.

At some point during the ritual, the air had begun to feel heavy, and I realised my body was covered in goosebumps, my clothes stinging me as static clung to the fabric, causing a prickling sensation to crawl in my flesh. There was a pause, all of us closing our eyes, and although Morcant had told me to envisage a fiery angel so bright that it was impossible to look into the centre of its light, all that kept coming to mind was a silly man in a tight red devil outfit. It didn't matter so much, but I was annoyed at myself, so I kept trying, and Maredudd had to reach, and give me a poke to distract me.

"Goddess of the Moon, we do seek your guidance this night," Morcant uttered, the firelight flashing in his eyes, and illuminating his pale face between the two dark curtains of his hair. "We seek the location of Evan Vaughn, a long-time student of your wisdom. We seek to clear Geraint Clough of his disappearance. If need be, we seek your blessing in the work of punishing the guilty."

Silence. The wind was sweeping across the mouth of the cave, and the sound of the waves was audible over the hiss of the fire.

"Sit," he whispered, and slowly we moved to sit down on the salt-strewn ground.

A droplet of sweat dripped from my nose, but I resisted the urge to wipe my face in my wrist. My whole body was shaking with the strange energy that was beginning to hum in the air, and as we sat there, I felt an enormous presence moving between Maredudd and I. Instinctively I turned my head towards it, expecting to see a person standing there, but the space was empty. Maredudd was looking up into the same space, his eyes wide open, and his lips parted. Another prickle of goosebumps caused the hair on my body to rise. The flames of the fire blustered as though the wind was battering them, but there was no breeze. The rising line of smoke from the censer changed direction as though a hand had passed through it. The presence was so big, covering everything in the space of the cave, cupping us within its body as though a dome had been placed down over the circle in which we sat.

"Goddess, my queen, and my only muse. I beseech you with humiliation, and humble adoration. Please show us the location of Evan Vaughn's body." Morcant breathed, his hands gripping his athame so tightly that the veins in his trembling arms began to bulge visibly.

I closed my eyes as they were starting to sting. In my mind, I asked the same questions Morcant had.

Please show us, Goddess. I want to find my dad.

Suddenly, the pressure vanished, and my shoulders physically lifted as though someone had been pushing them down towards the ground, only to let go. The burning fire sprang violently to life, momentarily consuming the bubbling pan in a flash of yellow before it sank back to a comfortable glow. Morcant's cheeks were red, and his eyes were bloodshot again.

"She has spoken."He smiled.

"What did she say?"Mum whispered.

He pointed to the mouth of the cave. "She said look, and she will show us." He struggled to his feet, and I was surprised to see his knees were wobbling, so Maredudd rushed to help him up.

We grouped at the opening within the cliff-face and looked out at the dotted lights of the village that spread across the bay. Maredudd put his arm around me as the wind blew harshly here, sending a chill down my spine after being near the warmth of the fire. I felt stupid as everyone else seemed to know exactly what was happening, and yet I had no idea what I was meant to be looking for.

"What's hap—" I began, but my voice stopped when all the lights across the bay began to go out, gradually plunging the village into darkness.

Only one light remained.

"No... No, she's wrong..."Mum turned, and moved away from us, hugging her body, and rubbing her arms to stay warm. "I don't believe it..."

"Don't you dare say that, Wenda," Morcant snapped, raising his voice in a manner I had never heard him use before. Maredudd held me to his side, preventing me from following.

"What can I say! That's Geraint's house!" Mum cried, pointing towards the cave mouth.

"Then, are you saying the Goddess is lying?" Morcant tilted his head, his knife-hand hovering at his side. I felt that he was threatening her, and wanted to step in, and defend her, but Maredudd wouldn't let me go.

"No, I'm saying she's made a mistake." Mum folded her arms. Her eyes were glistening, and she looked worried to tears.

"She never makes mistakes."

Mum continued to shake her head, but she said no more. Morcant approached her carefully, and she allowed him to put his hand on her shoulder.

"Wenda. We need you in this circle. You can't deny what has been shown. Evan's body is in that garden, and it is our duty to unearth it. That is the Goddess's will. Think of Evan, think of your son. Is Geraint more important than them?" he asked, and her hand grabbed his wrist, squeezing it as though in search of support.

"I can't believe Geraint would hurt Evan," she whimpered, allowing Morcant to bring her into a hug, her face pressing to his waistcoat as he turned to look at us over his shoulder. He nodded, his eyes closing briefly.

"We are not finished here," he murmured.

Morcant summoned us once more to our places around the fire. He took up the knotted thread woven of Geraint's hair, and threw it into the pan upon the fire, the oily string disappearing beneath the simmering surface. I placed the wand on the ground before me, and Mum and Maredudd did the same. I could see the tears in Mum's eyes as they shone every time she turned her head, and yet it seemed she was still willing to go ahead with the rest of the ritual. She wouldn't make eye contact with anyone, not even me. Older relationships were at play here, relationships of authority, and studentship between her, and Morcant that I had never known existed, further revealing to me unknown tales from the past I had never been told. I wanted to reach out to her, but the circle Morcant commanded was rigid, and it left me feeling awkward, and clumsy. The relaxed mood we had shared before had been consumed by something else.

"Geraint Clough, you who would harm your brother, and lie to those who love you," Morcant answered with a voice much firmer than before, his hairless brows meeting in a frown. He lifted his athame, and knocked it against the rim of the pan, the metal clanging loudly. "Geraint Clough, you who deserves punishment for your wrongdoing!"

I flinched, alarmed as the candles that Morcant had arranged in a small circle around the fireplace suddenly burst into flame. The wicks cracked loudly, fire erupting as though a spark had been struck upon gunpowder.

"Lucifer, she who shows no mercy, she who burns brighter than the Seraphim. Lend us your strength," Morcant continued. He put down the knife, and opened one of the wooden boxes, taking out a small bottle of liquid, and after dabbing some of the sweet oil onto his fingertip, he used it to draw some symbols upon the red wax of the candle sticks. He then cut a cross through each of them with his silver blade. I wanted to ask what was happening now as he hadn't told me what we were to do after the casting of the circle, so I was surprised to hear him speaking of a different God. Replacing the bottle in the box, he held out both his hands, so Mum and Maredudd took one each, and offered their free hands to me. I looked at them both anxiously, before imitating.

As soon as their hands enclosed mine, I felt as though I had been plugged into an electric circuit as a violent vibration bolted down my arms and met in my very centre, causing me to let out a whimper of discomfort. It was as though all of us were connected now, sharing the same flow of energy, running between us through skin-to-skin contact as it radiated out from Morcant and poured into us.

"Owen, close your eyes and relax. I will guide the circle, just let the images come to you. Do not speak, you may ask questions later," Morcant murmured sternly, but when I looked at him to show acknowledgement, his eyes were shut.

I did as I was told, the light from the fire still reaching me through my eyelids. My heart was palpitating, and sweat was soaking my shirt. I was starting to feel exhausted. As soon as I began to still my mind, I became distinctly aware of another presence close by. It was different to the one before, which in comparison had been clear and glassy like the surface of a pond. This one was like popping static, and it made my hair stand on end. I felt even Maredudd was trembling slightly, his fingers squeezing my hand tightly to stop it from slipping free as his palms were sweating too. The presence moved, circling us, buffeting the flames of the fire, and brushing against us. I gasped as what shockingly felt like a feminine hand stroked over my face and head, a fingertip running from my chin and down my throat before vanishing. That's when the visions started to flash through my mind.

Suddenly, I was in the sky, flying.

"We come for you." Morcant's voice echoed, a sound as smooth, and sleek as the music of a clarinet. "We come for you... We come for you..."

I could see the village below me. It was dark, but I could see everything, feel the wind on my face, the cold air on my skin. Slate roofs, emerald tree-tops, the orange illumination of street lamps on asphalt still warm from the sun's rays. Gardens and pavements passed beneath me, and people were walking alone like tiny ants crawling. Terrified that I would fall, it took a great amount of effort to keep myself calm, to tell myself this wasn't real, but it was crystal clear, it felt more than just a vision. I heard other voices whispering the same words, and realised they were the voices of Mum and Maredudd, soft and spidery like wind through the boughs of the trees. The land below started to vanish as though being sucked into a hole, shooting and darting away, lights blinking out, leaving me surrounded by darkness. Only the wind breezed past, lifting my hair and brushing against my beard.

"You can't hide from us," Morcant whispered.

Suddenly, I was rushing forward. Down, down towards grass turned blue by the moonlight, towards a dense patch of woodland that looked so familiar. Tree trunks whooshed by, close enough to scratch me, but I was like air, like a formless breeze that passed right through them when they sought to block my path. Sweeping, sweeping, up over the hill. I heard the shrieking of birds and the rushing of ocean waves, salt slick in the air, and the grey motion of clouds above. I wanted to scream, but the sound was dead in my throat.

A glass door appeared, closer, and closer, my body tensing as I thought I would crash into it, but instead I flew through the solid surface like a ghost. We were in a dark hallway, we were in Geraint's house. Everything looked as I knew it, except it was dark, no lamps on to banish the shadows. A wall approached, and I clenched my teeth, knowing that like the door I was going to be taken through it, and as the plastered surface rushed past my ears, I had no choice, but to witness everything.

"I see you there." Morcant's voice became a thundering tumult.

"I see you!" Maredudd shouted. The noise was like a steam engine pumping past.

There he was, Geraint. He sensed our presence immediately, and turned, looking over his shoulder, and

I felt the penetration of dark eyes piercing me. His nude body was drenched in blood. Red on his face, in his mouth, between his teeth. His jaws opened, and he screamed.

"I banish thee!" Geraint howled, the sound assaulting me, pelting across me like bricks thrown out of malice, pain shattering inside me like a fallen teapot.

Maredudd's bellowing voice became a roaring quake, a bass rumble that rippled through the ground, and Morcant's whisper was like nails on a chalkboard. I thought I heard Mum crying somewhere in the distance.

"Upon thy face my claws open your flesh, marking you for what you are. Liar, killer, thief. Treacherous brother. I pierce your heart with the punishing blade." Maredudd's booming words shook me as though the ground itself was in upheaval. "Lay down your weapons. I see you."

"I banish thee! Be gone! Be gone!" Geraint kept screaming. Wind was tearing at his wet hair, and slapping at his body, sending spatters of blood to paint the cluttered cabinets, and worktables that surrounded his cowering form.

"I see you, brother!"

A sudden plopping sound snapped me out of the trance. I fell forward, my arms going out to prevent my face from hitting the floor, all the energy sapped from my body, and leaving me shaking, and drenched in sweat. As I pushed myself upright, I found everyone kneeling in the spots I had last seen them, but they were no longer holding hands. Mum had opened up one of the wooden boxes, and from it she was taking rusty old nails, tossing them one by one into the frothing milk-filled pan. A cold shiver ran through me, and I wiped at my wet face. Snot dribbled from my nose, so I licked it away. Maredudd looked at me, and his face was grave, weary. He didn't need to say anything. I could tell that things had become suddenly serious. I watched as

Morcant ran his athame through his clawed hand, opening a cut in his palm, and squeezing a generous drop of black blood into the mixture.

"Steady now." He breathed, looking across the circle at me. No sooner had he spoken than the walls of the cave shook, and I shrieked, shielding my head from falling stones that rained upon my shoulders. A few fell into the pan, but no one moved to fish them out. Mum continued her rhythmic motion, ignoring the stones that pelted upon her head, and arms.

"It's okay, don't leave the circle." Maredudd reached to hold my hand, crushing it in his grip.

"I'm scared," I cried. Something felt wrong. Very wrong.

The walls shuddered, and quaked again, more shards of rock pattering around us. There came a foul stench, a rotting stink that began to drift around us, drowning out the sweet smell of the milk, and the fresh fragrance of the incense. I wanted to get up, to run away, and hide somewhere far from here, but I couldn't leave them, not now. A rumbling groan spread through every surface, and I was convinced that the cave was going to collapse, and kill us, but the groan turned into a roaring noise. I pinched my eyes shut in agony, the volume hurting my ears.

"MAREDUDD." The voice was a buzzing vibration that filled me from the ground up. "I WILL COME FOR YOU. MAREDUDD. I WILL COME FOR YOU."

The voice echoed into a cacophony, the words becoming nothing more than an unintelligible shriek. The light from the fire, and the candle-flames did nothing to keep away the blackness that had begun to swell inside the cave like a mass of smoke, creeping, and swirling around the border of the circle we sat within. The cave shook again, another shower of pebbles, the blackness pressing closer still, enveloping our circle inside its core as it bloomed in every nook, and cranny, blocking the view of the bay from the cave mouth.

"Geraint Clough. I speak your name as the master addresses his slave. Be gone now." Morcant lifted his athame and pointed it into the air. "Be gone!"

A thunderclap rolled through the cave, and the darkness was sucked out of the cave mouth, drawn away as though on the currents of a harsh gale, extinguishing the candle-flames, and almost dousing the fire. I clung to Maredudd's hand as the sooty smoke dissipated, and was taken by the wind, leaving us coughing on its stench. The fire timidly grew once more, and Mum sat there with the box on her knees, her cheeks red, and her hair tousled from the breeze. Exhausted, Morcant used his knife to support himself, the end of the blade finding purchase in the bumpy granite floor. Sweat was running down his face, and at some point he must have removed his waistcoat as he was now only in his damp shirt, a few, buttons undone at his throat.

"He knows we know. But he also knows that he will be punished. I will keep this fire burning, and this pan bubbling until no liquid remains," he said as he moved to sit comfortably, his tail dragging along the floor to curl round his leg.

"He was meant to be in Cardiff..." Mum mumbled, her head bowed as she looked down at her hands upon her knees.

None of us said a word. I let go of Maredudd's arm, and got up, moving round the fire so that I could finally kneel beside her, and I put my arm round her shoulders, pressing my head to hers. I knew she felt betrayed. Mum always saw the good in everybody, and sometimes that meant she didn't see the bad, simply because she didn't want to see it. We had revealed Geraint for what he was, and that was painful for her.

Morcant and Maredudd performed the last rites of departure, declaring the ritual over, and paying gratitude for the spirits that had helped us. Mum didn't say a word. For a long time we sat there in the cave, and Mum wept for a while, so I comforted her as best as I could, but what could I say? It was hard enough trying to convince her that Geraint was in the wrong. Now came the obstacle of convincing her not to forgive him. Morcant was certain Geraint would crawl away and hide for a while. Maredudd had battered him cruelly, leaving him psychically wounded, and he would need time to regain his energy. I didn't understand how any of this was possible, and after being taken through the air by Morcant's trance, I was even more confused, and bewildered than before. Still, we at least knew now where to dig, but I also had to face that Dad really was gone. There was no longer any hope of his return.

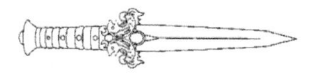

Mum decided to stay with Morcant for the night. Maredudd fetched some pillows, and cushions for her to rest on while his father knelt before the fire. We were all feeling pretty drained, but of the group, Morcant had taken the heaviest beating. I saw how his hands shook, and how tired his face was as he added more wood to the fire and stirred the frothing pan of discoloured milk. I wanted to offer some words of encouragement, or to tell him how amazing it had been, or even to thank him for teaching me, but I was speechless. I sat there with my mouth open dazedly as Maredudd draped a blanket round his father's shoulders and planted a kiss on his forehead. The white-faced wizard smiled gratefully, looking up at his son with warm fondness in his eyes. Even after everything that had happened, he was still going to sit awake, and watch the milk burn away, even while the rest of us went to find some rest. Mum was already snoozing, her eyes closed as her head sank in a feather-down pillow, a duvet pulled up to her chin.

"Come on, let's go," Maredudd whispered against my ear as he bent to help me up. I took hold of his hands, and he lifted me to my feet, my body aching as though I had just finished running a marathon.

The lights had all come back on across the bay, and I let the cool sea wind soothe my skin as we climbed the path up the cliff, the air fresh after the suffocating stink that had filled the cave. Neither of us spoke until we were inside the cottage, and Maredudd put the kettle on the boil.

"You did well tonight," he mumbled drowsily as he watched me taking some cups from the cupboard.

"Thanks." I made a lazy smile, accidentally missing the cup and dropping a teabag on the counter instead. "I had no idea what I was doing, but I tried my best."

"You had me fooled." He chuckled as he shuffled onto the kitchen stool with a sigh of relief.

"I've never done anything like this before. I'm still not really sure what I witnessed."

"It's always like that the first time. It was great to have you there. It's been a long time since we had a full circle like that. We'd be even stronger if we had a few more people join us," he told me as he rubbed his eyes with his thumbs. "It's a shame your first time had to be a violent one."

"Well, maybe next time it can be for something nice instead."

We took our tea to the bedroom, but Maredudd fell asleep before he even finished his. As soon as my head hit the pillow, I was out like a light. Our work wasn't done, not yet.

The next day, we showered, and dressed, and ate our breakfast together in the sunshine. It was another beautiful day in the bay. It was fortunate for us as it meant we wouldn't have to dig in the rain. Mum was in a better mood than she had been yesterday, but I could see she was just hiding her sadness, locking it away in the back of her mind, and putting on a brave face. Morcant was still present beside the fire, except during the night he had propped himself up on a cushion, looking rather Buddha-like as he rested his head in his palm. Mum must have brought the seagull up to keep him company as it sat beside him, its head hunkered down, and its eyes squinting while it napped.

The milk in the pan had become little more than a brownish gunk surrounding the pile of nails, and he must have taken the stones out at some point as they were nowhere to be seen. Morcant was glad that soon he could douse the fire and put the nails in a jar. It would give him a chance to rest after such exertion. Even though he called himself an old man, all I saw in him was raw power, but I suppose even raw power needs to rest sometimes.

When we were ready to go, we walked across the beach to Geraint's house. The only one who didn't seem nervous was Maredudd, but even he was behaving rather quiet compared to usual.

"I don't think he's here," he said as we climbed the path towards the house. The sun shone down on it, and birds were twittering in the trees; nothing seemed out of place or out of the ordinary. It was almost as though last night had never happened.

"Owen, you take Maredudd to get the spades from the shed. I need to feed the animals," Mum instructed as we stopped at the front gate. "You can bet Geraint didn't bother to do it last night."

"Okay. I'm sure the goats will be happy to see us." I smiled, hoping they were doing all right.

We went through the side gate into the back garden, and Mum climbed the steps to the rear door, fiddling with her keys before finding the right one to unlock it. For some reason, none of us would make a sound. It was ridiculous because there was no way Geraint was going to appear and attack us after being wounded the night before. Mum stepped straight into the kitchen and went about her business as though nothing was wrong, dumping her handbag on the kitchen table, and taking out the buckets to fill with animal feed. Maredudd glanced at me, making a hesitant smirk, and I rolled my eyes.

"Come on, let's get the spades." I gestured towards the small shed that shared a wall with the chicken enclosure. "Do you know where we're meant to dig? I mean, this garden is pretty big, so it would help to have a starting point."

"Dad said the Goddess told him the exact spot was in the goat pen," he told me, following at my shoulder across the lawn.

"Oh joy, we get to dig through goat poop too then." I threw my hands in the air. As if sensing they were being talked about, the goats came trotting over to the fence, lifting their heads over it, and watching us pass. Roger started beating, and kicking the ground with his hooves, tossing his head, and flapping his ears.

"Don't worry, Roger, Mum's bringing you food now." I stopped to stroke his head, but he was inconsolable, and started biting at my clothes. "Hey, stop that now. I know you're hungry, but you'll have to be a bit more patient than that."

"What's the combination for the lock?" Maredudd interrupted, and I looked over to find him waiting beside the shed.

"Oh—it's 2249," I told him, moving away from the huffing goat to stand at his side.

I watched as he turned the spools, and popped the padlock open, both of us grinning at each other. The shed was full of cobwebs, and spiders so Mum hated going in there, but the spiders didn't bother me at all. All of her gardening equipment was stored here, which meant she usually had to ask me or Geraint to take them out for her if she wanted to actually do any gardening, otherwise if she ventured in herself she'd end up screaming, and fussing with her hair, believing she was covered in bugs. There were only two spades, so one of us would have to be on tea duty while the other two did the hard labour. Mum seemed to know this already and designated herself as the tea maid since she came down the steps with a tray laden with a teapot, and cups, and put it on the bench, a cheeky smile on her face.

"There you are, boys. You get on with the digging, and I'll sort out the animals," she answered as she watched us heading towards the goat pen. "Uh, what are you doing? You're not digging by there, are you? It hasn't been mucked out yet."

"Dad said the body is in the goat pen." Maredudd paused as I unlatched the gate.

"Oh, well, suit yourself. But at least put some wellies on first." She pointed a finger at him as she turned to go back to the house.

I never thought I would ever end up digging the earth in search of my father's bones. I tried to steel myself, to distract myself from the thought as Maredudd, and I began taking up the earth together, my body aching with tiredness, and my skin hot with the sunshine. Fortunately, Mum had reminded me to put on some sun-block before we started. She kept the goats busy on the lawn with buckets full of food, and encouraging them to eat the fresh grass, cooing to them as she petted their heads, and stroked their ears. They seemed grateful for some human contact after being left alone the night before. Roger kept turning to look between us, his mouth chomping, and smacking as he ate, still pawing the ground with a rear hoof as though something was agitating him.

It wasn't long before we struck the jackpot. Maredudd's spade hit something hard, and as he turned the soil, we discovered a cluster of yellowed bones in the bottom of the hole. My heart lurched into my throat, and I moved away, unable to look as he bent to reach in, and examine them.

"It's alright. It's an animal." He assured me, holding out his hand to show me the lower jaw. It looked like it belonged to a small carnivore, a fox or a badger perhaps.

"Oh. I can't tell if that's good or bad." I breathed a sigh of relief.

"There are a few here," he commented, chucking bone after bone out onto the ground at my feet. All sorts of bits, skulls, leg bones, spinal sections, and ribs. All from different sized animals.

"Well he does enjoy his taxidermy. Not sure why he'd bother to bury it here though." I looked down at the pale bits and pieces.

"These had ritual use. Look." Maredudd held up a long piece and pointed to the patterns scraped into its surface, perhaps by a knife. "Probably parts he used to summon that thing he created."

I shuddered, thinking of Chief's staring blue eyes.

We continued to dig, refilling holes as we went, and discovering more, and more hidden heaps of animal bones. It made sense that he would use this area to bury these things since it was the only part of the garden that wasn't covered by lawn. If he buried it under the grass, it would be obvious he had taken up the turf. Mum watched us dig as she leaned against the fence with a mug of tea, reaching to pet the goats with her free hand. Despite the jolly face she was putting on, I could tell she was tired too, physically, and emotionally. We dug, and dug, and dug some more, but the only bones we found were animal ones. The pile we amassed was big enough to fill a bin liner. I wasn't sure whether to feel glad that we hadn't found anything human, because it could have meant that Dad was buried elsewhere in the garden, which would mean more hours digging by hand.

"I think she was wrong," Mum remarked as we sat down on the grass while the goats grazed around us, exhausted, and damp with sweat, our hands filthy with earth.

"No, she's never wrong. Why would she point us yere if it was the wrong place?" Maredudd shook his head and lifted his mug to his lips so that he could sip his tea.

"Maybe she's wrong sometimes. Or maybe she's being spiteful, and playing games with us," she suggested with a tilt of her head.

"Don't let Dad hear you say that," he murmured, his eyes half-closing.

"Maybe he's buried much deeper than we've been able to dig?" I intervened, sensing that they might start arguing at any moment. We were all stressed, and frustrated, and fighting wasn't going to make things any better.

"Then what can we do? Hire a machine? Call the police, and get them to tear up the whole garden? This is a waste of time." Mum shook her head, and I saw that she was rapidly losing faith in this entire plan.

"Wenda, please don't say that," Maredudd requested as he leaned his forehead against his muddy palm. "There has to be a reason why she pointed us here. We just need to figure it out."

"This kind of nonsense is why I gave up witchcraft. It's too cryptic. How hard could it possibly be for a Goddess of all things to communicate a message in plain English, or even Welsh? Surely she speaks either of those languages?"Mum huffed as she put her mug on the tray, holding her hands out at Maredudd despairingly. "Is that too much to ask of her?"

Maredudd wouldn't look at her. He stared away from her, towards the goat pen, his face frowning with annoyance.

"Mum, not everyone speaks English or Welsh. Maybe not even Gods. But that's not the point. What Maredudd is trying to say is that we can't give up. Even if the Goddess is wrong, we still found Geraint out to be a liar." I got up, standing before her to keep her attention. "I know you're hurt that he lied to you, and you straight up don't want to believe that he hurt Dad, but denying it isn't going to make it go away. You can't keep burying your head like an ostrich."

She shook her head slowly, unable to make eye contact with me, but her scowl soon loosened into an embarrassed smile. She sighed, turning towards me, and stroking my hair before pulling me forward for a hug.

"Oh, Owen, you sound so much like your dad when you tell me off." She chuckled, patting me on the back as she leaned back in my arms. "I know you think I'm just a silly woman shooting her mouth off all the time. But somebody has to play Devil's advocate. It just usually turns out to be me doing it."

"Nobody thinks you're a silly woman. I just don't want to give up on Dad. I know he's gone, but I can't rest until we find him. This is the closest we've ever been to figuring out what happened, and I'm just not satisfied with the suicide story. I don't believe Dad would do that, it's too out of character," I said, hoping she would understand me, and perhaps agree, but I wasn't betting on that too much.

She nodded sheepishly. "I'm sorry for winding you up, Maredudd."

"Apology graciously accepted. Please, let's not argue again. We don't have much time before Geraint is well enough to attack us again." He reminded her as he rose to his feet and put his mug on the tray too. "I think it's pointless digging by yere for now. I agree with you Wenda, this is a waste of time when we have only two spades, and a time limit. But like Owen, I can't give up on Evan either. He needs all of us to keep going for his sake."

Mum wanted to stay at the house, and when we had

finished digging, and put the spades away, she was already in the kitchen peeling vegetables for dinner. As far as she was concerned, she didn't think Geraint was any harm to us, her in particular, and I became annoyed at how difficult she was being. Maredudd said she was acting just like she used to when she was young. As Morcant's student, she had been disobedient compared to the three boys. We had to persuade her to leave, and we only managed to get her out of the door after she had somehow found the time to pack herself a suitcase of clothes, and essentials, insistent that she was going to stay in the cottage, and not down in Morcant's prison cell.

I could tell she was miffed that she had called into work sick for the day for what appeared to her to have been a waste of time since we had dug up nothing of substantial value from the garden. She was still complaining as we walked back along the beach, and I began to feel wary of her. The words she was saying, and the way she kept raising her voice was like Mum, but at the same time, not like her at all. Maredudd handled her like a difficult teenager. I could imagine him making a good father, not that I could see us having children together, not yet anyway. Perhaps that would change with time.

"Where are you going with that suitcase, Wenda?" Morcant's voice stopped us as we climbed the cliff path. We turned to find him standing at the entrance to the tunnel, his cloak wrapped around him, revealing nothing, but his pale face. He pointed a curled claw at the luggage Mum was carrying, and she looked down at it.

"I'm staying in the cottage," she replied with a baffled frown.

"No, you'll stay here with me." He gestured she come with him into the caves. "You're dirty with bad energy. I can smell it on you from here. I won't have you passing it to the other two like a disease. Come now, woman."

"Just who do you think you are, telling me what to do?" She puffed out her chest, almost losing her footing on the bumpy ground so Maredudd pushed her back by her shoulder.

"Wenda, come now," he repeated. "I speak your name."

"Go on Mum. You've been acting funny all day." I urged, placing my hand on the bottom of her back, but when I did, she flinched, and looked round at me abruptly. I shrank back when she looked into my eyes. Her face was glaring, and her lip was raised, a wolf waiting to bite. I had never seen her look that way before, and it frightened me.

"Wenda!" Morcant's voice was a barking echo that rang across the cliff.

As if snapping out of a trance, Mum jumped slightly, and motioned to shuffle along the narrow pathway towards him, leaving me clinging to Maredudd's arm for protection. I looked up at him, at the concerned expression he wore, creating lines on his forehead, and at the corners of his mouth. His lime-green eyes were focused on Mum's back as though guiding her towards his father.

"Sweetheart, I invite you for tea, and cake, and this is how you treat me?" Morcant said merrily as he put his arm round Mum's shoulder.

"I'm sorry, Morcant. I'm not feeling well, haven't done since last night," Mum confessed. She sounded so tired all of a sudden, and her head hung timidly. He held her to his side, his claws on her arm keeping her steady as he looked across at us. A silent conversation took place between him, and Maredudd, but I didn't know what was said, they simply made eye contact, and that was that.

"Come on, let's go home." Maredudd bent slightly to

whisper against my ear as he ushered me away from the cave.

"What's wrong with Mum?" I questioned as I continued up the path, picking my footfalls wisely, and using the outcrops to keep balanced.

"Don't worry, Dad will help her. Geraint must be trying to take control of her. She's weaker than we are because she trusts him, is willing to open herself to him. Dad will sever the connection," he reassured me, and I felt his hand hold onto mine briefly, giving it a small squeeze.

"It won't hurt her, will it?" I looked over my shoulder at him as we approached the top of the cliff. I had to raise my voice as the wind was buffeted against our faces, billowing our clothes, and playing with our hair.

"She'll be fine. She's a strong old bird. Anyway, Dad will take care of her so don't worry." He leaned close to give me a kiss, and I wilted, giving in.

"You just want to have me to yourself, don't you." I put my hand on his chest, keeping him from enveloping me in his arms. When he looked down at me, I grinned.

"Am I that transparent?" He grinned back, matching my mischievous smile with his own.

Shortly after we returned to the cottage, I decided I would make dinner since it was already gone four o'clock, and we both were quite hungry. Maredudd sat by the counter drinking a glass of cider, watching me cut the vegetables on the chopping board, but neither of us spoke. My mind was far away, following behind Dad's memory, and seeking Mum's wellbeing, hoping everything was going to be all right. I made enough food for four. It was like we were a family again, like it had been before Dad's disappearance, and I used to cook for three. But this time the roles had swapped around a bit, and I had gained a father-in-law. I wanted to take the meals down to the cave to see how Mum was doing, but

Maredudd was adamant that I stayed away.

He said that the energy could be passed onto me, and he didn't want to risk me falling under Geraint's control too. I sat in the living room with my food on my lap, waiting for him to return so that we could eat together, and for the first time in a while, I was feeling rather defeated. This was a lot more complex than just being positive, than just being strong enough to get over things, and move on. There were things taking place that I was too weak to have any influence over, and all I could do was rely on my new friends, to be taken along with the events the way the estuary currents had carried me out to sea.

The slowly setting sun filled the room with orange light, and I looked at the ornaments and candles everywhere, at least feeling safe in this cluttered haven Maredudd now referred to as my home too. I couldn't help feeling afraid though when I heard footfalls outside, but I was relieved when it was his voice that spoke to me from the kitchen.

"She's doing well. No need to worry," he called to me as he picked up his own plate of curry and came to sit down beside me. His hair was messed by the wind, and he looked as tired as I felt.

"I'm glad," I commented, looking down at my tray. My knife, and fork were in my hands, but I hadn't eaten a thing. He sensed this immediately, and I was grateful when he reached to stroke my face, touching my beard with his fingertips.

"Hey. Everything's gonna be all right. When Geraint next shows himself, we'll take him down. We just need Wenda to be well enough to assist," he said, his voice a comforting murmur that I was glad to hear after the silence he had left me in. "Dad's trying to find the location of the creature so he can destroy it. He said that early this morning, a fishing boat found a whale in the next bay over that had been pulled up out of the water, and partially eaten. Hoof prints in the sand."

"It's still killing?" I was surprised as I finally scooped some food onto my fork.

"Yes. Owen, there's something I should have told you sooner... But, you know the day your mam brought me to the house?" he said slowly, looking up at me through his eyelashes as he moved his food about on his plate, his fork scraping against the ceramic.

"When you were injured? Are you saying the beast attacked you?"

He nodded, taking a mouthful of rice, and chewing. I looked at him, knowing that he was telling the truth. I had seen the wound. I hadn't thought at the time that it looked anything like what a jagged rock could do to flesh.

"I was swimming in the bay. You've seen my seal pelt. Well, I like to swim as a seal. But that's beside the point," he explained cautiously, stopping between sentences to eat. "That morning, I went for a swim, and next thing I knew, I was being pulled under by my flippers. I thought it was a shark. It wouldn't have been the first time I've seen a shark by yere. As a seal, I make myself their natural prey. But still I didn't get a good look at it, so I couldn't be sure what had gone for me. But I managed to escape onto the shore, and there was Wenda walking along the sand."

"Didn't you put two, and two together?" I questioned. "Didn't you think maybe Geraint had sent it in after you?"

"No. I didn't think Geraint was responsible for these attacks. I didn't even think Geraint was still doing witchcraft. Even after I challenged him to his face, and accused him of killing Evan, he didn't make any moves to attack me psychically. He punched me, yes, but there came no curses or spells, and to create a monster from the parts of other animals takes a great amount of skill, and power. It was always clear that Geraint was Dad's star pupil, but I didn't think he would be skilled enough to do what he's done. It's almost impressive," he confessed, his mouth curving into a bitter smile.

I went quiet. I wasn't sure what to think or say, so I ate some more curry, and contemplated what he'd said. It made me wonder if Geraint had done more than just antagonise me when I was living there with him. It made me wonder if the arguments had been a front for something darker.

"Geraint must have been secretly toiling away all these years while he distanced himself from us. He wanted to do things Dad deemed as immoral, so Dad refused to teach him further skills out of fear that he would use them for harmful means. It seems he taught himself in Dad's absence," Maredudd continued in a murmur. "Geraint was never a bad person, he's just... Lost. Very lost. Dad thought he would save him from further hurt by withholding these teachings. I guess he failed."

"They say there's a fine line between genius, and insanity..." I commented in an undertone.

"Pity Geraint has taken a step too far over the line towards insanity," he agreed, and I managed a pessimistic chuckle.

They also say, 'speak of the Devil, and he shall appear.'

That night, after all the lights were off, and we were laying in the dark, I struggled to sleep. I was tired enough to sleep like a log, but every time I began to drift off, I found myself standing on a beach bathed in moonlight. My bare feet were on the soft, moist sand of the shore, and the waves were gently washing towards me, stripes of light flickering on their flowing surface as the moon cast its pale eye upon me. When I looked down, I saw that I was naked, and to my left, my clothes had been folded into a neat pile with my boots on top. The key, the copper key on Maredudd's hair string, was placed with them, and I got an itching sensation in my hand that urged me to reach for it as it sung to me in a delicate hum. Suddenly, my body lurched forward as though being controlled remotely, heading for the waves.

"No!" I shouted into the desolate night, and just like that, my eyes opened, and I found myself staring at the ceiling of Maredudd's bedroom once more.

Several times this had happened, and I was starting to feel afraid. Too afraid to sleep.

I rubbed at my eyes and groaned, becoming increasingly fed up, wondering if I should just go downstairs and make myself a mug of hot chocolate. Maredudd slept soundly beside me, the glow from the moon coming through the window, and casting silver highlights on the contours of his face. It was so quiet: no wind, not even the sound from the waves below. I shuffled from the bed and took a sip of water from the glass on the bedside table. The moonlight was so bright tonight that I could see every blade of grass, and every leaf of hedge when I looked outside. The ocean was calm, and barely seemed to be moving.

But something else was moving. My eyes were instantly attracted to the slow, stealth motion of something enormous slinking alongside the bushes at the far edge of the cliff, deliberate steps bringing it nearer to the house. For a moment, I froze, my eyes fixated on it until I was able to snap myself out of it, and back away from the window. I went straight to the bed, climbing on it, and rocking Maredudd by his arm.

"Maredudd! Maredudd! Wake up!" I hissed, shaking him until his eyelids parted, and he stared into space dazedly.

"Huh...?" He yawned, lifting his arm to wipe at his face.

"Maredudd, there's something in the garden," I whispered, too scared to look round at the window as though expecting a face to be there waiting for me.

He came to after a moment of confusion, his eyes now focused on me instead, and he sat up, his hair falling from his ears, and around his shoulders.

"What did you say? Something in the garden?"

The second he finished his sentence, we heard a loud thumping against the back door. Something big was pounding on it, the wooden panel rattling in its frame. Thud, thud, thud. The shuddering stopped, and we looked towards the bedroom door, both of us holding our breath.

"Stay here," Maredudd said as he climbed from the bed in his pyjama trousers and went across to the broad oak cabinet he kept facing the bed. I had never seen him open it. The only furniture I had seen him use besides the bed was the matching oak wardrobe in the corner where he kept his clothes. The rest of the room was remarkably bare compared to the other rooms in the house.

"Where are you going?" I clambered to the edge of the bed as he pulled out one of the drawers by its black iron handles, revealing the silk-wrapped objects inside.

"Downstairs. To see this thing face to face," he replied determinedly.

He took up one of the parcels, pulling the silk sheet from around it, and tossing it back in the drawer. In his hand he held his personal athame, an item I had never seen before, perhaps as he had not had any reason to use it until now. Morcant's athame had been plain, rustic even, by comparison. This one was made of highly polished copper, and it shone like a flashing flame even in this dim light. The handle was solid wood painted with a royal blue varnish, and the hand-guard was shaped into the likeness of two arching Medieval fish, their eyes inlaid with pale blue gemstones. I wanted to take it, and examine it, how pretty, and delicately made it was. I was so mesmerised at the sight of it that I didn't even register that he was leaving me. The bedroom door opened, and he darted out, slamming it behind himself.

"Wait! Don't go out there!" I shouted after him, stumbling, and falling to my knees as I rushed to follow. The thumping sound downstairs was getting louder, more frequent, and as I stepped into the hallway, the floor juddered, the walls moaning as though an earthquake was shaking the entire building.

Suddenly, the quaking stopped, and I heard Maredudd's voice like a howling gale that came blasting up the stairs, and almost knocked me off my feet, the wind forcing me against the wall, taking my breath away. A rumble of bass noise spread through the house, filling the air with static. I forced myself forward, clinging to the handrail as I descended the stairs. All of the ornaments in the living room rattled together as the tremor of noise was absorbed by the floor of the cottage. The back door was ajar, the wind rocking it on its hinges, and slamming it against the wall as I approached, and pushed it open.

I cried out when the charged metal of the door handle shocked me, leaving me no choice, but to use my bare toes to hold the door to the wall. The moonlight was as bright as a stadium strobe, and I had to shield my eyes from it as I gripped onto the doorframe, the battering gales whipping at my pyjamas, and pelting me with leaf litter, and garden pebbles. Maredudd's form was lit up as though under a spotlight, his arm held high, the orange blade of his athame pointed heavenward. The bass booming seemed to be emanating from the concentrated air around his sinuous form, swirling, and blustering in a whirlwind that was twisting about him in circles. I fell back against the door, and slid to the ground, the crackling electricity in the air snapping at my skin and lifting my hair to stand on end.

Beyond, near the edge of the cliff, there was a dark space. Within it I saw two luminous blue dots, a pair of staring eyes, and the blackness was sucking in every ray of light that came within its pull. As I squinted, I was able to make out the shape of the beast inside the dark aura, and when it opened its mouth, and roared, the cry swept towards the cottage in a wall of sound that made me believe the windows were going to shatter. I rolled onto my side, covering my ears, shrieking at the pain that left me momentarily deafened. Liquid spilled from my nose, and when I licked it away, I tasted blood.

Maredudd's voice had become so loud that I no longer heard a thing. Panting, I clawed away from the door, and rammed it shut with my heel, sobbing while I fought to hold it closed in a pathetic bid to protect myself. The ground was vibrating violently, and even the tiled flooring was starting to crack, small pieces chipping off and scattering here and there. As I attempted to catch my breath, I heard a heavy, groaning rush, the sound of something gigantic heading this way. All of a sudden, I heard water crashing, and it came rushing under the door, the icy ocean wave soaking my trousers, and causing me to screech, and lift my backside off the ground. The door shook against my back, trying to push me aside. I tried to hold it firm, but the wave was powerful.

I was sent sliding across the kitchen as the water forced the door ajar, and came gushing in, pouring through the room, and running through into the living room, leaving me pushed up against one of the kitchen cabinets as I huffed at the freezing temperature, my eyes wide, and cheeks red. The tide slowed, weakening, and then slowly started to retract. I lay on my back in defeat and watched as the water began to suck back out of the doorway as though the house had tilted, and gravity was drawing it out again. Every single droplet began to return from where it had come, even the liquid that had soaked into my clothes, and as I struggled to sit upright, I watched the liquid pooling around me, and running off in rivulets towards the back door. The noise had stopped, and my ears were ringing shrilly. Blood stained my lip, and I wiped it in my wrist, hauling myself to my feet, and heading towards the open doorway, heading towards the pressured silence, terrified of what I might find.

Outside, the wave had pulled the grass sideways so that it all pointed towards the edge of the cliff, and a few bushes, and plants had become uprooted. I staggered down the steps, the soles of my feet stung repeatedly by bolts of electricity still lurking in the surrounding ground, but I didn't care. Maredudd knelt on the grass, his back to me, his head bowed. As I got closer, the very air began to tick, and snap, biting at my flesh, pricking me with goosebumps.

"Maredudd!" I called to him, my own voice sounding distant to my deafened ears. When my hands fell upon his shoulders I was struck with a charged shock that made me flinch backwards with a restrained whimper. He was holding his knife in his lap, and blood was seeping from his nose, and depositing scarlet droplets on his bare chest.

"Maredudd, talk to me," I pleaded, ignoring the static that sprung to greet me as I cupped his face in my palms. "Please! Are you okay?"

His chest was rising and falling steadily. I rubbed at the blood on his face with the hem of my shirt, but more slid out into his stubbled moustache. Finally, his tongue emerged, and licked at it.

"Owen..." He breathed. His thick eyelashes parted, but he didn't look at me.

"Maredudd, what the fuck just happened, there was water, and a fucking wave, and the noise, and..." I blurted, tilting his head up and making him look at me. His eyes were glassy, dreamy.

"No need to swear," he whispered. He started to smile at me, and I sighed.

"You're bleeding," I told him, and he nodded slightly. "What happened? I was so scared."

"The beast came to pick a fight with me," he replied, his voice sleepy as he fought to keep his words steady. "I showed it what happens when you mess around with a witch who means business."

"Where did that water come from?" I asked, looking towards the cliff edge over my shoulder.

"The ocean, silly," he replied, and I let go as he moved to get up. He was trembling with exhaustion, and I got up too, putting his arm round my shoulders so that I could support him on the way back to the cottage.

I couldn't manage to get him up the stairs, so I deposited him on the sofa, and rushed to slam the back door shut. I didn't think the beast would come back, but one could never be too careful. I brought some kitchen paper for Maredudd to clean his bloody face with, helping him to sit up, and pushing a glass of water into his hand. He allowed me to take his knife, and when I accepted it from him, I startled at the heat that exuded from it. The handle was sweltering, and steam was rising from the blade, so I put it on one of the glass coasters on the coffee table. The last thing we needed right now was a house fire.

"Are you all right?" I asked, relieved that he seemed to be more conscious than he had a moment ago, and he nodded.

"I'm fine. It's always like this. It'll probably hit me in a couple of days, but that's natural." He shrugged a shoulder before drinking from his glass.

That's when we heard a banging on the front door, and we both looked towards it.

"Owen! Maredudd!" Morcant's voice called to us.

I hurried to the door, unlocking it, and pulling it open to find Morcant standing outside in his blue, and white striped pyjamas, his night-cap pulled on over his hair. He looked quite ridiculous, and cute at the same time, and if the circumstances had been different, I might have smiled.

"Wenda! I can't find Wenda anywhere!" he exclaimed, pointing across the cliff in the direction of the caves. "She's gone!"

Thirteen

The moon's eye watched us as we crossed the beach on foot, Morcant leading the group with knife in hand. We might have looked quite fearsome if it weren't for the fact that all three of us were in our pyjamas, but we didn't have time for fashion. The tide was out, and the ground was hard underfoot as the sand absorbed what little liquid was available, leaving the higher dunes dusty, and pale. The energy that had shocked me when I had touched Maredudd earlier seemed to have accompanied us, emanating outwards from his, and his father's bodies, and leaving me feeling rather normal, and boring by comparison. I wasn't sure how they did this, charged the air with electricity, but at least having them beside me made me feel safe.

The night was calm when we had descended the cliff to the beach below, but as we approached the other side of the bay, a chill wind began to whip around our legs, lifting our clothes, and caressing our hair. I thought I heard the sound of thunder coming from miles away, but neither Maredudd nor Morcant appeared to pick up on it. Geraint's house on the hill above the beach was dark. The windows yawned with shadows, and around the point of its roof, clouds began to culminate, hanging in the air like spectral air-ships, dark, and swirling as oil on water. The wind whistled in my ear and cooled my flesh. I held onto Maredudd's hand, holding onto it like it was the last time I would ever get to again.

We moved silently up the hill, keeping to the shadow of the hedgerow, and creeping in a line towards the front garden of the house. The thunder came again, and this time there was no denying it. All of a sudden, water began to patter on the track, pitching on our shoulders, and in our hair. I looked up at the black sky, relieved that I hadn't worn my spectacles otherwise I wouldn't be able to see where I was going with the lenses covered in rain flecks.

"Walk safely," Morcant whispered as he stopped beside the hedges, turning to look round at us. The glow emitted by his eyes was even more pronounced in this darkness.

"We are with you," Maredudd replied, and his hand crushed mine, reminding me that he would be there for me without needing to say it.

I felt like there was something I should have said, but I just couldn't find the words. They both looked at me with grim smiles. They seemed to sense it too, but none of us spoke. Morcant nodded, turning again towards the gate, his tail lifting so that it did not drag along the dirt road. His taloned hand reached for the latch, and as he pushed the gate open, a loud cry rang out from within the house, all of us looking up sharply towards the source of the sound.

"Mum!" I exclaimed, lunging forward in a bid to rush to the house, but Maredudd still had hold of my hand, and he stopped me.

"No, Owen. It's not safe. We have to stick together," he warned me.

"But he's hurting Mum!" I sobbed, trying to yank my hand free of his grasp. Morcant startled me by grabbing my other arm, and they squashed me between their bodies against the fence, Morcant pressing a claw to my lips.

"Hush. What did I tell you before? A chain is as

strong as its weakest link. We need you to be strong," he whispered, his face inches from mine. He smelled strongly of tea tree oil and burning paper. "Calm yourself, Owen. We must stay calm, all of us. For Wenda."

"But Mum... He's hurting her..." I tried to prevent myself from weeping as I heard her scream again.

"He's using her to draw you in—don't fall for it," Morcant said, stone-faced as he let go of me, and moved away. "Owen, you must be strong. Do you understand?"

I nodded, staring down at my bare feet on the muddy path, trying to fight back the urge to rush to Mum's aid. Morcant eyed me for a moment, before deciding that I was calm enough to continue, and gesturing that we follow. Maredudd kissed me gently on the cheek, his copper athame glinting as he moved past me, and pulled me along.

The front door of the house was unlocked, and Morcant opened it onto the darkness of the hallway. The house reeked of the putrid stench I had smelled before in the cave, and about two feet from the ground there floated a stinking, brownish haze that swirled round our legs as we moved through it. I covered my mouth, restraining myself from retching at the smell. It stank like someone had died in here a week ago, and I really hoped that wasn't the case.

Morcant seemed to know exactly where he was going, so perhaps he had visited this house before in the past, or perhaps he was following the stink towards the person that was making it. The sound of the rain died back as Maredudd shut the door behind us, and took up the rear, his presence behind me assuring me that he would protect me. I followed his father through the house, past the kitchen, through the back room towards the garage where the haze thickened into a suffocating smog, and even he covered his mouth then, his tail swishing in irritation.

"Owen!" Mum's voice shrieked through the door of the work room. The floorboard under which I had hidden the knotted thread had been torn up and was missing.

We paused before the door. Light was creeping around the cracks at its edges, and the faint sound of 70s Blues music stretched thin to our ears as we listened for movement. Mum's voice cried again, calling my name, calling for help. The desire to slam the door open and run in was overwhelming. My heart was pounding, and I felt damp with nervous sweat. The air started to crackle, and tug at the hair on my arms, and when I looked at Morcant, I saw him drawing a pentacle in the air with his knife. He whispered something under his breath and drew an invisible line down his body with his index claw before opening his eyes and reaching for the door handle.

The flash of static was visible in the shadows when his hand touched it, sparking briefly, but causing him no alarm. This door wasn't locked either; we were being invited in. The hinges scraped jarringly as the door was pushed inwards, and the yellow light glowing from the overhead lamps hurt my eyes, momentarily preventing me from seeing anything, but Morcant's black silhouette. The rotting smell in the air became coupled with the scent of formaldehyde, borax powder, and rubbing alcohol. As my eyes adjusted to the light, I saw the many staring faces of the mounted deer, and antelopes Geraint kept hung on the wall of the work room, their glass eyes shining as though alive.

"Morcant!" Mum screamed when she saw him enter.

I moved around him to look over his shoulder and was astonished to find Mum laying on the biggest work bench in the centre of the room. She was completely nude, and her wrists, and ankles were bound to the corners by loops of rope, causing her hands, and feet to turn purple with lack of blood flow. Tears twinkled on her cheeks. She looked as if she hadn't stopped crying since she'd got here. A dotted line had been drawn on her skin in marker pen, starting at her throat, going down between her breasts vertically along her body. Beside her lay a tray laden with an assortment of knives, and scalpels.

"Owen! No! No, leave, get out of here! He's here! He's in here!" She started shouting at me and shaking her head. "Please go! Run! Run Owen!"

"I can't leave you!" I gasped as I struggled to undo the ropes holding her down.

"Owen please, get out of here, he's dangerous, he's—" she pleaded with me, but her words were cut off by a deafening roar that erupted from behind the rows of glass cabinets at the far end of the work room.

All of us froze, our eyes trained on the shadowed area beyond. My hands began to shake; my heart skipped a beat. Glass crunched under a heavy hoof, and bristling fur hissed as it flexed. Without wasting another second to see what lurked there, I nearly knocked the tray off the bench as I scrambled to pick out one of the knives, and Mum panicked as I started to saw away at the rope, each second it took to cut the threads torturous, and agonising.

"Geraint Clough. Well, well, well. What have you done to yourself, my treacherous son?" Morcant chuckled as he and Maredudd moved between us, and the rising shape that was creeping round the edge of the cabinets.

A slithering tail slid along the ground, glass tinkling then crashing as it smashed down through one of the display cases, a rain of shards tumbling across the concrete floor. Taxidermy animals shuddered in their places, suspended birds rocking on their fishing wires from the ceiling. Chief's drool-wet snout appeared from the shadows, black steam puffing from his glistening nostrils, and globules of snot-like saliva hanging from his leathery lips. I let out a muffled squeak, horror and relief coupled as the first rope split free. Mum's hand lifted immediately, clumsily snatching at the nearest scalpel on the table-top so that she could start cutting the rope that held her other wrist. I moved to her ankles, my arm pumping back and forth, careful not to cut her with the razor blade as I sawed tirelessly, my rampant heartbeat racing in my ears.

"So it was you all along," Morcant continued. He seemed to be teasing the creature, taking pleasure in goading it. "After all I taught you, this is what you have become? A monster?"

The beast began to snarl, lips drawing back to reveal the rows of its dagger teeth. Then came a second snarl as another head curled round the furniture to stare at us with its feline eyes. It had two heads now—one was Chief's, and the other was that of a lion. The growls were low, rattling. Glass cracked as it moved forward, but Morcant and Maredudd stood their ground as it came, the humped back of its disproportionate cow torso revealing the new additions of multiple spikes of deer horn poking through the hair. The scalpel in my hand sparked me as electricity filled the air again, choking me, stinging my throat and burning my eyes.

The walls of the work room began to shudder to life, jingling chains and shedding mounted animal heads, jars, and bottles clinking musically on the many shelves and cabinets. Finally, I freed Mum's second ankle, and as I pulled her from the table, the beast launched forward. The front paws crashed through the table as it landed on it, narrowly missing her legs, its slobbering heads snapping after us as I dragged Mum across the ground, glass and razor blades slicing cuts in our knees. Mum was screaming, and she howled as Chief's jaws clamped on a mouthful of her hair, ripping it out at the roots, blood droplets flying into the air as I tore her away from it.

A huge scaly tail smashed through the cabinet facing us as we fled, glass showering on our bare feet, and as we backed away, I bumped into Maredudd's chest. Shouting, he guarded us, guiding us towards the door so that we could escape as his father held the monster back at knife-point. Its roaring bellow followed on our heels as we ran through the fog, fleeing through the garage and out into the kitchen. I slammed the door shut and leaned against it. Blood drenched the knees of my trousers, and the soles of my feet stung madly. Mum collapsed to her knees by the kitchen table, clinging to the edge of it to try and stay upright. I rushed to her side, grabbing her in a hug as we sobbed and shivered. Her hands and feet were reddened and swollen from being tied too tightly, and she had accidentally sliced her own skin as she had fought to free herself, along with some angry bruising caused by the rubbing of the ropes.

"Owen was going to kill me, I swear." She wept into my shoulder as I clutched her to me, blood seeping from her scalp soaking into my pyjama sleeve.

"It's okay, it's okay, it's okay," I repeated, my teeth chattering, the adrenaline making my whole body shake.

"Owen, listen to me." She struggled out of my arms and took me by the shoulders. "Owen, upstairs, where Geraint keeps his gun."

I breathed deeply, fighting to wipe the fear from my mind, but the stinking mist that filled the air made it difficult to think clearly.

"Fetch the gun and shoot that son of a bitch," she pleaded with me, shaking me back and forth by my shoulders.

"Okay." I breathed, my eyes staring at her, shell-shocked.

She stared back, her teeth biting down on her bottom lip. I nodded. For a second we didn't move, but then I struggled to my feet, and pulled her dressing gown off one of the kitchen chairs, carefully draping it round her shoulders. I felt light-headed, but I knew what I had to do. I must have been so high on adrenaline that I didn't feel any pain, only a springy spryness in my limbs that kept me shaking and active. I kissed Mum's forehead, and then went to the door, opening it a crack and looking out into the hallway. The vibration coming from the work room was reverberating through the walls of the house. Photo frames had fallen to the ground, and ornaments had fallen over, smashed on the wood floor.

I stepped outside and shut the door on Mum, turning away from the kitchen and heading for the stairs on hurried feet, my hand reaching for the handrail, a movement that seemed so normal after having lived here for several years. The mist was thinner here, but the smell hadn't dissipated at all. I crept into the bedroom Mum and Geraint shared, knowing vaguely where I needed to look. Suddenly, there was an almighty boom that rocked the entire building. I was thrown sideways, my body flying to land upon Mum's dressing table. My shoulder went straight through her dressing mirror, the fragile glass broken to pieces. Her jewellery box knocked to the ground, spilling bits and pieces on the carpet.

The rumble of thunder was coming from within the building this time, and when I got up, my foot fell on the metal handle of Mum's hairbrush. I shrieked as electricity bolted up my leg, crippling me for a second as I fell back against the wall to support myself. The static Morcant, and Maredudd were generating was spreading through the building, charging every metal object, and turning the house into a death trap. I staggered forward towards the wardrobe on Geraint's side of the bed, throwing the doors open, and pushing the clothes aside in search of the box in which he stored the rifle.

The ground quaked. Something in another room shattered. I seized the leather-bound case and threw it on the bed, undoing the brass latches and revealing the polished weapon within. I didn't have an athame, so this would have to do. I fumbled with the box of ammunition, stuffed a handful of bullets into my trouser pocket, and hauled the heavy weapon into my arms, I panicked as I couldn't remember how to load the damned thing. I would have to ask Mum.

I clung to the handrail as I took each step down the stairs, the house groaning and cracking under the torment the witches were inflicting. I screamed when the furniture in the living room began to slide across the floor towards the door as if dragged on strings, the sofas smashing into the doorframe as I was pelted with DVD cases, and doilies. The telephone table in the hallway slid past me, the phone itself still attached to its cable, preventing it from following like a dog on a chain. Everything was sliding towards the work room as if sucked by a vacuum. When I reached the kitchen, I had to fight to get the door open.

"Hang on, Owen!" Mum shouted to me from the other side as she pushed the furniture aside. The door opened a crack, and she squeezed out, the door immediately slamming back into its frame as soon as I let go of it. I could feel the pulling sensation. It wanted to suck us in too, rifle and all.

"I need you to load this thing." I thrust the gun into her hands.

"Yere," she grunted, and she made it look so easy, tugging the chamber open and ramming a shell inside. She pushed it back into my hands, her head tilting up to look at me.

"I'm going to put some clothes on, and then I'll try to help," she promised, turning and running off along the hallway.

I held the gun to my chest and went the other way,

towards the source. The furniture in the back sitting room had been overturned, and was crowded around the door to the garage, so I had to try and drag it away, just enough to let me squeeze through the door into the garage. Even Mum's car had slid across the concrete and shattered a headlight against the wall. I coughed on the stinking mist, disgusted by the flavourful scum it left on my tongue and in my lungs. The door to the work room was rattling violently. A crackle of electricity shot around the handle when I moved close, leaping towards me in a bid to connect with the rifle in my hands so I backed off, concerned that I might get fried before I even had a chance to fire this thing. Mum had left a bucket and rubber gloves out here after the last time she cleaned the car, so I pulled on a glove to shield myself from the current and cautiously reached for the handle. It popped loudly, and I could feel the glove melting on the hot metal. I turned it quickly, and threw the door wide.

"Shit!" I gasped as the churning wind blasted across my face.

The room was a tornado of glass and smashed furniture. Some of it spun out of the whirlwind, smashing across my chest and face, forcing me to step back. I put out my arm, shadowing my eyes as I looked into the light. Maredudd was kneeling on the ground, dark rivulets of blood streaming from the wound in his arm, and his athame on the floor at his side, his hair flying in the twisting gale as Morcant stood over him, his silver knife held high. His other hand was flung out before him, and his lips were moving. His words were the source of the bass rumble that was shaking the house. The crushing force of the noise was pressing the beast to the far wall, preventing it from moving. It convulsed and writhed, frothing from the mouth as its demented limbs clawed at the air. I clung to the door frame, forcing my foot round the corner to prevent myself from being swept away as I brought the rifle to my shoulder. I had fired it only once before, and that had been a disaster, but what choice did I have now? I had to try, even if the bullet got lost in the maelstrom.

My hand touched the metal barrel. It shocked me, but I ignored it, squinting one eye as I lined it up with the monster's bulging ribs. Sweat and blood coated my fingertips, making the trigger slippery. I took a shot. Bang!

The bullet ricocheted off the breeze-block wall. I shoved my hand into my pocket for another bullet, my breath chugging, sweat in my eyes as I fought to reload, and then aimed again. Another shot, and this one struck home. As soon as the chunk of lead hit the creatures' torso, it exploded. The resulting wave of ominous, ebony smoke that came gushing forth took Morcant off his feet and sent Maredudd sprawling across the glass-strewn ground as chunks of fur and tanned hide battered us. I fell back onto the garage floor, bumping my head on the side of Mum's car, the rifle clattering to the ground. The beast's roar turned into the feeble cry of a man, and as the whipping tempest began to die back, I heard Geraint's voice.

"Do you think you can kill me with a bullet?" He started to laugh maniacally.

I rolled onto my front and got up, crawling to the doorway to peer through. Geraint was crouched on the other side of the room, surrounded by the debris of his taxidermy, his naked skin smattered with shed fur and smeared in a green, oily substance. His face was the most frightening part. His eyes, wide open and shot with veins, revealed his madness, and the smile he wore was one of someone who had nothing left to lose. I held my breath as he looked right at me.

"You are without your armour now," Morcant wheezed as he dragged himself to his feet. Blood was pouring from his nose, staining his mouth and chin scarlet. "I don't want to see you dead, Geraint, but you must cease this madness immediately!"

"It is not madness, you stupid old bastard! It's the culmination of my life's work!" Geraint shouted at him. "You thought you could stop me from learning more! Did you really think you were the end all, be all of everything there is to know? Only a dumb old man like you would be so full of himself as to think that!"

"It was for your own good, to protect you," Morcant answered as he rose to his feet. He looked down at Maredudd who lay there unconscious, covered in glass, and splinters of wood, stepping over him to get between his motionless body and the madman he faced.

"There is no protection for those who think they can act without impunity." Geraint spat as he too rose and moved closer to us. "There is only punishment, for those who think they can ignore the weak when they need help."

"Do we deserve to be punished, my son? We, who have helped you? I, who took you, and nurtured you, put food in your mouth and clothes on your back?" Morcant tried to reason with him.

"No. No." Geraint began to shake his head, a bitter smirk twisting his mouth. "You protected them. You allow them to carry on as though nothing ever happened. Even after everything, you allowed the people who should have helped me to go about their lives. No one was punished for the way I suffered, and ignoring that makes you one of them."

Morcant swallowed hard, looking down at the ground as if out of shame. I thought I saw tears in his eyes. I understood now, why Geraint was so filled with hate. He blamed the village for not being there for him when he needed them most. But that didn't make what he had done right.

"That's why I have to kill you now. All of you. Because if I let you live, you will never let me follow through with justice," he added, bending to pick up one of the knives that had fallen from the decimated workbench.

Morcant searched the debris-covered floor in search of his knife, but it was nowhere to be seen. I got up, hauling myself to my feet as Geraint began to charge. Our feet seemed to strike the floor, completely synchronised, Geraint's nude form becoming the sole target of my vision as I pounded for him, ignoring the pain in my feet and the ache in my knees. His arm rose, poised with the carving knife high above his head as Morcant turned to protect himself. As my body struck Geraint and knocked the wind from my lungs, we were thrown to the ground in a tangle of limbs.

My bruised head struck the corner of a broken cabinet, and I rolled onto my back, my vision turning red. Every thought smashed into a thousand stars as I lay there reeling. Geraint's snarling face loomed above me, and I saw the knife shining in the lamplight, a flash of white steel surging towards me in one fluid motion, and in an explosion of luminous darts, the knife blew to pieces as it made impact with the copper key at my throat. Pieces of metal fired off in all directions, one penetrating his eye, and sending him falling away from me, leaving me curled there shaking, and bewildered. I heard Geraint shrieking, and scrabbling beside me.

"Owen, get up!" Morcant's voice shouted beside my ear, his claws digging into my flesh as he dragged me away. I was so dazed that I could only look up at his dark silhouette peering down at me from above. I sat up slowly, the hot metal of the key burning my chest as it touched my skin.

"What's... What... Huh..." I stammered, disorientated as I tried to get up.

"Fucking bitch!" Geraint howled as he clutched at his face, blood oozing from the wound in his eye, and as he lifted his head, I saw the chunk of steel jutting from it, but he didn't try to pull it free.

"Geraint, you need to stop this now or I shall be forced to tear you apart," Morcant threatened as he bent to pick up Maredudd's athame, the copper blade like a ray of sunlight in this dark, and smog-filled space.

"You don't want to be like this old bastard, do you?" Geraint sneered as he stared at me with his good eye, his hand opening, and letting the broken knife handle fall to the ground. "He'll suck the joy out of you. Turn you into a subordinate, a little witchy servant. Is that what you want?"

"Don't listen to him, Owen." I felt Morcant's hand on my shoulder, keeping me steady.

"I can teach you things he'd never think to utter to you. Power, wealth, sexual gratification. No need to shut yourself in a cave like a hermit, denying yourself love! Denying yourself good food, and wine!" Saliva spat from Geraint's mouth as he screamed at me. "You want to be a man, huh! You want to be a man! I can make you a man! You want to be like your dad! I can make you like your dad!"

I gulped, trying to swallow down the hard lump in my throat, my breath escaping through clenched teeth in a noisy wheeze as Geraint wobbled to his feet. We watched silently, Morcant stepping before me, and holding me back with a held-out hand as Geraint went to the metal cupboards built into the wall and pulled one open. He yanked out the contents, not caring as they fell all over the floor around his feet, until he discovered what he was searching for, and took it out into his arms. Unwrapping it from the plastic sheet it was wrapped in, he unfolded the long scrap of flimsy leather, and held it out at arm's length, his eyes boring into mine, desperate for a response as I looked at what he offered. My eyes were drawn to the ginger hair, a mop of it dangling from one end. Then I started to see the freckles that covered it, then the yellowed fingernails, and the holes where eyes should have been. I couldn't move, couldn't breathe. My whole body started to feel weak, and I thought I would faint there on the spot.

"You can wear your tada, you can be Evan if that's what you want so badly." He breathed, his teeth red with his own blood.

"Owen, don't look," Morcant whispered, turning, and putting his arm round me. I fell to him lethargically, my mind a desolate void of questions, and horrors as I buried my bleeding face in his sweat-soaked pyjama shirt.

"Geraint, I bid thee cease this madness at once!" He coughed, spluttering blood as he held the athame out, pointing its end towards him threateningly.

"Don't be stupid, Morcant. You've got nothing left in you. Nothing. You're gonna hurt from now until next year after this if I let you live. Without magic, you're nothing but a dried up husk," Geraint whispered before his uttered words merged into a cruel laugh.

I leaned back, lifting my head to look at Geraint standing there, the tanned skin of my father hanging from his hand like a worn jacket ready to be chucked on the coat-stand. I felt sick. My knees trembled, and I dropped to the ground, trying to push the vomit down in my throat as I gagged, my hand covering my groaning mouth.

"Ungrateful as always, eh, Owen?" He cackled.

I gasped as I threw up, unable to stop my belly contracting, and tears from streaming from my staring eyes. When I next looked up, Geraint was lifting Morcant's athame from amongst a pile of damaged stuffed animals, and when he turned, he howled as he ran towards us. Morcant stood his ground, and I felt static snapping the air again, but even I could feel his exhaustion, a black hole inside him that sucked his energy. I wasn't sure if he would be able to defend himself this time. Searching frantically, I skimmed the area around me for something to use as a weapon, seizing a large chunk of glass, and spinning round to rush to Morcant's side just as something big came bolting through the open door of the work room.

The goat's hooves left the ground as it leapt, sailing through the air, ears flapping, and head bowed, a torpedo that rushed straight towards Geraint's body. Ribs smashed, and spent oxygen puffed from Geraint's lungs as the goat's curled horns rammed into him with the power, and ferocity of a speeding car. Like a rag-doll thrown from a child's hand, he was sent flying across the room, limbs sprawling, and with a wet crunch he landed facing the ceiling upon an upturned deer head. The piercing antlers shot through his soft flesh, sinking into his back and emerging through his front, his arms, and legs falling to the floor, limp. Roger stood, huffing, and grunting, kicking the concrete with his rear hoof as he stared at the result of his heroic entrance.

The glass I was holding shattered as I let go of it. The noise shocked me into consciousness, and I crawled across the ground towards Maredudd, my breathing laboured as I struggled to turn him onto his back. He groaned when I moved him, and as I patted his cheek gently, his eyelids fluttered.

"Maredudd... Maredudd..." I squeaked, my voice cracking as I tried to wake him. "Maredudd, it's over..."

Maredudd's eyes opened, and he gazed up me dazedly, taking a moment to fully grasp what was happening as his pupils adjusted to the light. He smiled when he realised it was me, lifting his hand to stroke my hair, and pulling me closer into a hug, and I collapsed into his arms with a plaintive sob, allowing him to hold me as I noisily wept. The battle had ended, but from it there had sprung a number of difficult situations for me to face, just as from the one severed hydra's head there grew back many.

I clung to Maredudd, relief that he was okay flowing through me, but it did nothing to wash me of the terror, and grief that had tainted me when I had seen my father's pelt. I heard footfalls, and felt arms round my back, Mum's chin resting on my shoulder as she grabbed us both in a bear hug, and rocked us from side to side, her sniffles muffled by my filthy pyjama shirt. She was still wearing her dressing gown, except she now had slippers on her feet too. The bullets in my pocket clacked together like a maraca, and Maredudd's pulse throbbed against my ear as I pressed it to his neck, burying my eyes in his tangled hair. It was several minutes before we had calmed ourselves enough to open our eyes again and figure out what to do next.

"Owen, my brave man." Mum beamed at me with tear-stained cheeks as she held my head in her hands. I blushed as she kissed my cheeks, making wet, smacking sounds, and ruffling my hair. She then grabbed Maredudd, and he gasped in agony as she dragged him into her arms and crushed him tightly with a growl of affection.

I turned my head, and looked at the destruction around us, my eyes falling upon the stooped shape of Morcant who stood with his back to us, spikes of glass sticking from the scaly flesh of his tail. He was holding the two athames in one hand, but the other hand was stroking his chin as he looked down at Roger, who stood there proudly with his bearded chin held high. Breathing deeply, I crawled to my feet, and limped over to Morcant's side, both of us regarding the goat as he turned this way, and that, seeming to want us to admire him from all angles.

"Owen... I think this... Is your father," Morcant said slowly, the words coming out in short bursts as though he wasn't really sure whether to speak them at all.

"Roger? The goat? Are you serious?" I looked up at him in disbelief.

As if affronted by my answer, the goat reared up on his hind legs, and pretended to ram me with his horns, falling slowly onto his front hooves, and knocking my leg with his head. He turned again with his tail held up, trotting over to the sack of leather Geraint had dropped to the floor, and lipping at it with his pouting mouth. Morcant moved closer, bending to pick up the skin, and examining it carefully.

"We can try it, and find out," he murmured thoughtfully.

"What are you doing?"Mum questioned as she came over and peered at us both. She took some folded tissue out of her pocket, and started wiping at Morcant's gore-soaked face, and he grunted, trying to stop her from fussing around him.

"Wenda, I think the goat is your husband," he said grumpily as she held onto his shirt sleeve.

Mum looked down at Roger, and the goat seemed to smile up at her, his canny eyes twinkling. She curled her lip, and looked at me, apparently not seeing the resemblance.

"What's going on?" Maredudd asked from the other side of the room. Mum had helped him into a comfortable position, and he was sitting against the wall, his hands resting in his lap.

"Just wait a moment." Morcant sniffed, turning, and sucking air into his nostrils like a dog following a scent. He went to the metal cupboards, looking up and down at the contents, and selecting a tall bottle of greenish liquid. He winced as he lifted it, his arm obviously wounded, but he disregarded it as he laid the skin out on the ground and started pouring the oil over it. The herbal scent made our eyes water, and Mum pinched her nose disgustedly. Roger hurried over, and stood beside him, his tail wiggling, and his ears flicking about. He seemed so happy that he started rearing up again and prancing while Morcant massaged the liquid into the dripping pelt and lifted it up out of the puddle he had created.

"Here now, goat," he commanded, watching Roger cavorting in front of us.

The pelt made a wet slap as Morcant threw it over Roger's back. The alarmed goat bleated as he tugged it round him tightly. Then, a most curious thing began to happen: the leather began to stick to him, drawing tight to his shape and swallowing him whole as he fell to the ground, convulsing as if in a seizure. I wanted to reach for him, console him as he seemed to be in pain, but I was rooted to the spot with amazement. The shape beneath the pelt started to change, stretching and splitting, squelching as it was pulled like taffy to fill every inch of it. The goat-like cries began to morph into those of a human.

"Never..." Mum whispered as she held onto my arm, covering her open mouth with her hand as there on the floor at our feet lay Evan Vaughn.

Morcant crouched, taking hold of Dad's wrists and helping him sit up, placing his hand on his back as he groaned, and rubbed at his face. The horns had shrunk away, the fur was gone, the hooves no longer hooves, but feet. I couldn't believe what I had just seen.

"Evan?" Morcant asked cautiously.

"Years..." the stranger breathed before coughing abruptly. "Years I've waited...!"

"Evan!" Mum shrieked, rushing forward and practically climbing on him as he allowed her to envelop him in her arms, and suffocate his face in her bosom.

I stared down at his ginger hair, that freckled face that was so familiar, and when he looked up at me, I saw his eyes were still that of a goat. But when he smiled, I knew.

"Dad," I whispered.

"Owen, I want to thank you for scratching my every itch. I'm sorry I haven't been there for you all this time."He held out his hand to me, and I dropped to my knees beside him as Morcant got up and moved away to see to his own son.

"Dad, is it really you?" I was gobsmacked, unable to tear my eyes away from his face.

"Yes! It's really me! What, did you think the bloody goat could talk like this?" He laughed, and the sound brought forth a riot of memories all charging through my mind, and leaving me speechless with astonishment.

Mum was crying hysterically, her hands near enough clawing at his bare shoulders as she wept into his neck.

"It's okay, boyo. There's a lot I need to explain to you," he said as he put his hand on my shoulder.

"No, it's okay. I know about it already. About the witches, and everything." I smiled, tears bubbling at the corner of my eyes, and blurring my vision as I gripped onto his wrist.

He laughed, and I allowed him to pull me into a hug, and for the first time in years, I felt complete again.

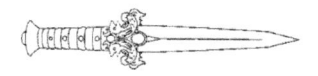

Even as we watched the ambulance reversing up the lane, I still couldn't believe what was happening. I stared at Dad as he and Mum talked to the police, my eyes wide, and unblinking, and my hands warmed by the mug of hot chocolate I held in my lap. My injuries were bandaged, and I hurt all over, but I had never felt so happy. Happy to see Mum with her life partner beside her, happy to see Dad's grinning face, and hear his infectious laughter. I never thought I would see him again, couldn't believe that the goat I had fed, and looked after all this time had been him there waiting for me, showing me affection, and listening to me talk nonsense when I felt lonely. I didn't hear what they were telling the police officers, but I didn't care. We were a family again.

"How are you feeling?" Maredudd's voice purred against my ear. I looked up as he sat down beside me on the porch step. His words were strained, and I saw how he cringed in pain as he moved. I smiled at him, leaning forward for a kiss, which he offered adoringly. I had to put my hand on his chest to remind him we weren't alone.

"I'm okay. Are you?" I asked.

He nodded, lifting his good hand to stroke my bruised cheek. "I'm all right. What doesn't kill you makes you stronger, right?" He chuckled, leaning his forehead against mine and gazing into my eyes.

"Right." I agreed, brushing noses with him. "I love you, by the way."

"By the way?"

"Yeah. I couldn't remember if I told you, but I've thought it all along. I thought maybe being a witch you were telepathic."

He laughed, shaking his head.

"I wouldn't read your thoughts, anyway. I'm too pure for that. Who knows what kind of sordid filth lurks there." He smirked, and I pretended to slap his leg. "And yet despite that fact, I love you too. Actually, I love you very much, Owen Vaughn."

I beamed at him, leaning to kiss him again before we both gazed down the front garden, the flashing lights of the police car lighting us up in a shade of blue. The police headed back to their car, and Mum put her arm round Dad's shoulder as he clutched the blanket round himself.

"Are they gone yet?" Morcant's voice whispered from the shadows of the hallway.

"Not yet. We'll be in, in a minute," Maredudd replied, and we both giggled to each other. I glanced over my shoulder, spotting Morcant's pale face peering round the corner of the living room door. He had managed to find his nightcap, and had put it back on his head, but it was the only part of him that wasn't dirty and blood-stained.

"Well, who fancies fish and chips!" Mum cried, flinging her arms into the air as she followed Dad up the garden path. We all cheered in agreement.

In the living room, Morcant sat in Geraint's armchair, surrounded by broken furniture and smashed ornaments, cradling Jojo's sausage body in his lap as he stroked her short, silky fur. She looked quite pleased with herself, and raised her head for a passing stroke as Maredudd and I moved by. Mum had found her in a shut box in the work room, hidden away out of sight. Fortunately no harm had come to her. As soon as we had let her out, she had jumped up at us barking and vibrating, her stumpy tail wagging a mile a minute.

When the ambulance came to take Geraint's body away, Dad was quick to comfort Mum, which still struck me as very odd after everything we'd been through. I still didn't understand how she could feel anything, but contempt for Geraint. Even Dad seemed ready to forgive him.

"That night, I went back up to the house after a few drinks at the pub, and he ambushed me. Cracked me right over the head, yere." Dad pointed to the back of his head as he sat on the sofa, dressed in some of my pyjamas with a tray heaped with fish and chips on his lap. "Clobbered me and chucked me down the stairs. Well, the next thing I knew, I woke up and found myself covered with hair. I only found out he'd faked my death when you lot turned up and moved in with him."

"We always knew something was amiss," Maredudd declared as he poured gravy over his cheese-covered chips.

"Go on, go on, go on," Mum teased as she tried to feed Morcant a chip, nearly climbing onto the chair with him and Jojo as he turned his head away.

"Stop it, you mad woman!" He batted her away, and Jojo barked so she fed it to her instead.

"We're a family again," I murmured, my mouth full of food. "And we've got Geraint's house. He can bugger off."

Dad laughed, wiping at the tears in his eyes.

"I just want to thank you guys. If it weren't for you, I'd still be out in the garden, bonking those old nanny goats." He snorted, and everyone started to laugh, except for Morcant, who seemed to find the whole idea rather alarming.

After that night, things changed for the better. There were still obstacles to overcome, for example, when sitting at the dinner table a few days later, Dad suddenly transformed back into a goat after the salve wore off and left him sitting there with his hooves in his food. Morcant said there was no permanent way to change him back without skinning him the way Geraint had, but he wasn't prepared to risk it, so it meant Dad would probably have to live the rest of his life knowing that at any moment, he could return to his caprine form. But, that didn't matter. I said he was like me now, except he was a man trapped in a goat's body instead of a girl trapped in a man's body.

Mum and Dad continued to stay in Geraint's house while they searched for somewhere else to rent, and I successfully moved all of my belongings over to Maredudd's cottage, which had become my permanent home. Morcant packed up his cave, and got on a train to Scotland, intending to holiday there until next Spring. I started working at Mrs Bryn's shop, and everything was looking up for me.

The animal attacks had ceased, but that didn't mean the village wasn't alive with the sound of delicious rumours as, naturally, there was plenty of new gossip for the wind-bags to spread about. I didn't care. I walked down the street beside Maredudd, holding his hand with my head held high, because I was proud to be his, and proud to be who I was. He had given me a new use for my camera now that there were no more animals to photograph. Instead I ended up with a bag full of film rolls containing picture after picture of his handsome face.

"Fancy going for a walk on the beach?" Maredudd greeted me as I left Mrs Bryn's shop and stepped out onto the street outside.

The sun was starting to set, and the sky was lavender, and blue, lazy streaks of motionless clouds making stripes across its face. He stood there before me looking radiant as always in shorts and a button-up t-shirt. He offered me his hand as I joined him to walk along the road, but I took his arm instead, smiling when he chuckled down at me.

"I'd love to, and I know of a certain porcine friend that might want to join us," I remarked as we wandered towards the lane.

A couple of weeks after I had moved into the cottage, the village held a farmer's fair, and we had all gone to visit it. Mum had come to fetch me while I stood with Dad sampling some of the local beers, and when I followed her to another stall, we found Maredudd standing in front of a small pen. There on the grass was a cluster of little pink piggies, and when he saw that I had come, he grinned at me excitedly. How could I say no?

"I'm sure she will. Anyway, not much of the summer left. I can taste Autumn in the air already," he said, both of us gazing down the hill towards the ocean as it rose and fell peacefully.

"Me too," I agreed, breathing it in deeply. "It's never tasted so good."

Fin

Bonus Chapter

The summer sky was a haze of deep sapphire-blue and vanilla streaks, fading to a celestial white that surrounded the shining circle of the sun. Glittering light twinkled on each gentle wave, shimmering like precious jewels that rolled and sparkled with every motion towards the shore, where the bubbling surf swept up around our bodies, engulfing us in its frothy embrace. Salt water and sweat coated our skin, warm from the midsummer heat and cold, simultaneously, wherever the ocean's reach touched us. The chitting of numerous birds in the bushes that populated the overhanging cliffs were occasionally lost in the delicate breezes. It was a gorgeous day.

Maredudd lay beside me, diagonally, so that the tide played with the long strands of his hair, sliding it up and down each time it came in. He didn't care that it washed up around his ears or even onto his face sometimes. I wasn't so relaxed about that; I lay slightly higher on the sand than he did, keeping my beard and my eyes dry. My skin was red from the sun, covered in sun-block though I was, but Maredudd's skin had turned a beautiful shade of gold and little copper highlights had been picked out in his hair, which somehow made him seem more youthful despite his greying.

This tiny cove was hidden from the beach, inaccessible to tourists who weren't aware of the tunnels where Morcant lived, so we had no worries about being interrupted. We swam naked together, bobbing in the waves that grew rougher in the deeper waters, and floated on inflatable rings when we grew tired of treading. Our cooler was packed with plastic ice cubes, chilled bottles of cider and soda water, so when the heat grew too intense, we popped off the bottle caps and sat drinking together on the rocks. We watched crabs scuttling amongst the drying seaweed and tiny fish darting through the rock pools, trapped until the tide rose again.

Lately, I had had the feeling that Maredudd wanted to ask me something. Mum and Dad had talked about renewing their wedding vows, and for some reason, he had become quite awkward when we had headed home that evening after dinner. I had asked him if there was something wrong, but he had simply shaken his head. I began to worry. We had never talked about marriage before. Our relationship was approaching its one year anniversary, so in my mind that was still too early to be discussing something of the like, but even then, I wasn't sure I wanted to be married. My relationship with Maredudd was so easy and relaxed, like water flowing smoothly through a creek, swerving around obstacles without effort. Adding something like marriage to the equation would complicate things somehow.

On top of that, Morcant had talked about arranging for me to go and study. There was room for me in a coven in Scotland, a coven specifically focused on the element of Fire. My element. But there was no room for Maredudd. I would have to leave him for a year or two, only meeting with him on holidays or special occasions. I wasn't sure how I felt about that. I wasn't sure I could expect him to wait for me for a couple of years. It felt wrong, somehow.

"You keep breathing in like you're about to speak," Maredudd commented beside me, causing me to open my eyes in a flash. I hadn't even been aware that I was doing that while I lay there thinking to myself.

When I didn't answer, he spoke again.

"What's on your mind?"

"It's nothing, really," I murmured. I felt guilty that I was ruining the mood. We'd had such a lovely day together; I didn't want to ruin it now. We still had a barbecue planned for this evening.

"Tell me. I can tell something is bothering you. I know you well enough now to tell when there's something stuck in your mind," he persisted, rolling onto his side with a grin.

I looked down my chest at him, my eyes half-closing with a smile. He was so handsome, I couldn't bear it.

"Promise you won't think I'm being silly?"

"Why would I think that? I never think you're silly." He made a bemused grin.

"Last week, you seemed kind of awkward after Mum and Dad were talking about renewing their vows," I began slowly, giving him plenty of room to interject.

"And?"

"I wanted to know what you thought. I mean, about marriage, that is."

He eyed me for a second, the tide washing between us and dotting his cheeks with fresh water droplets. His expression became thoughtful.

"I suppose I was worried you might ask me about marriage at some point," he said. I couldn't tell what he was thinking or feeling; his eyes had darkened.

"Why?" I prompted.

"I've thought about marriage a lot over the years. But, I realise it's not really for me. I was worried that if you brought up marriage, I would have to tell you that I didn't want it, and I didn't want to hurt you. I didn't want you to think that it was because I don't love you," he explained, this time making eye contact with me.

"Maredudd..." I trailed off, shaking my head.

"It's really not, I promise you. Marriage, the kind that Wenda and Evan are talking about, is just a contract with the government. To me, it's meaningless. Do you understand what I mean?" he added, seeming confused by my reaction.

"You know, I was worried that you were gonna ask me about it, too. And I was worried that you would be hurt if I told *you* that I didn't want it," I told him, watching as his smile curved into a wry smirk. "I don't feel like I need that from you. I feel like I have you already and that's enough."

His smirk broke into a broad smile as he toyed with a piece of seaweed in the water. I thought I detected a faint blush on his cheeks but it might have just been because of the heat.

"Now I feel quite stupid."

"You're not stupid. I was stupid," I laughed, sitting up slightly so that I could press my forehead against his. "Maybe we can talk about it again in a few years if we start to feel differently. But right now, I'm happy with what I have. I'm happy with you, just *you*, as things are."

"Me too," he replied. He tilted his head, leaning into me for a kiss, and I met him half way. His lips tasted of salt and his tongue of cider.

"I've spoken to my dad about you going away to study," he spoke as soon as we parted. That made me nervous.

"What about it? I'm not even sure I want to go, anyway." I shrugged.

"Because you're not interested in studying, or because you don't want to leave me?" he questioned, and I became coy. He arched an eyebrow. "I've seen how you pour over those ancient books of his. I've seen you absorbing every scrap of information he has to offer you. I know you want to study; you can't hide that from me. And I think you're an amazing witch. You're a natural; it's like you were made for this. So don't pretend you're not interested."

I shrugged again. I felt embarrassed; was I really that transparent? "Okay, I see your point. Then I guess I will admit that I don't like the idea of leaving you for such a long time. You make me feel like who I really am when I'm with you; I don't know if I could handle being separated from you now."

"That's why I had a chat with him."

"About what?" I glanced up at him, confused.

"There's no room for me in the coven. You know that already. They wouldn't allow me to stay with them when I'm not a member of their group. But I could live close by. It's not far outside of Edinburgh, so I could come on the train to meet you when you're not busy," he suggested, watching the excitement growing in my eyes. "I've never left Wales before, but I think it's time I widen my horizons a little bit. A change of scenery would be fun, and I could be there to support you, too."

"Really? You'd do that for me?" I was surprised. I had never expected that Maredudd would want to leave this seaside village that he loved so much.

"I love you, Owen. I want you to follow your heart and study like you want to. But if you weren't yere, the sun wouldn't shine so brightly. The ocean wouldn't be so pretty. My days would be empty without you. So, the logical thing to do is to go with you. Because I need you just as much as you need me," he spoke softly, lifting his hand and stroking my jaw, his thumb sinking in my beard so that he could touch my skin.

"Thank you," I stammered. "I love you, too. I don't think I could manage without you in Scotland. I'd always be so busy thinking about you that I would never be able to focus on my work."

"As long as I don't become a distraction while I'm there," he declared.

"Of course not. Well, maybe only on my days off. You can distract me all night, then."

We smiled and gazed into each other's eyes, closing them only when the water splashed against our bodies, and in the lime green of his irises and the darkness of his pupils, I saw our entire future together, and what a long and happy life it would be.

About the Author

Nem Rowan is originally from the UK, but despite Brexit, he still considers himself to be European. He was born in the West Country of England, but later moved to Wales, where he lived for almost a decade before deciding to move to Sweden in the summer of 2019. He shares his home with his wife, his girlfriend, their rapidly-growing triplets, one cat, and a demon.

Nem started writing when he was very young. He always loved Horror stories and has an undying fascination with the creepy, the bizarre, the shocking and the unusual. Coupled with his enjoyment of love stories, his writing became a fusion of Horror and Romance, often with characters that have been through terrible hardships but who eventually reach the happy ending they deserve.

nemrowan.com
nem.rowan@outlook.com

A Gurt Dog Press
Publication

2022

Printed in Great Britain
by Amazon